NITE'S PASSAGE

An American Odyssey from
Appomattox to Lake Erie

Charles J. Koutnik

CJK-ART-E
Colonial Heights, Virginia

ISBN: 978-1985576704

DEDICATED TO

my dear family and friends, some of whom gave me
material needs, some who gave spiritual support,
and some who have just been there enriching my life.

PREFACE

Sam Nite's decades-long odyssey from Appomattox to Lake Erie begins in what was a "truly ugly place": the Howlett Line outside Richmond, Virginia. That is where readers first meet Sam, a fourteen-year-old enthusiastic conscript to the south's doomed effort to protect its capital from the despised Yankees. By the time Sam joins the line in the waning months of the Civil War the battle zone is a wasteland. The reader is introduced to the horrors of trench warfare around Richmond and empathizes with Sam and his colleagues as they face the disgrace of their defeated army. Sam's immediate post-war experiences are ugly, too. Upon his heart-rending return to his family's Virginia farm, Sam realizes he can never return to the life he had before the war. He then begins his journey, west to Tennessee and eventually north to Ohio.

Sam's odyssey takes the reader from the war-torn rural South of the 1860s to the industrial north of the Roaring Twenties. Along the way, Sam grows to manhood, searching for a profession, love, and enlightenment while meeting some of the period's important historical figures and pondering the significance of historical movements and events.

In Tennessee a horrible incident brings Sam face-to-face with General George Thomas. The general, not well-known to readers today, was famous in his time. Known as "The Rock of Chickamauga," Thomas was born a southerner, a Virginian like Sam, but fought for the north and became one of its greatest heroes. To Sam, the general was "a traitor," a turncoat who helped defeat his native land. But the general takes a personal interest in Sam and plays a major role in directing his fateful journey.

Sam goes to Ohio and works as an assistant to Cleveland Abbe, a meteorologist trying to perfect the science of weather prediction. Abbe, another important and little-known historical figure, today is known as "the father of the National Weather Service." Abbe helps Sam further his education and find employment.

Another Ohio resident important in Sam's journey is Sherwood Anderson. Though not on bestseller lists today, Sherwood Anderson was one of the most popular authors of the early 20th century. Among his popular books was *Winesburg, Ohio*.

Through Sam's eyes, readers of *Nite's Passage* experience the challenges and excitement of life in Ohio in the late 19th and early 20th centuries. Readers are introduced to characters as wide-ranging as John D. Rockefeller and Johnny Appleseed, and historical movements as diverse as industrialization, unionization, and the development of professional baseball. There was a lot going on in Ohio and readers are treated to Sam's perspective on all of it.

Readers will root for Sam as he struggles to become educated and employed, as he searches for love, and as he looks for meaning in all he experienced. His journey highlights the importance of human kindness and shows that "some good always seems to come out of something bad." Though a work of fiction, readers are introduced to many fascinating and true historical figures and events. Whether or not the reader is a student of history, every reader will find something new in *Nite's Passage*.

John Halliday

ACKNOWLEDGEMENTS

This book is possible due to my sister Dianne Pruden. She is the true scholar of the family, having become so by being the direct pipeline of my late mother's thirst for knowledge. This book would never have been written without the support of my wife Sharon. Much gratitude to Sue Hannibal and Tilly Conley for helping Dianne with the editing of my manuscript. And much thanks to the following people who connected me with the right people to get this done: Bob Gillette, Kathleen Grissom, John Halliday, Steve Winn, Francis Wood, Will Green, and Tom Kelechi. I offer sincere thanks for those joining the effort to make this project a success. This group includes Steve Winn, Bill Luton, and Neal Rupright. And finally my thanks to my most important connection on this particular "Passage" no matter where it may lead, Jon Marken.

The Sapling

A bolt of lightning set the woods ablaze. When the fire went out the land lay barren. It was not long before new life, aided by the rain and sun from above, took form upon the blank canvas of land. Rejuvenation began with the appearance of low-growing weeds, which in turn gave way to a grassy meadow. Eventually shrubs followed and then young pine trees. The last of the meadow disappeared as the trees grew to form a canopy over the land. New species of plants, requiring less sunlight, took possession of the forest floor. It was at this time that a seed arrived by way of an animal's scat. The small rodent ritualistically kicked dirt over the scat and seed and then went his way.

The pines grew tall with age, and below them the seed pushed its tightly packed contents above ground and burst open into a small seedling. The seedling was alive, but soon it would be gone whether it was transformed into nutrients under the ground or changed into a different form above ground. Change is the interplay of life and death. Only the trick of memory fools one into thinking otherwise. The seedling changed into a sapling because it received the right combination of sun, shade, and water. The sapling now faced a multiple of possibilities. An animal could eat its tender shoots and leaves. Something like a larger tree might eventually block out the sunlight. An old or young diseased tree could crash down upon the helpless sapling. A tornado or fire could destroy it in less than a day.

None of these things happened and the sapling grew into a mature tree. Life in the forest changed at a slow but constant pace. However, the swiftest agent of change was yet to arrive. A few men over the years passed within a hundred yards of the tree as they traveled a path along the shoreline of the great lake to the north. Soon, however, many men of a paler skin came into the forest. These men stayed and cut down just about every tree in the area to build boats, houses, barns, and churches.

The sapling that grew to become a tree remained in the form of a tree only because one day a group of the white-skinned people gathered around its base and dug two rectangular holes in the earth. They placed a box in each hole and filled the holes with the same dirt. This was followed by much talking, singing, and weeping. Someone said, "We must keep this tree here to provide shade for our departed love ones."

Humans struggle against change. Not only do they fear death, but they fear what tomorrow may or may not bring. The fear is controlled by a vain desire to control the next moment. They go to war over control and the certainty that they alone know the truth. Truths change and peace constantly changes to war. In early 1865 men at war stood yards apart from each other on the barren lifeless land. They asked themselves if the misery was worth the pain.

Five Hundred Miles South 1866

Captain Tilly gave me some last advice. "Sam, just stick to the facts. The General is a very busy man. He knows all about fighting and dying. What he needs to know is how you became involved in all this trouble."

Well if facts were what was wanted then that is what I'd try to give. Not knowing exactly how I could tell everything that happened to me in the last year without describing all of the little things that go into creatin' one big mess, I took a deep breath and gave it a try. I figured the first fact in his report should be my full name. So I began.

My name to the educated is Sam Johnson Adam Knight. We spelled it N-I-T-E though, because my Pa, not being able to read or write, and always impatient when his work was interrupted, told a census taker to write our name on his paper the shortest way he knew how. So the man suggested "Nit," but then thought better of it and told my pa that he would add a silent "e" at the end. Ma remembered Pa's exact reply: "How about just a regular 'e' and let me get on with the farming around here." So Nite is the way we spell it and Ma never got tired of telling the story about how it became such.

BOOK ONE
MANHOOD

PARKER'S BATTERY

The Howlett Line was truly an ugly place. The trees were cut down, pools of standing water in the wet season, and blowing dirt with the slightest breeze in the hot summer. In time trees will grow again, and the bushes along with all our lousy earthworks and forts will be swallowed up by the forest. I suspect it is already overgrown with weeds and small trees, like what happens when you leave a farm field alone for a spell.

Back where I was born and raised in Nottoway County we had a nice place with fields giving us crops of tobacco and food. It was no plantation, but sure was nicer than a tent home in Jeff Davis's Army, which is where I was with the Parker Battery, a group of the old and young mixed in with veterans of the war. We were part of the Howlett Line. We were supposed to make sure no Yankees got past us, either coming from City Point or from Petersburg to the south. We were supposed to stop them Yanks from getting to Richmond. None did get by us, but then again they didn't need to, because Old Robert E. Lee's main concern was to hold on to Petersburg. The Yankees had no need to fight their way into Richmond. The city just wasn't that important anymore, so I guess what we were doing wasn't so important after all.

Even though there was little fighting where we were at we could hear the war. Cannons were always booming, whether they were firing at boats on the James River, or shooting down in Petersburg. Sometimes we'd even hear guns from the fighting across the river by those forts due east of Richmond.

Just about the time I joined the unit there was some serious shooting at our spot in the line. The Yanks fired at Parker's Battery from a church that wasn't too far away. Sergeant Taylor, Corporal Verlander, and Davey Brown volunteered to take care of the problem. In the dark they crept through the no-man's land, slowly made their way through the few thickets that could provide cover, and came out where the church sat on a muddy road. Seeing no Yanks there, they proceeded to burn the church down. Without the building for protection, the Yankee boys didn't bother Parker's line from up close again.

The next day a minister came to complain about the church being burned down. Being a religious man, Captain Parker politely listened. It takes some kind of man to stand in one spot constantly shooing away relentless mosquitos and listening patiently when he knows there is nothing to be done no matter what gets said.

After a bit, the Captain called on Sergeant Taylor to explain why he and the other two fellers did what they had to do. From the way I heard it, the Sergeant, being less God-fearing than the Captain, wasted no time interrupting the minister and telling him the way it was.

"You may be a man of God and I reckon that gives you the right to not have to fight the Yanks, but you could at least understand that while we are doing all the fighting we will be damned if we just sit by while Yankees take pot shots at us from your precious church."

Captain Parker interrupted Taylor at this point and took great pains to again explain the necessity of the unfortunate burning. He also gave assurance that as soon as the Yanks were chased from this area, his men would rebuild the church.

Well, that whole story was repeated around the evening campfires many a night, much at Sergeant Taylor's expense. It needed a lot of tellin' because it was the only exciting thing that happened on the Howlett Line until the day we left.

I knew I was lucky to have arrived here with the major fighting being carried on at other places. To be honest about it, for me army life was not that bad. I always liked sleepin' out in the open air. It wasn't as nice as doing it back home where the land was shaded by plenty of mature trees. The brooks were clear, and it was quiet out there in the woods without thousands of soldiers around.

Me and the few nigger boys we had (I've since learned to more properly call them Negroes) would hunt, fish, and just run around them woods. More than anything, though, I loved it when we would take off at dusk into the woods for a mile or so to sleep on the ground with maybe just an old blanket or two. I remember laying there and looking at all the stars.

To this day I love a clear night sky. It ain't just all dark. There are stars and there is also the blackness. That dark just wouldn't be dark if it wasn't for the stars, just as those stars would not be little spots of light without the dark. It occurred to me then and still does today that ain't that like living? We wouldn't know what a good time was or how some things are so special if we didn't also go through a great mess of not so good things.

One thing the war could not change was the sky. Looking at the sky at night was my own private time. It's not that I didn't also have a lot of fun with the other new soldiers who, like me, joined the battery after all the major fighting was done, but the sky was reliable; whereas People, mostly young loud people, are the most unreliable thing there is in this life.

During free time when I wasn't lookin' at the stars, I would be keepin' company with some of the other new fellas around my fifteen years of age. We would carry on something fierce. There was Harry Fenley, Bobby Craddock, Roy Dalton, and a guy we called "Old Hairy" because he had the exact same name as one of the veterans of the unit and needed distinguishing from him. He just about had hair everywhere on his body and so it was a good nickname.

There was this one guy named Owen who thought he was quite funny, but he really wasn't. Owen loved to fool with my name. It was all just the same tired joke coming out of Owen's mouth. When retiring at night he would say, "Have a good night Nite." Come morning he'd actually search me out, just to say, "Did you sleep well last night Nite," or, "That was quite a stormy night Nite."

I'd constantly have to tell him, "I understand the joke Owen, stop it now would ya? If you keep on I'll see to it that you don't bother me again." But I couldn't do that no how, for I felt somewhat protective of Owen. He didn't have any idea on how to get along with the other soldiers, and he took it from some of the tougher and rougher fellows for just being the way he was. I could see there was more to him. I thought about talking to him about it, but I knew he would just end up feeling hurt. So, when he came up with a stupid joke, I just tried to smile and thus somehow let him know it was funny once, but not a second or third time.

One way Owen and I fit in with the rest of the soldiers in our group of newcomers was that we professed no fear. We talked plenty of times about how if General Butler's Yanks tried to march through here from City Point we'd run them all the way down the peninsula to the old towns of Governor Dinwiddie down by old Williamsburg. We would catch that fat old Benjamin Butler and teach him for all his atrocities in New Orleans. Captain Parker told us all about it. You see, after the Yanks took New Orleans they set up old Ben Butler as head governor of the city or something like that. He somehow, I didn't fully understand how, made the fair ladies of the city into something like them kind of women who hang around outside taverns. Butler, it is said, forced our women folk to be nice to his Yanks and I reckon that means in every way if you know what I mean. Now, Butler was handpicked by Grant or Lincoln to march right by us and head up to Richmond where he could all over again degrade our women folk. We never found out what we'd do to him if he crossed our path, 'cause as I said he never did.

Indeed we all felt pretty good about our chances of whipping any Yank army that tried us. This was all well and good excepting for those times we would be bragging in front of some of the seasoned soldiers who were with the battery through the roughest fights. You see, if you have done nothin' to prove your bravery, you had to brag that when the time come you would have no problem showing it on the battlefield.

We did all the talking around the campfire while the veterans sat there listening, taking it all in. I couldn't tell if they were bored or just doing like I noticed some other smart people doing, that is saying nothing because they knew better.

One day we did get an answer to our carrying on. One of the older fellas we were talking to, I forget his name, but he was friends with Tom Forsett, finally said to no one of us in particular, "Whatever you say boy." Now down South, unless you were friends, "boy" meant more than "hey you" or "fella." It meant you was on the same level as a Black man. Some of us less-than-aristocratic types would have let it go and been done with it, but not Jefferson Whitehouse. He came from a plantation down in Charles City County where being called a "boy" was definitely fighting words. Jefferson, in an increasing louder voice, told this feller that he better take them words back or else.

"Or else what, boy?" he answered. "You gonna whip me like you are going to whip the Yanks when you meet 'em? Well if that's what you're planning to do, let's commence with it. But, before you do, let me tell you this, in my first battle up at Sharpsburg I ran three times when the firing started. Each time though I ran less farther. Now by the time of Gettysburg I was done running and I was there at the Peach Orchard where the Yank's artillery was giving us Hell. Just ask Forsett here who was wounded at that fight. We made a charge there too, and I killed two Yankees with my gun. Not shooting, but using my hands and my gun as a club. So if a rich planter's son like you is ready to jump right in and take on a guy who don't care anymore if he lives or dies, then let's get on with it."

It was a good thing that one David Crockett Richardson came by at that time. He was almost a neighbor of Jefferson's living in the adjoining county of New Kent. Davey, as we called him, fashioned himself a scholar. That description fits him for he'd done something most of the rest of us wouldn't have done. After he was injured at the Second Manassas, he lay in bed for all that time and did a lot of thinking and he decided what he wanted to do with the rest of his life. After returning to camp you'd always see him carrying around a book or two. It turns out he was studying the law. I believed he would do well as a lawyer after the war, and also be quite good in politics if he chose.

He indeed showed off some lawyering skills back that day when Jefferson was calling out that feller. Davey stepped in and gave Jefferson an easy way out. I remember his words. "Listen everyone, I imagine we will all have a chance to fight the Yanks again and we are going to need the high spirit and act like the brothers we are and not fight among ourselves. We must not underestimate our enemy. In these modern days with the new accurate weapons, like the repeating rifles the Yankees have, we face a formidable foe." Davey then slowly looked around at all of us. I remember feeling a chill go all through me as he did so. He settled his eyes directly on John Moodey and asked, "Is that not true John? You were there for just about all of it, were you not?"

Moodey looked up. All he said was, "Yep, I was there." And then he said nothing for the longest time. Finally, he spoke again. "Only a fool would choose to get in a fight. Every day I don't have to fight is a good day."

These were not the inspirational words Davey had hoped for. They left him and everyone else speechless. It did accomplish stopping the fight though for one by one, veteran and new recruit, got up and wandered off into the landscape of mud and little more, their shadows looking like ghosts returning to an unreal world.

I headed back to the tent I shared with Owen. He was still awake. "Hey Nite," he said, "How'd you get signed up into this unit coming all the way from Nottoway County?"

"Well, Owen, the old fellas back in Nottoway Court House who sat on the drafting committee were running out of boys to make into soldiers. They was hesitant to sign me up for I just turned fourteen, but after waiting as long as they could, they sent a letter to my parents saying they had no other choice and I was to report to the courthouse two weeks from that day. My mammy and pap didn't like it none much and they went and talked to those old men. One of them was Colonel Bradshaw who wasn't an active Colonel any more but had fought the British back in 1812 when he was about the same age as I am now. He said to my folks that if I would immediately volunteer, they would try to find for me as safe a spot as possible. Because it was late June of 1864, Colonel Bradshaw was aware that some batteries had settled in near a place called Chester Station. Being a smart military man he guessed that the hardest fighting would be either at Petersburg or closer to Richmond. So somehow he arranged it all that I come join Parker's Battery here right outside Chester."

"Because the vast majority of the boys are from Richmond," Owen remarked, "I wondered how a fella from way out in the country ended up with Captain Parker."

"Well Owen, how about you," I said as I playfully jabbed him with a stick. "How come a city boy like you is down here instead of up in Richmond helping block the road from Washington?"

"It's because near where I lived is where Captain Parker was a doctor and he was the one that organized this battery."

I hadn't needed to have asked Owen why he was here. I had heard from others the story. Owen, now also fifteen, was put into the army by his ma because she had some doctoring done by Captain Parker and she'd rather have him in his unit than drafted in with some strangers. You see, Owen's father was killed way back in the First Manassas battle. Owen was merely twelve at the time and his ma felt that at least she need not worry about him ever going off fighting. But then it was three

20

years later and the fighting was still going on and Jeff Davis needed soldiers real bad. Didn't matter if you was an old fella in say your forties or like Owen and myself just getting to the age where we just started learning to become men.

The story goes that Owen's ma always watched out special-like for him. For my part she didn't realize what she was doing. By being so protective she made it harder for him. The other fellas around here who are fifteen or sixteen years old are a much different sort. Most of them are conscripts, that means they didn't bother joining, instead they were told to report or else. Most of them had to be rounded up and brought in against their will. These types don't care about Owen's situation and because of all the coddling and protecting he is not really ready for dealing with these fellas. If Owen was down in the Petersburg trenches, these types would make his life intolerable. As is they are always saying things around here like, "What a pretty boy you is Owen. I think you might really be a girl. Would you like to be my sweetheart?"

To show how different it is around here and why Owen's ma trusted him with Captain Parker, you just need to see what happened when the Captain heard about this one soldier saying such things to Owen. You see, Captain Parker is a strict person, a very devout religious person and a man of very high principles. You wouldn't know it right off but he also has a special concern for those like Owen who would easily be taken advantage of. The Captain, therefore, wasted no time in ordering that tormentor of Owen to ride the rail from sun up to sun down the next day. Riding the rail meant being forced to sit atop a narrow rail that was just set high enough so one's feet did not touch the ground. The fella laughed about it at first, but by the end of the day he was crying and begging to be let off.

The next day Captain Parker asked to see me. Now the Captain had never directly talked to me excepting in line inspection to tell me to straighten up or sew back on a button or something like that. So I was scared stiff as I walked to the headquarters' tent. There I was met by the Captain's servant Joe Mayo, who looked to be at least part Negro. For certain he was much loved by the Captain and you soon knew that you best treat him with the utmost respect. I saluted Joe and he immediately snapped at me, "Put down those fool arms son and don't be saluting me. I'm no officer. I ain't even officially a soldier. And don't be looking so scared. You ain't in no trouble. Now wait here and I'll let the Captain know you reported."

Joe made me feel so much better about things that maybe I was too relaxed when I entered the tent, for I almost forgot to salute the Captain. "OK son, be at ease," Captain Parker told me. "Nite, I have been observing you and I think you are going to make a pretty good soldier. I have also noticed you in the company of Private Owen Butterfield." After a short pause he looked directly into my eyes and made me feel that somehow he knew every little thing about me. "I made a promise to Private Butterfield's mother that I would watch out for her boy. I am able to do a fairly good job of it at this camp. The war has not really come here up to this time, but I suspect one day it will and then I will not be able to keep as close a watch. I am therefore ordering, well in this case better put, asking you, to help me carry out my promise to Mrs. Butterfield. The cold weather will be coming soon and if you could build a shelter for you and Private Butterfield it would be much appreciated. I know that you are new and have no experience building a shelter for winter camp, but I will see to it that you receive some assistance."

Now there are always the good sides of a deal and the bad sides. The good side was the help to build a shelter. A good shelter with a built-in stove is a luxury only a veteran knows how to build. The bad part of the deal is that I wouldn't get much peace with having to be around Owen more than I was already. In this case though, the good outweighed the bad in that I still had a liking for Owen even though he could be a bit tiresome. So, not that I really had a choice, but I told Captain Parker that I'd be happy to do as he asked.

This all happened around the middle of August 1864, which made it somewhat odd that the Captain talked about cold weather coming up soon. The thing was that the two thoughts didn't add up. On one hand it sounded like Captain Parker expected us to be here a long time, worrying about winter in August and all. From this I suspected that there would be no more invasions of the North, no more Sharpsburg's or Gettysburg's. We were strictly on the defensive and that ain't so bad. I'd rather be behind fortifications, walls, or anything else while shooting at fellers running across open fields than it being the other way around.

However, the other thought turned my mind in the opposite direction. Asking me to be serious about taking good care of Owen, knowing he wouldn't do very well on a march, let alone in a battle, Captain Parker seemed like at the same time to be figuring we would be on the move someday soon. Now I git it. I guess that is why he is an officer. He must of been preparing for both ways things could go. The fact of the matter is that as time went by, it seemed more likely we were going to be here for a long while. Maybe we were here for good. The cannon and rifle fire from the places around us seemed to simmer down to almost nothing.

Owen and I with the help of Davey Richardson decided to build our shelter a short distance behind the gun placements. This was pretty much unheard of but Davey, who was assigned by Captain Parker to help us, said that some of the boys had been informally meeting with the Yanks down at the springs. They were trading tobacco for some coffee and things like soap and candles. They had all made kind of an agreement not to be shooting at any soldiers' huts. Not all the officers were agreeing to this idea, but nobody saw anything to be gained by killing each other when we all was just trying to be as comfortable as possible.

A hot summer turned to fall and fall gave way to winter. September was memorable, thanks to General Wade Hampton's Beefsteak Raid. We began having good meat to eat for quite a spell after Hampton and his boys rode way around Yankee lines to steal a herd of beef on the hoof and drove them back in a daring fashion circling around Grant's forces.

During October the skies opened up and we had to live with heavy rain, flooding, and the misery of mud. December and most of January was cold but did not present an unbearable hardship. At the end of January though it got incredibly cold. Thanks to Davey's expert help, Owen and I were quite warm in our hut. February wasn't bad at all as winter approached an end.

Time on the Howlett Line continued to be spent being called up to the trenches on the rare occasions that there might be one or two shots fired between the lines, the usual drilling day in and day out, and listening to the veterans tell the latest rumors they heard while swapping goods with Yanks at the spring.

More than anything though, my time was spent jawing with Owen and watching over him. Since the time the Captain made the unfortunate bully ride the rail, nobody dared mess with Owen. This was good, but I was figuring that in this war, these good times would end for both me and Owen. So we'd sit in the hut and I'd try to help by responding to all of Owen's questions and remarks.

To escape all this for a while I would disappear from the hut in the night time just to be alone with my thoughts. I'd stare at those stars when it was clear and wonder how those could be just like our sun as Mr. Connelly back home would sometime talk about after he gave us a Bible lesson on Sundays. He'd do this while we were waiting for the adult church to let out. It was funny because Mr. Connelly would be kind of boring and he seemed somewhat uninterested himself while he told us all about the happenings of the Good Book, but when he got talking about stars or plants or rocks, he just seemed to light up. From being at his house once, I saw that it was full of books.

Now I can't read excepting for a few words here or there, so I didn't know what Mr. Connelly's books was really about. Pa said reading is for those with time to do nothing. Instead of schooling, he would say I was needed on our place so that we'd never lose it. We had gotten to the point where we could afford the three or four Negroes we had, but when Pa bought our place he had nothing except the willingness to work from sunup to sundown and to him that's the way life is. It was amazing that he would even allow me and ma to attend church on Sundays.

Mr. Connelly told me I should be attending his school because he could tell I was not only smart, but that I had that certain kind of excitement when hearing about new things. I recall best how he showed us how far away the nearest of them stars was. He lined up sheets of paper with what must have been a hundred blocks on each page. He said each block was equal to a hundred million miles. He put the Sun in the first block and the planets Mercury, Venus, and our Earth in the second. Then he put the planets in boxes right up to putting a funny sounding planet named Uranus in about the twentieth box. He even said that recently a couple guys in Europe said there was another planet even farther away. Then he really got me to wonderin' when he showed us a whole bunch of pages he blocked off with nothin' in them until about the tenth page. On that page he had marked where he said the nearest star, not coutin' the sun, was. And just think each of those blocks were equal to a hundred million miles. Ever since then, I just can't help from starin' at that sky and thinkin'.

Again though pa saw no use in knowing such things. He said the whole thing was a waste of valuable paper. I love my pa, but I feel I always was fated to be a big disappointment to him. At times I thought things about my pa, things a boy should not feel. I mean I would think to myself that he was a stupid man. That is because it is ignorant to not care about learnin', and all the things there is to learn.

I will never forget him catching me trying to read some of a simple book Mr. Connelly let me borrow. I was sitting on a rock taking time off from plowing a piece of land that was so hard and rocky that me, the ox, and the plow had been just worn out. Out of nowhere a shadow spread over me. Causing the shadow was pa looking like he could kill me. "What the damn hell are you doing?" Rarely did pa use words like this.

I was emboldened by his sharp words and replied. "I am trying to make something of myself. Don't you know you have to read these days to not be considered ignorant?"

He turned all red, or at least redder than his sunburn already made him, and that was pretty red. "You have a good life here and none of it has come from books. And you think I'm ignorant, your own father. I'll tell you what ignorant is, it is all those fools in Richmond and Washington, and even just down the road in Blacks and Whites. They are so learned they do not have the common sense to leave things alone. Instead they take in all this blabbering from books and listen to professors or whatever, who haven't worked a day in their life yet know all the answers.

"Why it is for sure you won't make any kind of farmer and this place will be not worth one of your damn books when I'm gone. But, I will not let this happen. I'd like to whip you good you lazy mama's boy. But, then we would have to endure a big thing around here with your mother crying and all. So you do this. Take that book to Connelly and tell him if I ever see one of his books on my land again I'll consider it some type of trespassing and ruining of my land because it is and it should be just as much against the law as reading to niggers is. Now go and get back because I don't care if you have to work all night during the full moon. You are getting this field plowed by tomorrow. You see idiot son of mine, I don't need to know how to read a Franklin almanac to know there is to be a full moon this evening. Now get out of my sight with that book."

By now I could only look at the ground. The idea passed through my head that if my pa did try to hit me I was getting pretty big for a twelve year old, which I was at the time, and I could fight him back. He was still strong yet a bit worn out from age. I had thought on it some in the past and figured I could be fast on my feet and avoid a couple of his attempts at blows and then sneak in a couple of solid hits. But, despite these thoughts, I kept my head low for it was just terrible having these thoughts about giving your father a beating.

Just then, with me in such a sorry state, I heard a slight noise coming from the Negro cabins. There three of the boys had just returned from their fields all finished for the day. They was just standing there looking and my sorrow turned to humiliation and then anger. I shouted at my pa that he was a bastard and before he could take a swing at me I run off with the book to the road leading to Blacks and Whites.

All along that road I hated my pa more than ever before and more than ever after. It was good that he treated the Negroes well enough so that he didn't expect any more work from them than me. But, there was not another place in Virginia from the largest plantation to the smallest hill farm that would allow their Negroes to watch a family squabble as it was then happening. You see after that I always felt conflicted. On one hand I greatly respected my pa for treating the Negroes well and I considered them part of the family. On the other hand, I felt anger because the Negroes never again gave me full respect because of the way pa treated me.

I arrived at Black and Whites and went to the modest house next to the church. I walked almost all the way around the house before finding a side door. I didn't feel at all like going to the front and having Mrs. Connelly fuss about me like the fine Southern woman she is. No, a cup of tea and a piece of cake while being all polite and neighborly was not what I wanted at that moment. I wanted to give back the book and get back on that road.

I could see Mr. Connelly through the side door. I knocked and quickly said, "Here is your book back Mr. Connelly, or I mean Preacher sir." Now, feeling even more humiliated, I attempted to get quickly away.

"Sam, what is your hurry?" Mr. Connelly said before I could get away. "Were you able to make any sense of the book, especially the parts that tell how to see signs that the weather is about to change?"

I wasn't going to say anything, but I broke down. "Mr. Connelly, I didn't get to fool with the book much at all. My pa said it was a waste of time, actually even worse in that reading books like this make men lazy and worthless."

The kind teacher did not look overly concerned about the revelation. "Sam, your pa is a hardworking man who loves you dearly. He can only see that hard work has enabled him to succeed. More than anything he cherishes your mother and you so much that he wants to instill in you what it will take for you to have a good life when the farm is yours."

Before I could say anything, Mr. Connelly continued. "That is not to say you should give up on learning. Sam, life is learning and if you pay real close attention to things you will already know much about life when you begin to read books. You do not need to discuss this with your pa for he won't understand. The truth is, however, no one can do anything to stop a determined person like you from learning."

I started back on the road home. It hadn't rained in a while and the dirt was packed firm and easy to walk on. I felt better as the sun began to set. A June sunset can't be any better than on a Virginia road heading west. By the time I could see our place, just beyond our two oak trees, I felt better and I wanted to go make things right with my pa again.

The problem was he wasn't at any of his usual spots. He wasn't down by the slave quarters talking about farming with the Negroes. He was not on the porch or in the barn working on the farm equipment as he would do often on warm nights. The last place to check was at the eatn' table where ma and pa might stay after dinner talking a bit.

There I found ma alone looking upset. She saw me and holding back tears gave me a plate covered with cloth. A slab of beef with some fried taters was below that cloth and usually I would be eating it before sitting down. "Where is pa?" I asked ma.

"He took off in the buggy towards the Courthouse. He is mighty upset Sam."

"I know ma, but…," I stopped. "I understand how he feels."

"Do you Sam? Your father loves you so much. You need to love him back."

This hurt me so much. Didn't they know I loved them both? It seems that what they wanted was proof. They just lived their lives too much through me. I just could not respond to ma. If they didn't see it was important that I become educated, at least learn to read and write, so be it. But, they should not think because I had dreams of my own I did not care about them.

When I saw pa the next day we exchanged just a few words. I never did find out what he went up to the Courthouse for. Maybe, just riding on the moonlit roads like I hear he did in his younger days. He loved to ride and I think that was the part I inherited from him, that is getting out and seeing things that others didn't bother with like how it looked and felt different to be out on the buggy during the full moon when you could see where you were going. He just couldn't see how my wanting to learn things in a book was the same thing.

After a few days he eased up a bit and began talking normal to me again. He talked again about how this place would be mine and if I took care of it right I would have a wonderful life here. He even talked about how it might not be so terrible if we lost this war for he was sure the Negroes would want to stay and help work the land. "After all," he said, "We have been real good to them."

This made some sense to me, but then again, it had to gnaw at them not being able to make up their own minds about things.

So, I secretly kept my dream alive about going to school. I have to say that with all the thinking I did back on the Howlett line I got mighty down about the prospect that I never would be attending school if I got killed in the war. Thinking about all this distracted me from the comfort I usually got looking at the night sky. Often I would return to the shelter at night somewhat in a bad mood.

I remember one such time, sneaking in as quiet as possible. Owen was sitting up wide awake. "Nite you been looking at the night sky again," he said.

"Yea," I answered, "now why don't you get some sleep. We'll be chopping wood again most of tomorrow."

"OK, but what is it you see up there?" asked Owen.

"Well, I see something kind of peaceful up there, something that don't give a damn about Jeff Davis and Abe Lincoln, something that is beyond all this thing where we have to kill each other and we have to put up with big mouth's that don't really know nothing.

"Who knows anything?" responded Owen.

"Well either way it's a good question Owen, but they all sure act like they know it all and we are likely to die for what others are so sure of."

"Don't say that," Owen near pleaded with me. "You have been such a good friend that I'll pay you back some day and you'll have a fine life."

That's when I realized what I'd seen in Owen. He just had such a good heart. That made me scared though because I just knew this here war was going to destroy him somehow. I also knew it wasn't only Owen who I feared would be ruined by this war, but that I would somehow be a victim of it too, and it wouldn't be long.

The End Of Peace

I recall the last morning spent on the Howlett Line like it was yesterday. I remember slowly turning over in my bed roll. It was barely light out and I could just barely see out through a crack between the logs the other shelters and the still cannon. I looked harder and noticed in the distance the sentry for our area leaning against a hitching post. He didn't move an inch the whole time I watched. Whoever it was, he must have been sound asleep. For a second I thought it my duty to go wake him. But heck, there hadn't been any activity at night since, well, I guess the beginning of winter.

It felt good just doing nothing. The air, even with the terrible odors of me and my two shelter mates, had that unmistakable feeling in it that lifted the spirits of every country boy. It was the smell and feel of spring. Back home it was a time when chores felt less like work and doing anything outside felt good. This day I even looked forward to getting up and falling in for drills, having some lousy grub, and following that with some digging work detail.

It was the first day of April in the year of 1865. As I went through the routines of the day, I noticed the others were also in good spirits. It was a clear and pleasant day after an all-night rain. The war seemed a long ways off. Maybe this would be the year that everyone would come to their senses. The Yanks had to be sick of trying to make us see it their way. I mean, what was so important to them that they were willing to die by the thousands? For us it was different. This was our land and we just want to be left alone.

Little did I know that it would be the last day of the war that I would really feel good about being an army man, for I was about to do some serious soldiering. That meant no easy camp life, no regular eats, and no comfortable shelter to sleep in at night.

After supper that evening, Owen and I were the first into our shelter and we were settling down telling some tall lies and the like. Soon, Davey came in. He too was in a joking mood, which was unusual for him. He didn't even pick up the law book he was studying as was his usual habit before the last light of the sun went away. Instead he made a crack that if we didn't wash our uniforms soon they could be propped up on the line and we would have no worries. He said the Yanks would not dare go near them because of the smell of them. We joked some more as the day turned to dusk and then night. It seemed like I'd just gone to sleep, in the spring air, when all of a sudden I jumped up to the sound of lots of cannon fire in the distance.

I had never heard them this loud coming from Petersburg excepting maybe the time the Yanks mined under the line and blew a huge hole in the ground. This time it had to be an even bigger fight, for it was coming from farther away, west of Petersburg, where our lines were trying to protect the railroads coming from the south and the west. It sounded like the end of the world was taking place some twenty miles away.

The three of us sat up but didn't say a thing as dawn slowly came upon us. Then the barrage of cannon fire stopped. Owen anxiously asked Davey, "It is just some testing out the guns, you know showing off for some general or something, isn't it?"

"I reckon," answered Davey, but I could tell he knew better.

There wasn't much use just lying there in our blankets, so the three of us quickly dressed and went out to prepare some breakfast. We roasted some green apples and made some weak coffee from a few grounds a Yank had traded for some of Davey's tobacco. Suddenly Sergeant Taylor came running over. "Get that fire out and report to the line," he barked. So we did as he said and when we got there we could see why. The Yanks were rushing about in their camp about 100 yards from us. I noticed our veterans fussing with their guns. They was giving their weapons some extra cleaning and making sure they was loaded, and had extra cartridges ready. More than anything I noticed that they made sure their bayonets was properly fixed. Nervously I began preparing my gun. Owen just stood there looking scared stiff. "Come on Owen, get your gun ready," I yelled,

"What for?" he shouted back as if we were about to engage in a game of rounders and he just wasn't interested in playing.

Now the Yanks were all up at their front trenches. Our pickets had retreated to our lines since we didn't need anyone to tell us the Yanks were about to charge. It was real quiet. Then our veterans started hollering one after the other things like, "Yank, you are about to see the elephant now." Or, "It sure is a shame you came all the way down here just to be shot up and sent home to mommy in a box."

At that time I felt it was awful cruel to say such things. Later, I figured out that most of the Yankees were young new recruits or more likely conscripts. A veteran soldier knows that a scared man who is about to get into his first fight is a man likely to run away when the battle begins. I looked down again at Owen and I realized that the Yanks were not the only scared soldiers on that field. Owen was shaking badly, and his gun was nowhere near ready to fire.

Seeing Owen so scared made me feel a bit braver. I was about to tell him again to get his gun ready when the Yanks commenced whooping and jumping out of their trenches. They came a running right towards us. Then I felt a hand on my shoulder. I looked back to see standing there steady as a rock Major Parker who had recently been promoted from captain. I must have just been the nearest shoulder to him, but I felt honored that it was mine he planted his hand on to announce, "Now steady boys, and wait until I say fire."

I waited as told and fired my musket, reloaded and fired again. I was so nervous at the sound of all the guns going off my first shot kicked up the dirt only 20 feet in front of me. The veterans must have got off four rounds by the time I took my second shot, which I reckon missed everything since I aimed way too high trying to correct the mistake of my first attempt. Before I could take a third shot, the Yanks had retreated to their original line. That was all the fighting I did during the war. I reckon you can see why I don't even count that as really fighting. Those Yanks never got anywhere close. The dead bodies were so far away I couldn't even feel they was real.

I just know I was happy the battle, if you could call it that, was over. However, I realized things were about to change for good. I saw Major Parker and I could tell he was plenty concerned. I knew in my gut that the easy days on the Howlett Line were over. All through the late morning officers were meeting. Once in a while, a courier would ride up and give some papers to Major Parker. I could tell it wasn't like other times when this might of meant we were about to get some fresh rations. No, not this time, and to make matters worse, one could just feel a certain excitement over at the Yanks line even though they had just took a whipping. All in all, these things did not add up to good news.

Owen, however, appeared to be in a good mood. He heard some scuttlebutt that General Lee won a big victory that day. Well, we had heard that rumor almost every day, but, when the facts came in, we got news that Sherman was in North Carolina, General Hood's Army virtually no longer existed after being totally defeated at Nashville, and Sheridan was burning up the valley west of the mountains. One day at the spring, I heard one of our boys telling a Yank that we was winning. The Yank said, "Then how come we're seeing officers from The Tennessee Army here like General Wilson? They ain't here because they are whipped; they are here because there is no one to fight in Tennessee anymore." That's one of the two reasons I never talked to a Yank. It would just be them telling us bad news and the other reason being I might be called on to kill a Yank. I had been fearing that enough without having to know the feller.

Later in the afternoon, while Owen was carrying on about how Lee had whipped Grant, we was told what I feared. We were ordered to pack and be ready to fall in and march. We were abandoning the Howlett Line. Owen came running asking, "Are we about to join up with our victorious army, do you reckon?" I just said that we were about to do some serious marching for the first time, so he should pack up good and only take what he would need to survive. It was about nine in the evening when it was all dark and quiet that we was ordered to fall in a few at a time and not make any noise. After each group formed, they headed west away from our little fort and onto a dusty road where we commenced marching in the darkness. I actually enjoyed this until I got so tired I could have slept standing up.

We got to the place called Chesterfield Court House just before dawn. Major Parker decided we could stop there by the roadside and sleep for a while. Soon, we heard tremendous explosions coming from the direction of Richmond. Even Owen knew the truth now. This could only mean the city was under attack or had already surrendered. Word was soon passed along to the men that indeed Richmond had been taken by the Yanks. It was only fair to be told this news for most of our battery was from Richmond and they all had family there. In the meantime, we was told that we would keep moving west to join up with the main army that had evacuated Petersburg. No one knew exactly where we was trying to get to after that.

Owen was now in tears. "Sam," for once he called me that instead of just Nite, "Do you think my mama is ok?" I was real concerned for him, for no one in the army would dare be overheard calling their mother mama.

"Now listen Owen," I said, "Your ma is a civilian, and even Grant himself respects that. She had plenty of notice since yesterday and I'm sure that she is fine." I said this while thinking the whole time that I didn't really know if this was true or not, but my words did seem to calm Owen and helped me too because I felt I was doing something worthwhile by carrying out Major Parker's wish that I look after Owen. After a short rest, we started marching again, and in the daylight we could see that we was part of a long line of troops. Besides the units that had been near us on the Howlett line, we were joined by other units coming from the north and south. Now Owen and I experienced first-hand the drudgery of marching. It was just as the veterans had told us it would be.

We slept somewhere that night. Darn if I knew exactly where, but I remember what it was like the next morning. It was beautiful out and the spring fields smelled wonderful like early spring always smelled in Virginia. It would have been a grand day to be back home instead of marching all day. It didn't help one bit that we had hardly eaten' a thing, only a little parched corn. We started marching and kept at it all day until we come to a place called Goode's Bridge where we stopped for the night. Owen and I huddled up just about shivering to death under the clear cold sky. Owen started talking about slippin' away. "Come on Nite," he said. "I know we are just going to die out here and I have to find out if my mother is ok."

"Don't you even think about that Owen," I replied. "If you do and get caught you'll be shot. We're marching now and no one would fool with the rail. You'd be facing a firing squad! Just stick with me, and I'll take care of you."

Owen calmed down enough to fall asleep. I never felt more like a man and a soldier. I was sure Major Parker would be proud of the way I was carrying out his request to watch over Owen. The weather remained clear and I got up to stretch my legs. It was a beautiful night sky and even though we were on this terrible march I felt okay. The sky was still there just as it had always looked this time of year. I fell asleep thinking about what Mr. Connelly had told me about the stars back home. Peace existed somewhere, even if it was millions of miles away.

By noon the next day we were in Amelia Courthouse where a train load of supplies was supposed to be. We found nothing but plenty of other soldiers who had been fighting with Bobby Lee and General Longstreet. As tired and hungry as we were, we looked like wealthy planter folk next to these fellas that had been in the Petersburg trenches for nine months. Now they were getting even less food and the disappointment of there being no food supply train in Amelia had everyone moaning. Suddenly, Corporal Gibson Clark approached and said, "Men, I need one of you to report immediately to Lieutenant Brown. They are splitting us up here and one of you two needs to join the Lieutenant right now."

"Corporal, may I point something out?" I spoke up before I could think about it.

"Yes, quickly, private, speak up."

"Major Parker has requested that I keep an eye on Owen here,"

The Corporal looked around like he might find the answer somewhere in the town. I figured he hoped to see someone of higher rank so that the responsibility of making a decision wouldn't fall on his shoulders. Then he spoke, "OK, Private Butterfield come with me. Nite if you can find Major Parker to countermand the Lieutenant's order before we leave, then so be it, but get back here on the double." Obviously, Corporal Clark was doing his best not to disobey orders and not get in trouble with the Lieutenant or Major. Army life was like that. Displease someone above you and you could be busted in rank or worse. So, off I went a looking for Major Parker but soon was stopped by Davey Richardson. "Sam, didn't you hear that if you weren't called to go with Lieutenant Brown, you were supposed to fall in near Major Parker's tent?"

"It's Owen, Davey; he's gotten separated from me. It's the one thing I was supposed to do in this war and now I've failed."

Davey said we should go find Major Parker and he would recall him. We done just that, but this was a different Major Parker from before. "Son, you did a good job," he told me, "but Owen had to grow up sooner or later, and I have no time to deal with such a matter. Just about the whole army is here fighting for its life. Now fall in with the rest here, for it is time to do our duty for state and country and pray to God that our friends and loved ones, as well as ourselves, survive this trying time." That was it, whether the Corporal was still back along that road with Owen or not. Owen was headed one way and I another.

I don't know about Owen, but I had left all my gear, as meager as it was, back at that place where the corporal hailed Owen and me. Of the things I left behind, it was that lousy musket I missed the least. I no longer had any appetite for fighting, even though the extent of my battling had been shooting off my gun twice when those Yanks charged us at the Howlett Line. We tramped through the dust thirsty and hungry like runaway slaves. At least we had been dry, but to tell the truth a little rain would have been welcomed. The next morning of April 6th it was cloudy and looked like we might get some rain, but it never came. We were on the march again when we heard crashes to the south that at first I thought was thunder. The veterans knew the sound all too much better than a recent recruit like myself. It was cannon and as we continued to march, the more experienced soldiers quickly surmised we were steadily moving away from the artillery. We marched for the rest of the day and heard no more fire when we stopped at nightfall and slept wherever we could find a flat spot. The next day, the rain we desired began to fall. It was a very hot day and the cooling effect of the rain was welcomed. It was rather pleasant that evening and the next day I remember my body feeling strong after nearly a week of marching. I felt optimistic, why I do not know, when we made camp the night of April 8, 1865. It had been a week since we left the Howlett Line and if anybody ever missed a place like that it sure was us. Now, we was at a place someone told me was just outside a town called Appomattox Court House.

When I woke up the next morning, there was all kinds of hollering and directing. We was soon moving up to take position. I was about to see "the elephant," the name given to a battle by the veterans. All you could see in front of us was blue soldiers. The Yanks had gotten ahead of us, and if General Lee wanted to make it to Lynchburg or Danville then we was going to have to fight our way through. This was what I thought would never happen, since we was always fighting a defensive war since I signed up. Now, it looked like we would be the ones charging across an open field and getting shot to pieces. For hours, I can't rightly say for how many, we gazed at the blue soldiers across from us and everything else one's eyes could see. I looked around real good figuring this might be the last day for me to see this earth. There in the distance was a small town, much like Nottoway Courthouse near where I was from. Actually we wasn't too far from my home, but it now seemed as far away as you could get.

I tried to enjoy what I was seeing. I looked long and hard at the small wood buildings surrounded by spring fields. In the distance were rolling hills and even mountains. It was paradise compared to the muddy swamps of the Howlett Line, even though the land was torn up in places from thousands of soldiers trampling the ground as they gathered at this place. As I was looking around and getting lost in my thoughts I realized that it had become very quiet. It was a strange experience and some of the veterans said that things just didn't seem right. Before a big battle there were always lots of soldiers from both armies marching and counter marching as the generals tried to get everything just right. Then we saw a single soldier running up to us as fast as he could. It was Johnny Glen, who had been out foraging for anything at all we could eat. "O here it comes," said Davey, who was standing next to me. This kind of thing apparently meant something big was about to happen and in these circumstances, that something wasn't good.

But there were no thousands of blue clad soldiers, no yelling mass of men bent on killing you. And killed I surely would be now that I did not even have a weapon. This wasn't to happen, though, for Johnny didn't jump in behind us or holler to get down. Instead he stood there like he just seen a ghost.

"General Lee surrendered," he let out after catching his breath.

Immediately, the meanest things were yelled back at Johnny. Their sentiments were clear. There was just no way the Army of Northern Virginia could surrender to a Yank force no matter how big it was. Then Major Parker rode up amongst us on his horse. Amidst the groaning, in a firm yet sad voice, he said, "It's true men. It is all over." I looked down and then quickly up to see that I was standing next to Gibson Clark.

"Gibson," I said, "What about Owen, where is he?"

"I do not know. Soon after we left Amelia I was dispatched to find Major Parker. I do know this though; our boys got into the awful fight along a ditch called Sailor's Creek. Some boys from another unit told me so. They said many from our army were killed or captured." I then realized Owen had seen the elephant and how it turned out I wasn't to know for a good while. For me, the war was over.

HOME

The war was over and we lost. As a defeated army no one knew what would happen next. Even in defeat we trusted Robert E. Lee to take care of us, but in truth the Yankees were now in charge. Soon word came down that we were going to be allowed to go home. The Yanks knew that if General Lee told us the war was over then the war was over. We gathered up in a line and said good-bye to General Lee and the other Confederate heroes. Soldiers were crying and telling General Lee that if he changed his mind they would fight on. Not me, I had home on my mind. About three day's walk away was my bed and my old life. I was fine with the way it turned out. No time in a prison camp and no time marching under orders. I could go back to working on the home place.

I was going to insist my folks let me get some schooling. I now knew from seeing more than Nottoway County that the fella who would get ahead in this world had to know about reading and writing. And besides, I had met plenty a fool who could read and write, so why couldn't I. Major Parker thought I was bright enough to make a good soldier, so I figure I was smart enough to get all the learning I could. My Pa's way of thinking, that one should spend all his time working the land and he'd be provided for, just wasn't going to be true anymore. There were new inventions that would change everything. The war made you see it. The Yanks might have been wrong attacking our land, but they showed us what steam engines, the telegraph, and large modern factories could accomplish.

I wanted to get home and rest some and enjoy some good country living before I started the learning of subjects. Just a few days in bed and then later on some camping in the woods like the good old days and then I would be ready to get serious about life.

Just a few days after the surrender, I headed out on the road that ran from Appomattox County to Nottoway County. It wasn't a whole lot more than 50 miles to home. I could be there in three days, maybe less. The road was clogged with Southern veterans headed east, and there were Yankees too, on horses in clean uniforms acting special like. Some shared some food and water. Most were friendly until news arrived that Abraham Lincoln was shot. Then some of the Yankees turned real ugly.

At the time, I was a little past Farmville, no more than a full day from home. My first thoughts about Lincoln were that it was just one more dead. Everyone had suffered, so why shouldn't the leaders of this darn thing? But by this time, a whole week or so after Lee's surrender, Abe Lincoln had become more than just a person to the Yankees. He was now more like a legend. That made all of us Southerners suspects as evil doers. We all were considered guilty for the actions of whoever shot the Yankee president. I just tried keeping my mouth shut and my thoughts to myself when coming across a Yank, even if he had something bad to say. Late the second day after I left the army, I crossed paths with a Confederate veteran camped about two miles west of Burkeville Station. He greeted me fondly. "Hello friend. Where are you's headed?"

"I'm headed to…" and then I hesitated because I had heard stories about deserters and renegades just looking for places they could rob. I started again and told a lie. "I'm trying to work my way back to Petersburg."

"Good luck," he replied. "I will tell you though, you ain't going to find much there. The place is just a mess according to some Yanks who passed through here heading west. After months of shelling and fires breaking out the town will probably be unrecognizable to you."

"How do you know I wasn't there during the siege?"

"Because son, you look like you have had some food in your belly, and your uniform isn't totally torn up, and you don't have that faraway look in your eyes."

I could not argue that point with him, so I told him how I was up on the Howlett Line. We talked some more, and he told me he had been released at Appomattox to work his way back home to North Carolina. I didn't know still if I could trust him, for I wondered how he got to this place a couple days ago just about the same time they were releasing us to go home. He said he set up camp here to rest a bit and let a slight flesh wound heal. The fella did give me one bit of advice I did heed. He said there was a big camp of Yank soldiers down at Burkeville. They was guarding some prisoners who were not released yet. With the recent news about Lincoln, he said I'd best avoid that area if I could.

I was not about to chance trouble like one finds around a bunch of soldiers without much to do, especially if whiskey was available. Add to this the news about Lincoln and it just smacked of trouble. Sure, there were plenty of other Confederates heading east on the road, but that could make it worse. Drunk soldiers just might attack four or five of their former enemy if they appeared to be marching together.

I got off the road and headed due south through the fields. I knew of an inn down that way right on the county line between Prince Edward and Nottoway County. The place was known as Burke's Tavern and it sat right at the intersection of the road to Moore's Ordinary to the west. To the east it was about two miles to the railroad junction. If I could circle around it to the west, I could avoid anybody staying at the inn as well as the force of Yanks at Burkeville, or as we called it Burke's Crossing.

Evening was approaching and that was good. I could more easily slip by in the dark. The sun began to set and the fields were soaked with a brilliant gold brought on by the west setting sun. The days were springtime short so that by the time I could make out the burning oil lamps at the tavern it was quite dark.

The sounds traveled to my ears soon after my eyes made out the light. There was the hollering that I knew to accompany the drinking of whiskey. Then came a loud shrieking that caused my heart to start beating like it was about to bust out of my chest.

It turned out I was about 100 feet from the railroad tracks and a train from the west was speeding through towards the junction. I jumped off my feet and sprawled down flat on the ground. One car was lit up by lamps inside and I could see some important looking people wearing big hats with brims through the windows. I reckon it could have been General Grant and his staff for all I knew, but it flew by so quickly I couldn't tell.

The sky was clear, and under the moon I moved slowly in a big circle around the Inn. The night sounds were a strange combination of spring fields filled with the merry insect sounds of a new farming year and that of the ruckus being made at the tavern.

The closer I got, the sounds of nature were overcome by the drunken noise of young men. I steadily made my way around the building until I reached a point past where the only sound was again that of nature. I just stood there feeling good. The familiar sounds of all the local creatures let me know I was away from war and back home. It is funny, but the sounds there are different from those at the Howlett Line even though the two places can't be much more than fifty miles apart. For one thing here you could hear dogs and cows making their own kind of music. Closer to home you would even know whose dog was barking. You would know the name of the dog. Around a soldier's camp you didn't hear any animals except horses. Maybe you would hear an occasional pup that had become an army pet. The dog didn't start out as a soldier's pet. It was just a fact that if you had a farm near an army, and had a dog, you wouldn't be having it long. Near a place like the Howlett Line, the animals would be taken and the officers would move into your home. Nope, no sounds of regular people activity and no sounds of the animals normally found with people.

There was a brilliant sky filled with stars and planets that night I got past the tavern. I remember thinking that down here on earth the sounds, trees, and the lay of the land could all be altered by war and other doings of men like the building of farms and towns. Yet, the sky still looked the same at each time of the year whether man was down here fighting or plowing the land. I felt so small. I was glad I wasn't on that train that went by, for if you was on it, you would have to think of yourself as being big and important. By first light I had made my way down to Raccoon Crossing Road. I was about five miles from home.

There were a lot of Negroes on the road, most just keeping their heads down and acting like they didn't know what they were looking for. Maybe they were out exploring since before this they were never allowed off their owner's place. Some may have been searching, looking for family members that their owners had sold off years before.

I headed south on Lewiston Plank Road and then east on Hungrytown Road. I was just a couple of miles away now. One Negro man who held his head up passed me on the road. Unlike the others, he spoke to me, "There nothin' down that road fo' you. That land all ours now, especially with the killin' of father Abraham. You need not be goin', I tell you man." The words of this man scared me. What if the four Negroes I remember at our farm were now in charge? Jim, I reckoned, would be the oldest - not much older than me. Was Ma, Pa, and I going to be Jim's slaves? It couldn't be, could it?

Just then I passed another Negro man known as Jake from the Crittenden place. I remembered he was trusted to travel back and forth unguarded to get supplies at Nottoway Station. He stopped me and said, "Ain't you the Nite who went to war?"

"Yes," I answered anxiously and added, "Do you know if my Ma and Pa are doing ok?"

Jake said, "They was fine last time I was down that way about a week and a half ago. I haven't been that way since then because of all the commotion with the Yankees coming through." He added, "Don't be worrying none about Union soldiers, because there are not too many this far south of the main road." I figured he was right, because by the time the Yankees got here chasing Lee, they knew where our troops were and it was mainly to the north. And they were in a big hurry to try and get ahead of us, which of course they did at Appomattox.

I hesitantly asked Jake if it was true what that other Negro man had told me. "You shouldn't pay attention to that trash," answered Jake. "I know what fella you are talking about and he is just an ignorant field hand who worked his way up here from one of the Carolinas. The folks here are going to work together now. Yes we is free, but those of us who were treated right are going to pitch in with the White folk and we is all going to have to toil side by side. If we don't, none of us going to eat, free or slave, white or black. Don't you worry. Your folks are good people. We all one, now, fighting to stay alive."

Feeling better, I continued walking through the countryside. I didn't see much damage and could tell that the army didn't pass through here, at least in large numbers. It was a beautiful spring day. I got more and more excited as I neared the road that turned off to the right towards the Crittenden place, and the small town of Black's and White's, called that because of two taverns there, one owned by Mr. White and one by Mr. Black. Sounds strange, but that's why they called it as they did. I'd go up there once in a while to see Mr. Connelly, who taught school there, and that was who I was going to have teach me to read and write.

I wasn't going to bring it up to Pa right away. I'd settle back in working the farm and doing more than my fair share. Pa would eventually come around. Right at that moment, though, I was ready for one of Ma's meals and maybe sitting on the porch with Pa afterwards. I figured we probably wouldn't say nary a word to each other. That's because we would be glad just to be back on that porch together again.

And then there it was just up ahead, that beautiful dirt road on which I grew up. Again, I know I complained about Ma and Pa not letting me attend school and just staying put on the home place, but that is because they loved that place so and loved me too, they just wanted us together. No one ever had better folks. Ma's cooking was the best and Pa taught me plenty about farming. He loved the land, and I think that's where I got my appreciation for the outside world.

I remember how sad they was when I set off for the Howlett Line. Now this was going to be a happy day. I was just about a mile or so from our place. A nice house it was with three rooms upstairs, a parlor downstairs and another room with easy access to the cook house, spring house, the barn, and storage buildings. And it had well-built comfortable slave quarters, three slave houses for four slaves. We had slaves yes, but we treated them good.

I would soon be seeing our tall barn. It was visible from the road where it made a turn about a half mile away from the farm. As I was thinking and walking, I came to where it was a slight ways down to a little creek and up the small hill and around the bend. That is the location from where one could see the barn. I got down by the creek and hesitated a bit. I stared at the small rivulet of water just the same as when I left for the war. It was like it was alive and it seemed to be at peace. Peace again, I thought. This little creek knew nothing of war or what evil people could do. And now I was headed back to my peaceful life as I knew it before the war. I felt lucky because I didn't see much of war, just enough to be thankful to get back away from it and return to the good life.

I now left that creek of my boyhood and ascended the small hill and rounded the bend prepared to see that good 'ole barn. But once I got there, I couldn't see it. Sometimes a hazy day would obscure it from view, but it was a clear sunny day. My mind started racing and so did my feet thinking that the closer I got, it would appear.

Finally, about halfway to it from the bend in the road, I could plainly see where it should be. There was a black outline around what was once the foundation of the barn. I moved closer and could now clearly see the rubble that had once been the barn. I could also see only charred timber and broken bricks where the house and every other building stood except for one slave house that remained intact.

I can't say what I did next or felt. I just remember walking around the farm. It seems to me now that it could not have happened a long time ago for Jake said he had seen my folks a week and a half past. None of that really mattered at the time. I could not think. I felt and it was the worst I ever felt. As I look back at it, I had to be the first soldier who would taste the total darkness of what man was capable of in war — not during the war, but only after it was over. I didn't have to go to battle, but I felt worse than any soldier did as I stood there in the field.

The next thing I remember was waking up in the field. I hadn't bothered using the one blanket I had. I was just lying there in the dirt, now moist from the night. The sun was coming up. I slowly stood and walked around a bit still in a dazed state but now able to mix a little thinking in. First thing I realized was that it had been no accident. Pa had the buildings set far enough apart so that if a fire broke out in one of the buildings it would not spread to the others. No, the fire was set on purpose and now only the one slave house that still stood was there because someone wanted to use it.

Then I had to do a thing that I'd wish on no one. I had to search through the ruins to see if ... I can hardly say it now ... my folks had burned up in the house. It didn't take long before I found some bones that were human. It just had to be my parents for next to them were the remnants of the small pen knife my pa carried in his pocket day and night. It had the letters RW on the metal blade. It had been Roger William's knife, his grandfather, the father of his mother. I just broke down and wept for what seemed like hours, and then I must have fallen asleep again on the ground. When I got up, I pulled myself together and looked around the burnt slave houses. I'm not saying for sure, but there were no bones there. At least I sure didn't find any.

The one house still standing looked untouched. The old table and chairs were still there and a few of the older slave clothes. This was Jim's place, and he never kept much to begin with. I sensed though that

45

somebody had been in here more recently than a week ago. I can't say for sure, but It was too orderly like somebody was staying here going to great pains to make it look like no one had been here. I spent the next two nights in Jim's house. Mainly I just sat there asking why. I was set to resume my life here, the life I loved as I loved Ma and Pa. So after the second night in the slave cabin, I headed up the road towards Black's and White's.

Our place was the only one on this here road. That's why we had little contact with folks unless we headed into Nottoway Station or Black's and White's. I got to Black's and White's about three hours later. I banged on the school house door, but there was no one around. Then I could hear some wood chopping going on not too far away. You see, the school was on about two acres of land with plenty of woods in the back.

It turns out Mr. Connelly was back there getting some wood. As I neared him, he greeted me friendly like, "My gosh, is that you Sam? You have come home from the war safe and sound! Well, are not your parents blessed?"

"No they ain't neither," I replied.

"Now Sam," Mr. Connelly quickly responded, "The times I have seen your parents is all they talked and prayed about was your safe return."

I began to feel sick; I saw a log and sat down on it.

"Is there something you need to tell me Sam?" asked Mr. Connelly. He had a soft kindly voice and I believe there was no finer man on earth than this old school teacher. I pulled myself together and told him what happened. He sat down next to me and put an arm around me. "I'm sorry son," he said. "I had no idea. With the war coming close to these parts and ending so abruptly, nobody has dared travel very far from home. No news has come from anywhere except down the main road, and that news is all about the end of the war, the assassination of Lincoln, and rumors about what will happen next."

We sat there silent for a good long while. You see, Mr. Connelly knows when it is time to talk and when it isn't. So, I spoke up next and asked him who could have possibly done such a thing. He took his time and answered that there had been reports of folks' slaves going crazy after hearing they was free. And of course, there were plenty of

46

Yankee patrols through all these parts. Or, it could have been robbers and thieves taking advantage of the lack of official authority in the area. Two words stood out from the whole bunch Mr. Connelly was telling me. Those words were slaves and Yankees. Sadness was turning to anger and Mr. Connelly could tell that. "Sam" he said as if physically shaking me, "You must move forward. Why you could stay here and finally learn to read and write like you have always desired."

"Aw, the hell with that," I responded. My words seemed to shock the kind teacher. I didn't care and continued with my rage. "Besides being a waste of time it's too late anyhow. I just wasn't meant for reading and writing. I'm a farmer like my pa."

"Sam," I vaguely heard Mr. Connelly speaking now. "Why the new president of the United States, Mr. Andrew Johnson, did not learn to read and write until he was 18 years old."

I didn't answer because my mind was far away. I kept thinking about our slaves going crazy when they got the news they was free. I would think of those fool Yankees, like those across from us on the Howlett Line, probably just going off and killing innocent people and burning their places just because someone they didn't know shot Abe Lincoln. I thought if that's the way they want it, that's the way it will be. I knew I was going back to our place with a shotgun and be ready for the first Black or Yank who dared set foot on my parents' property.

I went to Gardner's Hardware and asked what I could get in terms of a firearm on credit. I didn't have to ask to know that the two dollars I had in Confederate money was worthless. The clerk, who I didn't know, asked me a bunch of questions about our place which just confused me. I couldn't tell him what our expected crop yield would be or what we were planning to plant in what field or any of the other blasted questions I needed to answer to purchase a lousy gun on credit. I did know that if I said our place had been burnt down, I sure wasn't going to get a firearm, and as is I got nothing, anyways.

By the time I left town, it was late afternoon. Mr. Connelly had one of his students find me and give me a sack with some food in it. That was good since the little I had from the Yanks at Appomattox was about gone. Besides, just the thought of eating Yankee food now made me sick.

As I walked to what I could hardly now call home, I had plenty of time to ponder my new-found hatred for Negroes and Yankees. It got dark, and as I got close to our land, I saw what looked like a campfire burning on our place. I should have been more cautious, but the anger burning in my soul hurried my feet along. I had it set in my mind that it would be Jim and the other Negroes and they better be able to prove to me that it was Yankees and not them who committed the crime. As I approached, I could see it was three white men in tattered clothing, maybe Confederate uniforms like mine, that is they barely looked like uniforms anymore.

"What are you fellas doing on my land?" I surprised them. They all pulled their guns and I figured this was it. But then, one spoke up saying, "This don't look to be much of anybody's land anymore. And, you don't exactly look like a well-to-do plantation owner." The other two started laughing. "I'll say this though. You got guts coming up on us like this with no piece. Are you a remnant of our glorious army of Jeff Davis?"

"That I be," I answered. "And yes, this is my land, for what it's worth. If you were colored or Yankee, I wouldn't care that I had no gun, for I'd charge so fast that the one shooting better have damn good aim."

The same man answered, "Wooie! You sure do have guts, or you're crazy. Most of the folks around here have given up and talk about getting along with Yanks, even with the niggers." Hearing that word reminded me that I had stopped using it and I just couldn't startup using it again. I don't know why. I stopped because I didn't like being called names so why not call them coloreds or Negroes and not niggers? Even with the hatred I had I couldn't say it again. But that didn't cool off my hatred any.

"Well, I'll tell you what…," he tailed off and stopped for a moment and instead asked me what my name was. When I didn't answer he said, "Why you sure don't trust anyone, but all the same my name is Billy, that one over there is William, like me, but I goes as Billy. And the one with the brown bay is David. We ain't Yanks and sure as hell not niggers. Why we're on your side. We ain't given up. We rode in from near the Tennessee-Kentucky border and once we get some rest and supplies we are going back there. You can get lost in those hills and give the Blue Coats a whole bunch of trouble. So ya see, we are on your side."

"Well I reckon' you are, but that still don't explain you coming on my land."

"We're hungry and tired," Billy said. "You don't have to keep fighting, but if you really hate the Yankees and niggers, you could at least let us stay on your land here and rest awhile and tell us your name." I was too tired to argue, and they seemed to be what they said they were, so I told 'em my name and welcomed them to camp.

After a month's time, they were still camped on the land. Every day Billy would ask if they could look around and help try and salvage what might be left in the burned houses. He said he understood me not wanting to do it myself, the remains of my folks being in there and all. I didn't know what salvage meant, but if they could find something that would help I thought why not. He added that if they found some remains like bones they would gather them up so I could conduct some kind of decent burial.

As they looked around, I dug two graves for Ma and Pa. The whole time I dug I felt my hatred rise for Yanks and Negroes. I felt the same way as I attempted to work in the fields, trying to take care of whatever Pa had planted in the early spring. I had no seed or money to buy seed so that was all I could do. Even though I loved the land and knew about surviving out in it, I never was much of a farmer, at least not up to Pa's expectations. Pa didn't have much patience when it came to teaching and usually ended up just giving me jobs like feeding the hogs and cows, repairing fences, or prying out rocks. I also had done some plowing under Pa's eye, but checking the fields every day to see how the crops were doing I knew nothing about. When Pa did it I had no idea what he was looking at and why.

William and David knew how to use their guns right well and did some hunting, mainly rabbits and other small game, so we ate. Some strawberries were growing and middle to late May we ate our share of them. About the last week of May, Mr. Connelly showed up with some provisions. When he arrived, I was setting on a rock out near the small dirt path leading up to what was the main house doing what I did every day, brooding, and wondering how I could ever avenge what happened here. Meanwhile, Billy and the boys were doing their usual digging around in the remains of the house.

Mr. Connelly came up the path and I hardly noticed. "Sam," he startled me by saying, "What are you doing and who are those men up by the house?"

"What house?" I asked.

"The house where you were born and raised of course," he replied.

"That is no house," I said with an angry tone in my voice. "That is a pile of stuff busted up by the enemy just like places I seen on the road to Appomattox. I told them fellas up there they could search through it and see if they could find anything to help us live on this lousy piece of land."

The teacher replied, "Sam, you cannot go on like this. You must move on. Why are you trusting those strangers who...."

I interrupted him with anger in my voice, "Those men are my business and I kindly ask you to regard your own business."

But he was quick to say, "Those are well-spoken words Sam, actually remarkable for a man who can't read and write. You have to make something of yourself. You have a natural intelligence; use it for God's sake. Get off this rock and come back with me to learn!" I just sat there unmoved. After a while Billy came over and asked if there was some trouble. "I suspect, young man, there might be," responded Mr. Connelly. "Who are you and what is your business?"

"Why old man, my business was fighting your war while you sat safe and dry in your fine house." Then Billy turned to me and asked if I wanted him to "run this old coot off."

"No, just let him be!" I screamed. "Why don't you all just let me be?" I walked off into the trees and when I came back Mr. Connelly was gone and Billy and the two others were packin' up.

"Hey Sam," Billy called, "why don't you come riding with us? We are heading out for a while; maybe we will even get some revenge on the Yankees and niggers for ya."

I told him thanks for the offer, but I was stayin' put to see if I could get the crops in. "O yea good luck," David chimed in. "I don't know anything about farming, but I sure know it ain't done by sitting on a rock all day. You should be helping us look for something worthwhile like silver or gold."

"Shut your mouth David!" hollered Billy. "You know we agreed to help Sam here since he's a grieving and all. If we could have found some coins we'd given them all to the righteous owner. In fact Sam, here, you take a little of this dried beef. We will be back to check on ya. But we got to go now." And off they went and to be honest, I didn't care what they were talking about or where they were going.

Spring quickly turned to summer. Nothing grew. I occasionally received some supplies from Mr. Connelly who just left them, for he knew it was no use talking to me. Then, one day in the middle of August, I was there hanging around doing nothing when a skinny young man walked up my path. I asked what business he had here. That doesn't seem courteous, but it is more than I extended to the occasional Negro who came around. I'd tell 'em to get off my property and be in a hurry about it. I had only one small troop of Yankees stop by. I knew better than being forceful with them. But when they saw there was nothing here but the slave cabin I was staying in, they had no interest anyhow.

The skinny fella spoke up. "Don't you recognize me Sam? It's Owen."

"Owen!" I replied, "What in God's name are ya' doing here? Why are you not home where you belong with your kin? If you want anything from me you is outa' luck because I don't have anything to give."

He seemed taken back a bit, but he must have gotten used to the war changing people because he just continued talking to me. "What happened here Sam?"

With those few words of concern I broke down and told Owen the whole story. I must admit, it felt good telling it to Owen. For the first time, my heart softened a bit. Maybe it was like one of those instincts about taking care of someone because you took care of them before. Whatever it was, it got me to tell him to come on over to my sitting rock and rest for a while.

Then for the first time since I returned home I asked someone about their life. "Owen, I thought you might be a goner from what I heard about the battle you was in!" Before he responded, I told him why I couldn't come back for him.

After he assured me there were no hard feelings, Owen commenced telling me the whole story about what happened after I left him in Amelia with Corporal Clark. "Lieutenant Brown ordered all soldiers assigned to his outfit to fall in and get ready to move out on the double. We fell in line with Lieutenant Brown's two cannons and marched out sometime in the early afternoon. We didn't stop that night because the word was that General Lee feared we would get intercepted by the Yanks. The problem was we were with General Picket's men and we steadily fell behind General Mahone's troops. We got to a stream named Sailor's Creek and we got across it and up a hill when we halted with the guns. We were placed back a mile or so behind our line on the road. We weren't there long before the battle began in front of us. A column of Yankee cavalry headed right at us. It was us and the four guns of Captain Taylor and about six other guns under Officers Huger and Smith. We had no infantry to help us and no time to effectively employ the guns. I saw Captain Taylor get shot dead when he refused to surrender. And before I knew it, the rest of us were captured.

We were kept in an open field. Some Yanks took pity and gave us some hardtack. After a miserable night, this General named Custer showed up and galloped around us with a captured Confederate Flag with his band playing all the while. I heard one of our men mutter that someday he would like ride around Custer after defeating him in battle and see how he would feel about it.

Anyways, we were marched rather quickly so that in about three days, we were at City Point. Up to this time, most of the Union soldiers treated us well because they were fighting soldiers who knew how hard it was fighting all the time. It wasn't so at City Point. Here the Yankee soldiers were support troops and they had all the hate and foolishness we had on the Howlett Line. They felt cheated because they didn't get a chance to prove themselves in battle and took it out on us. They were barking orders and acting like real swells. When night came, they expected us to sleep in the open with no food to fill our bellies. The next day we were packed like slaves onto a ship named the Neptune. I was crowded with the others down below with nothing to eat and nothing to drink. The voyage was sheer misery. If it lasted another day I'd be dead for sure. As it was, we arrived at Point Lookout just in time."

Owen went on to describe the prison at Point Lookout. He said a good many of the guards were black men who had it out for the white Southern soldiers. However, Owen had it better than most because his mother got a little money to him. At this point I blurted out, "Owen, why are you not home with your mother?" He replied that there was lots of reasons, but he didn't feel like talking about it much. "Well, at least tell me about Point Lookout," I said.

Owen waited a darn long time before he slowly began to talk. "The guards, both White and Black, treated us as if we were to blame for everything that happened, especially the shooting of Abe Lincoln. For those of us who got some money, things were not too bad. I had some from mother and I was able to pay for some food, some soap, and blankets. More correctly, I was able to pay for not being roughed up and starved. But, then something happened..." Owen became quiet for a long time. Then, taking a deep breath he started up again. "You see, we were crowded into big rooms and at night we all slept where we could on the floor. One night, I fell asleep and suddenly I was woken up by one of my fellow prisoners. He whispered, "Let me under that blanket with you, you beautiful boy." He was much bigger than me, and I tried to pull away, but somehow he had a knife. He held that knife on me and then he started touching me in places he shouldn't and then...." Owen stopped, then suddenly got up and said, "I gotta, I gotta, I got a just go over in the trees a bit. I just have to." He ran off and I let him. I did so because I had no words to tell him back. I didn't fully understand what happened to him, though I had a pretty good idea. Also, I already had enough of my own problems. Why did he have to come here and tell me his problems? A bit mean yes, but I had become mean.

A couple of hours later he returned, sulking like he was ashamed. I put my bad attitude aside for a bit and told him that with everything that happened, with this war and all, he had nothing to be ashamed of. It was just another case of people acting their worst.

Owen then started talking again. "Sam," he said, not calling me Nite as he usually did in the past, "I told my mother what happened and before I knew it she was back at the prison with a Yankee officer. They made me point out the fella who did what he did to me. Then they took him out of the prison to do to him I don't know what. They then told me I was getting out. As I gathered my few things, some of the other prisoners told me they were going to get me soon and I better have eyes in the back of my head. That wasn't the worse of it though, for when we left it was in a fine carriage with that Yankee officer at the reins."

"What was so bad about that," I interrupted, "other than the fact that those Yankees are all pigs?"

"Well that was just it," Owen went on. "You see my mother used her charms with that fellow and he liked it so much that he went all the way back to Richmond with us and stayed right in the house with us."

I knew what Owen was saying, but my meanness was coming back and all I could think of was how his ma's house was in Richmond and it didn't get destroyed and his ma was ok and yet my folks were away from the war and look what happened.

So it turned out that Owens's ma sweet talked this Yankee and gave him some favors so that he would get Owen out before the others were released to go home. And Owen came here because of the shame of his ma living with a Yankee, plus the fact he was scared of being found by the prisoners who said they would get him when they got out.

This all got me to thinking about more stuff. I'd never have told my ma about something like what happened to Owen if it happened to me. I don't know what I'd do, but I wouldn't have run to ma like a boy. On the other hand, Owen seemed to know just what was going on. He knew right from the start that his ma did a little more than just ask that Yank officer for some help. It was confusing, but I got the idea that Owen wasn't quite telling everything just the way it was. After all this thinking I decided there was probably no way of figuring it all out, so if he needed to be here, why not? Two can be as miserable as one.

I turned to Owen and told him it was ok if he stayed and added, "Listen, first of all, those soldiers don't really give a damn about that rascal. When they get out they are all going to go their own ways and think about their own problems. Secondly, your ma was doing what she felt she had to so she could get you out. I'll admit I wouldn't want to be in any house with a Yankee, but he'll get what he wants for a while and then get out."

"Sam," he said, "there ain't nothing to go back for and I just gotta get away. With what happened with that fella', that is, what he did to me, I just gotta get away, I gotta get away to somewhere, somewhere where I can get back to being who I was before it happened."

All I could think of was I wished it was back in the days that Owen would never call me Sam, but would always greet me with a stupid joke about my name Nite, like, "That sure was a windy night Nite," or, "You sure were snoring like you were working on a pile of logs last night Nite." Just to hear one more awful greeting like that would do me good.

54

But the war had come and the funny thing is that for the two of us it came when it was over.

I told Owen it would be fine for him to stay awhile. "Just like old times," I joked, "That is the two of us staying in a hut together," seeing that the old slave cabin wasn't much more than a hut. So for the next month or so, we'd hang around pretending we were farming while we really weren't doing anything.

We didn't talk much like in the war days. We were both scarred, at least I know I was, and didn't care much about philosophizing like we used to. Owen did ask me how I was getting food, and I explained that Mr. Connelly would send one of his students over with food and supplies, and I'd give him some Union coin for payment. "Where did you get money from?" he asked. I told him that even with the fire I knew Pa always had some Union cash buried by an old oak tree in a glass jar. He said that there was no telling how the war was going to turn out and we may need that Union money someday. And he was right.

Up to this point I had told no one about the coins excepting Mr. Connelly. I told Owen, "Don't tell anyone about it especially if these three fellas named Billy, William, and David show back up here. I reckon' they are ok, just soldiers like us with nowhere to go, but they seem awful anxious to help look through the ruins to see if there was anything of value left. They did give me some food, and I figured they came here because the well was still providing water. After they left, I dug up the jar. I was surprised to find it, figuring that the way things were going the last year of the war Ma and Pa would have needed it. I was shocked to find near fifty dollar gold coins in there and some smaller change that I was using to pay Mr. Connelly." I knew my numbers a little bit, so I figured all together there must have been sixty dollars.

Owen and I continued to spend our time sitting around doing nothing. Obviously, the farm wasn't exactly prospering. A few things grew, but basically Owen and I were living off the money from Ma and Pa. One thing we now shared was hatred for the Yanks and Negroes. Owen hated the Yanks for sending him to prison and for one of them being wooed by his mother. As for Negroes, he said he hated them for "acting so high and mighty" at City Point and Point Lookout. I figured that more than anything Owen was just full of hate because of what that fellow did to him at the prison.

The summer months went by and it was soon September and then October. The nights were getting miserable as we looked forward to a winter on what you couldn't rightly call a farm no more. Once in a while, someone would go down the road but it was pretty clear that there was nothing here worth having. Then one day, Owen found me out near the woods and said three riders were galloping towards our miserable slave house. Things were about to change.

Across Western Virginia

The riders approaching from the southeast were Billy, William, and David, all in a great hurry. They rode right by the slave house and came right to us where they jumped off their horses. Billy spoke first, handing me a sack with some dried beef and other victuals in it. "Hey good buddy Sam, we got something for ya'. We got it from some nigger named Jake. He said it was for you." Before I could say a thing, the three riders pulled out their guns. "Yes sir, we'll have to talk about Jake right after the fight," Billy growled.

"What fight?" I asked.

Billy said nothing. William spoke up and asked, "Who is this ugly kid with you?"

Before I could answer, Billy hollered, "Here they come."

I still didn't have a gun, but Owen disappeared and was back in less than a minute with a service revolver. He crept up behind a little ridge with the other three, and I found a safe place to hide behind some of the house ruins. Coming towards the farm on foot were about six black men. They wasted no time rushing to the spot where Billy and the other three were behind the ridge. It was apparent who had fought and who hadn't in the war. Six against four were poor odds for the six if they were in the open and the four were behind cover. Soon two of the black men fell and the other four retreated. One of the black men shouted, "You be sorry. Now the law's on our side and we'll be back."

"Bring on the whole nigger town if you want you Prince of Africa," Billy shouted. At this the Negroes retreated from the scene.

The four defenders came towards me and David spoke first. "I don't know who this little guy is, but he is some shooter with that pistol. I think he got that one guy."

Billy chimed in with, "Yes siree. But right now we got big problems and so do you Sammy."

57

"Why do I have problems?" I responded.

"Well, number one, when they return with a lot more niggers, they ain't going to stop and ask questions, especially with word about that you don't like them so much these days. And number two, you ain't going to put up much of a fight with no gun. So if I was you and this other fella' here, I'd pack up and fast."

I stood there speechless for a moment and then saw I had no other choice. A shot suddenly rang out. William had finished off one of the two men who lay in the field. As we watched, he walked to the other one and pronounced him already dead. I turned to get what I could from the ruins of my lost home. As I walked away, Billy said one more thing that put fear right into my bones. "And Sam, don't forget that glass jar."

I knew I was lucky we were leaving in a hurry and Billy had no time to make sure I got the jar. What had just happened raised a lot of questions in my mind concerning Billy and the other two. I knew one thing for sure, they found out about the jar of coins when they met Jake on the road. Jake was about the only Negro I trusted at the time. He always helped Ma and Pa get things from town and even do chores on the farm without them even asking. To avoid questions from the officials in Black's and White's, I only told Jake and Mr. Conley about the jar of money hid on the farm, though not where it was hidden. Jake was such a good fella that Billy and his gang must have done something terrible to get him to talk. At that moment, however, there was no time to think any more about what happened to Jake. Owen and I had no horses, and Billy told William and David to take turns allowing us to ride with them so as the horses would not be overburdened. At other times, we would have to walk alongside. It was worse than marching in the war.

We was scrambling, so that even with us leaving late we must have made near 25 miles that day. We kept moving after night fell and came up on a town with nothing much more than a tavern. The place, it turned out, was called Green Bay even though there wasn't any water anywhere around there. Billy told everyone to stay put, keep our mouths shut, while he went in to see what he could find out. He came back out after what seemed like maybe half an hour.

"Let's push on a couple miles up the road where we'll find a place to camp," Billy announced. We found a spot, maybe 500 yards off the road. I had brought a couple of blankets along and I gave one to Owen. No one had barely spoke a word from the time we left the farm until we was all standing around the fire we built trying to get warm. Finally, Billy spoke. "Well Sam, you want to know what happened? I'll tell ya' what happened. We were riding back to check on how ya' been getting along. We come up on a nigger and we asked him his name. Nigger tells us he is known as Jake. We asked good 'ol Jake where he was headed and to do what. Well, at first this uppity nigger didn't want to tell us, but we did a little persuading, if you know what I mean. So he tells us he is dropping some food off for you sent over by this fella Mr. Connelly. The next part surprised us some when he told us you were paying for it with Union coin you had squirrelled away in a bottle somewhere. Here all this time we thought you were just flat broke like us. So what's the deal Sammy?"

I started out belligerent like, "I never promised you fellas anything. I did let you stay on my land and do all the looking around you wanted to do."

"Stop right there Sammy," Billy let out as if he never had been more insulted in his life. "We have done nothing but try and help you. If it wasn't for us, some highwaymen would have come by and killed you for a bite of beans, or worse yet, some Yanks or niggers would have got you. What did we have to gain by staying by you so long? In fact we was all surprised to find you alive when we got back here. I insisted that we look in on ya' in case though. Ain't that right David?"

David just stood there and didn't say a thing.

Billy in a louder voice repeated his question. "I said ain't that right David?"

"O yea that's right Billy. That's what you told us all right."

For just a second or two, Billy glared at David. He turned again towards me, and in a quieter voice said, "Now let's forget this here squabble with each other like the sons of the South we are, and pledge never to give up until the Yankees again let us be."

I didn't believe a word of it and was finally beginning to see the truth. Like a fool I said "Bull shit." Billy took a step towards me when suddenly Owen spoke up.

"Leave Sam alone. He lost a lot and if his folks wanted him to have some money, so be it."

David and William both started towards Owen like they were going to kill him, but Billy raised his voice and told them to back down. "Owen earned his say by fighting with us back in the gun battle and he knows we best be all together now." Looking at me again, Billy continued, "Yeah Sam, in it all together. What we got, you got, and the other way around too. We can survive together, for we all got the same mission—to get back at those who did us wrong—the Yanks and niggers. So Sam, did you bring that jar of money?"

I now was happy I didn't have all of it. I had 10 coins on me, but the rest was buried back in the hiding place on the farm. I told Billy so and gave him the 10 Yankee gold coin dollars.

"We oughta kill ya' right now, ya' pitiful son of a bitch. Ya' ain't good for nothing. You got no gun, no horse, no money. Now listen. Here's the way it's going to be. You and your friend Owen is going to have to prove yourselves before we are done riding together. We're going to all work together for what we are all after, that is, getting back at the Yanks and niggers. And after things have cooled off back on your farm, we will go back and get the rest of the money. You and Owen are going to follow orders just like you did back in the war, and if you don't, you'll end up like that nigger Jake."

Billy was done with his speech. I didn't want to know what they did to Jake, and, I knew Billy and his gang was dangerous. But, as long as I was the only one who knew where the coins were buried, Billy was not completely in charge. It sounds like I was just waiting for a chance to get away. Actually, I still felt dead inside and didn't care much one way or the other. It was more of a game at this time. I was miserable and it made me feel good that Billy and the others in our so called gang were too. Before I could think much more on it, Billy said him and William had something' to do and they would be back before the sun rose. I really didn't care much about what he was going do and what he was saying. I just wanted to lie down and sleep. And that's what I did.

Owen came towards me like he wanted to talk, but I pretended I was asleep so he wouldn't bother me none. Soon, I heard him and David snoring. After a while, they weren't making any more noise, but they were still asleep. I turned on my back and stared at the sky like I used to in the army. There must be an answer up there somewhere. Was Ma and Pa up there? I saw a shooting star, and just for a moment, the pain

I had been feeling left. Soon again, I was thinking of the predicament I was in and I said to myself that maybe I could live and get through this if I didn't care. Now that sure don't make sense, but somehow I knew it to be true. Not caring can make one unable to feel pain, but to be sure, the deadness is still a kind of hurt, but a duller ache than when you care about what happens to you. Still, it is a deep pain just the same. I wasn't, for some reason, convincing myself that I shouldn't care. I thought "the Hell with it" and fell asleep on the cold ground with nothing but a dirty blanket I brought from the farm. The next thing I knew, William was shaking me and saying "get up." Next to him was Davey on horseback holding the reins of another horse. Owen was rubbing his eyes, already up and standing next to the new nag.

"Let's get going" said Davey. "Sammy, I figure you can ride this horse, and this fella Owen can ride with ya'."

"Where did ya' get the horse?" Owen asked.

"Let's just say a kindly nigger lent him to us," snorted Billy, joined in sneering laughter by William.

To this day, I don't know exactly how they got the horse. I can't say I cared that night, but I slowly started feeling more and more like my old self as days passed. Gradually, I started to have more feeling for others, starting with Owen. Maybe it was that shooting star. I woke up with it on my mind like I was dreaming about it. I heard everything being said by Billy, William, and Davey; but my mind was somehow stuck on that star. As we rode away, me and Owen fell far enough behind the other three so that I could have a quiet conversation with him.

I started by saying, "So what's got into you Owen, running up to that ridge with that gun that I didn't even know you had?"

"What's so different about that?" he answered. "Don't you have a gun?"

I told him how I tried to buy one when I first got to Black's and White's, but when I couldn't my disposition changed from killing to just wanting to be left alone. Even after I found the jar of money, I didn't care about having a gun. After a pause I said to him, "So, back to my question about what's got into you."

"I got to prove I'm a man," Owen said with some anger in his voice. "After what happened at Point Lookout when they removed me from the others, I heard lots a talk and was called lots of names.

"Owen," I responded, "that fella forced you no matter what others said."

"I don't care Nite, I have something to prove and besides I hate Yankees and niggers just like you do." As he told me this, his voice got louder.

"Quiet down," I told him. "Let's just ride a bit and we will talk later."

We rode on till mornin' and kept going most of the next day. We camped at night and every so often I'd hear Billy go on about how we would have to prove ourselves. He told me I'd get a chance to avenge my folks. I could thank them later by sharing the money I had when we got back to Nottoway County. He told me he understood it was my money, but they were friends and I ought not be keepin' secrets. All would be right again, he added, once we finished our work on this trip, got back and treated each other like friends should. Slipping back into my sour mood, I didn't care enough to even think about what he was telling me. I was again losing my taste for living except once in a while when I thought about that shooting star.

Owen and I grew more distant as he started talking more to the other three fellas. One day, he started riding on the back of David's horse, and I didn't seem to mind a bit. After a few days, we got within three or four miles of a place called Austinville. Here two paths crossed at what looked like a tower from the days of the knights in the old country. Billy told us this was the old shot tower where fellas like Daniel Boone made bullets. It seems they would drop hot lead from the top so it would form into bullet shapes and then hit a pool at the bottom, cooling off into shot. We camped not too far from the tower and Billy announced that William and I should stay and watch the horses. Along with David and Owen, he was going into Austinville for some supplies. Neither William or I said a word and didn't for most of the night. That was OK with me for the stars were out and I just wanted to lie there and look at them.

Again, I felt comforted by the night sky and actually was feeling at peace that night. But with the peace, the caring about myself and fellow humans again started to creep in. I forced my mind to stop such thinking. I knew if I did, I'd realize that Owen and I were in a predicament. I had closed down my feelings so that I didn't think of how Billy and the other two were not at all interested in us and once they got hold of my money ... again I refused to think of it. To keep from thinking about the real situation, I started thinking about gals I've seen, ones I never talked to, being way too scared for that. I was wondering if I'd ever get the nerve to talk to a gal. This all caused funny feelings in me all through my body. I kept on thinking on this because it was comforting in a strange way. After a good while of this, I finally fell asleep.

Suddenly, I was startled out of sleep by the sounds of pounding hooves. I heard Billy saying to William in bits and pieces, "At least I kept my mind straight enough to bring all the horses back. The little guy is hurt. I don't know how bad it is. Davey is a goner. We need to get going right now." I got myself awake and stood up to see Owen lying close by on the ground. I soon could see he was shot in the leg.

"What happened?" I yelled.

"Let's just say some niggers have guns now," Billy casually replied. "Look at the sunny side. Now you got a horse, and as for those niggers, you hate so bad, well now there are two less of them. Of course we lost David, and Owen here ain't in the best shape."

Feelings of caring were coming back to me fast and I said, "Well, we got to get him to a doctor."

"Sammy," Billy again speaking in a calm voice said, "you are the only doctor that boy is getting and this gun says you will get him on a horse, get on one yourself, and along with us get moving." Then he turned to William and told him, "If we put our minds to it, we could be in Tennessee at the Ross house in three or four days." So we rode the rest of the night and the whole next day in a cold rain that went right through the bone. Owen kept on bravely, but he was hurting bad and losing a lot of blood. The others refused to stop for me to change the bandage made with pieces of an old shirt I had brought along.

The going was real tough, not only for Owen, but for us and the horses. We were now in mountain country. Staying off the main Wilderness Road so that the wounded Owen would not draw any unwanted attention, we followed small trails that only Billy knew about. The October rain made them muddy and slick. Up and down hills we went, Billy pushing us towards our destination. Finally, we stopped outside a place called Abingdon. Owen was running quite a fever now and I covered him up the best I could holding him in my arms under a canvas. The only dressing I had for the wound was scraps of the dirty shirt. I think the bullet had missed the bone and a doctor could have saved Owen, but now it was too late. I had begged the other two to let me get him to a doctor, but Billy would have none of it saying, "O Sammy, you was a big man talking about how you hated Yanks and niggers. You didn't think there was any risk in your hating. Well I'll tell ya', this hating has a cost and you're paying it now. If you want to do something for your buddy, you'll continue on our mission of hate and as I said, you will prove yourself." The first part made some sense. The second part did not because I could not see how continuing on this mission and proving myself was going to help Owen one bit. I was beginning to see that hating was never going to do anyone any good.

That night, Owen moved in and out of consciousness as Billy and William snored under their makeshift tent. At one point Owen told me he was sorry about the way he was the last few days. He said I was his best friend and after what happened in the prison he knew he had to come see me. But once he did, he didn't know what to say and he could tell how bad I was feeling and ... then he just went unconscious again. I said something meaningless and stayed up most of the night holding Owen. About an hour before daylight, I checked on his breathing and heartbeat, and there was only silence.

Before any emotions could take over, I moved fast, using sticks and some sharp stones, to dig a hole for Owen's body. Once I finished, I dragged the corpse and placed it in the hole. For about a minute, I stared at what was once a living breathing human being. I could not help but feel a failure, for I had, what seemed long ago, accepted the responsibility to take care of Owen. I snapped out of my mood to do what next had to be done, that is secure the grave. There was some old railroad tracks not far away, which trains hadn't traveled for a long time. I figured it met its fate during the war like so much else. I gathered some big rocks from the bed and made several trips carrying them to where Owen was laid to rest, just as sure a war casualty as those tracks. I piled the rocks over the grave in an attempt to keep animals from digging it up. And that was it.

Owen suffered much the last 24 hours. At the time though, I was so tired I could not feel a thing more about it. I heard Billy say over and over that the Negroes had killed him, but I couldn't feel any more hate. Plus now I realized I didn't know the whole story. Without a word I hopped on a horse and left when Billy and William said so, and again without a word I grabbed the reign of the now rider-less horse and brought him along.

Tennessee

A few days after Owen died we arrived at our destination. Up to this point Billy and William just called it the Ross house. I was so upset and angry about Owen that I had ridden along without speaking a word. Billy and William were the type of fellas that had no problem not talking about things anyways. Others would ask you if something was wrong, or, maybe try to start up a conversation. Most folks just wouldn't feel right being with somebody three days without talking to them about anything. Then again, there were those like Billy and William who just lost along the way any human feelings they might have had. It for sure happened to me for a while.

I knew I was in trouble when we dismounted and Joe Ross stepped out of his crudely built house. The man and the house suited the country we was now in that is a country of mountains and deep valleys. The forest was thick with all types of trees, such as firs, chestnuts, elms, and walnuts. One could easily get lost up here. One thing I remembered the most was the clean smell of the cool dry air. Except for occasional wood smoke it sure beat the scorch and humidity of the flatlands. Now, this Joe Ross fella, he fit this country fine, for he was a big, rugged man who looked like he could easily handle climbing up and down these hills hunting for food. He stood maybe six foot and had a long mane, a big bushy beard, and a stone jug in his hand. He didn't crack a smile at all when he saw the three of us, but just said, "Who the hell is this pitiful looking work of the Devil," obviously referring to myself.

"Don't mind him," answered Billy, "He is a veteran of Jeff Davis's army who owes us a favor, and he hates Yanks and niggers just like us. Ain't that right Sammy?"

Before I could say something, Joe Ross spoke again, "Where is that other runt Davey? His ma comes up here once a week looking for news about him."

"Well you can tell her there won't be any more news about Davey. He is dead and done for, shot and killed in Virginia." Billy made this statement with a big grin on his face like it was something to be proud of.

"Damn you," snarled Ross. "I told you to stay out of trouble until after this job. That kid had two brothers who fought for the Union. Now it might not just be his ma showing up." No one said anything for the longest time. Finally Ross spoke up again. "We will have to be out of here tomorrow. And, I don't like the looks of this new fella with you. Veteran of Jeff Davis's army, my ass."

He never looked or spoke to William. In fact he called Billy over and talked private to him. When Billy came back, he told me I could bed down in the barn with William who began to complain. Right away he was cut off by Billy. "Shut your big trap and get in that barn." I hadn't seen Billy so forceful in speech with William before. I quickly figured out that Billy felt he had to show Joe he was a tough type. I was seeing that Billy was scared of Joe Ross and for me that could be either a good thing or a real bad thing.

All through the night William and I tried to sleep in the barn but couldn't because of the loud carrying on in the house. There were at least three other fellas in there. After I finally slept a little bit, a drunken Billy entered the barn. "OK soldiers of the great Southern cause, we have our assignment."

"What is it Billy?" William asked.

"Well," Billy began, and then with a grunt fell face first on the ground and was passed out as good as if someone took a rifle butt to his head.

In the morning I got up and looked around a bit. I knew we were now in Tennessee and I sure liked this mountain country. Suddenly a voice snapped at me. "Listen you half-pint of horse piss. What do ya' think you're doing? This ain't your place to be walking around." It was another tall fella who also had a big bushy beard and looked just as mean as Joe Ross. I turned to get back to the barn, but he called to me again before I took two steps and he signaled for me to come closer.

"Hey, do you know what trouble you are in? Billy, that fool, said more than he wanted last night because he was drunk. He tells us that he's keeping you along because you got something back in Virginia that

67

he wants. After that, he'll have no use for you. That idiot is stupid, but he is an extra fool when drunk. If you want a chance at living boy, you tell me what he wants."

Seeing that Billy was afraid of Joe Ross and this fella was one of Ross's buddies, I quickly decided to tell him what I knew. It was like being cornered by a bear and wolf together. Both could kill ya' but the bear would for sure, so I told the bear what he wanted to know. The fella scratched his beard and thinking out loud muttered, "Union gold coins, nearly 35 dollars of them huh? That will interest Joe." Then looking towards me he said, "After the job in Nashville, you pay close attention. At some point, your friends Billy and William are going to mess up and get killed or something. Yep, maybe join 'ol Stonewall and J.E.B. Stuart in the great beyonder. Watch me in any event and you may get out of this alive. Now get and don't say a thing to anyone especially to Billy or Joe."

This man was confident or just not afraid that I would say something to Billy. It was even more puzzling that he didn't want me to say anything to Ross. I couldn't figure out why he was telling me about all this. Why partner with some fellas if you don't trust them? And why didn't they force the information about the coins out of Billy last night? To these questions I soon got some of my answers. Billy woke up lying in the dirt he fell onto the night before. As if everything was normal, he told me and William to get over by him. He simply said, "I got our assignment. You understand what that means Sammy. It's just like back in the army. I'm the officer and you're a shit private. What I say, you do with no questions." The plan was for us to travel in two groups to Nashville, about 50 miles away. The three of us was one group and Ross and his gang the other. We was to ride right to Market Street where there was lots of stores, taverns, and other businesses. We was to be there two days hence at eleven in the evening. Ross gave Billy a pocket watch and had him set it exactly to his own time piece to make sure we rode onto the street right on time. At fifteen minutes past eleven Ross and his men were to be hid out on Cherry Street two blocks away.

That is all Billy told us, but I figured that Ross had to be using us to take attention off his gang. Whatever the case, I was sure he couldn't care less about what happened to us. Soon we mounted up and rode off. We spent a long day and night of riding first on some winding mountain paths and then leveled country as we got closer to Nashville. It was more like home but still was a lot different. There were less pine in the woods and the country was less settled than around Nottoway County.

We were exhausted when we got about three miles out of Nashville at about 6 p.m., according to the watch. We found an old abandoned farm building set a piece off the road where we could hide out until dark. It was getting on towards winter, so we didn't wait long. "OK boys," said Billy, "Our job is about as simple a one as we could have. Right at ten minutes after eleven we are going to leave William holding the three horses at the corner of Jackson and Market Streets. Sammy, you and me is going to go up Market a ways and start raising some Hell. We will commence shooting in the air and making a general ruckus. We do this until the soldiers over on Cherry Street come running."

Not being a city boy, I began wondering what these streets was like and all when William spoke up. "That's it? Come on Billy. That ain't worth 15 Union gold dollars each."

"William, shut your big mouth," yelled back Billy. "First of all I get 15, you get 13 and Sammy you get two since you owe us some from your glass jar. It's a kind of insurance, just like some dude in a fancy shirt would be selling ya'."

I said nothing, for the worst of my worries had to do with the mess I was in. It looked bad in every way. If I was lucky enough not to get hit by a Union bullet then either Billy or Ross would kill me once I showed them where the jar was hidden, and I suspect if we was still alive we would be riding hard to Nottoway after this stupid caper was over.

"Second, William, you big dumb Son of Benedict," or something like that said Billy. "We are important for starting what is called a diversion. Ya' see, Ross has information that the Yankees are bringing in a shipment of gold coins tonight to pay the soldiers stationed here. He knows from one of his fellas the exact place and time. The Yanks are riding in from about three miles out of town where they are getting the money from the train. Once they get back to Cherry and Jefferson, they will carry it in by hand so as not to draw attention with the horse's hooves and all. We have good information that they will be going down Cherry Street right about 15 minutes after 11."

William said, "Oh I get it. We start shooting and the soldiers with the gold will head right to us where we will be waiting for them."

"No, you idiot," responded Billy, "They ain't going to tote boxes of gold to us. The plan is that the soldiers posted on Cherry Street to watch the route will come down here and there will be just a few soldiers for Ross and his gang to take care of."

"Hey, I ain't no idiot, but the Yanks sure are if they just don't unload the gold at the downtown station."

Billy looked at William like a fool, but for once I thought William made sense. Billy turned and looked at me. "Sammy you're a lot smarter than this sack of shit. So I'm going to tell you so that if he does not understand it you can explain it to him. The reason this job is going to work is because the tracks into town have not been fixed yet and that is why the Yanks have to bring the gold down these roads by wagon."

I started wondering who were really the idiots. How exactly did they know all these details? What if the soldiers who heard the shots thought it more important to stay on the route of the shipment? And, from what I already knew, how could Billy trust Ross? But, there I was right in the middle of it and I knew it wasn't good. I had begun to have some notions that maybe I could still get away if Billy got distracted, but even with that I was sure that four years of war made the Northern army too smart to let me get away. Look how fast they rounded up all the people who were involved in killing Lincoln.

Once it got dark, we rode into Nashville and hid out in some trees about a half mile from our destination. As the eleventh hour approached we took the horses and crept into town, and what a town it was, the biggest I'd ever seen! You could see the huge state capitol building. The scale of everything, what we was about to do, and my poor chances of living, was just too much for me. I started thinking about my folks, about Owen, and even Jake. I suddenly stopped hating so much and just saw the tragedy of it all. There were no bad folks, that is, at least they weren't made bad when they was born. I'd never seen a bad baby.

Before I could think any more, Billy said it was time to move up to the end of the block. There he instructed William to stay with the horses. "I want to go do the shooting one time," William suddenly whined like a kid.

"You take orders," Billy said in a whisper. "If you went, you'd be dead faster than David and that kid Owen. I can do enough shooting with these two pistols by myself." I wondered exactly what I was going

70

along for. Billy was not about to give me a gun. It was real quiet on the street. Billy said we would find a saloon down there where it just made sense shooting would take place.

It was nearing the time for Billy to start making a racket when, walking ahead of Billy, I came to the front of an alley. A voice called out, "Halt right there." I got so scared that I tripped on a small hole, and when the man in the alley stepped towards me, Billy clubbed him on the side of the head with one of the pistols. We dragged the man, a Negro soldier dressed in a Union uniform, into the dark of the alley.

The soldier began to moan in great pain. Billy stood at the edge of the alley and threw me one of his guns. "Now Sammy old boy, it is time for you to prove yourself. Shoot that nigger." I looked at the man twitching in pain and I knelt down beside him. I figured we would both be dead soon. Suddenly, I felt more courage than ever before. It was not the hero kind, but the kind where I could no longer do wrong. I stepped out of the shadows and threw the gun against the wall.

"Go ahead Billy, kill me," I said. "I'm sick of it all."

Billy looked dumbfounded and said, "I will if you don't tell me where the money is hidden back on the farm."

"What for, you think I don't know you will kill me either way?"

Billy stood there a few seconds looking confused at what to say next. Then he told me what I'd already known in my heart. "You fool, with your hating Yanks and niggers. We killed your folks and your slaves. If you would have looked more closely you would have seen a lot of bones in that shit hole of a house we burned down. Now I'll give you one last chance. Where is the money hid?"

I said nothing, and with that, Billy stepped towards me with the cocked pistol. This was it. He would shoot me and then the Negro, who was now quiet, probably passed out from the pain. The pistol was about three feet from my head when suddenly a voice from the shadows said, "Move now man." I quickly stepped to my left and then a sound like a cannon ball exploding shook me from head to toe.

With my ears ringing, I looked up and saw Billy back in the street about five feet from the entrance of the alley. The Negro soldier had shot him and the force of the bullet had carried him back into Market Street. Billy was on the ground twitching something awful and I'll never forget what he was saying. "Forgive me mother, please forgive me,

I love you. Mother please…." His voice faded away. Now there were a few grunts and then quiet. The soldier behind me was groaning in pain again. He must have forced himself earlier into being quiet so that in the shadows of the alley he could get his revolver out of his holster and shoot Billy. He kept crying "O my head, my head, it hurts so bad." Next, I did a peculiar thing. I went to the soldier and put my arms around him and said, "It will be ok. Just calm down, I gots you, and help will be here soon. Just rest now and think good thoughts." Then I started humming to him a lullaby tune that Ma used to comfort me with.

Soon, I heard the stomping of horses. At first I figured it was William, but then I realized it sounded like more than three horses. Soon lots of horses and men appeared in the street near where Billy now lay. "Corporal, this one is dead," a voice said.

"All right private," another voice answered and continued, "Men, there in the alley is another one. Grab him and put him with the others. And then bring the nigger over to the wagon."

Suddenly another voice, deep and self-assured, interrupted, "Corporal that Negro is not a nigger and you are looking at a higher rank. That soldier is a Sergeant in the United States Army."

The Corporal turned around quickly like he was about to tell the fella where to go when all of a sudden he spoke very sheepishly. "General Thomas, I am very sorry sir, I could not see clearly that he was a soldier, and a sergeant at that."

General Thomas replied, "I see. But you could tell that the color of his skin was black."

Before the corporal could make another excuse, the General asked where they were taking me. The corporal answered that they were taking me over to the jail wagon that I could now see held William, Joe Ross, and three or four others. A funny thing was that the fella who talked to me at the Ross house was outside the wagon talking to a Yankee captain like they were good buddies or something. Two privates grabbed me and started walking me to the cart when the Negro sergeant spoke up. "Sir, with your permission," he said.

General Thomas replied, "Yes sergeant, speak freely."

The sergeant continued in a shaky voice, "This man refused to shoot me and did his best to help me. From the way the one lying dead in the street talked, I don't think this man was one of them. The dead man had talked about how he killed his parents and done some other wrongs to him."

"Very well then," said the General, "take him to a separate holding place and keep him under guard until you hear from me in the morning. Now, help this sergeant and treat him with the respect you would give a soldier who has just heroically performed his duty."

As the general began to walk back from the alley, he stopped very sudden like and looked lost in thought. After a short while he went and talked to the Negro sergeant who was on a stretcher and about to be placed in a wagon. After a few moments more, he started to walk away only to stop again and go over and talk softly to what looked like a medic who had just came on the scene. Finally, he moved back towards the opposite sidewalk where there stood a group of Yankee officers. He stood next to one of them and began what looked like a serious conversation. Then the fella from Ross's gang who had talked to me the night before was called over by the General. The three of them were conferring and occasionally one of them would look over towards where a couple soldiers were putting wrist and leg chains on me.

Before they finished chaining me up, the officer talking to Ross's buddy and the general came over and told the soldiers that it would not be necessary to shackle me, whatever that meant. I now reckon it means chaining one up. The officer, accompanied by one Yank private, asked me to go with them and of course that's what I did. We went to what looked like a hotel on the same street. The officer stepped in the door and woke up a man sitting at the counter. I couldn't believe what I heard next.

"This man will be requiring a room on the inside with no windows. The private here will be posted at the door for two hours and then be relieved. I want some food sent up to his room and also the bath filled with hot water. The charge will be to the United States Army in care of General George Henry Thomas.

"Yes Sir Captain McGraw, I will get right on it," responded the clerk. Afterwards, I could hear him mumbling about, "first being woken by the shot and other commotion up the street and now this." And so I was soon eating the best meal I had in about three years and enjoying a good wash in the tub for the first time since I was a boy. After that I looked around for some place to curl up on the floor when the private knocked and entered to ask if all was ok.

"Sure," I started to tell him when he noticed I was set to lie on the floor.

"Old Pap is sure smart," he interrupted. "Who would want to escape from this setup? And you, ya' darn fool, sleep in the bed not on the floor. You ain't behind a pile of dirt now like you was fighting in the war again." Into the bed I climbed and fell dead asleep.

Morning came quickly with a knock at the door. I got up and slowly opened it. A man on the other side introduced himself as Captain Tilly and asked if he might come in. I was in my skivvies and requested to first dress real quick like. To this the captain said that he had some clean clothes for me which he handed through the door. "I'll wait here a moment then," said the captain as he stepped back into the hall.

After I dressed, I opened the door and there he still stood. He stepped in and said, "All right then, again my name is Captain Tilly and I am part of General George Henry Thomas's staff. I am trained in matters of the law and I am to gather information from you." He hesitated as I stood there confused. "In other words," he explained, "on these sheets of paper I need you to write down your story from the time you entered the war. From information given us by Johnson Callison you were a member of the Confederate Army. Is that not true?"

"Johnson Callison! Who the devil is that?" I asked.

"Why, you don't even know that, do you?" replied the Captain. "He is the man who infiltrated the Ross gang and gave us the intelligence about last night's planned raid." I thought on this a minute and even though I didn't know the big words I figured it out that Callison was the fella who talked to me at Ross's house and last night was talking to the Yanks like they was all good buddies of his.

"Yes, Callison was right," I finally answered.

"Fine, then let's sit down and you will write your story on this paper."

With these words by Captain Tilly, I turned a bright shade of red and said, "You see it's darn right embarrassing to tell someone, especially an educated man like you, but I can't read and write."

Tilly put an arm on my shoulder and said, "It's all right if you can't write, son. Why don't you sit here on this comfortable chair and I'll sit at the desk and write down what you tell me?"

I said ok, and thought for a way to start. And so I began, "My name is Sam Nite. Nite ain't much of a name. It sounds like dark or black. Now I'm a white man, but I've found out that ain't much to brag about."

Headed North

The sudden jolt of the train woke me up, and the newspaper fell off my lap onto the floor. I looked down and read the bold head-line: "Congress Debates Impeachment of President." Above the headline, in fancy italic type, were the words *The Louisville Courier-Journal*. In the upper right hand corner of the page was the date May 10, 1868.

I picked up the paper and started to read about the attempt to remove President Andrew Johnson from office. After reading a few paragraphs, I put the paper down, put my head back, and stared out the window into the darkness. Farm houses, marked by the flickering light of candles and oil lamps, sped past. To be correct, they were not passing, but instead the train was passing the houses. Actually, since the earth was moving in its orbit, everything was moving, just at different speeds. This was the type of thinking encouraged by Professor McCarthy at the academy in Nashville, with his use of the Socratic Method, an educational practice of constant questioning and answering. It can keep the mind occupied for hours, but I felt too lonely and exhausted to continue. I turned my mind to more comforting thoughts like how I came to be on this train bound for Cincinnati.

I thought back to that cold winter morning in late 1865 when I was sitting outside the office of one of the most celebrated generals of the Civil War. I was frightened. My heart felt like it was going to pound its way out of my chest when the door opened and General George Henry Thomas appeared. The general motioned for me to come in. I entered wondering if this was to be my end. I knew only that he had received Captain Tilly's report concerning the attempted payroll robbery. My fate and future were in the hands of this general from the South who fought for the North.

"Please take a seat Mr. Nite," General Thomas began. "I see that you are a fellow Virginian, from I believe, Nottoway County. That is not far from where I was raised in Southampton County."

"Yes sir," is all I could find in myself to reply as I took a seat in his plain but well-organized office. The only decorations were leaves pressed carefully against paper in picture frames. As I learned later, the general had collected plant specimens from all over the country.

"Well, first of all," the general went directly into business, "I need to inform you about why you are before me. " At this point he picked up a piece of paper, gazed at it for a moment, and without looking up read the following: "As the military governor of this district, it is my duty to keep the peace and apply justice. You were involved with a group of men, who like many outlaws across the South, are taking advantage of the post-war situation and thus the vulnerability of the depressed population. However, because you refused to obey the command of one of your associates to kill a soldier of the United States Army, and by the testimony of our agent, Mr. Callison, there is reason to question whether or not you were a willing accomplice of the group of outlaws who attempted the robbery of a government payroll." General Thomas stopped and looked up from the paper and stared directly at me for what seemed like a full minute. Finally he spoke, "Son, you don't understand much of this do you?"

"Sir," I answered, "I understand enough of it to know that I was involved with some bad fellas. The problem was I didn't care about anything after the murder of my parents. I did not stop and really think about what I was doing."

"From reading your statement, Mr. Nite, as transcribed by Captain Tilly, that point is clear." After another long pause he put down the paper. "Son, from the report it is obvious that you are a thoughtful and intelligent young man, despite never having learned to read and write. Further, it is clear to me that before being involved in this unfortunate business, you desired not only to master the grammar and elocution of the King's English, but be educated in the scientific and philosophical arts. "

Forgetting for a second in whose presence I stood, I blurted out, "I don't even know what those words mean and I am just a damn fool who is now going to pay for his foolishness." General Thomas did not look stunned or angry as I suspected he would. Instead he looked at me differently, still in the official manner one would expect from a general, but also with what felt to me a kindness, a feeling that this man actually cared about others.

After another eternal pause, he said, "Come, come, son, one may have taken a walk on the wrong path, but they may also be presented with a chance to travel on the road of redemption. You may now be presented such an opportunity, but you must offer me a reason to give you a second chance." Following General Thomas's words, I just bowed my head saying nothing and tried to prevent the tears that were welling up in my eyes. To my surprise the general now stiffened up and in an officiating manner announced, "I have a choice and great latitude about how to dispense justice in these matters. What I need to know is your choice in the matter."

Slowly looking up, I answered, "I'm sorry, Sir, I don't quite see how I have any choice here. You are the one in charge."

"Mr. Nite, perhaps it is true that most of the time and in most matters we do not have a choice, especially in regards to military and legal ones. However, when presented with one of those few occasions to influence a decision, one must seize the opportunity. As a lifetime member of the army, I am used to following orders, but now and then, opportunity presents itself. Such times are the most important times of each and every one of our lives. You made such a decision when you did not shoot the sergeant in the alley. Now, I am presenting you with another opportunity to have input concerning the decision I must now make. I suggest we start by you telling me what path you can now follow that will lead to a life that will benefit yourself and your fellow human beings." After a long silent spell all I could say was that I had never thought about it. Thomas did not accept this as an answer.

"Think," he told me, but I could not come up with any words. "Perhaps," the general continued, "an illustration from my life will help. When I was around your age I decided I wanted to be a soldier, in particular an officer in the United States Army. Next, I had to take steps to accomplish that goal. I needed sponsorship from a congressman, I needed to do well in my studies at West Point, and after that I needed to continue working hard to master my craft as an army officer. It all started, however, with my identifying an interest and taking advantage of the moment of opportunity. I can tell from your report that a life in the army is not your destiny, but what interests do you have that may enable you to seize the moment?"

Again, the general was talking a bit over my head, but I began to see what he was hinting at. He stated earlier that he had figured out from my report that I had an interest in science or some kind of arts. Suddenly, it came to me, and I said, "I am interested in understanding how things like the planets and stars work and how it all fits together with other things. I want to learn all of the new things coming about like how a steam engine on wheels can travel fifty miles in one hour's time and how one can receive a telegraph message in less than a minute from a hundred miles away."

"Very good," said General Thomas. "You are interested in science, perhaps philosophy. Now how are you going to follow up on this interest?"

Suddenly it all became clear. "Sir," I said, "I want to learn to read and write, to go to school, and to be able to do something worthwhile in my lifetime."

"Very good, very good," George Henry Thomas said as he looked directly at me. "Then I will make the following decision in this case. You will attend the academy being established here in Nashville by Mr. and Mrs. Lawrence of New England. They are looking to set up a school to teach recently freed Negros and other victims of the war. I will arrange for you to have a room at the school in exchange for work you will do around the academy such as keeping the place clean and orderly. I will expect periodic reports from Captain Tilly and I will expect progress from you, young man, which will enable us to pass a final verdict concerning your case in no more than two years' time."

"Captain Tilly," ordered General Thomas. Up to this time I was unaware that the captain had quietly entered the office and was sitting in the back of the room. "I want you to see to it that this order is carried out. I also want you to find out from Mr. Nite where the body of this young man, named Owen, is buried, so that the family may be notified and can give him a proper burial. Also, see if you can contact Mr. Connelly of Black's and White's, Virginia, and see what can be done about recovering the money Mr. Nite has hidden on the farm. And, make a note for two years from now to again correspond with Mr.

Connelly about selling the land in the hopes that Mr. Nite will be in a position at that time to accept the cash value minus fair compensation to Mr. Connelly. Does that sound agreeable Mr. Nite?" I nodded.

"Will that be all Sir?" asked Tilly.

"Yes, that is all," said General Thomas returning to his desk work.

Without thinking, I turned around and said, "General Thomas," and then I couldn't say anything. He looked at me in a manner that made me feel like he had never seen me before.

"Yes?" he replied.

All I could say was "Thank you."

As we walked out of the building, Captain Tilly told me that I probably got more conversation out of General Thomas than anyone else he has ever seen in his office. I replied, "He is nothing like how I pictured a traitor."

"General Thomas a traitor?" he responded. "Why he was one of the few Southerners who was not a traitor. The General still loves Virginia, but he honored the oath he made to his country. The rebel leaders, including Lee, Jackson, and Longstreet, did not go to West Point to become officers in a state army. They pledged their loyalty to the flag of the United States of America."

"So," I asked, "what made him so special to side with the army invading his homeland?"

"Special!" said Tilly, raising his voice in defense. "The General never considered himself to be special. He simply believes in carrying out his duty." Tilly stopped for a second and then said, "I don't know why I am wasting my time trying to defend General Thomas to a Reb who came within a quill's point of swinging on the gallows; but I'll tell you this, General Thomas does not do things for personal profit. Back in 1862, after the Battle of Perryville, he was offered the command of the Union forces fighting in Kentucky and Tennessee. I cannot think of another man who would have turned down such an opportunity. General Thomas did, though, for the simple fact that he felt General Buell, the commander he would have replaced, was not guilty of the allegations against him. That's the kind of man General Thomas is and I'm damn proud to be on his staff."

I didn't have anything to say in return. Captain Tilly was not done though. After a short silence he spoke this time in low, measured tones making the same point. "If anyone should know General Thomas to be an honorable man it should be you. Most of the district commanders would not have wasted a minute on your troubles, especially taking the time to help an ex-Rebel found in the company of thieves and killers. There is nothing in this matter for the general's own benefit. He is trying to help you son. He is a soldiers' general. He was during the war and he still is, whether you fought for or against the Union. Now let's get on with this business Nite. We are going to make a man of you."

I thus began my formal education in December of 1865 at the Lawrence Academy. Captain Tilly made all the arrangements. He set it up so that in exchange for free tuition I would work as a janitor at the school, which was located on Nashville's Jackson Street. Despite Tilly's straight talk and no-nonsense manner, I could tell inside he was a man with a kind heart. His original report certainly influenced General Thomas's decision to give me another chance. Now, Tilly was always checking up on me, and not just out of duty. He took special care to see that I had all the things I needed like clothing, books, pencils, and paper.

I was placed in a beginning reading and writing class along with some freed slaves, a few Confederate veterans, and some other victims of the war willing to be helped by the victorious Yankees. I was determined to do well. After three weeks, I was reassigned to the intermediate English Language class. By June, I was able to read on what Mr. Lawrence termed an advanced elementary level.

The first six months, I studied, practiced my lessons, cleaned up, made small building repairs, ran errands for the school, and reported on my progress to Captain Tilly. My only other activity was to visit Joe White, the Negro soldier who saved my life in the alley on Market Street. I felt I owed it to Joe to visit him in the army hospital, and make sure he was being taken care of properly. I usually visited him after rubbing down and feeding Mr. Lawrence's horse.

Many of the times I visited Joe, he would have such bad headaches that I could only say hello and be on my way. Other days we would talk a little about our lives. Looking back on those times, I must admit that Joe was more honest and willing to talk about his feelings than myself. I would talk about the old farm and what the land was like; Joe talked about his family and the circumstances that led to him becoming a Union soldier.

Joe grew up in the southern part of Illinois not far from the Ohio River. From the way he told it, that area was not much different from the South except in one detail: slavery was illegal. That did not stop slave catchers coming up from Kentucky to look for runaway slaves. Often they would accuse free blacks of being runaways and take them back down South to be sold into slavery. Things got worse in 1852 when Illinois made migration of free Negros illegal. Growing up in such circumstances caused a free Negro, like Joe, to be especially alert.

One day, Joe was feeling quite well and we shared a couple of jokes. Without thinking I began talking about my parents. I remember telling Joe about my problems with Pa, especially him not wanting me to go to school. "At least your Pa wasn't hunted like an animal," Joe replied. "My Pa thought he went to heaven high above when his owner in Kentucky set him free. He came up to Illinois and set out to work in Cairo hoping to get some money and buys him some land. He was working at cleaning out stables until a white man from Kentucky came in one day to get a horse. He was drunk and all, and said he was headed up state to bring back a runaway. He looked at Pa and said it be a lot easier to just take him back. He said one black man was as good as another. Pa ran and told the sheriff about what this slave chaser said. The sheriff told Pa he would protect him, or at least that is what he told the judge later. The fact is no one tried protectin' Pa, for he was found dead in an alley with a bullet in his back. The slave catcher admitted he shot him, sayin' it was because Pa was not who he said he was, but instead was a runaway slave from Alabama. He told the judge that he shot Pa when he tried to escape. The sheriff claimed Pa never showed him any papers. It made things easy for the judge to let my Pa's murderer go.

"At the time I was only six years old. A sympathetic family found my mother, and me and my sisters, a farm to live and work on a short distance outside Marion, Illinois. It was farther from the river and safer due to the white owner's presence, but it was barely a step up from slavery. Any pay we got was taken by the owner for rent and food."

"I guess at least you felt you had a chance to be your own man?" I asked Joe.

"Farm work is hard and when you can't enjoy the fruits of your labor it is real extra hard. I saw no future in it, so when the Yankees started recruiting Negro soldiers, I begged my mother to let me go join the Union Army. Mother understood, but struggled with whether she wanted a possibly dead son, or one who might make enough money to get us our own farm someday. Her love made her say no at first, but she finally relented when she saw it was my one chance to be a man. In August of 1864, I found my way to Paducah, Kentucky, a Union stronghold on the river. From there I travelled with a small group of Negro recruits to Camp Nelson in Kentucky.

"I worked hard, whether it was helping clear land at the camp, or drilling on the parade ground. An officer at Camp Nelson told me I would make a fine soldier. This officer was friends with Colonel William R. Shafter, commander of the 17th U.S. Colored Troops. Arrangements were made for me to join the 17th in Nashville. Roughly two months later, on December 15, 1864, the 17th led a charge that overran several Confederate positions in the Battle of Nashville. I guess they were pleased with the way I brought in five captured Confederates, because they made me a sergeant. Colonel Shafter told me I was a natural born leader."

Joe next said something I would never forget. "You know Sam, I was plannin' on a good career in the army. Most of the white soldiers treated us like we was less than human, but after the battle some of them began to treat us like real soldiers. The officers, like Colonel Shafter, always treated us like regular soldiers. They was tough, but no more or less than they were on white soldiers. General Thomas came down and shook hands with many of us after we captured them Reb, I'm sorry Sam, I mean them Southern positions. I felt like a real man for the first time. Ol' Pap Thomas was like a father to us all, and that meant we were all brothers, black and white soldiers alike. That feeling didn't last long as things returned to normal, but I'll never forget that feeling."

"Joe," I said, "you can call Confederate soldiers Rebs. Back on the Howlett Line I heard soldiers talking at the spring calling each other Reb and Yank all the time."

"Yea, that's white soldiers talking to other white soldiers. Us Negro soldiers never had any conversations with white Southern soldiers, even after they were our prisoners. So why is it different with you Sam? Why are you up here talkin' to me?"

"Joe, don't you recall you saved my life?"

He laughed and said, "Well it's the least I could do in that ya' didn't shoot me with that big gun in your hand."

"Yea, I do suppose that was the first time a Reb would have acted as such to a black man in a blue uniform." We both laughed, but Joe's head starting hurting, so I told him to get some rest and I'd see him the next day.

That night I thought about how that day was the first time I carried on a conversation with a Negro like he was my equal. Suddenly, I felt real strange, like you do when something happens for the first time in your life, such as shooting your gun at a living thing, or releasing your manhood for the first time while dreaming. I didn't go see Joe the next day. I was scared to because not acting superior to Negroes felt foreign and even wrong. I had never talked that way to the slaves on the farm. We would laugh a lot for sure, but it was always at them and they would just laugh along. They would never dare make a joke about me, at least not in my presence. With Joe, I felt I had done something wrong like changing religions. You just don't change that way. After a day of staying away from the hospital, I decided to go back. This time I would keep the conversation less personal. We would talk about the war, maybe what I learned in school, and see if the food they gave him was any better.

None of this happened. It turned out that during the night Joe's head wound, from the butt of Billy's gun, was causing him the worst pain he had since the night in the alley. I had seen him in bad pain. Some days it was so bad that all I could do was sit with him for a few minutes as he groaned before I was on my way back to school. This time a corporal explained to me that a surgeon decided the only hope "for my Negro friend" was to operate and relieve the bleeding around his brain. The corporal said this was by no means a common operation and it held great risk, but he reckoned the surgeon saw it as a great opportunity having a Negro to try it out on. They used chloroform to make Joe unconscious and then drilled a hole in his skull. After that, I visited Joe in the special unit for those recovering from surgery. He was in a small room that was for Negro soldiers. Joe never came back to consciousness. He lay there alive, like maybe a tree or plants is alive, until he died three days later.

I went back to my room and just sat in my chair. I could not study. I cried and told myself I'd seen enough sorrow for a lifetime. And then

I thought about how Joe never gave up and how he had it worse than I did growing up, but kept giving it his best. I ended up studying harder that night than ever before. I stopped studying about 2 a.m. and went outside. It was a cold cloudless night. It felt good. I looked up and wondered what Joe, Owen, or my Ma and Pa now knew about the mystery of life. I wondered about Billy, the way he called for his mother as he lay in the street dying. I didn't even hate him anymore. Besides, no good would come from hating the dead or for that matter the living either. I had learned that much since the war. Now I also learned that the color of one's skin does not matter. I had said as much to Captain Tilly when he took my report, but that was just sayin' it. After Joe's death, I knew it in my mind as the truth.

The next day, I recited to the teacher every letter and the various sounds they make. Soon I was reading easy books and then harder ones. With the help of a dictionary that I found in my room, a gift I suspect from General Thomas, I read several books. None of these were major novels such as those written by Charles Dickens, Washington Irving, or Nathanial Hawthorne. I did, however, try and read a book called *Moby Dick* by Herman Melville. It is a great adventure story set on the high seas. Although I could not understand the exact message, I just knew it was more than an adventure story. It was sort of a mystery in much the same way the sky is mysterious. It's like the stars are real, but in another way they are not. From here they are little lights in the dark sky. They have some type of a meaning more than the scientific facts. Sure, they are just big rocks or whatever, but trying to comprehend how far away they are just puts one in touch with feelings that cannot be explained. They are feelings that make one believe there is much more going on than what one sees and hears here on earth.

The whale Moby Dick is like that. Mr. Melville somehow makes it bigger in meaning than any real sea creature. The crazy pursuit of this one white whale is the act of a crazy captain. He pushes his crew towards disaster. I have already met a lot of people like Captain Ahab who get stuck on something like that in their mind. The funny thing is that it is often the thing that kills you. Look what happened to Billy. He wanted that lousy jar of money so bad that he did terrible things and then suffered a miserable death himself. It almost happened to me because of my hatred of Yankees and Negroes. Now I was headed up to

Ohio to become a Northerner myself. I could not hate Billy anymore. Getting your mind to think and see what is really going on causes you to not hate so much. It is like watching a tough guy, like Billy, crying to his mother and realizing that we are all suffering and anyone can make one or two stupid mistakes that can destroy your whole life.

On the other hand, what do I know? I told this viewpoint of mine to a girl named Mary at the school. She was really pretty with dark red hair. I'd found myself not being able to sleep at night thinking about her. So, one day I got the nerve to talk to her and with one sentence she ruined my attraction for her as well as my personal philosophy. She said, "So Mr. Nite, I guess you are saying your ma and pa made a stupid mistake and so did Joe who you are visiting in the hospital?" I stood there dumbstruck and before I could say anything more, Mary exclaimed, "Rotten people don't always get what they have coming, but when they do, I am all for them getting everything they deserve." She stared at me for a minute and then told me she had to go to class.

I had wanted so bad to leave hate behind. Now I was again confused. How could I like Mary if she believed the opposite of me? Did I really know the truth? I was and still am scared to think hard about it. If I let go and start hating again then I see no hope for my life.

I looked again out the window as the train continued through the sparsely populated Kentucky countryside. It was totally dark when the pitter patter of rain began to hit the windows. Not a single star was visible in the sky. Feeling lonesome, I got up and carefully made my way back to the lounge car. There, amidst the heavy cigar smoke, I found my traveling companion, Mr. Birdsong. He was sitting in a comfortable chair talking to a well-dressed civilian and a soldier in a captain's uniform. I tentatively approached the men, for I felt totally out of place in my surroundings. The car had furniture like that normally found in a rich person's parlor. There were men in white waistcoats serving drinks and food to the passengers. The car had brass lining the windows and several brass spittoons on the floor. Only well-dressed men relaxed in the car with not a woman or child in sight. I wanted to turn around and leave for fear that I was not welcome in the car, but Mr. Birdsong saw me first and greeted me in a loud voice so to be heard over the many conversations in the car.

"Hello Sam, did you enjoy a good nap?"

"Yes, I did Mr. Birdsong." I answered.

"Well, my boy, this is Captain Oliver of the Seventh United States Cavalry and Mr. Doss of the Taylor Shoe Company." I exchanged greetings with the two gentlemen and at their invitation sat down. Mr. Birdsong told the men why we were traveling together to Cincinnati. As he spoke, I half listened and politely nodded as Mr. Birdsong told the story. He missed many of the finer details for he could not possibly know the whole story, like the time General Thomas came down to Nashville from his new headquarters in Louisville to visit Captain Tilly and me at the academy.

My mind drifted away to that day and recalled General Thomas saying to Captain Tilly, "I cannot believe the difference in Mr. Nite's speech after only a year at the academy."

"Sam has worked very hard general," Tilly replied.

"Indeed," answered the general and he gave me a look that was not quite a smile, but still one of apparent pleasure. I later overheard the general tell Mr. Lawrence that he had made too many decisions that sent fine young men to their deaths. I think he was pleased to have made a decision that resulted in something positive for an individual. I'll never know for sure, because the general remained a man of few words and I never heard him again speak on the matter.

"Isn't that right Sam?" Mr. Birdsong interrupted my thoughts of that day in Nashville.

"What is that sir?" I replied.

"That we met in Nashville upon the request of General Thomas."

"That's right; Mr. Birdsong and I met at the academy of Mr. Lawrence of Massachusetts."

Mr. Birdsong continued telling the story. "I had recently visited General Thomas in Louisville, working out a contract for the army to purchase candles and soap from Procter and Gamble. The general asked if I could help find a young man employment in Cincinnati. Now when a war hero and man of stature, let alone a huge client for our products, asks you to help find a job for a man, you help find that man a job." The two men politely nodded and Mr. Birdsong continued. "So I got on the next train for Nashville, found the young man, Sam here, and said to him, 'Son, how would you feel about accompanying me to Ohio the day after tomorrow?'"

I started to talk, but could not get a word in before Mr. Birdsong continued the story, telling how I was still in my night shirt when he found me at my room at the school. His version of the whole affair was embellished in the way that a salesman tells stories. One thing that was correct was that I did not have to think long before agreeing to accompany Mr. Birdsong to his main office of business in Ohio. I was excited about the prospect, for I had read that Ohio emerged from the war as the most powerful state in the Union with some of the best farm land in the country, and industry was prospering in places like Cleveland, Akron, Toledo, and Dayton. This was my big opportunity.

I remember asking Mr. Lawrence if he believed I was ready to leave school and go to work. "Mr. Nite," he replied in his usual formal manner, "You are our best student. I would be pleased to give you a certificate and letter commending you for your accomplishments at the academy. I believe you need the experience of work, but I beg you to save some money and do not wait more than a year or two to continue your education at a school of higher learning. You have the gift of curiosity and a good practice of study. Please take advantage of these talents."

So here I was on the train travelling through the night to a new life. I was leaving the South behind and in less than three years I had gone from hating Yankees to becoming one myself. It was a new world and I wanted to be part of it. The days of slavery were over. Everyone was free up North to succeed on their own terms. My experience with Joe had changed my way of thinking. I wanted to be in a world where everyone was considered equal and given a fair chance. I was sure such a world existed in Ohio.

The conversation had now switched over to a discussion of General Thomas. "You know," stated Mr. Doss, "From my sales route in Virginia, before the war, I covered the territory down along the North Carolina border not far from Suffolk and where General Thomas was raised. The Thomas family was fairly wealthy and indeed owned several slaves. They were at great risk when the Negro Nat Turner led a bloody slave rebellion in those parts around 1830 or so."

"Yes," spoke up the talkative Mr. Birdsong. "Thomas, over dinner on one occasion, spoke of his upbringing. It was one of the very few times he seemed a bit annoyed with his treatment by the army. He was quite aware that he was not fully trusted at any point during the war because he was a Southerner by birth."

Captain Oliver, who had been quiet up to this point, interjected, "Why, he should be suspect, growing up a Southern land and slave owner. In my view the man had to be seeking personal gain from the war, or he was of an overly rebellious nature, to turn on his family and neighbors. I am sure at some point he will return home to claim confiscated land and property. He has to be clever in the sense that he wagered on the right side and now has much to gain. If he does not have a financial motive, then he is not worthy of trust by any party, for what type of man would not side with his family and friends?"

Now it was my turn to speak up. "Captain, I politely disagree with your assumptions about the general."

"And what would you know about the matter?" interrupted the captain. "How old are you, or let me rephrase the question to ask how old were you April of 1865?"

"I was 15 years old," I answered.

The captain continued, "Well unless you illegally entered the army, you did not partake in the War against the Rebellion, unless you were a drummer boy. We didn't send mere boys to war like the Secesh did. We had common respect for the sacrificing mothers of the Union."

My dander was up and I interrupted the captain. I kept my head, though, being careful not to reveal that I fought for the South, and hoping Mr. Birdsong did not know, or would not let out my secret. I carefully said, "I may be younger than you sir, but I have had more than one audience with General Thomas and Captain Tilly of his staff."

My gamble worked in that Oliver did not respond that he knew either Thomas or Tilly personally. Oliver simply responded, "Well go on then, let's hear your expert opinion of the man."

"That I will," I responded. "The general secured an appointment to West Point, and due to duty he remained loyal to the Union. His true home was the United States Army. He fought Indians in Florida, the Mexicans under Zachary Taylor, and Indians again out West. He taught at West Point. He served as a cavalry officer in Texas right before the war, and in fact, travelled with Robert E. Lee on duty assignments in Texas. Like General Lee, he had a decision to make after Virginia seceded from the Union. Whereas Lee put duty to his state above the country, Thomas was a Union man through and through."

"Why you do indeed seem to be an expert on the man," Captain Oliver spoke up without backing down. "Are you of some blood relationship or did you serve General Thomas in some official capacity?"

"What does that have to do with the truth?" I shot back. "He is a fine man and as the record shows a first rate general."

"I am not disputing that he could make a defensive stand with the best of them, but if he was in charge instead of General Grant we would still be holed up in Chattanooga waiting for Bragg to make the first move. Why he wasted so much time in preparation for Nashville that only with Grant's insistence did he attack. We had the numbers and Thomas, just like McClellan, Hooker, and Burnside, simply would not use our superior manpower without delay. He was afraid to shed the blood necessary to get the blasted war over with."

Mr. Doss reentered the conversation and I began to like him more and more. "Captain, from my observations, what distinguished General Thomas the most was that he could organize an army and win a battle, and all the while see to it that casualties were kept to a minimum. His army's hospital and sanitary conditions were ranked the best. His men loved him. Without orders, his troops overwhelmed the Confederate forces on Missionary Ridge in Chattanooga. He never was defeated in battle, and in fact, may have saved the war for the North with his stand at Chickamauga. He defeated General Hood so decisively at Nashville, and I might say in his time and his way, that he virtually ended the war in the West."

Oliver stood up and said, "I will not speak of military matters with a boy and a sutler anymore tonight. Believe what you must, but in the words of our great Lincoln, 'the truth is self-evident.'"

"That little twerp," exclaimed Mr. Doss after the captain left. "He didn't even get our martyred president's words right. Lincoln's speech after Gettysburg included the line, 'We hold these truths to be self-evident.' I know all about Captain Oliver. He served with Schofield, who would have done anything to get Thomas's job after the Battle of Franklin. Why General Schofield only escaped to the safety of Thomas's forces at Nashville because Hood had him trapped and then let him go. Oliver is cut from the same cloth. Why if he saw any action it was well hidden behind a brick wall while Hood foolishly charged the Union lines. Truth be told, Thomas was little appreciated by many, especially the top brass. Grant, Sherman, and Sheridan had a simple philosophy of warfare: take the superior numbers of Northern troops and throw them as quickly as possible against the South's shrinking army. Casualties would be high, but the result would be certain victory. General Thomas could never look at it that way. He wanted as many of his soldiers as possible to survive. This meant careful preparation and training. Time and time again, Thomas proved his ability and courage. He never complained about his superiors. He did his talking on the battlefield.

"Well, that is enough of my speech making for the night. I may not be a military expert, but I spent the entire war with the western armies trying to secure contracts for my company's foot wear. Most contracts went to those in Washington pushing shoddy and worthless products. General Thomas and his staff were the exception in that they wanted the best for the men. To a man like Oliver, though, I am a mere sutler with no right to speak on military matters." Doss slowly stood up and extended his hand to me. "Gentlemen, I believe it is time for me to retire back to my seat and sleep a little. Good luck, Mr. Nite, on your endeavors." He then turned to Mr. Birdsong, who had been rather quiet during the conversation, and said, "I will see you Birdsong on another train somewhere soon I'm sure. Good night."

Mr. Birdsong, a Kentucky and Tennessee sales representative for the Cincinnati candle and soap firm of Procter and Gamble, excused himself to use the water closet with the promise he would quickly return. He was an important man and I was hopeful that his influence would help procure me a decent position with the firm. With a recommendation from General Thomas and my papers from the Lawrence Academy certifying my completion of two years of studies, I had reason to be optimistic. I needed to be, for I had moved out of my room in Nashville, and everything I owned was in my bag. One way or the other, I would have to establish a new life in Ohio.

Mr. Birdsong returned to the seat next to me and lit a cigar. "Sam, Doss is quite a principled man and he knew what he was talking about. I think, though, he was a bit hard on Grant and Schofield. After all, the strategy of using the North's superior numbers won the war.

Nonetheless, you must be one special person to have General Thomas look out for you. There is not a better man. I first met the general back in April of '64 in Chattanooga when he was purchasing supplies for the Atlanta campaign under Sherman. I had dealt with many purchasing agents, but I can't ever recall dealing with a top general until that time. He wanted the best, and believe me, there were plenty of things sold to the army that, let's just say, weren't the best. I never had any problem with the Procter and Gamble products, but sure enough the general found some cracks in the wax of some candles and I had to replace them. Which I did, and from then on we have gotten along just fine. I am telling you this because the general would not waste any time on you if he had detected any flaws in your character."

"Well Mr. Birdsong," I answered, "I have got my faults. No one is perfect, not even General Thomas, I suppose."

"This is true," he replied. "In fact, for my taste General Thomas treats the nigger soldiers a little too well. I mean, they've never had it so good as they do in the army. They get three square meals a day and a roof, or at least a tent, over their heads. I'm all for their freedom, but that does not mean they are our equals and should be free to leave the land they were born and raised on and come up north. I am really scared that more and more of them will be coming to Cincinnati and taking away jobs from white men."

I sat there quiet. A real nervous feeling came over me. After Joe died, I began to believe all people were equal. I was not prepared for a northern gentleman to think otherwise. I thought I should challenge Birdsong's remarks, like the way I defended General Thomas to Oliver. But I didn't. I did not know how to react, or maybe I was just too scared I'd sound like an abolitionist. In my youth that was just about the worst thing you could call someone.

For the rest of the trip we exchanged harmless talk on subjects like the weather, or what the fields were like back in Nottoway County. It was uncomfortable. I felt like I did when Mary put me in my place back at the academy. My self-confidence was gone and by the time we got off the train in the morning, I didn't even care about seeing the sights in Cincinnati. I was afraid it might not be the place I supposed it to be.

CINCINNATI

After stopping at a hotel to freshen up and eat a large breakfast, all on the credit of Procter and Gamble, we headed off to the company offices. Mr. Birdsong and I took a seat in the beautiful waiting room. There were paintings of people in fine suits on the walls and columns with the wood carved at the top to appear like bunches of flowers. Back at the academy, the only things I studied were language plus a smattering of American history, and oh yes, a little practical mathematics. After I learned to read, I did study the sciences some, especially astronomy or the study of the sky. I knew nothing, however, about art, especially what I was seeing now. As it was, the little I knew about history, science, and math amounted to less than a hill of beans. There was just so much to learn.

While we were waiting, to make conversation, Mr. Birdsong began to tell me the story of Procter and Gamble. "Sam, this is a great opportunity to work for one of the largest and fastest growing companies in America. The idea for the company came in 1837 from a man named Alexander Norris, who had two daughters named Olivia and Elizabeth. The daughters married two immigrants who settled in Cincinnati, one named William Procter, a candle maker from England, and the other James Gamble, a soap maker from Ireland. Wanting a good life for his daughters, Mr. Norris came up with a plan for his new son-in-laws. He called a meeting and recommended that together they form a company.

"With power and transportation provided by the Ohio River, Procter and Gamble quickly prospered making soap and candles. By 1859 they were employing 80 people and had a million dollar business. The following year the war started and profits increased even more, due to the needs of the Union Army."

I mentioned how I remembered seeing Procter and Gamble soap

and candles being used by soldiers at the Howlett Line. In fact, some of our boys traded tobacco to the Union boys for P&G products.

"Yes Sam," Mr. Birdsong continued. "The P&G label was seen across the country. Growth was steady. And that growth still continues thanks to former soldiers introducing Procter and Gamble soap and candles throughout the land."

It was as if Mr. Birdsong was giving me a sales pitch. He talked about the future of the company, how they would create more types of goods and build factories outside of Cincinnati. "The company's future could be your future," he said. "When that door opens, grab the bull by the horns. Impress Procter and Gamble by telling them how much you believe in America and free enterprise, how you want to be part of that future, be a player in the game. Tell them how you are a good investment."

I was feeling better as I listened to Mr. Birdsong, and for a moment it did not matter to me what he had said on the train. I now liked the way he made me feel important. Besides, maybe I just misunderstood what he said about Negroes on the train.

It is funny how you can make excuses for people when they have something you want. I would often hear the phrase, "It is just business," as if those four words could justify anything and everything. I was of that mindset when the office door opened and a secretary called my name. I shook hands with Mr. Birdsong. He left and I have not seen him since.

The very properly dressed and poised secretary took me into a small office. It was very quiet, unlike on the streets where I could hear animals screaming and smell a burning odor I recognized from the war. A small balding man named Jurgen Swartz shook my hand and asked me to take a seat.

"Well Mr. Nite, this is quite a recommendation I have here from General George Henry Thomas. You know, many an Ohio man fought for the general and loved him like a father. I am lucky to have two sons who were in his army and I believe that is why they both survived the war. Now tell me Mr. Nite," continued this man with a heavy German accent, an accent I would soon hear quite a bit on the city streets, "What are your ultimate goals?"

I became nervous and scared to death by this new experience of a job interview. The "sales pitch" by Mr. Birdsong, given just two minutes ago, might as well never happened. I was again just a country boy in the presence of an important man. My mind searched desperately for a strong reply. All it came up with was, "A career in science, sir."

"Very good then," he answered and quickly started telling me how I could start out in the stock yards delivering oil, bones, and other things that would be used in P & G products. "Later you would move up to the packaging line, and then the mixing room where ingredients were carefully measured and blended together. If at this point, you proved to be a good worker, you might get a chance to assist in the lab room. If you continued to show potential, you might even be considered for an administrative position."

None of this sounded like "taking the bull by the horns" as suggested by Mr. Birdsong. It sounded more like again being a private in the army, doing the dirty work, until one day in the distant future they put a second stripe on your shoulder.

I said nothing during or after Mr. Swartz's speech. Finally, he asked, "Young man, does this not sound like a wonderful opportunity for someone who just a short time ago could not read and write? Your diligence at school, according to General Thomas's letter, makes me think you would jump at this offer. There are many well-educated men who would see ahead to the future and how this is their chance to grab the brass ring. Do you need a little time to get settled before starting?"

Now I was ready to speak up as my thoughts suddenly became clearer. "Mr. Swartz, I have not yet given my answer."

He quickly responded, "Mr. Nite, I have been told that in the South business is conducted in a very slow deliberate manner with plenty of custom that implies a Northerner is acting discourteous when he is merely trying to save time. Time is what it is all about. We only have so much. Take the war for example. Thank God, General Grant took our plentiful resources and wasted no time in defeating the South. Could there have been another way?"

Without thinking I blurted out, "You mean such a way as deployed by General Thomas? Why, was not Nashville a great Northern victory? Yet, General Grant was impatient and wanted General Thomas to attack before he was ready. Thomas instead risked his command and waited until the situation was right for both victory and the survival of as many soldiers as possible. Still, an impatient Grant cabled and even started out himself from Washington to replace Thomas. Luckily for your sons, the weather conditions improved and Thomas with every detail worked out attacked before he was replaced. As you know, the result was a total victory that cost the Union very few casualties. And, as you said yourself, all of your sons came back alive."

I was expecting Mr. Swartz to have me forcibly removed from the grounds. Instead, he leaned forward in his chair, put his head in his hands and silently wept. This awkward moment probably lasted 30 seconds, but it seemed like an hour. Finally he spoke. "Not all my sons survived. My youngest son died at Spotsylvania Court House."

"Oh my God, I'm sorry sir. I should have told you right off that I'm only interested in science in terms of what it can tell me about life. I'll be leaving now. I apologize for wasting your time and I'm sure General Thomas will not be pleased either. I'm so sorry, I mean about your son and my being so impolite."

I got up to leave. When I reached the door, I heard, "Wait, Sam, if I may call you by your first name, please come back and sit down."

I slowly walked back to the chair and sat down. Mr. Swartz spoke. "When I arrived from Prussia twenty years ago and found employment here, I was the happiest man in the world. I soon married and had three healthy sons. I advanced in the company and I could not have hoped for more in life. Then the war came, and now you know how it affected my family."

I sat there not knowing what to say, and mercifully I didn't have to say anything, for Mr. Swartz again spoke up. "Sam, when I was younger than you living in Prussia, I was quite idealistic. Most of the men talked about the importance of military training and considered you weak if you thought about anything different. I loved creating beautiful candles made of the finest beeswax. I wanted to be free to see the beauty of the world, not a world based on might. Coming to America, I hoped for a different life. Alas, I found much the same attitude here in this country. Before I knew it, there was talk about going to war with Mexico. Still, one could more easily mind their own business in America, at least until shortly before the recent war. All my sons served in the war. Two of them lived.

"The point is," Mr. Swartz said in a now gentle, but forceful voice, "you don't have to work here. My son Ronald went to work on a surveying team out West. A good steady job with regular advancement was meaningless to him after living through Chickamauga and Missionary Ridge. So, he is working for small government wages in the far West."

Mr. Swartz paused for a long moment. He seemed to have another thought come to mind. "I'll tell you what. Recently I attended a function for a Mr. Abbe, the new director of the Cincinnati Observatory. Here, let me find the newspaper. I saved it somewhere here in my desk. It has a quote concerning what he hopes to accomplish as the new director." He shuffled through papers in each of the desk drawers until he pulled out the section of a newspaper. He looked at it a second and then said, "Ah here it is, let me read it to you: *If the director be sustained in the general endeavor to make the observatory useful, he would propose to extend the field of activity of the observatory so as to embrace, on the one hand, scientific astronomy, meteorology and magnetism, and, on the other, the application of these sciences to geography and geodesy, to storm prediction, and to the wants of the citizen and the land surveyor.*"

Mr. Swartz put down the paper, looked at me with a smile on his face and said, "Now Sam, that is an idealistic dreamer if I ever heard one. Imagine predicting a storm before seeing the obvious signs. So, do you want to see if Mr. Cleveland Abbe can find you a job to meet your idealistic tastes?"

I was totally caught off guard. From the little I could understand of the newspaper quote, this man Abbe wanted to make weather predicting an everyday science. After a moment's thought I told Mr. Swartz it would be perfect. "Very good," he replied and added: "Meanwhile you must stay at my house. My poor wife Anna passed away shortly after news of our boy dying at Spotsylvania and Ronald is away. So there is just my son Bruno and the housekeeper. There is plenty of room for another. If it becomes more than a temporary arrangement, we will work out some terms. So sit down, and I'll compose a letter and give you detailed directions to the observatory and my house."

I was shaking. I could not figure out how so much could happen in such a short amount of time. As I sat there, I pondered the change in Mr. Swartz from a gloomy straightforward businessman to a benefactor acting like a long lost relative. Why the change? Why did he take such a liking to me after I hardly said a thing? Then it dawned on me. He probably wanted another young person in his house since so much had been taken away from him recently. He saw a chance to fill the void in his life and I must have reminded him of Ronald, at least in terms of our idealism. Or maybe it was that I reminded him of a time long ago when he arrived in Cincinnati a green young man from a different land. Still, these were nothing more than assumptions on my part. I learned later that one should never assume to know the mind of another.

It was apparent that Mr. Swartz was taking great care in writing the letter. After about twenty minutes, he stopped and asked if I would like to read an article on Mr. Abbe that was in a scientific journal. "It's only fair that you know something about him as well," he said as he handed me the rather thick document opened to what turned out to be a short but interesting biography.

It told me that Cleveland Abbe was born in New York City under somewhat privileged circumstances. This I gathered since he got a good education, including a Master's Degree at the University of Michigan. He was 21 years old when the war broke out and despite his background, he tried to enlist. He was rejected, however, because of poor eyesight. I found this somewhat puzzling because he went on to become an astronomer or one who observes the sky. In any case, he was able to join a government project headquartered in Massachusetts that studied the shoreline, which had something to do with the measurement of the land and the sea.

I was having trouble reading and understanding the article, for it had lots of large words beginning with "geo," and it also contained several unfamiliar mathematical formulas. I was able to comprehend that in 1864 he went to Russia to study at the observatory of a famous astronomer. He then came home after the war and was appointed director of the Cincinnati Observatory. According to the article, Abbe worked to advance the observatory from being merely a museum to a great research center for meteorology, the study of weather.

This excited me, and at the same time, worried me because I had only a slight general knowledge of science. Before I could think much more on it, Mr. Swartz exclaimed loudly, "There, that ought to do, Sam. I think this is a good letter incorporating what I know of your ambition and interests, and it will complement General Thomas's letter quite well." He then handed it to me to read. I looked at the words on the piece of paper before me. One sentence stood out. It read, "Mr. Samuel Nite is a rare individual who believes that not all worthy endeavors translate into one's personal economic gain." I didn't know exactly what that meant, but I knew for sure that I would rather not work in a dark, dirty, and dangerous factory all day.

I thanked Mr. Swartz and took the letter. He gave me his address and directions to his house and told me to come over for supper. After dinner, we would work out arrangements for me to stay on as a tenant. My head was spinning. It had already felt like a full day since I got off the train from Nashville, but there was more to come.

My immediate destination was the Cincinnati Observatory on Mount Adams, which Mr. Swartz estimated would be a 45-minute walk. If I thought this northern town was paradise, I was wrong. There were no slaves for sure, but the workers I passed didn't look like country gentlemen either. They were dirtier than the men of Parker's Battery were after six months on the front lines. The sky was dark with smoke, and garbage lay rotting in the streets. The downtown stock yards echoed with the cries of unhappy animals.

I slowly made my way to the foot of Mount Adams. There I saw a group of White lads and Negro lads not exactly playing together. In fact, they were throwing rocks at each other and calling each other hateful names. They seemed to despise each other in a way I had never experienced in Virginia. Then again, Negro boys in Virginia never would have dared throw rocks at White boys.

The air got better as I made my way up Mount Adams. There was a sign when I reached the top that said the hill was named for John Quincy Adams, who dedicated the observatory. Before that time it was known as Mt. Ida. Now the observatory stood before me. It was a very small building, but its grounds served as a great place for a magnificent view of the city. Below, the mighty Ohio River snaked past the famous Roebling Bridge, one of the first suspension bridges in the country. Across the river was the Town of Covington and beyond it the forests of Kentucky. Cincinnati itself looked like a power hungry, dirty monster. Smokestacks were everywhere. From above, the city looked like nothing I had ever seen before. It was not a new place, it was a new era.

I took all this in and then entered the darkly lit observatory. At the door, I was greeted by a young woman dressed not nearly as formally as the secretary at Procter and Gamble's. She looked to be about 20 years old and she introduced herself as Sally Johnson. She was what you would call spunky and I liked her right off. She asked me what I wanted and I told her I was there to see Mr. Abbe. "Oh him," she said gloomy like and then cracked a big smile. "He is a good man. Always has his nose in a book though."

It didn't seem that she was excited about being there, so without thinking I blurted out, "So how did you end up in a place like this?" I immediately felt embarrassed to say such a thing to a person I did not know. I could not even imagine how a Southern woman would have reacted to such forwardness.

She giggled, but then quickly answered. "It's because my parents are what you call progressive. They want me to get an education."

"Even though you're a girl?" I let out.

Sally responded, "Well, I now see that you're not progressive. Where are you from anyway? You don't sound like you're German and you don't sound like an Ohio pioneer either."

"Why I'm from Virginia, the most powerful state in the Union," I said with confidence.

Sally was quick to say, "Hey, haven't you heard? You lost the war."

I now was getting a bit annoyed and I told her that war was men's business and that she didn't know anything about it. She started to reply when a man about 40 years old walked in. "See here, what is going on? Miss Johnson, is that man here for a purpose, or is he another one of your suitors?"

"Why Mr. Abbe, he is not. He is here to see you about men's business of which I know nothing." I did not miss the obvious sarcasm in both the words and the way she spoke them.

Despite a certain distracted manner and way of talking, Cleveland Abbe was a pleasant enough looking man with a kind expression and a slight smile hidden behind his full beard and spectacles. "So, come in young man," he offered and I entered his small office. I thought back to the article and wondered how he could have such great ambitions for this small place. As I took a seat, I found my mind on Sally outside the door.

"So who sent you?" Abbe's words snapped my mind back to my true purpose.

"Mr. Swartz of Procter and Gamble sent me and gave me this letter to give you," I said as I handed him the papers.

"What's this? It appears to be two letters."

"Oh, I'm sorry sir. The other letter is from General Thomas," I apologetically replied.

"George Henry Thomas? Yes, I hear he was a wonderful general. What unit were you in son?"

Without thinking, I responded, "Parker's Virginia Battery, under command of General Longstreet." I thought about what I said and quickly spoke up again before Mr. Abbe could react. I explained my situation in detail and how I came to meet General Thomas and how it changed my life. After listening to me for about ten minutes, the scientist said nothing for what seemed like an eternity. I was sure he was wondering, even after my story, whether or not he should take a chance on a Confederate veteran.

Finally he spoke. "Tell me, has the war changed you in any way, besides being reformed by the general?"

I carefully thought about the question and then answered, "Sir, before, during, and after the war I did not know anything except for what I was told. Study and learning has begun to show me that I can find my own answers. That is why I want to do something in the field of science. I want to learn on my own terms and not according to what I am merely told."

Abbe looked at me for a spell and then back at the letters. "I can let you clean up around here and prepare for an assignment later on. With my guidance, I'll expect you to continue your studies for a general education above the level you attained in Nashville. I'll expect after a year's time, or less, for you to impress me with your knowledge, and then at that time only will I consider you for a scientific assignment. In exchange for this I will see if some compensation can be given to Mr. Swartz to house and feed you. Mr. Swartz made mention of such a possibility in his letter. And one more thing, I demand that you apply yourself and not engage in any foolishness here like having long unnecessary conversations with Miss Johnson. I must tolerate her due to her family's generous contributions to the observatory, but I don't have to put up with others engaging in useless and distracting behavior. Are there any questions?"

I stood there too weary to think of an educated reply. I just nodded and said, "Yes, I mean no, I don't have any questions, but yes I want the job." Mr. Abbe said, "Fine. I will see you here in my office at 8 a.m. tomorrow."

I walked out of the office thinking of how only 24 hours ago I was boarding the train in Nashville. As I headed for the observatory door, a voice behind me said, "How did it go big britches?" I turned and there was Sally, quite the pleasant sight. She was of medium height with beautiful chestnut brown hair hanging rather freely about her shoulders; much different from the women I saw working at the hotel and at Procter and Gamble. Their hair was tied up either in what they call a bun or in a net. Although earlier I spoke rather boldly to Sally, I now returned to my shy ways around women. "Cat got your tongue, gentleman from Virginia?" she asked.

Being almost five feet and eight inches tall, I towered over her, but I could not find a good reply. All I came up with was, "It went quite well. I am going to start work here tomorrow."

"Well, that will make four of us staffing this place. We are going to make the biggest discoveries since Isaac Newton," she replied.

"Who?" I asked, immediately regretting my quick response.

Sally's quick judgment of "Oh boy, you have a lot to learn," caused me to turn red in the face. "Don't worry Sam, Timothy and I will help you get along."

I had never had a woman other than my ma call me Sam, and this made me even more embarrassed. At the same time, I had a strange feeling of joy that I simply could not explain. All I know is from that moment on I would be constantly thinking about Sally and looking forward to seeing her every day at the observatory. Like a fool, I did not know how to gracefully depart; I mumbled something without even asking her who Timothy was. I somehow found my way out into the sunlight. In reality, it was a gray day, but I felt like the sun was shining bright. I read the directions on the piece of paper from Mr. Swartz and I could see that it was not far to his house in the area known as Over-The Rhine, named so because it was a German neighborhood. It was a thirty-minute walk to his modest brick house on Vine Street near where it intersects Liberty Street.

There I was greeted warmly by Mr. Swartz, who left work early to be home when I arrived. He treated me like a friend he had known forever, maybe even like a son, though I had just met him a few hours ago. I cleaned up and reported for dinner with his son Bruno and his housekeeper Gretchen. The rest was a blur as I nearly fell asleep at the table. Mr. Swartz, who at first asked me all types of questions, soon stopped asking them and had Gretchen show me to my room. He promised to awake me in time to report for work the next day.

I awoke the next morning to a knock on the door. Before I could get out of bed the door opened and there stood Gretchen. "Why excuse me for being so informal, but I thought with you being so tired last night it might take more than a knock to wake you." I felt very embarrassed and did not know how to reply. Instead of leaving, Gretchen sat on the corner of the bed and told me Mr. Swartz had left for work and Bruno was sound asleep. Perhaps I was not familiar with the customs of a northern city, but I felt very uncomfortable. Finally, Gretchen said, "Well, I guess I'll let you get up and dress while I go to the kitchen and prepare you a good breakfast for your first day of work. Is there anything you will need first Mr. Nite?"

At that moment the downstairs clock struck seven times. I was to report at the observatory by 8 a.m. and I was determined to be at work early the first day. "No Ms. Gretchen," I said, "I must hurry, please go attend to my breakfast and I will be down in a few moments." With a sigh she got off my bed and left. I hurriedly cleaned up at the washbowl and put on my other clean suit of clothes and hurried down to the dining area. Gretchen smiled at me like it was the first time she saw me that morning. At the table was a note from Mr. Swartz wishing me good luck on my first day of work. I quickly ate a bowl of oatmeal, two poached eggs, and some fried potatoes. I washed it all down with some milk from a pitcher and out the door I went to work. On my walk to the observatory I thought a little bit about Gretchen's behavior that morning, but for the most part I was too nervous about my first day of work to dwell on the subject.

I arrived at the observatory expecting to be the first one there and have some time to compose myself before the doors were opened. To my surprise Sally and Mr. Abbe were already there when I arrived. I rushed in past Sally barely saying hello and there was Mr. Abbe sitting at his desk. Without looking up he said, "I know, Mr. Nite, it is your first day and you assumed work begins here at 8 a.m. when we open the doors. In the future, however, unless I specify that you are needed for some evening observation tasks, I'll expect you here at 7 a.m. What I need you to do first today is organize these papers on which Timothy and I were recording observations last night. Please arrange each paper according to the time marked on the top from the earliest to the latest. I will need them when Timothy reports back here in about two hours."

Thus began my first day of work. The second day and thereafter I would arrive at 7 a.m., but I was never asked to be there at night. The days soon became weeks and then months as the year progressed rapidly. As far as work went, Mr. Abbe quickly showed me the areas he wanted cleaned each evening after 4 p.m. Once in a while he would have me sort or arrange papers like the first day. For the rest of the time I was to read the *Encyclopaedia Britannica*. After handing me Volume One, Mr. Abbe explained that he himself was about halfway through reading the 17 volume set, and he could not think of a better way to learn about the accumulated knowledge of mankind.

So I began reading. When I came across a word or concept I did not understand, I asked Mr. Abbe or his assistant Timothy for help. After a few weeks of this, Mr. Abbe said he was pleased with my attitude and my ability to follow directions. He told me if I continued doing good work he would have an important assignment for me in a year's time. I would be sent to a location where each day I would observe the weather and telegraph my observations to Mr. Abbe at the observatory. Amazingly, from this information, and that of other observers, he would be able to predict the weather for Cincinnati and other locations hundreds of miles away from the observatory.

In the meantime, I was to continue with my reading. Mr. Abbe told me on several occasions that, "A good education is the best insurance against an observer wiring in incomplete or false observations. This is not because one needs to be well versed in scientific details. Instead, it is important because knowledge creates a thirst for more knowledge and interest in one's work. Enthusiasm results in better outcomes whether it is fitting horseshoes or discovering new planets."

Eventually, Mr. Abbe shared with me why he was constantly going over the papers on his desk and the books on his shelves. "It is the finer work of meteorology son." From him I learned that many factors controlled the climate and weather. The climate, or the typical weather condition of an area, is caused by things like the axis and rotation of the earth. The changes in the weather within the climatic parameters can be predicated by the current conditions of the air being held in by gravity, or what is called the atmosphere, as being stable or unstable and moving according to the interaction of areas of high and low pressure. These interactions result in what we experience as temperature, precipitation (rain, snow, etc.) and the force of the wind. Mr. Abbe, by knowing exactly where the weather was coming from, could predict what type of conditions could be expected the next day or two in Cincinnati. For example, if it was raining in Chicago, about 300 miles from Cincinnati, and the wind was blowing towards us at 20 miles per hour, and the barometer indicated that the air pressure was dropping at a specific rate, than he could accurately predict in how many hours we could expect rain in Cincinnati. The catch was that someone would have to be in Chicago and points in between to be able to tell Mr. Abbe with accuracy the conditions between the Windy City and Cincinnati.

A war is a terrible thing. But some good always seems to come out of something bad. I suppose something bad will usually come out of a good thing, too. One good thing that had come out of all the death and destruction of the recent war was the refinement of the telegraph. For Mr. Abbe, that meant he could station people at different places and they could use the telegraph to send the weather conditions to him in Cincinnati.

I enjoyed my time reading and talking to Mr. Abbe at the observatory. Things were not going as well away from work, however. First of all, there was Gretchen. She constantly made me feel uncomfortable. She made a comment my second or third day about me trying to gold dig the Swartz family. I did not know what that meant but soon figured it out, because she showed me what it meant. Gretchen was, let us say, offering her affections to Mr. Swartz's son Bruno. She also thought I had some plan to gain special favor from Mr. Swartz. Once she realized that I was not trying to be friendly with Mr. Swartz in order to get some of his money, she suddenly stopped sweet talking me. She no longer figured I might be her means to a better life. I should not judge Gretchen. Inside she had to be a sad person. One evening, Mr. Swartz told me her story. Her father was killed at the battle of Stone's

River in Tennessee. A month later, her mother died giving birth to her brother. She was ten years old at the time with no relatives in America, so she and her brother were put in an orphanage in Hamilton, Ohio. Eventually, Gretchen was placed by a relief agency with Mr. Swartz. She seemed to be a good housekeeper and getting to know her better was tempting. She had a shapely figure, attractive red hair, and a pleasing face. As I look back on it, I'm lucky that she scared me more than a Yankee bayonet charge. To be with her, as she would try any means possible to get her "share of the pie," as she called it, could have only led to trouble.

Another difficulty was living in such a large city after growing up a country boy in the South. There were immigrants everywhere speaking unknown languages or with accents that were so hard to understand that they might as well be speaking German or Russian. To make matters worse, many had trouble with my Southern accent. My speech and grammar had improved dramatically since entering the academy in Nashville, but I still spoke with a twang like the farm boy from Nottoway County that I was. There were many transients in Cincinnati. Those were people who came in to the city by way of the Ohio River, or came across it from the South, looking for work or some means to travel farther west, or in many cases get back to where they came from. These were often people who didn't mind committing a crime to further their plans. I once met such a fellow who openly bragged to me that he would commit a crime, if he had a good plan, in order to get some money to return to Indiana and buy back his family farm. In spite of his thieving plans, he seemed a decent and trustworthy man. I had met him sitting on a park bench one Sunday and we talked quite a bit about life in the city, which he hated. I lent him two pennies to get something to eat figuring I would never see him again. Three days later he was waiting outside the observatory at 7 a.m. with the money he borrowed. After that I saw him on occasion just walking the streets. One time, over coffee, I told him my story and how crime does not pay. I remember his answer, "That may be true in most places and most circumstances, but this city ain't one of those places and the circumstances of me landing here because of some dirty rotten bankers taking my Pa's land makes it okay in my mind to take back from some bank what is mine. I'll tell you this, when I get back home and buy back the farm, the first thing I'll do is jump in the creek and wash off this filthy city dirt." I never saw him again after that. I suppose he made it back home, or more likely was dead or in prison.

I heard other stories about criminals or just plain tough guys. A coachman told me that once a man offered to pay him fifteen gold dollars to take him all the way to Detroit. They were about 20 miles out of the city when a sheriff and some men arrested the man for robbing a bank. After a good while, the coachman was cleared of any charges of abetting in a crime. Another time, I was in a little workingman's café in the city where a teamster was bragging about running over a dog. The owner threatened to kill the teamster the next time he committed such an act. He meant it too. He grabbed the teamster by the collar and threw him into the street. It was a simple case that the café owner loved dogs.

The city was indeed a rough place, especially down by the wharves. On the other hand, for the most part, the German community was made up of very intelligent, hard-working, and highly principled people. There were watchmakers, sausage producers, furniture craftsmen, and quite a few master brewers. Yes beer, a beverage I was quite unfamiliar with, is a staple drink among the Germans. Mr. Swartz warned me of the evils that could come from drinking too many beers at one time, but he certainly enjoyed the one he allowed himself with each meal.

Mr. Swartz treated me well. However, I soon realized that I was not helping him deal with the loss of his son from the war, the son who was out west, or Bruno, his disappointing son. I was more of a reminder of what he lost instead of serving as any kind of replacement. He also knew that someday soon I would leave. Then he would be left only with the problems of Bruno.

As far as I could tell, Bruno was interested in three things: women, beer, and the emerging new pastime of baseball. He played what was called the second sacker position for a team called Live Oak of Cincinnati, but his real ambition was to play for the Cincinnati team known as the "Red Stockings." He talked about it all the time so that near the middle of May, when the Live Oaks were scheduled to play the Red Stockings, I was willing to spend one of my valuable nickels to go to the game.

The May 30th match was at the Union Grounds, a pretty good distance from Over-the Rhine. I compensated by leaving quite early on

Saturday morning, having secured permission for a rare day off from Mr. Abbe. When I arrived, the start of the game was an hour away. Still, a huge crowd was already assembled. Bruno had arranged to sell me a nickel ticket beforehand, which I clasped firmly in my hand. I worked my way through the crowd and got to the grandstand with the mysterious name "Old Duchess." When I ascended out of the dark stairway into the seating area, before me was a most pleasant site. Clad in gray were some of the Live Oaks doing something called calisthenics in order to stretch their muscles. Others were throwing a ball to each other to prepare for the game. A little beyond them were the magnificently dressed Red Stockings. They wore white red-trimmed shirts, red belts, pants fastened at the knees, and the clothing for which they were known, red socks pulled up to the bottom of the pants. I took a seat and watched the teams perform drills and practice hitting the ball with sticks that were shaped with a thin handle that expanded to a large barrel at the end. They were also quite proficient in catching the ball with their bare hands. Before I knew it, the hour was up and the game began.

It was not much of a contest. Standing at his position, Bruno saw more Red Stockings round the bases than I saw Confederates retreating from Petersburg. I soon figured out the basics of the game. One team had a player throw, or pitch, the ball to a player from the other team, who tried to hit it with that stick of tapered wood they called a bat. If the ball was hit and not cleanly caught by the other team, the fella who hit it could advance, running in a square, touching the bases or corners. A batsman scored a run, or point, if he made it all the way back to the corner from which he hit the ball before being tagged or hit by a thrown ball. At least that's the way the game seemed to be played. The Red Stockings, led by manager Harry Wright who did some of the pitching, were magnificent and won the game 72 to 5. Other players who impressed me were Asa Brainard, Fred Waterman, John Howe, Johnny Hatfield, and J. Williams Johnson.

I enjoyed the game, and in a manner of speaking, I became a "fan" of the game. My enjoyment, however, was tempered by the actions of Bruno. I could tell he was not good enough to play for the Red Stockings, yet that is all he talked about. He was friends with Asa Brainard, who was as good a pitcher as one would hope to see. They called him "The Count." I think it was because he was so important to the Stockings. Mr. Abbe told me a count was a nobleman in Europe. Asa was a big man and he could throw the ball very fast. He also had what they called a "twist" ball, which would bend after he threw it, making it very difficult for an opposing player to hit.

Brainard also enjoyed life, perhaps a little too much. And this I believe was not a good thing for Bruno. Some nights Bruno would come home late after drinking beer with Brainard and other baseball enthusiasts. At such times, he would cause Mr. Swartz much sorrow. Bruno would often bang on Gretchen's door until she would oblige and let him enter. Mr. Swartz, in my mind, denied to himself what was happening. He would lecture Bruno at the dinner table, which often resulted in Bruno abruptly leaving the house. He never talked about Bruno when speaking about his family. I believe he had experienced so much sorrow with the loss of his youngest son and his wife, as well as Ronald going out west, that he could not bear the fact that Bruno was not a hard worker. In fact, Bruno, did work very hard at baseball, but Mr. Swartz would always exclaim to him, "A grown man cannot make a living playing a game!" And I'm afraid in Bruno's case he was right.

During the times Bruno would enter Gretchen's room, I would lay in my bed both disgusted and curious trying to imagine what was going on in there. I cannot deny my manhood. Like other men I had feelings and longings for women. But I wanted to meet the right woman, one I could settle down with, taking her as my wife. One day, as if hit by a bolt of lightning, I realized I had met that woman. It was Sally of course, Mr. Abbe's secretary. I acted awkwardly around her when I first started working at the observatory. I had never before worked at a formal job where you were expected to behave in a professional manner. I tried to fit in, but felt like the farm boy I was. Sally would laugh at me, but in what seemed to me a good-natured way. When one of her male callers came by, it was different. Her beau would make fun of me and mean it. Sometimes Sally would join in, but at the same time try to also say good things about me. Her jokes never felt cruel like those of her suitors.

As time went on, Sally stopped kidding me and became much kinder. She seemed happy to see me each morning. She started asking me questions about my life and even made a point to come outside and sit with me at lunch time. I remember one grand time in particular. It was a beautiful summer day; the breeze blew the city smoke from the valley south into Kentucky. The view from Mt. Adams was extra spectacular, and the temperature was perfect. Sally and I were sitting at the park bench eating some cheese and bread, talking, and laughing, when she suddenly, out of nowhere, asked me, "Sam, have you ever had a gal; I mean a girlfriend?" I turned all red in the face and I just couldn't say anything. "I didn't think so," she said. At that moment Mr. Abbe walked past on his way to get something to eat at one of the nearby taverns. He looked at us and shook his head, but I noticed a little smile on his face.

"It certainly is a beautiful day for two young people to be sitting together on a park bench," he pronounced.

I had just regained my composure, and just like that I turned red again. After Mr. Abbe was a few yards past us, Sally leaned over and whispered in my ear, "Some gal is going to be real lucky when you do get around to courting." I even think she might have given my ear a little kiss. I never felt like I did at that time in all my prior eighteen years of living. I still couldn't say anything. But I guess I didn't have to, for Sally just sat there with the sweetest smile I had ever seen. And she was looking directly into my eyes.

The spell broke when a factory steam valve shrieked in the valley below. "Come on," Sally said as she stood up. "People will begin to talk about how improper it is for two people of the opposite sex to be whiling away time on a park bench in the middle of the day." Hearing the word "sex" from the mouth of a young woman set me to another round of blushing and feeling light headed.

We started on what would be one of many walks we would enjoy together over the next few months. Sally was so different from other women I had met at the academy in Nashville. She was what you could call a modern woman. She spoke to me of how women should be allowed to vote, how we owed it to the Negroes to give them land and houses, and how the government should pay for free schools, libraries, and Art museums. I was overcome with her talk, and I had fallen in love. At night I tossed and turned trying to go to sleep. When the sun came up in the morning everything looked and smelled different. As I walked, I felt five feet off the ground. Yet, I could not believe Sally would have any feelings for me. She was two years older than me, and besides, there was the other fella who worked at the observatory.

Timothy was a different kind of person than the men I met in the Civil War. Well, maybe Davey was a bit like him. Timothy was very serious, yet knew how to act around other men his age. He seemed confident, that's what it was. Timothy also seemed to be beyond petty behavior. Instead of making fun of me, he would help me when I had trouble understanding one of the encyclopedia entries.

I liked Timothy, but as time went on I could see that he also liked Sally. And, unlike me, he was not afraid to act upon his feelings. Sally told me that he called on her, and when I look back on it now I know she was hinting for me to do the same. I don't know who she would have picked, but I never made it a contest. I was just too damn, excuse the language, shy or stupid. She right out told me she was attracted to my innocence and my kind heart. She said I was real brave when I told her about the stuff that happened after the war. She told me I was one of her best friends. And even though I started feeling more and more like not only her best friend, but something much more, I just could not tell her so. As I look back on it, I was a fool.

Bruno sometimes came to the observatory. One time, Mr. Abbe came out of the office and said, "Honest to God Miss Johnson, please go off somewhere this afternoon with this young man. That way Samuel, Timothy, and I can accomplish something." I always felt special when Mr. Abbe called me Samuel. This time, however, I really felt terrible when Sally said, "All right I will. Just so happens Bruno wants to take me to a game of baseball, which I have always wanted to do. So let's go Bruno." Now, not only Timothy, but also Bruno was taking off after Sally. And, yet again, I just backed away and carried on while my heart shattered. I continued thinking and asking myself why I couldn't ask Sally to go somewhere. Every time I thought of doing it, I would get frightened that it just could not be true that she would like me in a way that was more than a friend.

That afternoon, after Bruno took Sally to the baseball contest, I did not act like my usual self. I did not even want to talk to Mr. Abbe about my latest readings in the encyclopedia, nor did I have that special feeling of honor when he would speak to me about his latest studies. "What's the matter with you son?" he finally said in a raised voice. "You are not jealous are you?" This really caught me by surprise because I never thought in a million years that Mr. Abbe would speak to me of romantic matters, him being such a studious person.

"No sir, I'm not jealous."

"Well," he retorted, "only a fool could miss the signs of a love triangle around here. It is more obvious than the warning of a red sky at morning to bring on a tempest later in the day." I looked confused and he just looked at me, meeting my eyes.

"She is that interested in Bruno?" I finally asked.

"Heavens no, a woman like Sally is too sensible to get seriously involved with that roughneck. It is you and Timothy. Whether you know it or not, the two of you are vying for Sally's affections." As was my habit at such a time, I once again turned red in the face, felt clammy, and must have appeared quite distraught. Mr. Abbe suggested we take a break and sit on the bench outside the observatory. I mumbled something and slowly followed him outside. For the first time, I saw Mr. Abbe's kindness and warmth. "I'm sorry," he started, "I feel terrible now, for I thought you knew that Timothy has been seriously courting Sally. Sally is attracted to him very much, but she is also attracted to you; how much I can't tell. It is certain, though, that this has confused the poor girl and given her second thoughts about Timothy."

"Are you sure of this sir?" I asked the scientist.

"No, it is just a hunch, Samuel. Now what do you say we get back to work?"

This was the only time Cleveland Abbe spoke to me about something personal and non-scientific. He raised the question, but since I was the only one who could prove the hypothesis correct, he dwelled on the matter no more. A distinguished scientist like Mr. Abbe would never consider speaking to a young lady of Sally's age about romantic matters.

As time went by, Sally spoke to me more and more. She began to talk openly about Timothy, how he intended to enter a college soon, perhaps a prestigious one like Harvard or Princeton. Ironically he eventually decided on the University of Virginia. During these conversations I would often become quiet or moody. One such time, Sally said, "I feel like I'm destroying you."

Like an idiot I replied, "It's fine. Timothy is a great guy." She could have hit me over the head with a hammer and I still for some mysterious reason could not reveal my love for her in words. Yet my actions were so obvious.

Now that I look back on it, indeed she would have had to hit me with a hammer and carry me off. A woman can't do that of course, but if one could have, Sally would have been the one. As it was, she soon gave up on me. In September, Timothy left for Virginia to begin college, and I had Sally all to myself. We would still eat lunch together, take interesting walks down Mount Adams after work and just enjoy each other's company, but it was obvious though that she had made her commitment to Timothy. She talked about him more and quoted from the many letters he sent to her. I was in Ohio with her, but her man was in Virginia.

I was just too shy when it came to women. I just could not believe that a woman like Sally could be interested in me. A couple times, before she had decided on Timothy, she invited me to her parents' fine home for dinner. After the meal she would sit with me on the porch swing afterwards. She would sit so close to me that looking back upon it, I knew she wanted me to kiss her. I was so afraid of doing the wrong thing that I did nothing. Even her mother and father, I think, could sense that our relationship was going nowhere. This must have made them feel quite comfortable. They treated me in a fine manner because they didn't have to worry about their Sally going off with an office boy like myself. No, she would properly be married to a college man.

Fall became winter then spring. In May of 1869, on a beautiful spring day, as I walked Sally towards home, she told me that she was to marry Timothy and join him in the fall at the University of Virginia. I was invited to the wedding, but made up some silly excuse for why I could not attend. Heartbroken, I worked harder in order to take my mind off Sally. I threw my whole being into my studies under the tutelage of Mr. Abbe.

One day in September, rather nonchalantly, Mr. Abbe said to me, "Samuel, it is time for you to become one of my information gatherers. I have men posted at the usual places that allow me to predict Cincinnati's weather. Now, I need to experiment and see if I can forecast from here what the weather will be in another place. I'm thinking of the Ohio Valley, east of here, say between Pittsburgh and Portsmouth,

Ohio. I have the opportunity to station you at a town named Mount Vernon, Ohio. It is the perfect location. Westerly winds pass through the Mount Vernon area in a direction leading to the many small river towns on the Ohio. Imagine the importance of alerting a boat captain whether or not it is safe to attempt passage between Pittsburgh and Cincinnati on any given day. A retired professor, who must be about 65 years old, has a modest home in Mount Vernon with a fine library. He has stated in a letter that you can stay with him for a very reasonable rent. There you may continue your education in his library and at the same time learn to read conditions that can be telegraphed to me here at the observatory. His name is Professor Pennington. "Are you ready Samuel?"

Mount Vernon

left Cincinnati on a cool autumn day. In the morning I said goodbye
to Mr. Swartz as he left for services at the Lutheran church. Over the
past few months, we had talked less and less. We both worked late
and whoever got home first ate and went right to bed. Still, it was an
emotional farewell. This good and wise man not only opened his home
to me but encouraged me to follow my dreams. He told me it was okay
to be different. He did not have the common attitude that there was
only one right way to live.

Gretchen, the housekeeper, prepared breakfast for me. While I ate,
she cleaned my room just like she had every other day. And, like every
other day, there was no good-bye. She had lost interest in me a long
time ago, which was fine by me. In so many words, she had told me
I was worthless. When I had first told her of my ambition to learn as
much as I could about the known world, she laughed for what seemed
like a full minute. Then she said, "You are a complete fool. You are
choosing to be poor. Some day you will be doing menial labor like me,
with no time for your useless books."

Bruno, who was still in bed, would likely have shared Gretchen's
opinion of my life. However, his plan to become a professional ball
player was not likely to offer him any more financial gain than my
own current path of education. Even if he made it as a professional ball
player, by thirty-five he would be too old to play, and he would have
no experience in a useful trade. The little money he now earned doing
odd jobs, like selling pretzels and beer at Red Stocking games, was
spent the very same day in one of the saloons. He still figured to inherit
something from his father, but he likely would spend it all in a year or
two. Gretchen had figured that out, and I had not heard Bruno gain
entrance to her room in a long time.

Of the three, I felt the most sadness leaving Mr. Swartz. There was something unfulfilled about our relationship. It happens a lot in life when you meet somebody and you have high expectations about your new friendship. Then, for one reason or another, you never become close friends and you feel regret. Probably, it just wasn't meant to be. On the other hand, it may just be the result of how the city changed family life. On the farm a family grew close from being together all the time. In the city, men, women and even children worked ten to twelve hours a day away from home and family. It was a different world both North and South. In a sense we were now all slaves. If you were not rich, deserting the city and earning a smaller, but steady, pay seemed to be one's only hope for freedom.

After leaving Mr. Swartz's home, I soon reached the foot of Mt. Adams. It was a Sunday morning and no one was about. Having plenty of time, I walked to the top, and from the observatory grounds I gazed one more time at the city below. The most prominent feature was the Ohio River moving on its muddy green path past the city. The air was relatively clear, much more so than on any of the other six days of the week. Not all the smoke stacks were emitting billowing long dark clouds into the sky. Those that did created an interesting pattern of skinny vertical lines rising into the bright blue sky. On the ground, trees of beautiful red, rust, and gold autumn colors dotted every spot where man had spared them from the frontier axe. I felt a strange sadness about departing. The city was not the paradise I imagined it would be, but it was my first home of independence. I held a job where I was encouraged to think, and that placed me with a small minority of men.

Soon it was time to descend the hill that represented the highest scholarly ambitions of the city. It was the hill where I worked for Mr. Cleveland Abbe, a true man of science who believed that scientific applications could solve every human problem. I still shared this belief, but with reservation, for I had seen the use of science in war and the resulting death and destruction. I also saw the peacetime dirty underbelly of the city. In my mind, for every answer science provided, it held an equal number of dangers because everything from filth to deadly injuries was tolerated in the name of progress.

I made my way to the station and boarded a train on the famed Baltimore and Ohio Railroad, the first railroad in America to carry passengers. With that innovation, railroads provided connections between every town in America. No longer was there one central place from which everything started and ended like ocean ports. The rails connected people and enhanced the sharing of information. In one article I had studied with Mr. Abbe, the author said that the term railroad was too narrow for what they meant for the future. He preferred a term beginning with the prefix "inter" followed by a word, which I think might have been "lines" as in "interlines"? I know it had something to do with the tracks connecting all of America like a great spider's web.

Mr. Abbe told me this was just the beginning. The wires of the telegraph had begun an era where people communicated with each other even faster than letters being carried by fast trains. He liked to say that eventually an age of communication, though never replacing the age of industry, would dawn upon the land. Already, the telegraph, not the railroad, was the key to Mr. Abbe being able to correctly forecast the weather.

One day I asked Mr. Abbe what he thought of me becoming a Morse code operator. He answered that no one could predict how long such a skill would be needed. He recited a long list of communication systems, noting which ones lasted a long time and which did not or would not. He said operating a printing press would provide a long and comfortable lifestyle, while riding with the Pony Express would not provide security once the railroad and telegraph lines became established on the Pacific coast.

My thoughts drifted back to the present as I found a seat on the train. The engine waited, impatiently puffing smoke that drifted back to my car. I felt the train, like me, was more than ready to get started, ready to pull four passenger cars, a dining car, a lounge, two baggage cars, and a mail car to destinations north and east. The train started turning its wheels ever so slowly and then gradually picked up speed. In no time at all we were far out of the station. It had been a long time coming, this second train ride. And unlike the first one, it was day time and a beautiful autumn day to boot. The countryside quickly became flat, unlike the hills of Cincinnati. The crops were being harvested, even on this Sunday, in order to be done before the long winter set in. There was so much to see, and I enjoyed being out in this country bursting with an energy not seen in the slow slave system of the Old South. Poles heavy with telegraph wire ran next to the tracks. In the distance there appeared one farm house after the next, where less than fifty years ago had been wilderness.

I pulled out of my bag a Cincinnati newspaper. On page nine was a short story about my great benefactor General George Henry Thomas arriving in San Francisco to assume command of the Military Division of the Pacific. The writer proclaimed this a great honor, but it was simply a convenient way for the new president elect, Ulysses S. Grant, to move General Thomas farther away from Washington. Captain Tilly had told me that Grant thought Thomas, like the South itself, was too careful and too slow. But Thomas had proved him wrong at the Battle of Nashville. Now, a president cannot afford to have people who proved him wrong close by or in strategic positions, so the important military positions went to Grant's good friends and proponents of total war, Sherman and Sheridan rather than General Thomas.

The treatment of General Thomas, a man who so valued human life, caused me to ask myself if this was a sign of things to come. Were the farms of Ohio to become forces in the dehumanization of man like the factories and stock yards of Cincinnati, where a man was no longer measured by the quality of his work? Instead, the word of the day was "quantity." Workers were forced to work faster in order to turn out products that could be sold back to them at just the right price so that they would be willing to keep working at low wages. This way the worker never got ahead. Huge profits were being made by the few at the expense of the many. Progress was a two-sided sword. Mr. Swartz once confided in me that he thought things were changing too fast. At his desk he received more demands from the higher-ups. At one time he was able to walk into Mr. Gamble or Mr. Proctor's office just to talk about their families or how a new worker was getting along on the job. Those easy going conversations ended with the war. He said he could understand the extra push to manufacture goods for the army during the fighting, but once it was over he had hoped things would return to the way they were. Instead, more young college educated men went to work at the offices. These "new captains of industry" displayed as much interest in Mr. Swartz as Grant did in Thomas. There was no time for friendliness. They had to quickly find more ways to produce more products. The men doing the actual work were merely parts of the machines in the factory, and a man's safety did not matter. If he suffered an injury he could be replaced. I always assumed factories and places of business existed for the people, but after the war, it seemed the other way around. Man now existed to produce, like a honey bee in a hive, and nothing more, quickly replaced by another bee once he could no longer work. The factory workers were the new soldiers of the day, being used up much like the thousands who attacked at Spotsylvania and Cold Harbor.

Reading encyclopedia articles under the tutelage of Mr. Abbe, as well as books, magazines, and newspapers, is what caused me to start thinking on such matters. Mr. Abbe told me not to worry so much. "Science will find a way to make machines serve man. There are always growing pains," he added. This did not help, but instead produced feelings of self-isolation.

In Cincinnati, away from the observatory, I felt a deep loneliness. People did not question things; they did not seem to reflect on their lives. I still believed in the hope of scientific and industrial progress, but I wanted to discuss its dangers. Most people in Ohio never understood my negative feelings towards the factory system. Once I was talking to a man at a baseball match about these matters, and he told me to "either accept it or become a lousy 'do good' reformer." This made me feel like I could not speak my mind to most people for fear of becoming an outcast. I never wanted to argue with people or push my point of view on them. I was the newcomer and veteran of the defeated enemy. I could not chance being seen as a troublemaker. So I kept things to myself. I felt totally out of sorts in my new world. Everyone else seemed to accept things as they were despite their struggles working long hours to stave off poverty. Only on Mt. Adams did I enjoy the freedom to ask questions and discuss issues.

The train rolled on. I tried to quell my depressed thoughts by going to sleep. Eventually, I succeeded out of plain exhaustion. When I woke up it was night. I walked out to the platform between the cars and I looked at the stars. The night sky was so clear in the country, even clearer than the sky as seen from Mount Adams. The city sky was always hazy with the factories constantly spewing smoke and steam. Gazing at the clear sky made me feel better. I thought that perhaps I could find God out there. I had not been to church in a long time. It just did not make sense to me that we could have so many churches and religions and only one of them would know the truth. I read about many religions in the encyclopedia. Mr. Abbe said religion and science had been at odds since Copernicus said the earth goes around the sun. But science does not answer questions concerning why there is life and there is death. Church people say that God is testing us. At the academy, a test had a purpose. When I learned how to add numbers, it was so I would be able to do things like manage my finances. But why would God test us? Is it so that after we die, we will be rewarded or punished, or simply be evaluated for the process of learning? No one had a satisfactory answer.

Maybe I had learned too much too fast at the academy, reading the encyclopedia and talking to Mr. Abbe. Everything I learned just led to more questions. Then there were the things I could not learn from books. I sure didn't learn much about women. I started thinking about Sally. Would I ever see her again? Even if I did, she would be married. I was and still am a fool. I fell more deeply into my depressed mood.

The conductor came through the car shouting, "Next stop Columbus! Columbus in ten minutes!" Since the train had left Cincinnati, I spent the whole time alone trying to make sense of life and my particular place in it. Now I needed to stop thinking for I had taken a beautiful day and ruined it by spiraling into a vortex of negative thoughts. I would have a two-hour layover in Columbus, and I was ready to see something new and stop thinking. Better put, I decided starting right then and there: I would change my attitude and make the most of my life in Mount Vernon. I would work hard and study in my free time so that I could eventually enter an institution of higher learning. The hell with Gretchen and her condemnation of knowledge!

I felt much better as the train, swaying back and forth, rattled into the Columbus station. It had been a bumpy ride, yet I still marveled at how I had travelled a hundred miles in five hours. We left Cincinnati at four p.m. and were in Columbus at nine p.m., right on schedule. I was surprised at how many people were at the station, which looked like a huge wooden barn, except there were three tracks running through the middle of it. I soon learned after speaking to a ticket agent that there were plans to replace this wooden structure with a more suitable brick building. Away from the tracks and the rumbling and huffing of the trains, various stands were set up attended by people screaming out what they had for sale. I bought an apple for a penny. That left me $4.99

from the funds Mr. Abbe had given me in addition to the funds for the train tickets. Scared to death of losing my funds, I must have checked my pocket a hundred times to make sure I still had all my money. This money became more important to me than the gold coins buried on the farm in Nottoway, which, it turned out, were so well-hidden that Mr. Connelly was unable to find them and reported as much to General Thomas. These coins, even though of far more value than what remained in my pocket, were now only a reminder of the bad times after the war. The five dollars from Mr. Abbe, on the other hand, meant survival in a strange land.

The two hours and the apple disappeared quickly. Some dandy tried to sell me some perfume water, but once it became clear to him that I didn't have a wife or sweetheart, he left for better possibilities. Soon, it was announced that my train was boarding on the far track, the old CC&C route which stood for the railroad called the Cleveland, Columbus, and Cincinnati Line. I wondered which company owned the line at the time. Baltimore and Ohio may have owned it, but folks here still called it the CC&C. A man I tried to converse with screamed to me over all the din of the place that there had been so many mergers and big outfits buying out little outfits that from day to day no one knew who owned the line, so the easiest thing was to keep calling it the CC&C. Whatever its proper name, I was soon to be on one of its trains.

The train pulled into the Mount Vernon station in the middle of the night about two hours after leaving Columbus. It would have been quicker, but twice the train had to pull into a siding to let another train through. Only about five passengers exited at the Mount Vernon station and quickly dispersed into the dark. This left just me and a man tending a wagon with an attached sign reading, "Ten Cents to anywhere." That was an outrageous price, but I did not tell him so. Instead, I told him someone was to meet me at the telegraph office. "Well fella, there is the telegraph office," he said not very politely as he pointed to a window at the train station.

"Are they open?" I asked.

He replied, "Does it look like it is open? Where are you from anyway? You sound like some of the Negros around here, yet you sure ain't black."

Losing my patience, I momentarily discarded the caution that comes with being an outsider. Thinking this man ignorant and of little importance, I declared, "I am from the South, from Virginia. Have you ever heard of it?"

"Oh yes I have, and you rebels were whipped and you should have stayed where you belong. I have a hankerin' to go alert the pole-ece."

At that point, I was a bit frightened but decided to carry on with my superior attitude. Having had enough of this wagoner, I stated, "Sir, I have taken an oath to the Union and my citizenship rights are equal to yours."

"Now what are you talking about?" he said. "No one has asked me to sign an oath."

"It is because you were, I assume, a Union man throughout the war. Now good night my good man. I would like to be alone to enjoy the autumn air."

I walked away, but he stayed right where he was on the wagon watching me the whole time. My bravado turned to worry. It was not a good start to my new life in this small but industrious Ohio town. I could only wait in the dark shadows until morning and the arrival of the telegraph operator.

In about an hour, a train arrived from the north. The only passengers exiting the train were a dandy and his two beautiful female companions. The dandy was wearing a top hat, a broad tie, and a fine jacket. He carried a cane even though it never touched the wooden plank floor of the station. I stepped out of the shadows and paced nervously on the platform so that I would not appear to be a robber in waiting.

"Good evening my good man," he said looking me right in the eyes. He could not have been any more than four or five years older than me, yet put on airs of a man of importance. "My name is Mr. Thomas Handly. Perhaps I may be of assistance?" He continued staring at me, but I was now preoccupied stealing glances at his two beautiful and stylishly dressed companions.

I came back to his attention and clumsily introduced myself. "I am Sam, and uh that is Samuel Nite, lately of Cincinnati."

The wagon driver was listening the whole time and rudely entered the conversation. "He is not anything of the kind. He is a Virginia rebel."

"You stupid fool, Williams," Handly spoke up in a loud voice. "I can perceive the Southern dialect. Here is 20 cents to take these fine ladies home. I'll see to Mr. Nite."

The wagon man grumbled and rode off with the two ladies muttering complaints about being shipped off like some load of cattle. I told Thomas, or Tom, as he insisted I call him, why I was in Mount Vernon in the middle of the night. In return, he gave me no details of his life, except that his family owned the Handly store, a local dry goods emporium. Tom recommended we walk over to the store, which was about four blocks down High Street in the center of Mount Vernon. I had never seen such a fine town anywhere in the South. Expertly built brick buildings lined the street offering everything from a haircut to the best cigars from Cuba. It was ironic that the town was named for a plantation in Virginia, the home of George Washington. The rude driver I imagined never thought of that as he insinuated that I did not belong in Mount Vernon.

Where High Street met Main Street there was what Tom called a public square, but looked more to me like a circle with a green park in the center. Along the outside of the circle was a road with a three-storied courthouse surrounded by several lawyers' offices. Tom explained that Mount Vernon was the county seat of Knox County and most of the legal business was conducted in the courthouse. As I looked around, I noticed one prominent non-legal business on the square; the sign there read "Handly Dry Goods" and this is where we were headed.

The building was dark. Tom pulled out a key and unlocked the door and lit several oil lamps. "You see this oil in these lamps, Sam? That is where the money is. I have just returned from Cleveland where I mixed in a little business with pleasure. There is a gentleman in Cleveland named John Rockefeller who has just built his second refinery. That is where the oil taken from the ground is made suitable to be used in these lamps. Somehow I want to get in on that oil money." Tom offered me a cigar, which I politely refused. I was determined not to take up smoking. Sure, I had heard how smoking is good for you, how it soothes the mind and such, but some of those cigars cost as much as four or five cents. I'd go broke if I got attached to that pleasure.

"You appear to be a cultured man, Sam," Tom went on. "I would not speak of this to just anyone. It is when I heard your accent that I meant to get to know you. When a stranger comes to town, most of the locals like Williams, the idiot with the wagon, see them as a threat. They have no imagination, no curiosity, and no hunger to welcome anyone new into their world. You, on the other hand, have traveled far from your place of birth and I'll bet have improved yourself for it. You are the kind of man I like."

I had never met a man so forward and sure of himself. I did notice in Cincinnati that people were quick to get to the point, but not like Tom. Down South, a person would be very friendly, yet it would take a long time before they would ask a lot of personal questions. Could I trust this person? Having a key to this fine store, he was obviously the man he said he was.

We talked a little more as he showed me around the store. The place had everything. There was a huge section with tools, nails, and other construction materials. There were plenty of dry goods, bolts of cloth in many colors, and fully made clothes, like dresses and britches. Bins of penny candy and a big pickle barrel stood near a huge counter. After a while we sat in two comfortable chairs back in what must have been his father's office. Tom told me what he had learned about the oil industry in Cleveland. He explained that right before the war in 1859, a man named Edwin Drake went to western Pennsylvania on behalf of a small oil company. Drake and the company believed drilling was the best way to locate and retrieve oil; and they proved their theory by successfully drilling the first oil well near Titusville, Pennsylvania, in August of 1859. The next four years saw many more drillers come to Oil Creek. Then John D. Rockefeller, a business man from Cleveland, entered the oil business. He had the good sense to see that an oil company could get a jump on the competition by investing in support operations such as oil tank railroad cars, barrel factories, and timber tracts.

Tom said he was up in Cleveland mostly to have a good time, but he always kept his eyes and ears open for when men talked business. He made it a point, he said, to meet and converse with businessmen. One thing he learned was that there was a lot of money to be made in the oil business. The trick was to do business on a small scale so that you would not draw the attention of a man like John Rockefeller to your operation. "Why?" I asked Tom.

"Men like Rockefeller want the whole pie. They are not satisfied with a part of a business. You saw that in Cincinnati with companies like Procter and Gamble. My family's store has made us rich only because it has not drawn the attention of a big concern. If we tried to open another store in Columbus, a big outfit would buy us up and drive us out. The key is staying small and not making too much money so that the big boys will leave you alone. It will not be easy, but if we can just stay out of the transportation path between the oil and the city it can be done. We don't have to become filthy rich to make enough money for what you want in life. This is the American dream," he said then, as he would say many times in the future. "If one can operate a store in Mount Vernon then one can run a small oil business." I think Tom revealed his plan to me for two reasons. First, I was not motivated by the prospect of becoming a rich man, and second, he knew I had studied with Cleveland Abbe. He believed I would make an ideal partner. I was trustworthy because I was not looking to build my own empire, and at the same time I added legitimacy to the business because I had worked with a respected man of science. It didn't really matter what I knew, but who I knew. Whatever the case, I found Tom quite charming and I was honored to be treated with respect. We talked through breakfast at an eating establishment on Main Street. Tom then accompanied me to the telegraph office.

The telegraph operator, Benson Bedlow, was at his post when we arrived. I greeted him with a warm hello in that I was in a good mood from my morning spent with Tom. Mr. Bedlow did not even look up. Tom, who was standing next to me, said, "Bedlow, what the Hell is a matter with you? Can you not see that you are being said hello to?"

"I can Tom," he answered, adjusting his wire rim glasses. "But I have no time to shoot the bull or any other darn thing with someone passing through town."

"Well, what makes you so sure he is just passing through?"

"Because no one, especially a man with a Southern accent, is going to stay here for any reason."

Tom smiled just a bit and then turned serious. "You used to be a nice fella Benson. But now you think yourself something special because the army taught you how to make the wires sing and everyone depends on you. Well, guess what, I heard talk in Cleveland that someday everyone will be able to talk through wires using their own voices and that will put you right back with every other common laborer in this town."

"That is 100% pure horse manure and you know it, Tom," Bedlow shot back. "Why, you are just angry that I don't clerk at your store anymore and you and the other Handlys can no longer boss me around."

I now discovered another side of Tom. It was the side I would see in plenty of men who had money, either through inheritance or personal industry. "There will always be suckers like you Benson," Tom said smugly. "You believe that you can work hard and because of that you will be taken care of. You get comfortable with where you are, just like my old man with the store. But it doesn't work that way. Once you find a comfortable profit-making position or enterprise, someone will be looking for a way to take it away from you. All you can do is stay one step ahead of them. You have to see what is in the future and get what you can from it and then move on." One day I would wish I had paid more attention to these words of Tom, instead of just enjoying his charismatic chatter about how the business world works.

Bedlow looked at Tom and replied, "I don't know what you are talking about Tom, but that is nothing new. I am ready to open the office, and I will now take care of your friend's business."

"Well, okay Benson. Sam, I will leave you in the hands of our capable telegraph operator. I look forward to seeing you soon so we can talk some more."

After Tom Handly left, Benson Bedlow seemed like a different person. "I'm sorry," he said, "Thomas Handly has his good side, but he tends to be demeaning with some of his old friends. I think he tries to defend the fact that his father is the richest merchant in town. What he wants to be known as is someone who made his own fortune. But that is just not the way it is. His father's money gets in his way, as odd as that may sound. Again, I like Tom, but I cannot tell you how many times he is here the first thing in the morning bothering me with his big talk while I'm trying to get this office open." Suddenly his face brightened up a bit. "Say, you're that fella from Cincinnati. I have been expecting you. Mr. Abbe of Cincinnati has made arrangements with Western Union to allow you to send up to three free telegraph wires a day that is if you are Mr. Samuel Nite."

"I am Sam," I answered. "Now, if it's not too much trouble, could you wire Mr. Abbe and let him know I have arrived? And, following that, please point the way to a Professor Pennington's house. "

"Pennington! Dear God, you have barely seen the sun rise in Mount Vernon, and you have made acquaintance with Tom Handly, and now you are going to see old Dr. Pennington."

"Actually," I answered, "I'm going to be living at Dr. Pennington's house."

"Oh, my poor man!" responded Bedlow.

"What is it?" I asked. "Is he another dreamer like Tom?"

Bedlow started laughing. "Whatever the opposite of a dreamer is, then that is Pennington. He arrived here two years ago after he had to leave the University up in Ann Arbor, Michigan. I don't know why he chose here or why he had to leave the university; I hear he was raised down around Urbana. Once he got here, he gave a couple of talks down at the old opera house on the great late frontier days of Ohio. The place was packed, but the talk was not what the town expected. Pennington raved for two hours about how George Washington, Thomas Jefferson, Anthony Wayne, William Henry Harrison, and everyone else you can think of stole the Indians' land." Bedlow paused and said, "Wait, you are not up here to agitate about supposed troubles we have caused, are you?"

"Benson, if I may call you that?" Bedlow nodded, but I had the feeling he preferred a more formal respectful greeting. "I know that at least three of the people Professor Pennington mentioned are from my home state. I am honored to be one more who only wants to pitch in and help. Ohio is now the finest and most important state in the Union. I am only glad the war is over and we can now all work together and make this country what Washington and Jefferson intended." This left Bedlow speechless. He acted like he never heard such a declaration from a Southerner, which in fact he probably never had. After this time, we got along fine, although cautiously, for the rest of my days in Mount Vernon. We were both very business-like concerning my wires to Mr. Abbe about the weather. We seldom talked politics; for he was a great supporter of President Grant and thought anyone who felt differently was ignorant.

Professor Pennington's house was on the outskirts of town across the road from an old coach house. Stage coaches still stopped here travelling between Cleveland and Columbus, but less frequently since the railroad arrived in Mount Vernon. As I approached his house, Professor

Pennington, shabbily dressed in an old suit and sporting a full head of gray hair, stood at the front door. "You must be the so-called weather observer sent my way by Cleveland Abbe. Well, if he wants to waste money on this project so be it. Are you coming in, or are you going to stand there all day?" Before I could answer, he disappeared inside. I followed and shut the door behind me. "You will stay in this downstairs room. Upstairs is my room and library, both of which are off limits to you." With these words he quickly excused himself and went up the steps.

After this odd meeting, I settled into the professor's house. He spent almost all of his time upstairs as my routine was quickly established. Every day, shortly after sunrise, at mid-day, and about an hour before sunset, I would walk to a small hill north of the house and observe the weather conditions. I would note the wind direction, the appearance of the sky, and if there was any precipitation. I would be specific noting how heavily it was raining or snowing by collecting a sample in a jar with measurement lines so that I could report how much rain or snow accumulated in the jar in a specific amount of time. Everything had to be exact and accurate in accordance with the scientific method, which above all requires accurate data collection. My first morning I noted a slight wind from the north-west, a few cumulus clouds in the sky, and dry conditions. After each observation, I would walk to the telegraph office and have Bedlow send my observations to Mr. Abbe. The whole process took two hours each time or a total of six hours a day. Mr. Abbe paid Professor Pennington for my lodging and meals. The professor was a worse cook than he was a conversationalist. Usually a meal would consist of some burned beef, a couple slices of bread, and glass of inexpensive wine. Thankfully, Tom would often buy me a meal at the place we ate my first morning in Mount Vernon. My only income consisted of five dollars that Mr. Abbe sent to me once a month. It seemed quite generous, but Tom told me I was being robbed. There was other advice from Tom. "Sam, you are a natural businessman. You pay close attention to everything and you know how to hold an intelligent conversation. I knew it the moment I met you. Once I get everything worked out I want you to join me in the oil business."

"Tom," I would reply, "I owe people like General Thomas and Mr. Abbe for getting me out of a lot of trouble. I can't just run out on this job."

"That's a bunch of horse manure," he said with much emotion. "They are no different than me."

"What do you mean?"

"While poor suckers like you were either getting killed or nearly getting killed in the war, I was nice and comfortable right here in Mount Vernon because I paid a substitute to fight for me. It's the same for your Abbe and Thomas. I guarantee you they were not up front where the bullets were flying."

"I don't know about Mr. Abbe," I strongly declared, "but I know George Thomas saw lots of fighting and before the war he was shot with an Indian arrow!"

"Okay Sam, calm down. It's just that in this world you have to look out for yourself because no one else will. Folks will pay you five dollars a month while they take home 500 bucks. It's called free enterprise and that is what won the war. If nothing else, it is better than a slave economy."

This whole conversation took place about two months after I had arrived in town. That night, when I got back to Professor Pennington's, I was quite upset. The Professor nodded at the burnt meat on the table and started upstairs. Without thinking I spoke up to him as I hadn't dared to in the past. "What's the matter with me that you can never say more than two words at a time in passing? Mr. Abbe said I could learn something from you. I don't see how, unless without knowing it I'm receiving information from you like a cell receives nutrients through osmosis."

This stopped the Professor on the steps. He actually chuckled a bit. After a long pause he said, "Son, why is it Mr. Abbe and not Professor Abbe?"

"I don't know. That is what he told me to call him. What does that have to do with what I just said anyway?"

"Well," he answered, "you know we were both professors at the University of Michigan. He was the one man there who treated me with respect, even though he did not share any of my sentiments. I was a Professor of Philosophy and History. I was not a flag waver, yet Professor Abbe not only treated me with honor, but has continued to watch out for me by occasionally sending a little money my way. As for other folks, it is like this: I have lived here for only two years. At first they welcomed me. They asked me to give lectures, which I did, carefully giving my views on the so-called civilization of this land. When I did not say what they wanted to hear, they no longer greeted me warmly or treated me with scholarly respect. Now, why would you be any different?"

"Well, I am here on behalf of Mr. or Professor Abbe, for whom you apparently have great respect," I answered.

"I don't know that I respect Cleveland. It is that he respects me, not for what I say, but for the fact that I say what I believe. Today, young men, like you, have come back from the war worshiping symbols, objects of idolatry like flags and eagles. Idolatry, I say, for they miss the point of God and country. God should not be confused with manmade objects. The evaluation of government should not be obscured by man's passion for so-called acts of glory that are nothing more than the bloody barbarian acts of murder!"

Now I became irritated with this old man who preached such idealism yet judged me without knowing a thing about me. "So professor, you have concluded all this about me? You are sure that I am back from the war singing glory hallelujahs, forgetting the bloody hell that war is, and wanting only to celebrate the acts of misery it brought forth?"

"Why not?" he answered. "I understand why a young man who has seen the terrors of war would want to feel that the experience was worth it, that victory was worth the price."

"Professor," I said. "One way you are like most teachers I have met is that you can explain why an apple falls to the earth, but you don't notice the obvious, like my accent. I'm not a returning victorious Union soldier!"

The professor became dead silent and then spoke. "I believe I heard you were a veteran."

"Yes," I answered, "but not for the side that won. Anyway, I don't care. We were fighting for a way of life that could not last. Jeff Davis and the rest of them were too blind to see that the future was about machines."

After a short pause, Professor Pennington slowly said, "Well I have finally heard some words of intelligence in Mount Vernon, but you and everyone else still miss the point."

"What point?" I asked.

"That it doesn't matter where you are from and what you believe. I simply don't want to associate with anyone. I'm treated like a fool because I am not a fool. I'm made fun of because I know Shakespeare and Euripides. I'm ostracized because I know that all through history man just can't work out his problems and move to a higher plane without killing his fellow human beings. And, if you speak out against this killing, you are a traitor. My tormentors declare Jesus to be their savior, yet they are the very same kind of people who would have screamed for His blood if they had lived in Jerusalem 2,000 years ago. Now damn it, I am going up to bed. Go check on the weather so that some fool boat pilot can get his barrels of nails down river in safety."

"Professor," I said, "Is it not better to have lived and seen the truth than die a fool?"

"Son, what do you know about truth? There is no value in the truth when you are fully discredited."

"Henry David Thoreau thought so."

"I'm a coward and cannot be compared to Thoreau. I am not willing to spend even an hour in jail like Thoreau for not paying a tax." He seemed calmer now after I spoke of Thoreau, for I think he realized that I would not give up and had the knowledge to back up my arguments. Pennington sat on a step. I looked at his face. It was the face of a man in such pain that he might as well have been riding the wooden horse in the army.

I had to say something. "You may not be Thoreau, but you are a teacher. And as long as there is one miserable soul on earth, like me, who wants to learn, then yours is a life worth living."

"Oh Samuel." The professor said my name for the first time. "Cleveland wrote in a letter that you had a penchant for learning. He also told me the rest about you. I knew you were an ex-Confederate soldier. I also know that sharing my view of the world with you will not help you. Instead it will set you a part, for I am not a good teacher. I am not objective. I have been hurt and I am prejudiced when it comes to the people of the frontier. It will be better for you to study on your own. I'll let you use my library and decide for yourself about the truth. Perhaps we can talk more in the morning. Please let an old man enjoy his evening with his books and in his comfortable bed. Good night." And with that he quietly plodded upstairs.

The next morning Professor Pennington was still upstairs when I returned from delivering my morning weather report to the telegraph office. "Is that you Samuel Nite?" he called. "Come on up here." I now entered a part of the house I had never seen before. On the second floor there were two rooms. The bedroom had a four poster bed with a raised frame, at least two feet off the floor. I later learned that he liked it that way so he could lie in bed and watch the people come and go from the coach house across the street. The other room was the library, filled with more books than I had ever seen in one room. The time had finally come when Professor Pennington was going to let me use his library. It would be on his terms though. First, he showed me where his poetry books were located. "I suggest you start with literature, especially poetry. Then, you may pursue your interest in science. I'm afraid you will not find many philosophy books. I gave those away a long time ago." I thought that odd since he had taught philosophy in Michigan, but I said nothing. I was quickly learning that the professor was someone who would constantly surprise me.

I looked around and saw a huge collection of history books. "How about these," I asked.

"I'd wait a while on those. Most are from a singular view point and will not help you understand the truth."

"I see professor, the writings of those who believe in glory and right and wrong."

"Exactly, and I'd be careful before you become too sure about right and wrong. It always has to do with who is telling the story. If you want to begin studying the truth of our history, then read books on the subject written by an American historian, a British historian, a French historian, and then histories written by the various Indian tribe historians."

I glanced at the collection and said, "I don't see any histories written by Indian tribe historians."

"Exactly," replied Professor Pennington.

I was not granted permission to spend any extended time in the library. Instead, each day after dinner the professor would allow me upstairs to pick out a book or two until I would return them the next day. I read everything I could get my hands on. I struggled with works like those from Chaucer and Milton. I did not struggle, however, with adventure books about life on the high seas or mountain ascents by authors whose names I no longer recall. I just read and read. I even read the history books that Professor Pennington thought to be worthless. I sometimes briefly discussed what I read with Bedlow. Usually, he just shook his head and liked to claim how it must be nice to be an author and not have to work to make a living. Tom Handly showed more interest. However, he always concluded that ideas such as those found in books were something to enjoy in one's older years after one had made their fortune. "Tom," I would say, "aren't the ideas in these books useful to one's development as a human being?"

"Sure," said Tom, "but with no money you cannot accomplish anything. If all you gain in life are good ideas from books, you'll just end up like good old Johnny Chapman." Since living in Mount Vernon, I had heard many stories about John Chapman. Local residents called him Johnny Appleseed. Real old timers, who were children when Johnny lived in these parts, gave a more reasonable account of the man as opposed to the legends being handed down. People who never met him liked to tell how he made children laugh by wearing a metal pot on his head, how he would not even harm a worm because he believed that all living things were equal in the eyes of God, and how he wandered the countryside indiscriminately throwing apple seeds on the ground so that the pioneers would have fruit trees. In truth, John Chapman was a businessman, albeit an eccentric one, who owned property in Mount Vernon and elsewhere. His business was developing apple orchards. He carefully imported and planted seeds and tended the seedlings until he had a profit-making product. Although he did not keep wolves as pets or sleep with rattlesnakes in his bedding, as people often claimed, he did hold animals in high regard. Old settlers remembered how in those days when their horses got too old to work they would release them into the woods to fend for themselves until they died. John didn't think that was right, so he would go find those horses and take care of them. John also looked after the settlers themselves. If he heard about a family having difficulties, he would find or buy some food for those folks and trek it out to their house. He was a very religious man and believed in charity as the main virtue.

"What are accomplishments other than people remembering and appreciating what you did for them?" I asked Tom. "John Chapman accomplished much in that regard."

"You have to look at things in terms of what lives on after a person is gone, Sam. Chapman was a poor business man, and he did not leave any type of legacy for the Chapman name. In Old Egypt, Rome, Israel, and right up to today in Europe, it has always been about what lasts after you die. The most important thing is your name, and your name endures only if you create a family dynasty. Sure, the idea of royalty in terms of kings and lords is now ending, but there is a new royalty right here in America and it is based on how much a family is worth in money. It's not easy to get there, but you can get there no matter who your folks were."

Tom's statement made little sense. There was more than wealth that could secure one's name in history. Nonetheless, I learned two things about Tom at that moment. One was that despite his claim to have little regard for knowledge, he was an extremely intelligent man. The other was that he was more than just the local son of one of the richest men in town who merely enjoyed the good life. He was quite serious about doing something that was important in his eyes. To clarify this point, I asked, "But, Tom, you are from a rich family. Your father has made a name here in Mount Vernon that will probably last forever."

"Sam, don't be foolish. My family is comfortable. However, the day will come when it will all be taken away. You have to do much more than own one store in one small town to join the ranks of the powerful. If you don't believe me ask the good professor you are staying with. He knows how easily the powerful can take away what you have. And don't get all sentimental about it. It's just the way it is. There are the few with power and the many without power. I want to be among those with power."

The next few days I pondered Tom's words. Here in Ohio, where the new post-war America was taking shape, I now knew two intelligent men representing two different Americas: one looking forward and one to the past. Tom represented the growth of America through a new aristocracy, not based on the ways of the Old World, yet basically advocating the same outcome of the rich ruling the poor. Then there was Professor Pennington, who may have once believed in equality and the power of knowledge, yet now spent his time in retreat staying as far away from the battle for the American soul as he could. I needed to find out what it was that happened to the professor. What was it that Tom said the professor could tell me about "them" taking it away?

One stormy night when I returned home from the telegraph office the professor was sitting downstairs, which was quite unusual. When I said hello he looked up and responded, "Hello Mr. Nite, I imagine Cleveland will be most excited when he receives your wire that it is storming here with the wind out of the northwest."

"Indeed he will," I answered. "Perhaps some good American souls will have their lives saved by a ship or two delaying passage down the Ohio River."

"Yes, indeed," he replied. "Whatever the case it will be safer than it was sixty or seventy years ago."

"Why is that?" I asked.

"It is because no one was safe on the river then. If you were white, there was always a chance that an Indian war party would attack you at any time. And if you were an Indian, you never knew when a party of white men might descend on your village with murder on their minds. Pregnant women of both races would be knifed in the belly and infants would be smashed on rocks. Torture was a cause for entertainment, with pure hatred as the only motive."

"Were the Indians really that savage?"

"Indeed they could be, but the whites were just as bad. They wanted the Indian to adopt the Christian way of life, yet when the fighting started, the white man adopted savage Indian practices such as scalping. In turn, the Indians readily adopted the white man's instruments of war like the rifle."

I noticed a tear slowly running down the professor's cheek. "Professor," I said slowly, "Tom Handly said I should ask you about how you had everything taken away."

"Tom Handly! Yes, he could not be fully trusted with a secret. Well, at least my story is best heard from me. As for Tom, he surprised me one night by appearing at my door after a lecture I gave on how the frontier was won. This lecture was met with disdain by the good citizens of Mount Vernon. Tom, however, was rather inquisitive about where I came by my ideas. This led to us spending much time talking about the unfairness of life, and eventually I told him my story. There is no reason I might not share it with you. Tom no longer comes by and

I'm sure you are not the first whose curiosity about my past has been piqued by what young Mr. Handly knows. After all, one must turn to page five to read the rest of the story emblazoned on the front page of a cheap train station newspaper."

"Professor, I'm not so sure he has told others. I have heard people on the street talk about you, but they only talk about your lectures. They seem to be angry that you spoke in a less than flattering manner about Ohio heroes like William Henry Harrison and Anthony Wayne."

"I never remember saying anything about Wayne. He was a soldier doing a job. Wayne didn't know anything else. He had no ulterior motives other than winning battles and a war. Harrison, now that is a different matter. He had political ambitions."

"What is wrong about that? Did not the Indian Chiefs have the same ambitions?" I asked.

"You make good arguments, and I like that, but there are many subtle differences between ambition, leadership, charisma, and doing one's duty. It is what separates men! You are so young and naïve, even with all you have gone through. Don't be discouraged though. For now it is a virtue to be an open book, to be appreciative of the goodness you have encountered more than discouraged by the evil you have experienced. Still, I think it will cause you some trouble later. You are too trusting. It indeed has made me trust you. Watching the diligent way you perform your duties for Cleveland has earned you my admiration. The last man I saw at your post would not go at the precise times required. He would fabricate his reports to make up for a lack of observation, and he would omit things when he could get away with it."

"But I thought I was the first one at this post?"

"You are, but three years ago when I lived in Michigan, I knew another. He did so poorly and lied so well that he was rewarded with election to a postmaster's job in a small town near Jackson, Michigan. I have already been around you long enough to know you would have no such luck in the political world. In the political arena a man must convince others that he is incapable of doing wrong while at the same time his opponent can do nothing right. You are too self-perceptive and honest for politics."

I sat down on the steps. It was silent for a full minute. I considered his last words. I knew I did not see much good in the world; actually I had formed the opposite opinion. However, I knew he was right. I did believe there was some goodness in everyone. Why did the professor see such little good in people? Before I could continue my thoughts, the professor, as if reading my mind, began to tell me his story.

"I was born in Southeast Ohio in the year 1803, the year Ohio became a state. By that time most of the Indians had been pushed west into the Indiana Territory. For the most part the land was still wilderness, and in a remote spot my father ran a trading post along with my mother who was a full Shawnee Indian. Behind the post was our house, which consisted of one big room where we ate, slept, and spent our time when we were not outdoors. Seven children were born in that room, I being the last. Things were difficult, but could have been worse. Two of my sisters and two of my brothers did not survive past their fifth year, but a three out of seven survival rate was not bad for those times. I was lucky to have had a loving mother and father. In 1812 came renewed talk of going to war with the British. This would also mean renewed conflict with the Indians. One night about twelve white men showed up at the trading post drunk on liquor and looking for more. My father gave them what they wanted, but after a few drinks their talk turned to the war and one brought up the inevitable."

With anger in his voice, the professor repeated the words the drunkard said to his father. "Pennington, how the hell can you be married to a Shawnee? They are good for nothing savages and thanks to good old Anthony Wayne they should all be out of this territory. Now tell me why your red bitch should be allowed to stay here, or for that matter you and your half breed runts, all tainted with Shawnee blood? All you are doing is raising more Shawnees to kill us and other civilized people."

The professor, changing to a sad voice, continued, "I was sitting near my mother playing with some carved toy soldiers. To me the words of the man were the same words I had already heard many times in the store. But my mother was listening very closely to the men. She sensed the immediate danger, and suddenly told me to race to the house and tell everyone to get out the back door and run as fast as we could away from our cabin. I did as told and we all started to flee when I heard the loud noise of something falling over followed by gun shots. After that I heard my mother frantically yelling for us to run, and then I heard my mother no more. My two older brothers made for the main road, but I hid in a thicket, a place only I knew about. Soon I heard horses on the road and then some shots, and I knew what had happened. I stayed in that thicket alone for the rest of the night, the next day and into the next night. I was too afraid to move, frozen in terror. I remember hearing movement at just about daybreak of the second night, and suddenly, there before me, was a Shawnee Indian, recognizable by the trousers and earrings that the males commonly wore. The Shawnee were angry and dangerous since their recent defeat by William Henry Harrison and the Americans at the Battle of Tippecanoe in the Indian Territory. Many had aligned with the British in the desperate hope that they could push the Americans back over the mountains."

The professor continued, "To this day I don't know if the Indian knew my mother was Shawnee, or if he was better acquainted with my parents than I knew, but in any case he had the bearing of a compassionate man. After a long moment he spoke to me in clear English. He said to me, "Come boy I will take you to safety." In my fright I could not think clearly, but I guessed I was to be taken to a Shawnee village and would be raised as a member of the tribe. Instead, about midday, travelling on horseback, we came upon a cabin set deep in the woods. It was summer and there was a woman tending a large garden in the front who, as we approached, showed no signs of fear. A white man stepped outside the door of the cabin and made no attempt to raise his gun. We slowly rode towards the front door. When we were about ten yards away, the Indian spoke to the man."

The professor remembered the Indian's words well. "Kenton, this boy is the only survivor of the murdered Pennington family. You know that we will be blamed for this even though none of my people are in these parts. I was here alone to see some of the places of my youth for what I am certain will be the last time. I am headed north to fight with the English against the Long Knives. It will be my last war and this will be my last time to see this country where I entered this world. The English show little heart. They fight with no conviction, but I promise that I will fight until the spirit is lifted from my body. You and I have fought as enemies many times, but you are a man of your word and we share mutual respect. I leave this boy with you. Not that it will matter, but he knows the truth of the murder of Pennington and his family.

May the Great Spirit watch over you and may you take care of this land that once was one with Tecumseh's spirit and that of his people.

"With those words," Professor Pennington said, "the Indian let me down and rode off."

The professor told me he was left standing before the house when the woman came from the garden and spoke, "Simon you must take this boy to Urbana and do so with such care that we do not get in trouble for whatever happened at the Pennington place."

The man named Kenton replied, "That I will do, but in my time, for I will not have my hand forced by any man who hides behind lies." The professor remembered Kenton deliberately saddling his horse only after making sure the horse was fed and watered.

Engrossed in the story, I asked the professor what happened next. He looked at me as if surprised I was there in his company. He composed himself and returned to his story. "Simon Kenton took me into the middle of Urbana, a small Ohio settlement at the time, which was not far from his cabin. He rode at a slow pace saying nothing until he stopped before a log structure that displayed a simple sign stating 'Town Office.'" The professor repeated the only words Kenton spoke to him that day. "Boy, I will find thee a civilized home for I am now too old and considered too uncivilized to keep you. However, if anybody treats you poorly, you know where to find me. Look back yonder at the path by which we entered town. And, one more thing, whatever the people in this town say about Indians, you remember the dignity of the man who brought you to me yesterday. There is not a man more civilized alive."

The professor continued, "With that, Kenton took me to the officials of Urbana, and I was placed in the home of a blacksmith. It was not a hardship for that family, for a young man was welcomed who could hit hot iron all day with a hammer. The family, named Wood, treated me fine. I was seldom beaten and fed well. But love I did not receive. I was for all practical purposes their slave. I worked and I was fed. Nothing more was given. I knew not to complain. On Sundays I would wander the woods for there was no expectation that I attend church or any other function. One Sunday I was approached by a rider. It was Simon Kenton. 'Boy, what are you doing out in these woods alone. You had a rare act of mercy bestowed on you last time, but no Shawnee is likely to do that again. Didn't those people tell you dangerous times are upon us?' Kenton motioned for me to get on the horse and we headed back to his homestead.

"I spent Sundays at the Kenton's thereafter for the good part of a year. On those days Simon Kenton told me many a story." The professor now spoke with joy in his voice. "Simon told me how he fled Virginia as a boy after he thought he had killed someone in a fist fight over a woman. How he learned to survive in the backwoods of the Ohio and Kentucky territory. How he was befriended by Chief Logan who saved his life after he was captured and tortured by the Shawnee. How he fought during the American Revolution against the British and their Indian allies. He told me about the defense of Boonesborough in 1777, the year of the bloody sevens, named so because of the all-out warfare between the Indians and whites. He mentioned in a modest manner how he dragged the wounded frontier hero Daniel Boone to safety at Boonesborough. Most of all he told me about his skirmishes and battles against the great Shawnee Chief Tecumseh. Tecumseh was a man of honor, and despite their many quarrels, Kenton and Tecumseh held great mutual respect for each other. The Chief, Kenton told me, was different from other tribal leaders. He believed that no chief could sell the land, and he sought to create a great alliance among all the Indian tribes."

The professor next told me what happened on the Ohio frontier following the American Revolution, and how it changed the direction of his life. He explained how after Anthony Wayne defeated a force led by Miami and Shawnee Indians in 1794, there existed an uneasy peace in frontier Ohio. As often happened, events from far away Europe served as a catalyst for trouble in Ohio. England was busy fighting Napoleon, and American sailors were being taken by force to man the British Navy. This angered Americans into declaring war with the British Crown. Frontiersmen saw the opportunity to secure more land for homesteads, maybe even conquer Canada. The British saw it as the chance to again control the land west of the Appalachians. And the Indians saw it as the way to take back their homeland. Unfortunately, for the Indians, the war in the Ohio Valley was mainly a side show for the armies of the King. Their main concern was defeating Napoleon. After Waterloo they wanted peace and cared little about what happened to the Indians.

Tecumseh knew this, yet fought like one possessed, leading his people on the warpath.

Returning to his own circumstances, the professor told me that, "Simon Kenton, at the age of 58, despite his respect for Tecumseh, was a loyal American and Ohioan. Following the American naval victory on Lake Erie, Kenton decided to join William Henry Harrison's forces for a fall campaign against the remaining British army at Detroit. Only the Indians acting as a rear guard, led by Tecumseh, fought the oncoming Americans as the British retreated into Canada."

The professor paused for a moment. It was obvious how much he cherished the time he spent with Simon Kenton, and how much he missed him after he left to join Harrison's army. In a quieter voice he said, "I was left without a protector. It was common knowledge by then that I was half Shawnee and every bully in town looked to give me a beating. The blacksmith and his wife did not care to get between me and the bullies. So, they rather bluntly suggested I get out of town. Having nowhere to go, I figured I could safely travel north with the Indians and soldiers fighting in Canada. My hope was to eventually find Simon. I walked along the military road established many years before by the army of Anthony Wayne. Soon, to my surprise I came across remnants of the already defeated Shawnee warriors. They barely gave me notice as they hobbled back to their villages located to the west of Ohio. I also met American militia men heading back home with the joy of victory in their steps. Occasionally, I would inquire if anyone had seen Simon Kenton. Finally a young soldier said that he had heard Kenton was called upon to identify the body of Tecumseh. According to this young man, many a rifleman took credit for killing the chief, but of the braggarts, none had ever come face to face with the great Shawnee chief. The soldier said that Kenton was the only one in the area capable of identifying Tecumseh's body. Years later I heard a story that Simon Kenton purposely identified the wrong dead warrior, so that the body of the great chief would not be desecrated. I'll never know if the story was true or not."

The professor continued, "I kept walking north, right into Michigan. No longer did I pass Indians or white men travelling south or west. The road turned into a path. It was now late November and with it came snow and cold. I sat down leaning on a tree and thought back to

141

the massacre of my family, the beatings by bullies, and the stories told to me by Kenton. I thought about the life and death of Tecumseh. I realized then that it was the great chief who took me to Kenton's house so that I could survive. Now, not only was Tecumseh dead, but so was the life of the Indians in what was then America. Being what is still called a half-breed, that is part Indian and part white, I knew wherever I went I would be treated with contempt just as my family was at the trading post. I lay in the snow and closed my eyes. I felt like sleeping even though I knew I may never again open my eyes. I felt like an old man in a boy's body.

"The next thing I remember was waking up in a warm bed with plenty of covers. I had been found by a Dutch family that had recently migrated to Michigan from New York State. They could not speak my language nor I theirs, but they nursed me back to health and put me on a stage coach headed to Detroit and what was called the Home for War Victims. Detroit was small, more of an overgrown fort at the time. The fighting had been fierce there and I was one of about 50 displaced young people needing care. I never found out how the Dutch family knew of the home and was able to make the arrangements for me to live there. I was one of the oldest in the home and about the only one who could write and read English. The Methodist missionaries, in charge of the home, immediately had me teaching other residents to read and write. In such a situation I read many books and applied myself to the education process. After I left the home, I had several teaching jobs in small towns in Ohio, Michigan, and Indiana; I eventually was accepted on a scholarship to attend the new University of Michigan. I was considered somewhat of a prodigy because I displayed an intelligence usually reserved for those brought up in the upper classes. I considered it an honor and worked so hard that I graduated in three years. I was invited to join the faculty and that is where I met Cleveland Abbe."

"It sounds like a wonderful life," I said.

Without giving me a chance to say more, Professor Pennington continued.

"Samuel, I guess I cannot complain to you since you also had your family butchered by some of the vermin of the world. Yes, Cleveland wrote to me everything he knew about your life. That is one reason I was hesitant to trust you. You seemed far too optimistic about life after having gone through the war and losing your family and friends. I suppose it is the strength of youth. But I have been discredited as a mature man mainly for being half Shawnee and for speaking the truth as I see it. It does not matter that I taught at a University. Instead it was as if I formulated my ideas in a separate part of my mind that is Indian, which to the settlers is an uncivilized place no more mature than a child's. Hours of reading books, collecting oral firsthand accounts, applying the scientific method, all means nothing to a man if you do not tell him what he wants to hear, and that is true whether he is a common laborer in Mount Vernon or sits on the Board of the University of Michigan. Wherever I went, soon after my arrival I was deemed incapable of teaching even at a local academy. So yes, with strangers I am mistrusting and unfriendly."

At that moment I had an inspiration. "Professor, I am optimistic because I have not had the time to sit and reflect on what I have gone through. I did get depressed riding on the train when I had time to think. But other times I keep busy because I have a goal to become an educated man and to share what I learn with others. Also, I did not experience the pain of brutality as directly as you did. At the end of the war, when I served, my unit saw very little action. My parents were indeed murdered, but not in my presence, like you, as you hid in the thicket. And, finally, I am young and have had good older men to help me, like General Thomas and Cleveland Abbe, and now I ask for your help. You are a teacher and you have a student. I believe in you."

The professor tried to hide his tears. "If you feel so inclined, you are still welcome to stay in my house. If you can tolerate academic discussions with a half-breed discredited professor, I would be honored to share with you fruitful discussions that may lead you on a path of self-discovery. That is the only honest way to learn. Otherwise you will just be another vessel taking in myths of a past as handed down to you by those who have long ago forgotten how to see life anew with all of its possibilities."

I told the professor it would be an honor to study under his tutelage. I looked forward to being an adult who would remain untainted by the games of men. I indeed had a lot to learn.

TROY

In early March of 1870, Mount Vernon experienced several days of cold westerly winds, typical weather for central Ohio that time of year. Despite the cold, I enjoyed telegraphing local weather conditions to Cleveland Abbe three times a day. Some days the reports would be nearly identical, including the regular daily constants, such as the sun rose in the east and set in the west. Other days there were pronounced changes between morning and evening. A day might start with a mild breeze and clear sky, but end with a large gusting storm. Winters are like that in Ohio. It was a long wait for the warm winds of spring, which usually arrived in May, about a month later than they arrived in Virginia.

Besides recording weather conditions, I read books and discussed what I learned with Professor Pennington, who told me that I was following a regular course of study in a non-traditional manner. The academy in Nashville, where I learned reading, writing, and math, was my elementary school. The reading of the encyclopedia, under Cleveland Abbe's guidance, served as my high school. And now I was in a college consisting of one student and one teacher, myself and the professor. We would talk about everything from amoebas to pyramids. I believe the professor was impressed by my determination. One day he announced, "Samuel, we need to set a goal for your acceptance into an established college so that you will obtain a diploma providing you the opportunity to earn a master's degree, perhaps even a doctorate."

I was excited by the promise of becoming a scholar. I longed for such a life, and I was in the right place to accomplish that goal. Ohio was a land of opportunity. During the fifty years following the Civil War, Ohio stood first among the states in innovation, led by an energetic group of talented young men all possessing genius, such as Edison, Firestone, two brothers named Wright, and Rockefeller.

Unlike Rockefeller, wealth was not chief among my aspirations, but I shared the same belief with the Ohio scientists and businessmen that knowledge was the key to success.

Despite his encouragement, Professor Pennington would slowly shake his head when I spoke optimistically about Ohio's future. One time I heard him quietly utter, "The boy has a hard lesson to learn." It was true that despite experiencing the horrors of war and its aftermath, I had regained my optimism, and like Mr. Abbe, believed in a future made better by science. I believed I would find happiness in this new world as I did when I first came to Ohio. But the professor knew better.

One morning in late March, with the weather feinting a false promise of spring, I walked to the telegraph office to send in my report. I enjoyed the walk as the sun rose warming the air and changing the frost on the vegetation to dew. Benson greeted me at the office. "Where have you been? I have a telegraph message for you from Mr. Cleveland Abbe."

"So what's the big deal," I answered, for I received plenty of telegrams from Mr. Abbe asking for the clarification of an observation, or sharing a discovery of his in the field of meteorology.

"You better read this one Sam." Benson rarely called me Sam, so sensing trouble I grabbed the piece of paper out of his hand and read the following message.

SAM — STOP — MUST CLOSE THE OPERATIONS AT MT VERNON — STOP — DESPITE OUR BEST EFFORTS RIVER CAPTAINS NOT UTILIZING SERVICE — STOP — IF YOU CAN STAY WITH THE PROFESSOR FOR NOW I WILL HAVE ANOTHER ASSIGNMENT SOON — STOP — C ABBE — STOP

I said nothing to Benson as I walked from the office deep in thought. Although I loved my work, especially on a clear evening when the stars were out against a black sky, I was tired of constantly relocating. In the past six years I had gone from my home in Nottoway County to the Howlett Line in Chester, to the Appomattox surrender site, back home to Nottoway, to Nashville, then Cincinnati, and finally Mount Vernon. I wanted to stay put for a while. I also wanted to continue my studies with the professor. If I did, however, it would be with no income.

Money was not my only problem. I also had no luck meeting a real lady, the kind you would be proud to show off at the opera house or even at the dining hall near Tom's store. In truth I had not tried very hard to meet a woman for my heart still belonged to Sally. Sometimes at night, when I was out on my weather observation hill, I would talk to her as if she sat next to me. I would even cry some for I missed her so. Other times I would feel angry at myself for being such a fool. Why did I not take the small risk of telling her how I felt? Now it was too late.

Instead of a wife, I shared a house with an old worn-out professor. Often after I finished studying in the library, I would find Professor Pennington lying in his special bed either reading or watching the people come to and go from the coach station across the road. Was this all one had to look forward to after a life of learning and sharing one's knowledge with others? Was this the reward of a scholar?

There was another option: a career in business. Tom Handly was offering me a partnership. He was indeed a good friend, always inviting me over for lunch, usually to discuss his plans for starting an oil business and trying to convince me to join his venture. I told him I had only a small amount of money saved for I was not paid much by Mr. Abbe, and Mr. Connelly had sent a letter apologizing because he could not find the jar of hidden Union coins I had buried back in Nottoway County. But Tom insisted that it did not matter. He said It was my brains, common sense, and willingness to work hard he wanted. Most of all, he said he admired my trustworthiness. I am not sure how I earned his praise, but it was a fact that I worked hard for Mr. Abbe without cutting any corners and filing accurate reports. Still, I wondered what Tom saw that made him so sure of my abilities.

On March 31st I was pondering my future as I picked up the professor's newspaper at the train station. It was my last day of telegraphing in a morning report to Mr. Abbe. As I walked, I glanced at the front page. In large type the day's headline read: "General George Henry Thomas, The Rock of Chickamauga Dead at Age 53." My first thought was that I thought he was much older. He looked well beyond his age. Then I felt a great sadness. I owed the man so much. What would have happened to me if he had not appeared outside that alley in Nashville? He had given me a second chance. Like all the soldiers he led in battle, I was important. He could have easily written me off as a criminal or a Reb that refused to stop fighting. Instead, he took a chance on me becoming a productive member of society.

I quietly wept all the way to the professor's house. "Here, here, Samuel, what is the matter?" said the professor with concern, as he greeted me at his door. I handed him the newspaper and he understood. "I see, I see. From what you have told me I know what a great loss this is for you." He then did something no one had done before; he embraced me. Now, an embrace between men is normally taboo. If someone were to see it, charges might be drawn against Professor Pennington. I knew, however, that his embrace was like that a father would give a son. Despite his cantankerous behavior, this man cared about me and he knew how much General Thomas meant to me.

Later that evening, I asked the professor how a good God could cause such pain. He removed his glasses and told me that we understand so little. "We can search but we cannot find. The Good Book and other great writings can give us insight, but ultimately anything man declares as the truth using our earthly tools such as paper, ink, and language is subject to conjecture. A great thought such as free will or sin is often carried too far until it becomes something harmful, something that instead of enlightening us makes us feel the need to control others. Mystery is good. I cannot say why you and others have to lose General Thomas at this time. It is just as it must be and that is enough to declare it not a bad thing."

I took great solace in these words, but I also recognized they were no more than words. I needed some way to validate my sorrow, some way to experience the occasion. I decided to travel to Troy, New York, where General Thomas's funeral and burial would take place the first week of April. Not only would this allow me to acknowledge my debt to the general, it would also give me time away from Mount Vernon to decide if I should accept Mr. Abbe's offer of a new assignment, stay and study with the professor, or partner with Tom in the oil business.

The day I boarded the train for Troy was the nicest day since October. It was a beautiful spring day, and I felt good as the train left the Mount Vernon Station. I looked out the open window and to my surprise there was Tom Handly running next to my car easily keeping up with the locomotive as it struggled to build enough steam to get the wheels turning. He yelled to be heard above the engine, "Make sure you have a safe trip, and Sam, when you get back be sure to come see me. I have a good business proposition for you." I thought it must be a new idea or angle on the oil business he so desperately wanted to start. Before I could say anything in return, the engine pulled the car away from the now out-of-breath Tom. I stuck my arm out the window and waved goodbye.

I was travelling on the Norfolk and Western line to Shelby, Ohio. There I would transfer onto a train on the Columbus, Cincinnati, and Indianapolis line, which would take me to Cleveland. At that point, I would board my third and final train, on the famed New York Central line, taking it all the way to Troy. Despite the solemn occasion, I was excited to be on the rails taking a trip through the states of Ohio, Pennsylvania, and New York. I would be seeing places that, up to now, had been mere dots on the railroad map posted on the wall of Benson's telegraph office. The first five hours were spent travelling through flat Ohio farmland. There were freshly plowed fields and farmers out everywhere working the land. From the bounty and riches of Ohio pastures, we entered Cleveland where smoke filled the air. When I closed the widow and gazed through the glass. I could see why Cleveland was one of the fastest growing cities in the country. Buildings, streets, factories, and houses were being built everywhere. It looked like everyone was in a hurry. I saw the oil refinery of John Rockefeller dominating my view from the train for what seemed like an hour. It was like a huge monster with smoke belching from several smokestacks. The factory looked mighty, but dangerous.

After a long slow trip through the city's rail yard, crowded with box and oil cars, the train arrived at the Cleveland station. I had an hour before the 2 p.m. train from Chicago was due to arrive on the New York Central tracks. The station, known as the Union Depot, was larger than the station in Columbus with a total of eight tracks entering and exiting the long building. I stood where the train was designated to arrive and spent an hour being pushed and bumped into by other passengers trying to make their way through the station. The train arrived right on time. It was pulled by a big steam engine and must have had nearly twenty cars. Luckily, I had a seat on the north side of the train for the trip. From there the great body of water known as Lake Erie was visible for a good portion of the first three hours of travel. From my readings I knew Lake Erie was the second smallest of the Great Lakes. I could not imagine one any larger. Despite the clear day, I could not see across to the other side where Canada lay.

We travelled through several towns, any of which made Blacks and Whites look like a mere crossroads. There was Painesville, Geneva, Ashtabula, and Conneaut. All had pleasant stations and they were all bustling with people at work. This was the fastest growing section of the country, and one could see why the South had lost the war. Pre-war Virginia was a land made up of a handful of wealthy planters in charge of countryside devoid of buildings, let alone towns. In Ohio there was an emerging small business class providing goods and services and enjoying the money made at their shops. Passing by my train window were hardware stores, barber shops, lawyer offices, dress shops, photography studios, even emporiums for sweets. In these prosperous towns it was no longer a matter of a few houses grouped around a general store and a church or two.

The North had the beginnings of a small but significant middle class. But, as I saw in Cincinnati, there were still plenty of poor people in the North. There were no slaves, but ten-year-old children digging coal and girls under the age thirteen operating huge sewing machines is not exactly freedom.

In the country I saw plenty of farms, much smaller than the plantations of Virginia, but with acres of fields for crops and grazing cattle. The farms looked no more than fifty years old and were being operated with machinery, steam engine tractors, and McCormick reapers. The farmers were beginning to produce an abundance of food, so that city people like those flocking to Chicago, Detroit, Pittsburgh, and Cleveland could be fed. They had migrated to these urban centers for the promise of the good life, but most were doomed to work in dirty factories for little pay. At least they might not go hungry. It reminded me of the beginning lines of a novel I read recently by a Mr. Charles Dickens of England. It went something like, "It was the best of times and the worst of times."

Progress is and probably always has been both salvation and damnation. Tom said I questioned progress because of my upbringing on the farm. I was used to daily routines that had lasted for centuries. He believed the lives of everyone would improve over time. For now, he said, work in the factories and the dirty cities was still better than being a slave or a share cropper. Professor Pennington addressed the subject differently. I remember him saying, "Sam, you are a true

Jeffersonian, as you should be, hailing from the great man's state. Jefferson believed that one day there would be no more slavery, though he probably didn't see it happening through warfare. He envisioned a country of farms and a few small towns. He knew what London had already become, and he would have been most disappointed to see the growth of our big cities along a similar line." Then he laughed and said, "So too would Tecumseh, Kenton, and even William Henry Harrison be shocked at the likes of Cincinnati. The Ohio of fifty years ago is disappearing faster than Georgia did after General Sherman's excursion through the peach state. Why I predict in a hundred years or so people will be running back to the South just as fast as they are now coming up North. People just like to move. So you tell me Sam, who really won the war?"

This was too much for me to grasp at the time, but I was beginning to understand. I looked out the window at the many prosperous towns we passed through. This landscape has drastically changed and it is bound to change again, and it runs deeper than just the land. Ohio has taken over Virginia's role of leading the Union in political influence. The once grand Commonwealth of Virginia was quickly becoming a backwater of little interest to the rest of the country. I read a Buffalo newspaper, as my train sped on towards Troy, more evidence of the power shift from my old state to my new state. A great Virginian was to be buried in Troy, New York the next day. Not one distinguished Virginian planned to attend. President Grant and Generals' Sherman and Sheridan, all Ohioans, would represent not only Ohio but also the United States government.

After a while I fell asleep. I woke in the middle of the night as the train made an unscheduled stop in Syracuse. The engine awoke and slowly puffed out of the station and followed the rails again into the darkness of the countryside. I rested my head against the back of my seat and the next thing I remember was a hand touching my shoulder. "Sir, we are in Troy. I believe this is your destination."

I jumped up and looked directly into the eye of the conductor dressed in blue. "You'll never take me prisoner Yank," I yelled. There was quiet in the car and then like an engine building up steam the car slowly filled with laughter.

"Hey Reb," yelled a passenger. "You here lookin' for trouble? They are burying the last good Southerner right here in Troy today and as I see it, you ain't him."

Another yelled, "Thomas didn't know where he was either, and just like this dumb son-of-a-bitch, Thomas fought for the wrong side without knowing it. Are you just another dumb cotton picker who doesn't know where he belongs?"

Most of the people laughed and I responded by yelling, "General Thomas was a better general than Grant, Sherman, and Sheridan put together. If the Confederates had him, you'd not be jowlin' about the South." I felt like I was back at the Howlett Line, wearing my torn and dirty grays, exchanging insults with the Yanks across the line. But instead of fifty yards of no-man's land for protection, I had only a conductor between me and a big fella who was up on his feet taking a swing at me over the conductor's shoulder, just barely missing connection with my head. Two or three others had made a movement to get at me when a gentleman dressed in a fine suit stepped in between, facing my attackers.

"Now, unless you gents want to spend the night here in Troy courtesy of the town constable, I would back off and allow this man to depart the train while you take your seats and continue on your journey."

"What makes you so sure we will be the ones ending up in jail?" asked a small mean-looking agitator.

"Because I am this man's attorney, representing the firm of Thacher Proffitt & Wood of New York City. Here is my card," he declared as he handed one to each of the men who were standing in the aisle. "Now maybe you men have a good attorney," continued my protector, "and you can wire him to be here today, willing to defer payment until he arrives. If such is the case it will be an interesting trial where the judge will rule the guilty party being one who merely woke from a nightmare or, you gentlemen, who tried to physically harm him because of his untimely dream?"

The car was quieter than at any other time I had been on a train. The well-dressed man claiming to be my attorney, whose back was still to me, said to the men now grumbling and finding their way back to their seats, "I thought so," and turned to face me for the first time. "Mr. Nite, allow me to carry your bag and escort you to our meeting with the other shareholders." As I pondered what he meant and what shareholders he was talking about, I recognized the man as none other than Captain Tilly, looking quite different not dressed in his captain's uniform. As he suggested, I quickly and quietly got off the train with the captain walking close behind. We stepped on to the platform and into a crowd of soldiers. They were everywhere waiting to march in the funeral procession. We slowly made our way to the center of town. It was finally quiet enough for me to ask Captain Tilly where he came from and why he was dressed in civilian clothes. "Samuel, I am out of the army and I am indeed an attorney with the firm of Thacher Proffitt & Wood in New York City. I was working on a case in Syracuse and was able to arrange boarding the train there to attend the general's funeral. I'll tell you what. Come on over to my hotel and I'll tell you all about my leaving the army. And then you can tell me how in the name of God you arranged to be here and what you are doing these days."

The hotel was a short distance away. Mr. Tilly or Raymond, as he now told me to call him, had reserved a room with an adjoining parlor. He said it would be fine if I slept on the davenport there. Before retiring, we had a long conversation. Raymond explained that he left the army when he had the choice either to follow General Thomas to the West Coast or resign. He said he was angry about the way the general was being treated. "He was such a good man, Samuel. He never complained. President Grant never went out of his way to honor his accomplishments. I am not saying President Grant is a bad man, but he always seemed to see General Thomas with a fearful eye. Unlike some others, the President would not resort to lies to destroy Thomas. However, he never recognized how important General Thomas was in winning the war. The truth be said, Grant has to feel relieved at Thomas's death."

"Raymond," I said, feeling awkward calling this man by his first name, "why was Grant jealous?"

"I think it was because things came easy for General Thomas. He knew how to relate to everyone from the lowliest private to his staff officers. He was a natural born leader who worked his way up the ladder by just being who he was. Grant, on the other hand, knew failure and had to always prove himself. Also, Grant was not a grand strategist. He could never devise and execute the perfect battle plan like Thomas did at Nashville. Now, mind you, Grant would have won at Nashville. He would have attacked soon and vanquished Hood thanks to numerical advantage. But, I also think many more men would have died for the victory. Grant would never be loved by his men like General Thomas. I think this hurt the President and caused him to withhold praise and find fault in subtle ways with Thomas, who will never have the chance to defend himself and set the record straight. Grant and other living generals will write the histories of the war, not the dead. Now tell me Samuel, why are you here?"

I thought carefully and then the right words came forth. "You were in the war. Nobody gave anyone a second chance. Soldiers were whipped and sometimes shot after making their first mistake. The cruelty only got worse after the war. I was in big trouble, an ex-Confederate soldier, riding with outlaws set on stealing government property. As you know, if not for General Thomas, I would either be in prison or dead. I never knew him like you did, but I'll never forget him. I can still see him in his office taking an interest in my worthless life; a Union general, a hero, taking time to help me!"

"Well, Samuel," said Tilly, "he was like that. And that was the world he came from. It is an irony that the South would administer a slave system and at the same time cherish the ideal of treating others with respect. I am indeed afraid that our country is entering a stage where human relationships are based on competition as opposed to respect. It is now hurry up and conduct business so that you can rush off and conduct more business."

Raymond continued, sounding apologetic when he revealed that his law office was one of the leading commercial firms in New York. His days were spent working on cases involving some of the richest business concerns in the United States. I told him about the decision I had to make concerning my weather forecasting position. He advised me to balance logic and intuition and once I had made a decision not to turn back and second guess myself. The light of dawn came through the window. We decided to try and get some sleep before the day's big events, and I quickly fell asleep on the davenport.

In what seemed like seconds after I fell asleep, Raymond, with a gentle shake, woke me up. He had graciously bought me breakfast and had it delivered to the room. He was dressed in his fine clothes and announced he was leaving for the service. I did not have an invitation to the church ceremony, so I ate, freshened up a bit, and went outside to take a place among the others waiting quietly for the church service to end and the funeral procession to begin. In a short time the service ended and a group of men, all in blue uniforms, carried the coffin down the steps of St. Paul's Episcopal Church to a wagon at the curb. Two well-behaved horses stood still during the loading and did not flinch until the wagon door shut and the quiet was disturbed by a sharp "Attention" shouted by an officer. Soldiers slung their rifles and began escorting General Thomas on his final march. The rifle-bearing soldiers were followed by brass bands and as I read later, 140 carriages of distinguished citizens. I did not recognize most, but I did recognize President Grant and Generals Sherman and Sheridan. It was soon over and before I knew it, I was back on the train for Mount Vernon. On the return trip, I looked at the night sky and pondered man's mortality, the meaning of life, and of course Sally.

The Mohican

When I arrived back in Mount Vernon, I had a decision to make. I could stay in Mount Vernon for the present and await Mr. Abbe's offer of employment in a new location, or I could find new work in Mount Vernon and continue my studies with Professor Pennington. A third option was Tom's mysterious business proposition. I decided my first step was to have lunch with Tom.

"Sam, I am going into the oil business," Tom told me before I had a chance to take a seat and look at the menu.

I responded quickly. "Well that's no surprise Tom, since that is all you have been talking about since I met you."

"Sam, at least my preoccupation will put food on the table. All you and your professor want to do is talk about history and how the North is not any better than the South. I know the professor's political outlook; we are turning into a nation of tin soldiers except they will be tin factory workers, and so on and so forth. Sam, I once believed his line of thought. The bottom line is that it will get you nowhere. You need to come out of the clouds and think about your future."

I answered unenthusiastically, "Okay Tom, I am all ears."

"Very good, here is the deal. Johnny Rockefeller is buying up everything he can for his oil business in the Cleveland area, like lumber yards and barrel-making factories. He is making special deals with the railroads. Trying to organize an oil company in Cleveland with my small amount of capital would be inviting either bankruptcy or being swallowed up by Rockefeller. Both of these results are equal to failure. On the other hand, a small oil refinery located well south of the rail lines between Rockefeller's Cleveland refineries and the western Pennsylvania oil fields would pose little threat to Rockefeller's monopoly and would not be worth the cost it would take for him to put us out of business."

"Assuming there will be a huge demand for oil, why would Rockefeller leave us alone?" I asked even though I knew full well about the future of oil. I wanted to see how Tom would respond. I wanted to test Tom's basic knowledge. Before he could answer I added, "I know when I was a growing up in Virginia candles and whale oil provided all the fuel needed for our lamps."

At this point, Tom looked directly into my eyes and said, "Listen carefully Samuel. That day is quickly coming to an end. It is very inexpensive to refine the enormous amounts of crude oil now being welled in western Pennsylvania. Kerosene is the final product. Candles provide poor light and they are messy and dangerous. Whale-oil lamps have a terrible smell and create a sooty smoke. Kerosene, on the other hand, is clean-burning and almost odorless. I guarantee you that everyone will be using kerosene ten years from now and I don't mean just in this country, but all over the world. And here we sit by the world's largest supply, a hundred or so miles away in Pennsylvania."

"Now hold on a minute or two Tom. I read the papers every day and all you say about kerosene may be true; however, it seems to me that you would have to go a long ways to escape the attention of Rockefeller. This year he created a big monster called the Standard Oil Company. I don't fully understand its operation but it is what they call a joint-stock company and has more money than you can imagine. He will have all the money, and established businesses as well as new ones will be crushed. I read that oil is slumping in the stock market, due to Rockefeller's effort. Standard Oil is in the process of gaining control of the railroads between the oil fields and their Cleveland refineries and thus Rockefeller alone sets the market price for oil."

"That is the challenge Sam. The key is that we are just far enough away for our small enterprise to be left alone. And we have a unique transportation opportunity. There are no railroad lines running from this area directly to Pennsylvania oil fields and none between Cleveland and the place I have in mind for a refinery. I cannot see Rockefeller building a railroad just to take over our small refinery."

"Our and we?" I questioned in response to the indication of Tom's words that our partnership was a done deal.

Before I could get in another word, Tom was talking again. "I have the money to get started, and the time to begin is now, when the market is down. Rockefeller will be buying up companies left and right. He is going to capture all the big money markets to the north and east. My plan is to stay away from those markets. Instead, we look to the smaller and poorer markets to the south. I need someone I can trust to help identify and set up contracts with the southern markets. Sam, you are that man. You are smart and you know the customs of the South. You instinctively know how to conduct business with people from there; it's your home for God sakes. In addition, you have a hunger for knowledge and self-improvement. You have been to many places and you know what is going on in this country. You are a born businessman."

I missed the irony, at the time, of how Tom started out criticizing my search for knowledge and concluded with praising me for having the asset of intelligence. Tom was indeed a first class salesman. He was an expert in the art of telling people what they wanted to hear, and apparently he believed I had the same ability.

Feeling an odd mixture of excitement and regret, I asked Tom to tell me more about his plan; I had to admit, it sounded interesting. Tom's idea entailed the opening of a small refinery in the Coshocton, Ohio, area. Coshocton sat on the Ohio and Erie Canal, which was doing very little business since the coming of the railroads. The plan was to ship crude oil from Pennsylvania on small private railroads to Coshocton, refine the oil there, and ship it to southern markets by way of the Ohio and Erie Canal and the Ohio River. We would stay away from Cleveland and shipping on the Great Lakes. The one tricky part was that the business contacts had to be made in Cleveland, the oil capital of the world. Thus, Tom needed someone he could trust to open a small business office in Cleveland that would draw little notice from Standard Oil. The someone he wanted was me.

There was much merit in Tom's thinking. He was not trying to become a rich industrialist. He just wanted to carve out a small piece of the oil production business. It would be a small local business in the tradition of his family's dry goods operation, except Tom's company would deal with select clients in poor post-Civil War markets that were not of chief interest to Standard Oil. Nonetheless, I was hesitant. I had not changed that much from the time I rejected a career at Proctor and Gamble. My heart was still with learning and education, and I loved reading and engaging in conversation with Professor Pennington.

On the other hand, I was at the age when I needed to consider how I would support myself. Most of my education had been informal, so that I would not be eligible for an academic career until I completed years of study. Maybe Tom's business would be a way to quickly earn enough money to go to college without depending on grants or, worse yet, loans. I asked Tom how soon he would need a decision. He replied that he would need to know by the middle of May or about a month away. I told him I would give it some careful thought and give him my answer. He was agreeable and we parted company on good terms.

I immediately went to Professor Pennington for advice, for he was now like a father to me. He listened, and like most wise men, he did not tell me what to do, but instead gave me guidance on how to make up my own mind. He suggested I seek some solace in nature. He said I should get out among the trees and clear my mind of the hustle and bustle of enterprise. All great thinkers from Jesus to John Chapman turned to the serenity of nature for contemplation.

I decided to take the professor's advice. I packed up a bed roll and supplied myself for two weeks in the woods. The next day, I walked all day on country roads using a crude map until I reached the small town of Loudonville. There I found a little store named Gillettes that was willing to rent me a wood bark canoe. I spent the next four days paddling local rivers with strange Indian names like the Mohican, Kokosing, Walhonding, Tuscarawas, and the Muskingum. It was a mystical journey that drew my mind to the history of the region. Not only had the Indians travelled these rivers in the near past, but so had Johnny Appleseed, whom I had learned about in Mount Vernon. Every time I would pass an apple orchard, I imagined it was one that he had carefully developed. Every old cabin I passed, I imagined Johnny stopping there to look in on the settlers.

The weather cooperated for it was unusually dry for this time of year. The insects were awful, however, and I had to use some salve to help keep them away. It was not like I hadn't gone through this in the army, but by the end of ten days the mystical aura of the forest wore off and I was ready for a soft bed. I was no closer to making a decision about what I would do next, but somehow I was confident that the answer would come to me when I arrived back in Mount Vernon. It took three hard days of upstream paddling to reach Loudonville, and

I had little food and drink left as I began my walk back to Mount Vernon. As I walked, a fever developed and I got weaker and weaker. I stopped for some water at a farm house, and all I can remember about my stay there was telling those kind folks that I was trying to get back to Professor Pennington's in Mount Vernon, tossing and turning in a cot, and having strange dreams in which I saw my Ma and Pa, Mr. Connelly, and Billy. I had one especially intense dream where Owen and I were marching together in our uniforms, except we were all alone and had no idea where we were marching to or from. I also remember seeing Sally sitting in a home with a baby. She no longer was interested in me and that hurt worse than a burning coal.

Then suddenly, I woke up in a bed with the sheets soaking wet and a smiling Professor Pennington looking down at me. Was I alive?

"Samuel, you are going to make it. The fever has broken. Here, you must eat a little something. I prepared some soup for you." It was the most kindly voice I had ever heard, so different from the first time I met him. "You have been in this bed for four days after a man brought you here in a wagon. We all thought you were not going to make it. But something pulled you through."

After a couple of days slowly getting my strength back, I pondered the Professor's words. I clearly remembered the rejection from Sally. I thought about Owen and me going nowhere. It really scared me. Where was I headed? Sure, Tom's proposition was not anything I dreamed about, but it would offer me the means to pursue other interests. And maybe I could do some good. I would be a competent businessman, and I would put people first. The success of the business would naturally follow if associates were treated with as much importance as personal profit. The journey to the forest had worked. I believed I understood the meaning of my dreams, and my mind was made up.

Book Two
A New Century

I t was June of 1890 and I was sitting on a small hill alongside the Cuyahoga River. Across a bridge that could be raised or lowered to accommodate large and small ships sat a large steel mill. The mill's location was perfect. It was in Cleveland, Ohio, where boats on the Great Lakes carrying iron ore from Minnesota met trains carrying coal from West Virginia. Steelmaking was an established industry. The Bessemer process, which combined molten iron with limestone and coke, a by-product of coal, revolutionized American construction allowing buildings and bridges to be built higher and stronger.

Up river I could see the Standard Oil refinery. I understood its workings because I had been an oil man myself since I left the town of Mount Vernon in 1870 until that very afternoon when my business partner informed me I was no longer needed. I left the office with no destination in mind. Eventually, I came to sit on that hill by the river where steel workers on lunch break were enjoying their time away from the hellish heat of the mill's huge furnaces. A boy they called Charlie was pouring beer from a pail into the laborers' metal cups and collecting a penny for each cup he filled. Several times he came up to me and asked, "Hey mister, don't you want some beer?" Each time I shook my head no.

It was a new America, and much had happened in the previous twenty years that reshaped both the landscape and the way people thought. It started progressively, with events like Hiram Revels and Joseph Rainey becoming the first Negro members of Congress, and Utah becoming the first state to grant women the right to vote, but such idealism soon gave way when hard times came a knocking. Between 1873 and 1879 an economic crisis known as the Panic of 1873 resulted in the failure of more than 5,000 businesses. Scandals about government officials profiting from tax evasion and the misuse of government funds marred the Grant Administration. New ideas needed to be carefully controlled, and so basic conservatism returned.

Immigrants were welcomed to life in the tenements. The Black man was free to join the poor rural and urban classes. The Red man fought on to keep his way of life. In 1876 the Sioux and Cheyenne surrounded and killed General Custer and his troops at a place called The Little Big Horn. I recalled Owen telling me how Custer triumphantly rode around his prisoners after the Battle of Saylers Creek. At the Little Big Horn it would have been the Indians circling Custer with shouts of victory. It all mattered little by 1890, when the few Indians left ceased to be a threat to American expansion. Now they could simply be ignored.

The words of radical thinkers like Thaddeus Stevens, Frederick Douglas, Walt Whitman, and Henry Thoreau were all ignored in the drive to make money. I was no different and cared little about the poor, the Indians, or anyone else. Instead, I was enjoying the life of a successful businessman, making my home in a fine hotel with running water and an inside water closet. I enjoyed good food and plenty of refined company, including women of good standing. On the surface, my politics did not change. I was against the Supreme Court overturning the Civil Rights Act of 1873, which once again allowed racial segregation in public places, and I felt a sense of indignation when seven labor activists were sentenced to death after a bomb killed several policemen in Chicago's Haymarket Square.

But I was all talk when it came to politics, and I only confided my opinions in the places one could afford to talk of such matters, like in the comfort of a good restaurant, or at a social function in one of the veteran halls. In reality I cared little of politics and social causes, I used progressive ideas as one uses one's wits in a parlor game. I would do so by demonstrating my intelligence and sophistication at just the right moment in a conversation. I dared not express my ideas in the streets, or at work, for what I really cared about was money and pleasure, both of which could easily be taken away if one lost favor with the rich and powerful. When I engaged in necessary political conversation in a meaningful forum, such as a civic meeting, I would ultimately agree with the safe and comfortable position that if the country would practice patience then all social problems would be solved in due time. About two years ago, I casually mentioned this point to a Black maid who I was talking to on a streetcar. She looked at me without saying a word. Confused, I turned away but suddenly had an epiphany. My words about time and patience were the same words I had heard in the South about slavery when I was growing up. I turned again towards the woman, but she was gone, an old white man with a long grey beard taking her place. He said hello to me, but I could only stare back at him, my eyes riveted on the small ribbon he wore with the letters G.A.R. on it, standing for the Grand Army of the Republic. I muttered to him, "This was my stop, I must get off," and I scrambled past him to the back of the car hopping off some twenty blocks from my residence. As I began walking, I passed several workers travelling in the other direction making their way home after a ten-hour work day. They evidently could not afford the nickel streetcar fare to ride back to their tenements in the middle of the city.

I eventually arrived at my hotel room and tried to put the incidents of the day behind me, but I could not forget the Black woman's stare, the G.A.R. ribbon on the man's lapel, nor the dirty factory workers on the street. I spent several restless nights lying awake trying to put all the pieces together. We had fought a great war, but had anything changed? Did it matter that I had fought for the losing side but now enjoyed the fruits of the victors while the fortunes of the common people remained the same? I tried to convince myself that I had no reason to feel remorse, yet I felt a creeping guilt, like a shadow. Eventually this guilt was replaced by the tedium of doing the same thing every day. Ironically, it could be said that my guilt passed away in due time. But there is no such thing as due time. There is just time, and although I again began to sleep, I was a changed man. Most noticeably, at work I was no longer enthusiastic about making a deal, reading about our profit margin, or monitoring the steady climb of our stocks.

Sometimes I told myself that I was going to quit the oil business and begin a life of helping others and making a selfless contribution to society. "Why not me?" I would ask myself. Over the years I read or heard about the accomplishments of old acquaintances. Cleveland Abbe played a key role in creating the National Weather Service and became the prominent weather expert in the nation. Two of my fellow soldiers from Parker's Battery were accomplished attorneys. Gibson Clark had an extensive legal practice in Cheyenne, Wyoming. He was active in politics and eventually was appointed to the Wyoming State Supreme Court. My old friend and mentor, David Crockett Richardson, attained a Bachelor of Law degree after the war and worked his way up to become the Commonwealth Attorney of Richmond. Eventually, he served four years as the mayor of Richmond. And Colonel Parker, our beloved leader, returned to his medical practice, publishing two informative medical papers in addition to treating patients.

Lost in self-pity and feeling myself a failure, I had lost track of the fact that I was sitting on the hill by the steel mill. Now someone was talking to me. It was Charlie. "Hey mister, what are you doing here? Are you okay? You sure don't look like a steel worker, not in those fancy duds."

I shook my head as if trying to wake from a deep sleep and I answered, "No son, I am not a steel worker or anything else. I am a 40-year-old bum."

"Come on, you're not at all. You look better than a rich uncle at a funeral."

"Perhaps yesterday, Charlie," I told him. "Today I am bankrupt. I've had my dignity stolen and the little I have in the bank won't relieve that kind of poverty."

"Mister you just don't seem right," observed the boy. "Help me take these pails back to my folk's saloon and Ma will give you some free eats."

I began to try and explain that I actually had money, but to keep it simple and with nothing better to do, I answered, "Sure boy, why not?" I grabbed two or three empty pails and followed Charlie down the dirty street until we reached the corner of East 49th and Guy Street. There, Charlie's parents ran a small grocery that included a long table, or what they called a bar to serve drinks on. In the last twenty years I had done a lot of things, but I had never developed a taste for beer. As I sat down I asked to see a wine list and Charlie's mom, along with three or four customers, broke out in huge laughter.

"Who is this dandy friend of yours?" asked Charlie's mother. And then turning towards me she said, "Mister, we are Bohemians here. We are from the Czech homeland where the best beer in the world is made. That is unless you believe the lies of our German friends."

"I'm sorry," I exclaimed and started to get up to leave.

"Wait," she said, "in this country you get to do what you want. I do have some wine here made from the grapes called Catawba. Would you like some of that?" I had heard of Catawba wine and understood it to be inferior to French and other European wine. Nonetheless, I nodded in agreement. At first taste I thought it must be what hair tonic tasted like. After two or three glasses, however, it started tasting quite delicious with a sweet yet sharp taste that distinguished it from a fruit juice.

I helped myself to the free food on the bar. I had a delicious Czech roll called a hoska or hoskie sprinkled with poppy seeds and some lunch meats. I found myself thoroughly enjoying the simple food and drink and felt more relaxed than any time I could remember. I began talking to Charlie's father who had joined his wife behind the counter. I told him my story, about how I had fought in the war, been given a second chance by General Thomas, had spent time in Cincinnati, lived with Professor Pendleton in Mount Vernon, and had finally moved to Cleveland. The sad part is I could summarize the last twenty years in about two minutes.

I explained to the Bohemian family that Tom Handly's plan had worked. We had set up a small refinery in Coshocton. I ran a small business office in Cleveland lining up customers, and we had avoided the attention of Standard Oil. We made lots of money. And then one day Rockefeller and his top associates noticed us, and in their customary manner offered to buy us out before they would force us out. Tom said yes. He was the president, and as he so often reminded me in recent years, it was his family's money that built the company, and thus he had final say. The company was reorganized with Rockefeller's people, except Tom was allowed to remain as president. I was out of a job. I was leaving after making quite a bit of money the past twenty years, but I only had saved enough to live on for a short while. I had become used to a comfortable way of living, which required more spending than saving.

"So you had everything taken away. Look," remarked Charlie's father, "now you can start a new business. Would that not bring back your happiness?"

"Well, not exactly," I replied, and then proceeded to tell him how I became disillusioned about being a businessman and wanted to do something that would truly help people.

Charlie's father said. "Look at you my friend. You wear fine clothes, you have money. Why you could run for office. Maybe you can get the streetcar fares down. Who knows."

I had thought about a political career, but I discovered that I really didn't know how to effectively convince those in power. I was fine in conversation with my peers in business but not with those who really had influence. So, I just shrugged off Charlie's father's suggestion. After a long moment of silence, I spoke, "All I really knew was how to be a salesman and convince others to buy oil. I don't consider that to be very prestigious, or of great service. When I did try traveling in higher social circles, I just made a fool of myself."

"Mr. Sam," said Charlie's father, "if you can convince someone to buy something you can talk to anybody."

"Yes, I once thought so, and I was full of self-confidence. I made acquaintances with some scholars and scientists associated with colleges and universities, but I found out the hard way that even though one could afford good things, there still remained class differences based on one's education and background. Unless some unusual opportunity arose, like military advancement during a war, or inventing something that would change the world forever, then one would remain on the outside, on the outside of those who matter. My partner Tom knew I would make a fool out of myself and three years ago he proved his point. He told me I was wasting my time taking an interest in academics, and that I would be humiliated by those who graduated from universities. He actually became angry the day I left the office early to attend a function at the Cleveland Central Armory celebrating the scientific experiments conducted by Albert Abraham Michelson, a professor of physics at Cleveland's Case School of Applied Science, and Edward Williams Morley, a professor of natural history and chemistry at nearby Western Reserve College. Michelson and Morley had successfully measured the earth's velocity as it orbited the sun. Using a special instrument, Michelson's interferometer, the two scientists had proven without a doubt that the speed of light would always be detected as the same regardless of where the observer stood. The problem was that their original hypothesis was that light waves traveling through the invisible and undetectable substance known as the 'ether' would be detected as speeding up when observed approaching the sun, the source of light, and slowing down when moving away from the sun. Instead their experiments cast doubt that the 'ether' even existed. It just did not make any sense since light, being a wave particle, could travel through empty space."

Charlie's father remarked, "Mr. Sam, you sound every bit a scholar."

I interrupted him and told him that was not what Tom had said. Instead, he said that Michelson and Morley's findings were the most worthless information he had ever heard. The only science, he said, that is worthwhile is the science used by geologists to find oil in the ground. Once the oil is tapped the scientist's job is done, because only the final profit matters.

"As much as I liked money, I also wanted to know, as well as be one of, the scholars of the world who do not crave knowledge to become rich, but instead want to learn for the joy of knowledge."

"Yes, I agree with you," said Charlie's father. "Tell me what happened that evening."

"The evening of the function honoring Michelson and Morley, I had the great surprise of seeing Cleveland Abbe, the scientist I worked for some twenty years ago. He was in the center of the room talking to some distinguished-looking people. He greeted me with a warm handshake and exchanged pleasantries. He asked me to sit at his table and tell him all about what I had been doing the last twenty years. I accepted and went with him to sit down. Already sitting at the table was none other than Albert Abraham Michelson. He sat next to us for about twenty minutes before he joined Morley and other dignitaries on the stage. Once introduced by Mr. Abbe, I acted like a silly school boy and started talking about my own life and opinions like they mattered. I even talked about General Thomas and told him that Ulysses Grant was not half the general or man that George Thomas was. Michelson stared at me a moment and rather suddenly excused himself to take his place on the stage."

Charlie's father asked, "Do you think he was offended by something?"

"Yes." I answered. "Sitting on the other side of Michelson's now empty chair was a large man who had a drink before him, some of it in a glass and some spilled on his shabbily knotted necktie. He looked at me with a smile on his face and said, 'Good for you, you son-of-a-bitch. Hot shot scientists like Michelson need to be taken down a notch now and then.'

"I looked at him momentarily, and then asked him what he meant.

"'What do you mean by that?' the man said. 'Stop playing; if I have listened to Michelson tell the story of how he and Grant became friends once, then I have heard it a million times.'

"I told him I had no idea what he was talking about.

"'Come on,' he replied, 'Michelson loves to tell how he went to Washington in search of opportunity. He took up standing around the front of the White House as much as possible. One day he sees Grant emerge to take his daily constitution, or as I would call it, his daily trip to the shit house. Michelson notices that Grant does so the same time every day. So Michelson begins to walk along. They start talking and it turns out that Grant is interested in hearing about Michelson's grand scientific theories. In fact, he is so interested that he eventually secures Michelson a position at the U.S. Naval Academy where he can continue his study of physical science.'"

I told Charlie's father that I looked dumbfounded at the man for a moment before an announcement was made and the hall lights, except for the stage, were turned down. I sat there ashamed of my big mouth for a half hour while listening to the speaker whose job it was to introduce the scientists. I began to fear that Michelson might mention my remarks once he got behind the lectern. I turned to Mr. Abbe and said, "I must go."

"But Samuel," he said, "there is so much for us to talk about." All I could do was again tell him I had to go. I anxiously moved away, knocking my chair to the ground with a big thud. The speaker stopped and everyone turned to look at me. Luckily it was dark. I bowed my head, quickly put the chair back in place and walked as quickly as I could towards the strip of white light marking the bottom of the exit door. When I reached the door, a man in an usher's uniform asked if he could help me. I asked him to please open the door so I could leave. The usher replied that he was not allowed to open the door until the lecture was over. Panicked and ashamed, I shoved him to the side and groped for the door knob. In the dark and in my state of mind, I felt as if an eternity had passed before I found the knob, turned it, opened the door, moved through it, and shut it behind me as I ran into the street and kept running until I got home.

Charlie's father remarked, "It sounds to me that the man with the rude language made a bigger fool of himself."

"No sir, don't you see, I wanted to be thought of as a scholar, not a person who enjoys criticizing men of education." With that I took another swig of wine and excused myself. Remembering the hospitality extended to me and being a little intoxicated, I pulled out a roll of bills and gave Charlie's father far more than I owed for the wine. He tried to refuse it, but I insisted. To change the subject, I repeatedly asked where the Catawba wine came from.

Charlie's mother who had been listening to the whole conversation at the bar, and eyeing the money in her husband's hand like the answer to a prayer, spoke up. "Some fella occasionally brings it in from out around Sandusky way. They grow the grapes near the shores of Lake Erie."

"Then that is where I shall go," I announced in a loud voice, and forced my way past the protesting husband into the summer night. Outside it felt good. A breeze up from the lake cut into the humidity and gave a relief that seldom was felt down South. With this thought of the South, I remembered how I used to write to Professor Pennington. I would tell him about some of my great accomplishments. Once I received a letter from him that simply asked, "But are you happy?" Soon after that Professor Pennington died.

Before I could head out on my journey, Charlie appeared with a bottle in his hand. "Charlie, where did you come from and where have you been?"

"Mister, I was upstairs in the house watching my baby sister. Anyhow, you don't look the same. I have to get right back inside, but first my pa said to give you this bottle no additional charge."

Not knowing what to say, I replied with a thank you and said, "Charlie you may live to see the middle of the next century. I hope that the promises of the big wigs come true and it will be a utopia."

"Mister," he said, "all I want to do is sell beer tomorrow and some-day be a streetcar driver, just to feel the power after pulling the throttle on a machine like that! Maybe if you try, you can get a swell job like that."

"Maybe Charlie," I answered, and with that Charlie ran back to the small store and saloon at the corner of East 49th and Guy Street.

Oberlin

After Charlie left, I found an abandoned crate on the bank of the river to sit upon and drink the bottle of pink Catawba wine. After finishing the bottle, I foolishly walked down the dark and dangerous streets of the river district called the Flats. Fortunately, my unsteady gate and disarranged clothing gave me the appearance of a down-on-his-luck, penniless drunkard and probably saved me from being the target of a thug. I soon discovered a bridge that crossed the river and found my way out of the valley to a major road called Lorain Avenue. I was away from where the working man forgot his troubles in bars and taverns and in a safer area where respectable people strolled outside to escape the heat inside their homes. Having sobered up a bit, I was able to make a somewhat logical decision. I knew that the city of Lorain was to the west, and it made sense that an avenue of the same name would lead there, so I decided to walk west on the crowded street.

As the physical effects of the wine wore off, my mood changed from euphoria to disgust. Amazingly, I was not physically sick or tired. Anger kept me walking at a quick pace away from Cleveland. I kept thinking of how I wasted twenty years working for the benefit of the company and not myself. It was as if I was a soldier again who sacrificed his life for an organization whose leaders saw me as mere fodder to be used until I could be used no more. I was expendable, but my work was not, for Tom would pass along my customer list to some minion of Standard Oil who would convince my former clients that it was a great privilege to do business with the company founded by the great John D. Rockefeller. Now I had nowhere to go and nothing to do. Most people have the notion that at the end of one's education, or apprenticeship, their life is set like the teeth that fit into a gear of a mighty factory machine. To be part of the machine though, you had to please the bosses the same as a slave had to please his master. A manager could fire you for any trivial reason. I at least had some money to show for my work. The poor had nothing to show for their work except the holes they dug, the clothes they sewed, or whatever else that was useful to someone who had more than you. In the end you would also get your name inscribed on a tombstone. The chemicals and soot from nearby industry would soon render your name illegible and the last trace of your existence would be gone. The Hell with Tom and Rockefeller, I was going to walk right out of the city, their castle, and find a place where other things besides wealth and power had value.

Finding the vineyards that produced a fine wine was as good a place to start as any. I had learned that to the ancients, wine was a sacred vehicle used to reach God, an instrument of awareness. It could take one on a journey to Heaven or to Hell where one learned their potential for evil. At times wine had the magical value of opening the mind to tremendous hope and happiness. The early Christians saw its power and likened it to the divine spirit of Christ, even going so far as to say it was the blood of Christ. If drunk in proper amount, wine could open a door of perception and aid in self-examination. This day, however, I had over imbibed and it was dragging me down to that dangerous place where people were harmed, even killed. Still, the lesson was of value, for it made me feel alive again and determined to decide my own fate.

I was trudging both by foot and in mind on a dark road farther and farther away from the city, that bastion of progress. It was the city where I had learned how easily one could be knocked off the pedestal shared with the select few who did not have to toil ten hours a day in filth and darkness just to spend a few hours at a home located on the fringe of the filth.

I, on the other hand, arose each morning in a modest but comfortable and clean hotel room on Payne Avenue. Using the water closet one floor down, I would wash up, shave, and comb my hair. The first several years I would catch an omnibus and ride into town, smelling the fresh steamy horse dung on the road, which was tolerable until we reached the poor neighborhoods where the smell of poverty mixed with the excrement of horses. The odor would clear once we reached downtown where the streets were raked daily. Entering my office on 6th Street near Superior, I would go to work sending and opening letters and telegrams. I would follow up such activity by making sure orders sent to the Coshocton refinery were processed and delivered. This work required a talented individual, one who could find the right words to convince a buyer, and one who knew how to organize large stacks of paper.

The first three years or so were more than satisfactory. When I started placing some orders, Tom and I were ecstatic. We had a real sense of accomplishment. Sometimes we met clients in person at the refinery. I would travel to Coshocton where Tom and I would show them around the refinery and shipping operations. Tom and I knew just how to handle potential buyers by displaying a united front. We each had our own lines as if we were performers in a play, and customers became very comfortable dealing with us.

Then in September of 1873 some banks failed and a panic followed. This came to be known naturally as the Panic of 1873. Many believed an inflation of American money by the government would solve the crisis. Congress, in response, voted yes to an inflation bill that called for the circulation of $18 million of paper money. President Grant, however, vetoed the bill. To many, it was evidence that Grant was more interested in supporting his friends and big business than the people.

The panic certainly hurt our business, and in early 1874 Tom and I sat down to dinner in Cleveland to discuss a strategy to deal with the down turn. We talked for three hours and our relationship would never again be the same.

The difference of opinion did not have much to do with our proposals for keeping the business alive; instead our conversation drifted to the role government should play in solving the crisis. I felt Grant and the Republican Party were merely following the wishes of those supporting them with money. Tom nearly hit the roof, exclaiming that the Republican Party had freed the slaves, and they must support business or else there would be work for no one. I countered that this argument was fine, but why not better compensate the workers and give them more money and time to enjoy their lives? I was not completely passionate about this belief, and would fall back on my "in due time" progressive philosophy, but Tom strictly believed that one should only receive what they were worth in terms of their contribution to the progress of the nation, which included the cultivation of wilderness and removing the occupying savages. The ground, after being cleared, was plowed by the engine of big business. This was the story of Ohio, which in a hundred years had passed from Tecumseh to Rockefeller.

The debate between Tom and me continued until Tom asked if we should pay the workers more instead of less while we were losing money. When I replied that it might be interesting, he stood up with a fury in his eyes. "Nite you're damn lucky I have given you this opportunity. Just let me run the business and you use that sweet Southern charm to make our clients feel comfortable with my so-called wicked Yankee ways. I'll see to it that the dinner is paid for. Good evening."

A couple of days later, I received a fine bottle of French champagne with a note of apology. However, things were never the same after that. Tom hired a man named Richard Kimmer who gradually assumed assistant director's status. More and more, I dealt with Kimmer instead of directly with Tom. By 1880, I would see Tom maybe once or twice a month. When he did visit the office we would often get entangled in disagreements, like the day I attended the Michelson and Morley event.

Yet, I stayed on because I had grown accustomed to the lifestyle that my position supported. I was not exactly living in high society. I was not a regular at events on Euclid Avenue where the really wealthy lived, but I was doing pretty well for myself. I called on several women of modest wealth such as Gwendolyn Matherson, whose father owned a local brickyard not far from the steel mills.

Gwen and I had some very good times together and she often hinted at matrimony. It was not love for me, however, for I knew what love was and how it made me feel. Yes, I still thought of Sally at least once every day. It was fruitless, yet somehow I felt she was still with me. Because of her, I never got excited about another woman. Sure, I would find my time with women pleasurable, enjoying kissing and caressing, but I was never willing to commit to a relationship just because it was physically fun. If there was anything I was not, it was a phony when it came to love. It had to have a certain feeling about it, the kind that would keep you up at night or cause you to walk into the middle of a busy street because you were daydreaming.

The only emotions I experienced were those of feeling like a phony at work. I still had my place in the business, yet Tom and Kimmer were the business. My job basically came down to making up lies about the company. We could no longer under sell Standard Oil in the South, so

Tom and Kimmer came up with stories about how our oil was better than others. We had a line about the Handley process of refining oil into kerosene, and how our product burned more cleanly and safely. It was the same ploy being used by the run-down shack masquerading as a restaurant that I was now approaching on this dirt road way out in the country. The sign out front read "Best Coffee in the Nation."

It was about 6 a.m. and getting light outside. I had been walking for over eight hours by the light of the moon following the road past flat, cultivated farm land. It felt like those days during the War, when we marched to our surrender at Appomattox, except now the night was clear and pleasantly cool unlike those rainy April days in Virginia long ago. I could still cover quite a bit of ground in a day. For a 40-year-old, I was still in pretty good physical shape. I looked up at the last few stars twinkling in the sky and thought to myself, "Just a bunch of rocks and burning gas." I then stepped into the café to taste the "Best Coffee in the Nation."

I must admit the coffee was indeed very good, so I decided to take a chance on the eggs, bacon, and toasted bread. The waiter, a fellow named Neil, who ran the place with his brother Paul, said they also had some pretty good potatoes, so I tried them too. Either I was extremely hungry or it was the best breakfast I have ever had the privilege to eat. Everything was fresh from the farms around those parts. Neil said they moved out here from about where I started walking last night on Lorain Avenue. "You can breathe the air out here and you don't have to worry about everyone coming through the door looking for trouble."

I asked Neil how far it was to Lorain. He told me about 25 miles and I asked him how that could be since I must have already walked over 30 miles. "Well mister," said Paul who had just stepped out of the kitchen, "I hate to tell you this, but Lorain Road does not go to Lorain. You are on the road to Oberlin."

I asked, "Where the college is?"

"That's the place," he replied. I pulled out my wad of cash and Neil looked at me in amazement as I gave him a dollar and told him to keep the change.

Paul informed me it was still 17 miles to Oberlin. "I have gone there many times to attend free lectures. The place is truly an oasis in a desert of farmland." I felt encouraged by this short conversation for here was a kindred spirit. I changed my plans and with a renewed energy of adventure and hope, I started down the dirt road to Oberlin and its famous university, which, having admitted women and Negro students with open arms, might possibly offer me some type of new life.

It was late afternoon when I walked into Oberlin. Like most Ohio towns, there was a large grassy area in the center of a square whose borders consisted of four dusty streets. It was quite ordinary except for the obvious presence of brick college buildings to the west of the local business area. Being summer, there were few students about. Exhausted, I sat on a bench in the grassy town center. I liked to walk, and was in decent physical shape, but the wine of the night before and lack of sleep caused me to fall asleep where I sat. The weather was clear and warm, totally pleasant. It had been dry for quite a few days. That was about to change, however, while I sat napping on the bench. Dark clouds moved in, which I became aware of only when the wind started gusting and blowing discarded pieces of paper about the bench. Jarred awake, I looked at the sky and recognized from my weather observation days that a cold front was moving in, and that likely meant a short but powerful storm was about to take place. Within minutes, I was proven right and was forced to take cover under a store awning on the town square. The awning began flapping violently in the wind and the rain began to drive in horizontally under the shade. The door to the store, which I had now recognized as a hardware emporium from signs in the window, like "Nails Five Cents a Pound," opened and I gladly followed the man's welcoming wave to come inside.

"This is a good rain," said the man, "but I'm afraid it will be over quickly, before the crops around here drink their share."

"Yes," I answered. "It seems to be that way with everything—it is either too much or too little."

"I don't know that to be true," the man replied. "Most of the time the good Lord provides just what we need. It is really a miracle when you think about it. Anyway, just make yourself comfortable, the rain will be over soon."

I sat on a wooden chair and found a recent local newspaper on the shelf. The news consisted of stories about people visiting relatives in Cleveland or Detroit, wedding engagements and upcoming church services. There was also some news about the latest labor strike in

Cleveland. From reading the article, I took it that most Ohio country folk were against the laborers, only because they didn't realize how badly the factory workers were mistreated. They could not grasp how unsatisfactory it was to put in long days for wages that offered little in return. Farmers and local business people worked just as many hours, but were rewarded with the self-satisfaction of governing their own lives and returning to fine homes in the evening. If one looked closely, however, you could see the beginning of change in the small towns. Less private ownership and less opportunity were slowly creating a change from post-war support of Republican leaders to support of so-called populist leaders like William Jennings Bryant. Perhaps the reform mood came earlier to Oberlin because this town supported the most liberal of colleges. I was interested in finding out.

Politically I was against just about everything the Republican bosses, like the Cleveland shipping magnate Mark Hanna, were for. Yet, as a businessman dealing mainly with Republicans, I usually kept my opinions to myself. Many people of the lower classes here in Ohio were also strong Republican supporters because it was the party of the nearly deified Abraham Lincoln. Because of the late president, veterans and Negroes held the Republican Party in high regard. I could not help thinking, however, that for the most part they were not voting in their own best interests.

The union movement was demonized by many as un-American. In my mind, all the workers wanted were decent working conditions, reasonable hours, and fair pay. Yet, they were called selfish by those who lived in large houses, owned several carriages, were catered by plenty of poorly paid servants, and enjoyed the freedom to work the hours they chose. Our country was entering another war, class rights were again the issue. I hated war. I hated injustice. Above all else, however, I hated conflict, especially the kind that could put me in disfavor with those in power.

I despised myself for what I considered the cowardice of not putting my beliefs on the line and speaking up about injustice. I was too afraid about losing my comfortable life. Professor Pennington had told me in a letter he wrote before he died that, "It is nonsense to loathe oneself for what one is not." He added, "Sam, you are the most important type of person because you know how to treat everyone with equal respect, something I could never do. One day when you are done with this damn oil business, you will be a leader, like a Jefferson or Adams. First you need people to ignite a fire. John Hancock, Samuel Adams, Patrick Henry, Frederick Douglas, and John Brown were such people. But those people had too much anger in them to lead the masses. The leaders who can carry through change are people like Washington, Adams, Jefferson, and Lincoln, who understand the needs of everyone." I could not believe the Professor compared me to such great men, but I was not surprised by his opinion that I was wasting my talents in the oil business. I wrote back to see what he thought I should do, but the letter was never sent for I learned of his death before it could be mailed.

Now I was out of the oil business, and the best I could do was walk into the country influenced not by great ideals, but by a quest to find the source of a wine I enjoyed. My decision to walk all this way with no practical plan was ridiculous and I needed guidance. I even considered engaging the shopkeeper in conversation about my impractical decision and see if he had any suggestions for what I should now do, but I knew him not and I feared he would only consider me a fool. Then the rain stopped and I realized I was in Oberlin, certainly a place where the exchange of ideas was honored. I didn't need to find it in a hardware store. Instead, I told myself that I would find it on the campus, just a short distance away. So I thanked the man for his hospitality and walked over to the college campus.

On campus I found nary a soul and little activity, as would be expected in the summer. Then I suddenly found myself in front of the place where questions, answers, and open discussion by thousands could be found. I was in front of the college library. I began to think I might find redemption on this college campus.

As I walked up the steps of the library, my mind raced ahead and dampened my spirits. I needed more than finding answers to justify my philosophical, political, and moral existence, I would need to make a living. I could not teach at the university, for I lacked a university degree. Obtaining a degree would take money and time, which I believed I didn't have.

Suddenly, I was at the library's front door with my recent euphoria and hope shattered. What now, but to enter and at least rest and kill some time? The hours were posted and luckily for me it was open until

6 p.m. This gave me an hour to comfortably sit and read until the library closed. I went inside to find no one there except a pleasant-looking woman sitting at the main desk.

"May I help you sir?" she asked. I explained that I was passing through and I loved to read. I half expected to hear about policy restricting use to students. Instead, I was graciously welcomed and, quickly looking around, I found a book on the exploration of America, not exactly the philosophical book I had hoped to find that would offer direction for my poor soul. Instead, I was reading about that which had already happened, and although history is the necessary starting point to examine the present, this particular book held few challenges. There was the usual praise for Christopher Columbus and his line of successors such as Pissarro, Cortez, Cartier, and DeSoto. It was written as a good adventure story and little more. As I read, the woman came up to the table where I sat carrying an "arm full" of books. "I noticed you were reading about the discovery of America, so I took the liberty to find these books for you." I thanked her and she surprised me by continuing the conversation. "Tell me, Sir, do you really think it is proper to say Columbus discovered America? After all, it is not as if there were not already people here when Columbus set foot on the continent." I paused for a second and thought quickly to myself, "Yes indeed, this is the famous Oberlin College bastion of liberal and progressive thought."

I replied, "Why Miss, I believe you make an excellent point." With that, we entered into a long conversation about history followed by information about ourselves. Her name was Kathleen and she was a senior at the college. She was from Erie, Pennsylvania, and was working one more week this summer, then going home for two weeks before returning for the fall semester.

She was studying literature and was hoping to secure a full-time position at a college library after graduation. I found her very forward in her thinking, and she believed strongly in such things as Women's Suffrage, the Temperance Movement, and the right of workers to unionize. I was careful not to mention that wine was responsible for my presence in town, but instead told her of my search for redemption after betraying my idealism of twenty years ago and doing nothing to help the unfortunate. She reacted by telling me not to be so hard on myself. To her, life was an adventure. Every moment was to be lived to its fullest and not wasted on regrets. "Mr. Nite, no matter what is changed in society we will always need businessmen in this world, and it sounds to me that you practiced your affairs in a highly principled manner. We need more men like you. Business is not bad when it is correctly applied for the benefit of all." Again, I indeed was at Oberlin. This was the type of statement Professor Pennington might have made except in the more pessimistic manner of advanced age.

The hour went by far too quickly. Kathleen said that we must find a place for me to spend the night. She knew a man near campus who rented rooms to male students, and this being summer, Kathleen figured he would be glad to have a paying tenant even if for just one evening. She was right and I agreed to a room for one dollar a night. As it turned out, I spent six nights in that room. Every day I would go to the library and read. Kathleen and I would have lunch and spend a little time together in the evening before she was required to be in her room at 7:30 p.m.

Yes, I felt awkward spending time with someone 20 years younger than me, but this was the first time I felt like this since my time with Sally. We talked about everything. Kathleen was so perceptive, down to earth, and idealistic. And she liked me. She was not a classic beauty. She had an ordinary figure and short sandy brown hair. Yet her smile was beautiful and her mind was as sharp as a bayonet. She was also very thoughtful with a kindness that was rare. I'll never forget one conversation we had about God. I gave my usual thoughts on the matter asking how a good God could allow the poor to suffer. I went on to criticize myself for lacking the courage to fight for justice, like the labor leaders who were willing to give up their lives for a just cause. At this point I was expecting Kathleen to tell me that I had done a lot of good and I shouldn't be so hard on myself.

Instead she told me something quite different. "Sam, I only hope God has compassion and understanding as he governs a world in which there is so much tragedy. The one time I knew what it might feel like to be God was a couple of years ago in Erie. We had a mouse in the kitchen and my father conceived of ways to kill the intruder. I asked him to give me one night to capture the rodent and release him in a far-off field. He agreed, so with string and an old metal pot, I set about capturing the mouse. On a hard piece of cardboard I placed a ball of cheese, and then I placed the pot over the top, carefully propping up one side with a pencil that had a long string tied to it. I sat about seven feet away with the string in my hand. I sat very still and was careful not to make a noise. Sure enough the mouse showed up under the pot. I waited until he got under the middle so there would be no chance of a quick escape. But then, the mouse stopped, looked around, and rubbed his two front paws together. Happy to have the kitchen all to himself in the night, I could almost sense the mouse saying to himself, 'Life is good. Here I am in this warm house instead of outside in the cold; there are no snakes and no hawks. Yes, life is good.' Then I pulled the string. The pencil fell, and with that the mouse was captured underneath the pot. I carefully taped the pot and cardboard securely together and carried the trap and mouse to a field about a mile away. The mouse rattled around inside the pot fearful of what was happening. I told him he should be happy, for I had spared his life and he would soon be free in the woods. And then my mind started imagining the mouse's reply. 'Oh dear, I won't make it through the night out here. Even mice who have lived from birth in the wild are quickly victims of owls and other predators. How I long for my warm dry comfortable home.' And I began to cry and kept crying all the way to the release point. I kept thinking how I would feel if dragged from my comfortable existence.

"As powerful as God in this situation, I had to let the matter play out like it must. I released the mouse that ran panicked into the woods and his fate. The only comfort I had was that I somehow cared. I loved the mouse at that point, yet I had to allow its probable demise to happen. But at least I cared. I had empathy for the mouse and somehow that meant something. And that is all I can hope from God." I looked at Kathleen and wanted to kiss her so badly. I knew I must not though, for it would not be proper for someone of my age to court someone of Kathleen's age. Then again I knew of others who married younger women. Perhaps it would be proper as long as I did not rush things.

As it turned out, Kathleen was not bothered by the age difference. It was obvious that we were falling in love and spent every moment we could together. In that glorious week we talked about how we would see each other when she returned to Oberlin in September. I was going to court her in proper fashion and meet her parents when we felt the time would be right. In the meantime, I needed to find some suitable employment in the area. My available cash would not last forever. Together, we looked through local newspapers in the library, but we could not find anything that I was qualified for or that I wanted in the nearby area. I did not want to enter the business arena again or work at manual labor where I would have to take orders from an uncaring boss while I worked 60 hours a week. I wanted time to read, explore new things, and of course see Kathleen.

I hesitantly brought up the idea of finding work at a vineyard. "That will not do Samuel," Kathleen replied. I was not surprised by her reaction. Kathleen had mentioned her belief in the temperance movement.

"But Kathleen," I replied, "men such as me know moderation and wine is used at Christian services."

She cut me off, and for the first time, spoke to me with righteousness in her voice. "The Anglican Church of my family substitutes grape juice for wine and with good reason. Can you not see how a man's addiction to wine always starts with one small glass? Pretty soon the man is out all night, abandoning his family, wasting the little money they have."

"But, Kathleen, it is not the man who is bad for drinking, but instead the reasons that cause him to abuse drink. The men in the city have had their pride stripped away. They work long hours in filthy conditions, and if they speak up they will be fired from their job."

"You are right Samuel; however, we should attack those problems and not give the opportunity to a man to treat life's pain by drinking. No, we must outlaw drink and improve social conditions so that our families will come back together and improve their lots by hard work and saving their money."

I let the matter drop by telling Kathleen she made a good point. In my mind I could never see how liquor could be successfully outlawed. It reminded me of back on the Howlett Line when we were forbidden to trade with the enemy. If someone was deprived of coffee and he could trade some tobacco for it with a Yankee, there was no way an order was going to stop him. Now, if it was so important you would execute a man for doing it, maybe you could stop him, but there would be a lot of executions and would a family be better off with a dead man than a drunken one? I dared not bring this point up to Kathleen. In fact I loved her so much that right then and there I decided I would never drink in her presence again.

With a job at a vineyard dismissed, Kathleen said she would like me to return to a business career, but she did understood when I said I was not ready to jump back into the business world. We both wanted to make each other happy. It was not a time to put undue stress on each other. Sure, I would have liked her to stay in Oberlin instead of returning to Erie before the fall semester began, and I'm sure Kathleen would have loved me to return to a respectable business position to help gain her family's acceptance of a 40-year-old courting their daughter. But we were in love and time and propriety could wait. We were just about to give up looking for the right job when Kathleen came over to the well — secluded spot where I read in the library. She had a small newspaper from a town called Clyde. An ad read "Needed Station Master. Responsible for two employees in operation of selling tickets, handling baggage, and keeping station in operable manner. Necessary qualifications include management experience. Apply at Clyde station."

"Good luck finding a qualified person in a small town for that job," said Kathleen. "I'll bet you could get the position."

"Well, where on earth is Clyde?" I asked.

"We are in a library, dear, let's look it up."

I got this tingling sensation when Kathleen called me dear and for a second did not respond. Then I simply said, "Yes."

Clyde was a town of about 3,000 people, which would have been a major city in Virginia but just average size for Ohio. The problem was it was about 40 miles from Oberlin. "That's too far away," I said.

"No, look here," Kathleen replied pointing to the map. "It is directly on a train line running through Oberlin and Clyde. You will be able to visit regularly and it will take under two hours, maybe less if the train does not stop for long in Norwalk. Besides, how will I finish my studies if you are with me all the time?" And then we looked in each other's eyes and we kissed, and then kissed some more. Now it was official, we were in love.

The next day, I saw Kathleen off on the train for Erie, with the promise to see each other again in three weeks. I then immediately packed my bags, checked out of my room to the chagrin of the landlord who was collecting unexpected rent money during the summer, and departed for Clyde. I figured I could walk there in two days and save the train fare. In truth, I could afford the cost, but I was feeling so special and everything looked so beautiful that I wanted to be out in the open air.

I had been walking 15 miles when evening arrived. Now I was about five miles from Norwalk. It was 7:30 p.m. and I figured I could be in Norwalk and find a place to stay by 9 p.m. As I walked, the stars slowly became visible. They were no longer rocks and hot gas. Once again they touched my soul with the hope that there was more to life than the daily struggle to survive. They made me feel whole again. My spirit was back. The great adventure of life had begun afresh.

When I arrived in Norwalk, I came across a rather run down noisy tavern. A sign outside read "Rooms Available." Even the raucous noise would not bother me now and I went inside. There was a room available for 25 cents a night. When I saw the room, I thought it was hardly worth two-bits, but I was so tired that without complaining I put a blanket from the chair over the bed's dirty linens and lay down on top quickly falling asleep.

When I awoke, the skies were gloomy. I started out without delay, skipping breakfast, in order to finish the final 20 miles to Clyde as quickly as possible. By the time I got to the western outskirts of Norwalk, it was raining, the type of rain I saw in northern Ohio quite often when the day starts out overcast with the bottoms of low, gray clouds touching the ground. You hope somehow it will not rain or be a brief shower, but experience knew the truth even in denial. It was going to start out slowly and then the rain would steadily get worse and last all day. To the farmers it was wonderful; to me it meant a hard day of travel.

I bought a couple of rolls with jam at a country store and ventured forward as the rain got harder and harder. The flat Ohio fields covered by the low, gray sky lost all of their bright color. It was as if the whole world was a low contrast black and white photograph. While I was thinking of Kathleen to keep my spirits up, a wagon pulled alongside me. The wagon's side, painted in black and red, read "Irwin Anderson: Painting and Odd Jobs." "You need a ride there?" a voice called out. "I don't have but a leaky roof to sit under yet it will keep you out of the mud." With little hesitation, I accepted and I was soon sitting next to Irwin himself. "Where are you headed, to Bellevue?" he asked, answered, and continued talking before I could get a word in edgewise. "Darn thing about Bellevue, they say the town sits on top of an underground river. Now I don't know, but that would make me nervous. When I was serving under General Grant at Vicksburg I saw whole hillsides of mud collapse. Just how sturdy can that ground be that Bellevue sits on? So what is your business in Bellevue?"

I had been in the North for over 20 years, yet I was still amazed at how Northerners get right to the point. In this case, Irwin was well ahead of himself for I never told him I was going to Bellevue. I did try to answer with, "To tell you the truth Mr. Anderson, I'm not going...."

But Irwin interrupted, "Mr. Anderson? Why as much as I like the sound of that, please as a friend, if I may count you as a friend, call me Irwin. Now, why did you say you were headed to Bellevue?"

I said as quickly as I could so to get the words in, "I'm going to Clyde."

He replied, "Why good sir that is my home and I am headed there today. It will be a pleasure to take you to Clyde." As he said this, I noted the rain had stopped after a fairly hard downfall. Well, it had almost stopped. The sky was still quite gray and it soon was drizzling again. Part of me wanted to get off the wagon and away from Irwin and the colorful stories I was sure he was about to tell me, so that I could instead enjoy the quiet and the scenery. But another part of me liked this man and wanted to stay because he was so friendly and entertaining.

I stayed on the seat next to him, and listened to one story after another. They were full of factual mistakes. He talked about meeting General Thomas at the Battle of Vicksburg (Thomas was never there). He said he fought with Thomas at Chickamauga under General McCook (McCook's men had fled the field with the commanding general William Rosecrans). And he claimed that at Missionary Ridge he headed up the hill with General Sherman no more than 20 yards to his right (Sherman was at a place called Tunnel Hill being contained by Cleburne's and Stevenson's divisions during the attack).

Despite this, Irwin was a likeable man. When I could squeeze in some of my story about serving in the Civil War, he cared not that I fought for the South. "We are all Americans now," he simply said. He even added that he wished more Negroes would settle in these parts. "They were good soldiers and I was proud to fight for their freedom.

Folks in these parts rarely if ever see a Negro, yet they are all so damn sure that they are lazy and shiftless."

Irwin also did not judge me when I refused a drink from his bottle. "I wish I could be disciplined like you, Sam. I know my family would appreciate it." He proceeded to tell me about his wife, sons, and daughters. All together there were seven children to feed. I quickly gathered this was not a prime worry of Irwin's. He knew he had to try and work to support the family, but his head was, as they say, "in the clouds." He played a coronet in the town band, he was engaged in town projects, such as local theater plays, but more than anything, he loved to tell stories.

Listening to Irwin's stories made time pass quickly. The road went through the small town of Monroeville, but not much was happening there as we passed through in the rain. Next, we safely made it through Bellevue, underwater river or no underwater river. When we were a few miles from our destination, I finally mentioned to Irwin why I was going to Clyde. "Oh dear," he said, "they hired Pete Johnson about a week ago for that job." My heart sank, but before it sank too far, Irwin added, "I'll tell you what though, few in town think Pete will last. He is smart enough having been a postmaster at one time, but Pete loves his drink. And I should know, for we closed up many a saloon on many a night together. For him to be at the station every morning by 5:30 a.m. to greet the west-bound Chicago train, well, that's just not going to happen for long." With that said, a small town appeared up ahead. I'd either be in that town working for a few months, or walking on this same road tomorrow headed east back to Oberlin.

CLYDE

The rain stopped by the time Irwin and I arrived in Clyde, and the sun came out, coloring the sky a brilliant orange before it set. I took it as a sign of hope after the all-day rain. The slow transition from day to night and the smell of the wet fields and meadows put me in a good mood that evening in mid-August of 1890. Irwin's remarks did not hurt either, for I felt there was a good chance that I would be hired for the station master's position.

Irwin insisted that I have dinner with his family. We rode through the center of town as the lamplighter illuminated the main street. It was not a particularly striking place, with little to distinguish it from other Ohio villages. We traveled another half-mile or so to a quiet street where Irwin hitched the wagon in front of a two-story house. In the yard a woman was taking down wash by the light of the moon. She must have hung the clothes after the rain stopped to catch the last rays from the sun. We strode up to her and Irwin announced, "Emma, my dear, this is Mr. Nite, a fine gentleman of Virginia. I have invited him to dinner." Politely, but unenthusiastically, Emma greeted me and then asked Irwin if they could have a few words in private.

I stood in the dark yard and looked at the damp clothes in the basket. A woman's day is never done I thought, especially with a man like Irwin who loved his drink and his fun. My mind wandered to Kathleen's support of the Temperance Movement, and I began to understand her feelings. My thoughts were interrupted when Irwin and Emma returned with the news that the children had already eaten and it would be a while before Emma could prepare us some food. It was apparent that Emma had not necessarily expected Irwin to be home that night. As for him showing up with a second mouth to feed, I sensed that Emma was quite embarrassed. Probably there was little food in the house to share. I had seen that look many times in Virginia after the war.

"You know what, Mrs. Anderson," I said, "I am so tired I don't think I could eat a single bite tonight. What I would like to do is get a room in town and be close to my planned appointment in the morning."

Irwin, most likely seeing an opportunity to get out of a sticky situation, said "Very well," and then asked me to wait in the yard for a moment. He entered the house and came back with a boy who looked to be about 12 years old. "This is Ray, one of my sons. He will take you to the best hotel in town." I told Irwin that would not be necessary, but he insisted. Ray and I walked silently for a block or two until we came to Buckeye Street. I decided to make an attempt at conversation as we headed east on Buckeye towards the center of town. "So, Ray, what is the finest hotel in Clyde? "

"You got me," he answered.

"Then where are we headed?" I asked.

"To the middle of town," he said in a matter-of-fact way. Before I could think up any other possible conversation, a tall lanky boy with a newspaper bag around his shoulder approached us from the other direction.

"Where are you headed Ray?" he asked.

"I'm supposed to take this man to a hotel or something."

I interrupted him by stating, "I'm fine, and I can now see where I'm headed."

The taller boy perked up and detecting my accent said, "Wow, you're not from around here are you?"

I answered in a rather unfriendly tone, "No, I am not," for I was tired of hearing that exclamation from others ever since I stepped off the train in Mount Vernon many years ago.

Undeterred, the boy kept on, "I would guess you are from down south."

I replied, "Right you are, I am from Virginia. However, I have called Ohio my home for the last 20 years or so."

"I sure would like to visit someplace like Virginia," the boy continued. "I'd like to visit the ocean, see where all the battles were fought, and go up into the mountains."

Becoming more irritated I ended his excited talk by saying, "Well son, if you don't mind; right now the only thing I would like to see is a nice comfortable bed."

"Hey," piped up Ray suddenly. "Jobby, can I go home now?"

Jobby answered, "Okay, I'll take this fine southern gentleman to one of our best hotels." The boy immediately reminded me of Irwin who I concluded was his father. Then again, as we walked and talked, I could see that he was also not like his father. He was called Jobby by everyone we passed. I later found out it was because, unlike Irwin, he was very industrious, looking for and accepting any odd job in town that was available. Also, unlike Irwin, he was interested in what I had to say. Irwin's conversations tended to be about one thing, himself, typically talking about some war incident that he probably never experienced.

I began to like the boy as we walked and became reenergized as I told him about my experiences fighting in the war, being helped by General Thomas, working for Mr. Abbe, and finally being fired by Tom and Standard Oil. In return, Jobby told me about his family, how his mother took in the neighbor's wash to make ends meet, and that his father had a good heart and a creative spirit, yet had no sense when it came to family responsibility. What I remember the most was Jobby telling me how one day he would get out of Clyde, make a million dollars, and take care of his mother in grand style.

"Making a million" was typical talk for those days, but I soon discovered that the fourteen-year-old boy did more than talk about it, for he took every job he could and worked hard for every penny he earned. There was, however, also a spirit of curiosity and adventure about him that led me to think he would never be happy in any one business for a long time. Instead, I concluded that Jobby had the spirit of an explorer or an artist.

We reached a corner with a saloon and next to it a building with a one-word sign that read "Hotel." Jobby said it was better on the inside than it appeared from the outside. He pointed out the train station and said if I was still around at 6:30 in the morning, he would see me when he picked up the morning newspapers from the Cleveland train to sell. I replied that he just might see me at that time and I gave him a ten-cent piece and bid him a fond good night.

The hotel room was Spartan, yet comfortable, and I certainly have slept in worse beds. I barely seemed to close my eyes when a requested "wake-up" knock on the door ended my sleep. It was close to 5 a.m. in the morning. Having only the clothes I wore when I left my apartment in Cleveland some ten days ago, I had no choice but to put them back on. They had been laundered in Oberlin two days prior to that morning, so at least they did not smell too bad. I cleaned myself up the best I could with a basin of water and soap supplied by the hotel clerk and made my way to the train station.

Upon entering the typical-looking station, which nonetheless was as important to Clyde as Grand Central Station was to New York, I saw a man furiously sweeping the floor. I approached him and asked if he was Pete Johnson. "Pete Johnson!" he exclaimed in a voice much too loud for the early hour. "I'll tell you about Pete Johnson. Mr. Pete Johnson was only late 15 minutes his first day as station master. The second day he was an hour late. The third day he did not come at all and I have not seen or heard from him since. Who are you, a lawman or bill collector? You certainly cannot be a friend, for Mr. Pete Johnson would not be able to associate with anyone at this hour." I told him my name and my business. He seemed impressed by my credentials at first but quickly became suspicious about why I would suddenly show up in Clyde for a job that paid far less than what I was making in Cleveland. Before I could attempt an explanation he said, "This is foolishness. Why would anyone want this job unless they had some strange and twisted motive? However, the worst that could happen is that you will not show up tomorrow morning. My name is Strom Martin of the Big Four Railroad. Are you ready to start work today?"

Concealing my excitement, I replied, "Yes sir." He gave me a uniform, consisting of a cap and blue jacket. In the future, I was expected to supply my own blue pants, a white shirt, and a tie. The job demanded that I be at the station each morning at 5:30 a.m. to open and staff the ticket window until the ticket man arrived at 6 a.m. It was also my responsibility to be sure the baggage man had the bags out and tagged to be loaded on the next train, see that the station was clean and orderly for incoming and outgoing passengers, and answer any questions about services. I would need to periodically check with the telegraph office adjacent to the station to inform passengers whether or not a train was running on time. The job was easy though the hours were long. I was expected to be on duty 50 to 60 hours a week with time off only possible by arrangement with the baggage and ticket man. If one of us was gone, it was expected that the other two would cover for him. Obviously, Pete Johnson made no such arrangements.

The passenger trains of the Big Four Railroad traveled east and west as well as north and south through Clyde. The Big Four had been created the year before with the merger of four mid-western railroads. Its formal name was the Cleveland, Cincinnati, Chicago, and St. Louis Railway or the CCC&StL. As impressive as that sounds, it was overshadowed by the New York Central that ran north of us on the shores of Lake Erie. Nonetheless, our line was quite busy serving as a connector to several big cities.

My first thought was we needed another worker or two, but the number of trains stopping in Clyde was small compared to the many expresses and limiteds that sped through the town without stopping. I found that we could even get by at certain times with only one of us working and, in an emergency, Strom could be called in from Norwalk where he resided. It would have to be a real emergency though. It was soon apparent that as long as there were no complaints, Strom was happy to let me run the station as I saw fit. After I established a routine, I planned to visit Kathleen every week or two in Oberlin. Train fare would be free, since I was now an employee of the CCC&StL.

My second night in Clyde I wrote Kathleen a long letter telling her about everything that had happened since I saw her off to Erie. The next few days I anxiously awaited a return letter. In the meantime I settled into my job. Woody Hanson, my ticket agent, was a big man more in girth than height and he was about 55 years old. Friendly and dependable, he did not move very fast, but he got the job done. Red Grommen was the baggage man. Young and an extremely hard worker, unlike Pete Johnson, he could drink at night and still be at work on time the next morning. Red's finest characteristic was his loyalty. He also was a good conversationalist because he was well-read and loved to talk about books. He especially loved novels that speculated about the future. His favorite author was Jules Verne, who wrote fantastic novels of men flying through the air and even reaching the moon. Despite his fine intellect, Red wouldn't hesitate to bare his knuckles or get down in the mud if there was trouble. And you did not mess with a friend of Red's. Red once told a local tough guy that if he said one more thing about me being a dirty Reb he would kick his behind from Clyde into Lake Erie, a good 20 miles away.

Jobby was a frequent visitor to the station mainly to sell his papers, but also to offer other services to visitors like carrying their luggage to the hotel. Jobby was somewhat fascinated with my presence in Clyde. He liked to compare my Civil War stories with those of his father, and because he was a seeker of truth, he seemed more impressed with my tales of digging trenches than his father's battle stories. Jobby also served as my one-man welcoming committee helping me get settled in Clyde. He found me a room at Mrs. Willard's Boarding House where the rent was reasonable and the food edible though not as fine as the cuisine I used to enjoy in Cleveland.

After a couple of days, I wired Cleveland to make arrangements to sell or give away my furniture, pay off my debts, and officially change my address. I transferred the money in my bank account to Clyde and had my stockbroker sell my stocks and forward the cash. Everything was falling into place except that Kathleen was scheduled to return to Oberlin and I had not heard from her since we separated in Oberlin. So, I decided to send her a telegram.

A few days later, I received a letter from Erie. It was not from Kathleen but from a Mr. Steven Jenkins, Kathleen's father. The letter read:

Dear Mr. Nite,

I am not familiar with the customs of where you come from; however, in this part of the country it is not proper for a stranger to arrive unannounced in a town and court a woman half his age. Mrs. Jenkins and I forbid you to have further contact with our daughter Kathleen. To assure this, your letters shall not be delivered to Kathleen and we have seen to her resignation from Oberlin College to prevent you from visiting her. I truly hope this will end the matter. If not, I promise you that there will be serious consequences.

Sincerely,
Steven M. Jenkins

Suddenly, my whole outlook and mood returned to the way I had felt prior to meeting Kathleen. It was as if I was again walking on a dusty road to nowhere. I was Samuel Nite, Station Master, Clyde, Ohio, nothing more. "I received an education in Nashville, Tennessee, for this?" I asked Red. "Here I am alone in a small northern town, probably disliked as much as Negroes are down south. Maybe I should return to my hatred of Negroes. If a Black soldier named Joe had not saved me from the bullet of a bitter renegade named Billy, I wouldn't be here living this cursed life. There would have been no disappointments, no falling in love, no being run out of business by the Rockefellers, and no miserable day-to-day struggle in order to just struggle more."

"Hee-ha," answered Red using his favorite expression. "Clyde is as good a place as any to rot and die, and besides we don't hate you, we like you just fine. You don't treat us with a swelled head, like you are better than us because you are 'Mister Station Master.' Now that you are no longer controlled by a woman you can join us for a drink once in a while. You'll see that some folks around here are not that bad. Sure, there are some 'upstanding fine individuals' who will look down on you, but if you look hard you will find them in some gal's bed while their wife thinks they are working late in one of their fine offices. Life is like that all over. Hee-ha, but you are okay; there is no special air about you."

That night, after work was over, Red handed me a paper bag. "Here is a gift for you, and in this other bag is a gift for me." My bag contained a bottle of Pink Catawba wine. His bag was a bottle of his favorite whiskey, I can't recall the name. We headed to a park out near the fairgrounds. The sun was setting earlier than mid-summer, but the September night was warm and Red knew plenty of places near the park where a couple of guys could drink without being bothered. Red was curious about how I ended up in Clyde. We both sipped out of our bottles while I gave him all the particulars and answered his many questions about the places I had been. Then I said, "Red it is your turn. Is this where you are from?"

Red laughed a little bit, for what reason I could not figure out. "I'm from just down the road in good old Fremont, but it might as well be a hundred miles from here." Before I could ask him why and what was funny about that fact, he continued. "I don't like to fight, but some fellas over there kept bothering my friend Don. We were drinking one night when three dandy dressers who worked in an insurance office came up to Don and egged him on because he never said much. They claimed Don thought himself to be better than them. Don ignored them and silently sat next to me at the bar drinking. After they drank a few more beers, those insurance salesmen thought they were real toughs, especially when the odds were three against one. They didn't figure on me getting involved because I always minded my own business and would occasionally drink with one or two of those office boys and talk about politics and such. Well, they started on Don pretty good, but Don travelled with the horse racing bunch from town to town and he knew how to handle himself. I watched for almost a whole minute once the name calling got down to actual scrapping. It took them a while before they finally got an upper hand on Don and one of them was about to hit him with a chair from behind. 'Hee Haw,' before he got a chance I grabbed the asshole from behind and tossed him, still gripping that damn chair, through the door and out into the street. Before I could get at one of the other swells, my good pal Joe showed up from I don't where and pulled one of those boys off Don and sent him flying over a table. Don was easily dispatching the other fella when suddenly more coppers than I thought were in Fremont rushed into the tavern and started manhandling Don, Joe, and me like we were the perpetrators of all the trouble.

"Joe was in good with a couple of the town big wigs and just got slapped on the hand, if you know what I mean. Don and I weren't so lucky. We both had been in trouble for drinking and creating what you might call "some unrest" a couple of times before. So, we were escorted to the edge of town and warned never to enter Fremont again. My friends had to bring my belongings from the boarding house I was staying at. You see, my folks were dead, and I had no other family in town."

"So what was your livelihood in Fremont and how did you come to work and live in Clyde?" I asked Red.

"You promise not to laugh?"

"Yes I promise."

"In Fremont I taught young kids how to read and write, and I was damn good at it. But, with my drinking and occasional fighting, the town was looking for a reason to get rid of me, and that night at the bar gave them all the justification they needed. I guess they also believed that a teacher of their children should not carry on in public like I did that night, especially a fella who didn't dress fancy like those insurance agents. Anyway, after I got my stuff, I just kept walking east since that was the side of town they took me to when I was told not to come back. Those jack asses. Fremont and Clyde always had a rivalry in everything you could think of, I mean the two towns hate each other, so those Fremont cops, I'm sure of it, thought it would be funny to drop me off on the road that led to Clyde. Don went with me, but he kept on going right through Clyde and ended up working the race horse circuit for some rich guy in Norwalk. I, on the other hand, was determined to prove those Fremont idiots wrong and I found a simple job in Clyde, the one I have right now, and decided to keep out of trouble.

"Sam, there are two reasons we are drinking out here in the woods. One is that I now only drink with folks I respect. And, don't worry, I know you are the boss and I don't expect any special favors. If you ever need to give me Hell for something, then give me Hell."

Those words summed up Red perfectly. He didn't do a good job because he had to, he did so because it was his nature and the loyalty he always gave his employer and boss. Sometimes I thought he might have been too loyal, for the CCC&StL wouldn't pause for a second if they thought they could get by without him. That's just the way it was.

After a short pause Red continued, "The other reason we are out here drinking is that…"—at this point Red stopped and let out a belly laugh and said—"there ain't no one out here to get in a fight with, and that keeps me out of trouble!"

Red abruptly changed the subject and said, "Come on Sam, with you being in the war and all, I want to show you another good place to drink. We can resupply ourselves on the way with medicine, if you know what I mean."

I'll never forget that night of walking on moonlit dirt roads with a full sky of stars and feeling an elation that was made possible by the wine. We stopped at a run-down store in the middle of nowhere and resupplied ourselves with more wine and whiskey. We reentered Clyde from the north end of town and walked through a field into the cemetery. There were strange trees silhouetted against the sky with limbs that looked like the knobby joints of old people. Then, coming into view was an even stranger site in this small country cemetery. Before us stood a magnificent monument with a Union general atop a horse marking the grave of General James B. McPherson, a native son of Clyde and a true hero. McPherson was a favorite of Sherman's and might have even been given the command to hold Nashville against Hood if he hadn't foolishly gotten killed on the Atlanta campaign. The story goes that McPherson was out scouting alone and found himself in the company of a group of Southern soldiers. He paused, gallantly saluted them, and tried to make his escape on horseback. A Confederate marksman, who probably grew up shooting squirrels, aimed and shot the fleeing McPherson right through the heart.

As I sat on the ground admiring the image of McPherson, Red headed off a short distance to relieve himself. My thoughts turned to what a strange coincidence it was that I'd be here before this cold granite memorial to a general who, if he lived, might have been in command at Nashville instead of General Thomas. If that was the case, the statue would not be here, I would not be here, and who knows what else would be different. Perhaps my life and the whole world would have been altered if that Confederate soldier was not standing in that particular place, or if he hadn't learned to be a marksman by shooting squirrels as a boy. Or, what if that soldier's great grandfather was killed in the great War of Revolution and thus he was never born? What if? What if? What if? My drunken mind was now spinning as I shared my thoughts with Red upon his return. I told him how my whole life could be different, and I looked at the stars and started shouting in frustration that comes with not understanding.

Red's facial expression froze for less than a second, but it seemed like an eternity to me. Then he screamed "HEE-HA!" The two of us broke into uncontrollable laughter. After we calmed down, Red said, "You know Sam, if it wasn't for that Don being so damn quiet, you and I would never be here together either. But Hell, life is one big mystery and then you die, 'Hee Haw.'" It's funny, but that was the last time I ever drank to the extent that I felt out of my normal mind, whatever my normal mind might be, and Red and I never spoke to each other of such serious metaphysical matters again, although after that night, Red and I formed a lasting bond of trust. We were in the minority, for the people of small towns across America did not discuss the big question of Why, as in why do we happen to be in Clyde and where will we go next? No, folks instead relied on the word of God as delivered by their preacher on Sundays. That was good enough.

I don't know what Red thought, but nights like that one made it clear to me that there was a purpose to life, but it was not to be found in a bottle of wine. Those good old Christians of the early days knew that wine could help turn the door knob, but it couldn't open the door. That night I approached an understanding of the fact that despite the myriad of ways things could turn out, everything still happens just the way it is supposed to. The thought was fuzzy because of the wine and thus hard to put in words, but it was pointing towards truth.

These were important matters, but after we left the statue, I can't remember anything except walking and telling Red how I would show Kathleen's father that I was deserving of his daughter. I had returned to the normal, sober concerns of life. The next thing I remembered was Red shaking me awake at the train station and telling me it was time to get to work. Apparently, we both fell asleep in my office in the early hours of the morning. Not being used to drinking so much like Red, and being at least ten years his senior, I was miserable that entire day after our night out while Red conducted his business the same as any other day. I felt better after a good night's sleep, but my days in the following weeks were spent obsessing on losing Kathleen and wondering what action, if any, I should take. I was able to suppress my painful feelings about Kathleen as much as I could for the sake of my job, for a job is a job and this one sure beat work in a factory. I was again extremely cynical. I was friendly and polite, but my important thoughts were kept to myself. An exception was made for Jobby. Just about every day he would ask me for more details about my life. One day the boy exclaimed, "Wow, your life reads like a book."

I could not hold back, "No it does not Jobby. If it did, there would be a happy ending. I would at least learn something. I would feel at the end that my life was important. Instead I am alone; my best years, when I felt most alive, are twenty years in the past. Even my time playing the part of an important businessman was a failure. What kind of book are you talking about, one that ends where the main character dies and no one notices? At least it would be an honest book because that is the fate of well over 99% of us." Jobby refused to accept my rejection of his notion that life is a great adventure with plenty of good and bad, yet all of it interesting. That is not to say Jobby was not aware of the dark side. One day out of nowhere he said to me, "A lot of people in this town pretend that they are not driven by human desire, and this fact makes them act strange." Despite my usual sour mood my interest was piqued.

"What human desire are you speaking of Jobby?" I asked.

"Sam, you know. It's what goes on between women and men."

It took me a second to realize he meant sex. "I must admit Jobby, I don't feel comfortable talking about it myself." I could see disappointment in his face, so I quickly added, "You sure are right though. Discomfort with the subject causes problems in everyone's life, because like those rivers under Bellevue, it is all going to rush to the surface one day. But I still don't know a way to broach the subject with others and if they would catch me talking to you about it, I would be run out of town as quick as a teacher caught putting an arm around a student as a gesture of care." Despite this, I continued with the subject because Jobby was the kind of kid that you did not want to disappoint. So I asked him to elaborate on his statement.

"Sam, it is just one of those things. Everyone has a drive for it yet they consider it wrong to even think about. It is just as bad, if not worse they say, than killing someone."

I said, "Yeah, I know what you mean," and then I told him about Owen, how Owen's shame led him to get the crazy notion in his head that Billy and his gang were heroes.

Jobby jumped in, "That's it Sam. The folks around here make up for their hidden thoughts and desires by coming up with crazy ideas about things, like they have a special knowledge about the meaning of life. I mean, it makes them crazy."

"I don't know if that's the right word Jobby." I added, "You know Professor Pennington had a word for it. He would say that people were all … something?" Jobby said he would look the word up and let me know what it was tomorrow. And then, he was off for home.

All that night I pondered the conversation. Part of me worried that it was too deep and dangerous a subject to be talking to a fifteen-year-old boy about. However, Jobby was no ordinary fifteen-year-old. Suddenly, the word dawned on me. It was "grotesque." Later when I thought about my situation with Kathleen, I could see exactly what Jobby was talking about. Her parents were so afraid of the possibility of my romantic intentions without knowing anything about me, that it caused them to lose their grasp on reality. They were so scared of their daughter's human feelings that they were willing to ruin everything

Kathleen worked towards by refusing to let her go back to Oberlin. If Jobby saw the grotesqueness of people, he also saw their beauty. I will never forget that I had the privilege to meet and know Jobby. I believed he had a special gift to see through all the pain and not be consumed by it. Great things were ahead for this talented young man from Clyde.

Over the next few years I saw less of Jobby. I think much of his time was spent chasing girls. In the meantime, I started going out more, usually spending time with Red, but being careful to limit myself to only one drink or two on such occasions. Red was a good man and respected my self-imposed limits. Red, too, began to put some of his energy into other activities. He began to play baseball with a local team that played games all around northwest Ohio, although he had to skip any game played in Fremont. He made some good friends on the team and introduced me to them, and several of them also became my friends. Playing games was the only thing for which he asked time off. Along with Woody the three of us worked out a schedule that even allowed me to attend some of Red's games while Woody looked after the station. We had recently been allotted a little more money, so that we could also pay Jobby to help on occasion.

Red's team was fun to watch. They had a fine hitting attack. Red led off and played centerfield. Chas Kerner, the first baseman, batted second. The big hitters in the middle of the lineup were shortstop Bob Taylor, the powerful Tom "Ed" Keetch, who played third base, and the slugging outfielder "Plank" Michaels. The pitching was strong with starters Carl Malco and Norm Bulzinski backed up by Mark Kristian, Vincente Mamonido, and a big guy simply known as "Duke." They were not the Cincinnati Red Stockings, but they were good. They did not have a base of operation but travelled a regular circuit to towns like Fremont, Fostoria, Bowling Green, Bucyrus, Upper Sandusky, Bellevue, Norwalk, and of course Clyde.

After I attended several games, the team asked me to serve as manager. Bobby Taylor, who was playing and managing at the same time, wanted to just play and not manage. Although I was not an expert, I had become a fan after my introduction to baseball by Bruno in Cincinnati. I attended several games in Cleveland and learned the fine details of the sport. I agreed to manage as long as it did not interfere with work and Woody was able to be at the station when we were gone.

I needed the diversion, for all I was doing was working and feeling self-pity about losing Kathleen. Several times I convinced myself to take a trip to Erie and look for her. I always decided not to go because I thought Kathleen must have wanted it this way or she would have found a way to escape her parents and join me in Clyde.

One day Jobby stopped by to say hello and I told him all about falling in love only to lose my beloved because of my age. I told him I was a fool, and he remarked that it was the second time I called myself such. He felt that I lacked self-confidence and I should be determined to find her again, or otherwise I would never know if she still loved me or not. I was about to follow his advice, but then thought it was ridiculous to be taught about love by a boy less than half my age. Still, he made sense and I told this wise boy that maybe he was right. At that moment Irwin walked into the station.

I had not seen Irwin much since that day he brought me to town. I don't think I ever had been together with Irwin and Jobby at the same time. Irwin barely acknowledged my presence and looked directly at Jobby and said, "Brad Miller was complaining to me that you and the Hurd boy have been calling on his two daughters. He says the other night they were out alone with you and Herman." I figured he was going to discipline or at least lecture Jobby right there in the crowded station. To avoid such embarrassment for Jobby, I began to interrupt Irwin, when suddenly he exclaimed in a loud voice, "Now that's my boy. You're a real chip right off the old block! Why I'm always for chasing a sweet gal myself." I realized three things at that moment. One, Irwin was drunk; two, Jobby was embarrassed; and three, Jobby was especially hurt for his mother to hear Irwin announce in public that he was unfaithful to her.

Jobby fled the station and was not seen in town for several days. Word got around that Herman Hurd was properly disciplined by his father, the town grocer. In more hushed tones others talked about Irwin's scene in the station. Since Red frequented some of the same saloons that Irwin did and would also see Jobby around Clyde, I asked him to keep me informed about any news regarding Irwin and Jobby. About a week later Red told me Jobby was back. He had gone to Fremont to work a few days and returned with quite a bit of cash and some beautiful flowers for his mother. That was the end of the story except I knew that there was more going on than Jobby's mother being humiliated by Irwin. Jobby also feared that a big part of himself was just like Irwin. I could see it in Jobby's dreaming of travel and adventure, which in my eyes was not entirely a bad thing, and I also saw Irwin's influence in how Jobby flirted with every girl in town. At the same time, though, Jobby had the sweetness and big heart of his mother.

Soon, after I once again rejected the idea of visiting Kathleen in Erie, I was managing the Ohio Shawnee Baseball Club as Red's team was now called. There were no Shawnee Indians on the team or anymore in Ohio for that matter. Still, I accepted the name and for inspiration I thought back to Professor Pennington's praise for the courage and humanity of the great Shawnee Chief Tecumseh. One Friday we left Clyde for a five-game series to be played in a place named Croghantown. The Croghantown fans greeted us graciously, but with each inning of each game they became more hostile. Everybody wanted to forget their problems and put all their spirit behind the home team. The first game was a 9 to 4 victory behind Norm Bulzinski's pitching. Ed Keetch hit a three-run homer in the sixth inning to lead the offense. We lost the next two games 18-7 and 12-6 before the "Duke" struck out the side in the ninth inning of the fourth game to preserve a 5-4 win. Red made a spectacular catch in the eighth inning with the bases loaded and the score tied 4-4. In the top of the ninth it was Keetch again homering for us to give the Shawnees the lead. Keetch had the only two home runs of the series.

On Sunday afternoon the second game of the day was about to start when a group of women led by a minister entered the ballpark. They carried signs protesting the playing of baseball on the Sabbath. The fans were angry at the protestors for interrupting their fun and threw apples, bottles, and rocks at these holier than thou interlopers. The police arrived and safely escorted the protestors away from the ballpark. Then the game got underway, but now the fans were in an ugly mood and started hurling the same kind of objects at our team.

I called for a timeout to discuss the situation with the umpires and the manager of the Croghantown team. The Croghantown manager was a good chap, and he decided to appeal to the fans to stop their rowdy behavior. At first it worked. Then we began to rally from a five-run deficit. With the score 8-3 in the seventh inning and two outs, Red singled, Chas Kerner walked, and Bobby Taylor reached on an error. Our big hitter, Ed Keetch, was up and he promptly hit a three-run double to center field. Next, "Plank" Michaels came to bat. With a count of two balls and two strikes, he hit a line drive to left field that hit the ground in front of their fielder. Coaching at third, I decided to send Ed home to get within one run behind the home team. Ed clearly looked safe as he slid into the home bag. The local umpire, perhaps fearing the reaction of the crowd, called Ed out. An argument between Ed and the umpire grew into a frenzy as fans left their seats and began to attack some of our players.

At this point the Croghantown players tried to protect us, and the fans were eventually pushed back. It was decided to end the game. Now, it was a matter of us getting to the train station as soon as possible. Some police came back out to the field, but most fans ignored the officers and remained on the premises. We were faced with a two-mile walk to the Croghantown station while verbal insults escalated to a rain of rocks, which left our faces and hands bloody. The everyday frustrations of living in late 19th-century America where most men endured too many hours of hard and dangerous work at low wages were being visited on us. Mark Kristian had a gash on his forehead, while Vincente Mamonido had apparently broken his arm after being violently knocked down. Some of our players decided to fight back with the one thing we had that the fans didn't, baseball bats. An angry Bulzinski with bat in hand warned the fans to back off.

Every Croghantown law officer available now arrived at the field, and along with the Croghantown team and some of the level-headed citizens did all they could to get us safely to the train station. Once we were on the train, I needed someone to help calm the team down. Norm Bulzinski was a very intelligent person who taught German at Heidelberg College in Tiffin, Ohio. He was especially upset with the incident because he could not rationalize why people would act as barbarously as they had in Croghantown. I could talk to Norm, however, and I managed to convince him that it was best if he helped me persuade the team that the best place to go when they got off the train was home and not to one of the "general stores" that illegally sold liquor on Sunday out in the country. At such a place, their report about the game would incite the local fans to plot revenge on Croghantown.

The truth was that the riot could easily have happened anywhere in the United States. People were fed up with their lives. They worked hard every day, and yet they didn't get anywhere. They no longer had the means to build a farm and see their land expand and their crops grow. They could no longer build a nice home to pass down to their children. Instead they worked for wages that never amounted to enough to get ahead. When they decided to enjoy the fruits of their labors, like attending a baseball game on a Sunday, there would always be a group of traditionalists finding a reason why they were wrong. However, the answer was not for the people to fight each other.

We succeeded in that most of the players said they would head home. Red and Ed stated that they would find their own quiet spot to drink away the nasty memories of the day. I thanked Norm for his help and sank into my seat and began to think about Kathleen. After this day of near-tragedy, I thought about how short life was, especially for the common man, and I asked myself, "Who was this Steven Jenkins to judge me sight unseen simply because I was older and did not have social standing?" I decided I would find Kathleen and be with her no matter what her family thought. The next day I checked our baseball schedule and saw that in August, almost exactly a year since I met Kathleen and moved to Clyde, the team had weekend games scheduled in Ashtabula, Ohio. The town was not much more than an hour by train from Erie, so I made plans to take extra time off that weekend and to visit the Jenkins after the games.

The date arrived for the games in Ashtabula and we won three out of the four contests to even our season record at 34 wins and 34 losses. It was nothing to write home about, but nothing to be ashamed of either. That Sunday afternoon it began to rain and as the rest of the team boarded the train back to Clyde, I boarded a train in the other direction for Erie. I had bought a new suit for the occasion and upon arriving in Erie I checked into the finest hotel I could afford. I made inquiries the next morning and obtained an address for the Jenkins home. Then, I sent a card of introduction to the home requesting permission to visit. I figured by following the proper protocol I would be given a chance to prove my worth.

About two that afternoon a carriage arrived with a driver and another young man who said they were there to take me to the Jenkins' home. As we rode to the west of town through some beautiful country, they explained that the estate was about ten miles away. After a while, I became suspicious when I noticed a sign that Conneaut, Ohio, was only ten miles ahead. Suddenly, the coach stopped and the door opened from the outside. "This is the end of the road fella," one said and then they both violently pulled me from the carriage. "Don't ever come back here, you understand?" one told me. Before I could form a reply I was struck several times and light turned to darkness. I returned to consciousness disoriented and hurting all over in a ravine. It was dawn when I somehow made it to the road, and I stood up to look for any familiar landmarks. At first I felt very dizzy and incredibly lightheaded and I soon "kissed the ground" as a guy I once met liked to say referring to the act of falling. Again light turned to black and a procession of events, some from my past, some that had nothing to do with my past, and some that seemed to have nothing to do with me, marched through my head. I can't exactly recall what most of these unconscious events were, I just know that they swirled through my mind unbounded by time and space. They were dreams and they were not dreams. Later I reflected on it and it was not quite like being alive, but it was not like nothingness either. I do remember one last dream with General Thomas and Joe, the Black soldier who saved my life all those years ago. "Joe," the general said, "Sam, here, has been treated rather rudely. He appears not to be viewed as an equal by these Northerners. The war changed us, but not the country I'm afraid."

"No sir," answered Joe. "I reckon those with money have the power no matter what and they will always find some way to keep it that way." And then I woke up. I was in Conneaut. At my bedside were Red, Norm Bulzinski, and Ed Keetch. They explained that I was found by the road and taken to a doctor's office. I was in a back room of the office where I had lain unconscious for three days. The doctor had found a card in my wallet for the baseball team and contacted Clyde via the telegraph. The three players wanted to find the thugs who beat me up and give them some of their own medicine, but I said to them, "Can't you see? Those thugs are just the paid help. The Jenkins did this with their money and there is nothing to be done in Erie that will gain us satisfaction. Instead we will just get in more trouble."

So, after I had a couple more days of bed rest we headed back to

Clyde. When we got off the train, I was greeted by Strom Martin. He was there relieving Woody and was on the verge of giving me a lecture when Red gave him a look. Strom did not want to tangle with Red, so he simply said "Welcome back," and asked if tomorrow morning I could be back on the job. The players spoke up and said that would be up to Doctor Hannibal. Before I knew it I was over at the doctor's office. Doc Hannibal was the perfect doctor for a small town. He had this very peculiar but optimistic attitude. He was aware of all the problems in the town and society, but he didn't let it get him down. He had enormous energy and never complained about taking care of people, including those who could not pay.

He laughed as he examined me and said, "I guess you're not going to tell me I should see the other guys. This fight certainly was one-sided. You should be okay though as long as you don't become a professional boxer. By the way, did you see that kid who boxed Junior Bell a month ago?" I didn't answer so he added, "Well, I guess you don't want to hear about a fight right now. But, gosh that kid was a real mess when he got to me." And so the exam continued with such comments that seemed inappropriate coming from a doctor but actually cheered me up. There were a lot of good people in town. That's what I found out when I was in trouble. The Doc finished with orders for me to get a good night's sleep and to take it easy at work tomorrow. "And, by the way, stick to the railroad business because I can't patch you up every time you try mixing in with high society folk." Yes, it was a town of good people, but on the other hand, a rumor quickly spread around town that I was messing around with another man's wife, and that's why I was bruised and broken.

Things eventually returned to normal, and my friendship with the team members became stronger after the incidents in Crogantown and Erie. They all stood solidly behind me. Norm was very self-conscious and overly sensitive, but he never let me down. He was a very caring person who "mothered" me back to health both physically and mentally. Mark Kristian was also sensitive, but in a more cerebral way. He was not surprised about human behavior and he took everything, like being hit by that rock in the face, in stride. Maybe this lack of fear and emotion is the reason why he was a very successful wire salesman? He had many interesting stories about attempted robberies and crooked card games that happened when he went on sales trips, but he never worried about such dangers, even when he travelled as far away as Boston. Ed was very daring, had a great sense of humor, and was ready to fight anyone who threatened a friend. He was somebody I would have wanted by my side back in the war. You might say that Norm and Mark helped with my emotional problems, while Red and Ed could be counted on for physical protection. These young men thought I lived in some kind of a fantasy world when it came to women, political issues, and enjoying life in a place like Clyde. One of the other players said, "Old man, you are like the other old drunks around here except you don't drink much. I don't get it." And so it was that as the hurt from Kathleen slowly left so did my ambitions. Life became day-to-day in Clyde, not unlike Cleveland, except I no longer believed I was working my way towards a goal. I was already there and it wasn't much.

Since we worked together, I was around Red more than anyone else, and we continued to discuss literature. Between trains, when there was no work to be done, he always had something to read. Besides books by Jules Verne, we also discussed books by Herman Melville and Nathaniel Hawthorne. He also had a keen interest in American essayists like Emerson and Thoreau. Yet, despite these intellectual interests, Red still seemed happy doing manual labor. When he drank, he could get very negative about things, especially when he was with his friend Joe who always seemed to be visiting from Fremont. Neither of them let drinking interfere with their work though, or cause them to argue or try and hurt a friend. Joe became quite rich from betting on the horses and eventually left the area buying a small horse farm near Canton, Ohio.

All of the players began to complain about travelling to the road games, because being some place on time depended on the train being on time. There was no other way to go. There was, however, something on the horizon that would make local travel much easier. Cities and many small towns already had street railroads which consisted of cars being pulled on rails by horses. Then, just before the 1890s, some places began applying electricity to their railways, eliminating the use of horses. In addition, these street railroads began to extend outside of the cities and towns into the countryside. Ultimately they began to connect the urban areas and thus began to be known as "interurbans." One of the first streetcar companies to connect towns was the Sandusky, Norwalk & Southern. This connection of about fifteen miles between Sandusky and Norwalk was a convenient route for passengers switching from the New York Central line to that of the Big Four. I found the interurban concept fascinating. I was also beginning to wonder just what I was doing in Clyde. I was always aware that the only reason I came here was to be with Kathleen. It resulted in a concussion and an increasingly bad attitude. I needed a change. I began thinking about a new career, maybe doing something involved with the interurban railroads.

By chance, in the summer of 1894, I met a young man named Frederick W. Coen, who was waiting for a train at the Clyde station. Three years earlier, Frederick moved from Indiana to join his brother in the banking business in Vermillion, Ohio, a town on the shores of Lake Erie about halfway between Sandusky and Cleveland. During our conversation, he told me about his involvement in a project to protect the bank's investment in the interurban line now known as the Sandusky, Milan, and Norwalk. I told Frederick about my past involvement in the oil business. Being a businessman himself, he seemed puzzled that I gave it all up for a station master position. He was an entrepreneur and believed in a bright future for America that included every town in America being connected by electric railways. He told me to visit him some day in his new Sandusky office and perhaps there would be a position open for which I was suited. I placed the business card he gave me in my wallet.

Soon there were other factors pushing me to leave Clyde. Since I mainly associated with young people, I felt like I would somehow be left behind in Clyde, growing old in my job and becoming a town fixture liked Woody who was still managing the ticket window at the age of sixty just as he had done at the age of thirty. Men who were boys when I had arrived in Clyde had married or left town. Once they married, they would either become devoted family men or stubbornly refuse to give up their independence, and like Irwin, spend too many nights in the taverns. Most women of such husbands accepted their fate, but a few joined the Temperance Movement. They were sick and tired of their men wasting the family money on drink, losing their jobs, and worst of all beating their wives when confronted over their behavior. Such happenings, especially involving men considered to be pillars of the community, were kept silent, but there was much discontent on the streets.

In the March of 1895, Red quit his job and went west to see the Rocky Mountains. He said that if he didn't go now he would never go. Perhaps he would find work in a mining town. The rest of the ball team also began to break up. Ed Keetch, still in his twenties, accepted an invitation to join a team in Hamilton, Ohio. Norm, after his parents died, decided to accept a position at Baldwin Wallace College in Berea, Ohio. Mark Christian moved to New York, taking an executive position in the booming wire and cable business.

In the May of 1895, Jobby's mother Emma died at the age of 43. Jobby, now approaching twenty, had nothing to keep him in Clyde. Although I did not see him nearly as often as when I first moved here, he occasionally stopped in to say hello. We had always remained on good terms. In fact I was the only one at the station when one day in 1896 he entered with a suitcase heading to Chicago to find work.

We exchanged pleasantries. I warmly shook his hand and wished him good luck. He thanked me for sharing some interesting stories. I was amazed at how he remembered them in every detail; things like how Professor Pennington built his bed so he could watch the people through his window, or how I was unable to tell Sally I loved her. Before Jobby got on the train, I said to him, "You know Jobby, I never learned your real name."

He looked at me and smiled. "The name is Sherwood, Sherwood Anderson. And you Mr. Sam Nite, if you ever get to Chicago, look me up." With that Sherwood got on the train and the ghost of Jobby was left to wander the streets of Clyde forever.

SANDUSKY

I reluctantly slipped out from under the four blankets on my bed. Hastily, I dressed in my uniform, ate two slices of bread with jam, and drank some spring water I kept in a jar. When I opened the door and emerged from the hotel, my exposed face and hands were hit by air so cold that it felt like a solid sheet of ice. This was Ohio in January. Slowly, head down, as if walking uphill, I made my way to the station.

It was January 1896 to be precise, and it had been over a year since I had met Frederick Coen at the station. But he had been on my mind for I was ready for a job with regular day hours, better pay, and the opportunity to better use my creative ability. On visits to the country, I had seen the cars of Mr. Coen's newly named interurban electric railroad, the Sandusky, Milan & Norwalk, speed along tracks through the fields, stopping at places the regular railroads bypassed. The average person was now able to easily travel in a short amount of time to the next town and beyond. Tracks were crisscrossing the countryside like a spider web. It was an exciting new era of travel, and I always enjoyed travel, so I wanted to be part of this new exciting development. Fred Coen had told me to see him if I wanted a job, and that time had come.

I was off early in the afternoon and had made arrangements by combining railroad and interurban travel to arrive at Mr. Coen's office before the end of the business day. Coen's office was located in Sandusky, a lake port close to twenty miles to the north. I decided to arrive unannounced, for I believed that once he saw me, he would remember making my acquaintance in Clyde. I arrived at the Sandusky, Milan, and Norwalk office a little after four, where I was greeted by a receptionist. I informed her that Mr. Coen had invited me to see him if I wanted a job. Looking rather stern with her hair pulled back tightly and perched on her nose, the woman studied me for a moment and then said in a polite, professional manner, "I am sorry to inform you, Sir, that Mr. Coen has moved to the Everett-Moore offices in Cleveland to work on the Lorain & Cleveland Railway project." Never having heard of Everett-Moore or the Lorain & Cleveland Railroad I lost some of my self-confidence. I just stood there not knowing what to say, when the woman sympathetically broke the silence. "Mr. Coen is still thought of very highly here. Why don't I see if Mr. Avery, our office manager, will see you."

"That would be quite satisfactory," I answered and took a seat nearby.

After a half-hour wait, a gentleman dressed in professional-looking but not expensive clothing asked me to come into his office. As soon as we got inside, he motioned for me to sit down in a chair in front of his desk. He looked at me for just a second, and then he spoke in an accent that sounded like he was from Boston, or maybe New York. "So, Fred told you to come see us. Are you an acquaintance from Cleveland?" I answered that I was not and explained how I met Mr. Coen in Clyde over a year ago. Looking a bit skeptical, Avery said, "I don't want to sound insulting, but I have never known Fred to invite people to the office from the, shall we say, working class caste." I said nothing and he began again with, "Caste is a reference from India referring...."

That did it. I was not going to play the fool for this man, especially since we were obviously sitting in the office of a low-ranking official with one chair for visitors and nothing on the walls save an old railroad calendar. I interrupted Avery, "I know very well what the caste system is, and I do not believe I am part of the untouchable class. I chose a station master's job for my own reasons. I used to work for a small oil concern in Cleveland that was bought out by Standard Oil. In fact I was a partner in the firm."

Avery now hesitated and seemed quite embarrassed, maybe even a bit fearful that I might be somebody of importance. After a brief pause, he asked, "Mr. Nite, will you be staying in town tonight? "

I had not planned to stay the night, but in order to demonstrate that I was important enough to be in control of my time and not tied down by someone else's schedule, I answered that I would be. When he asked at what hotel, with my confidence reinstated I answered, "I was hoping you would make a recommendation."

"Very well," he answered. "Miss Marchant, who you met in the outer office, will recommend a hotel. In the meantime, I will contact Fred and see what he suggests." I left the office and headed up Market Street towards the docks where Miss Marchant said I would find the West House Hotel. Because money was an issue due to my low pay in Clyde and the expenses I accrued over the years managing and travelling with the baseball team, I walked past the hotel and headed east on Meigs Street. After three or four blocks, I turned on to First Street, which had a line of old, large houses facing north. One of these might be a boarding house, I hoped. The fourth house down, a two-story Pre-Victorian-style mansion that was built in a simple, practical style had a sign in the window that read "Rooms by the week or night." I looked towards the north side of the street to clear my mind and decide if I was doing the right thing. Gazing out I was looking at a vast expanse of white, which was the frozen Lake Erie. I felt small and alone. I remembered that some of the old-timers in Mount Vernon still called Lake Erie and the other Great Lakes the English Lakes, but the wintry sight gave me no comfort, regardless of what it was called. I'm sure the lake looked the same as it did over 200 years prior when the French explorer LaSalle was credited with its discovery, ignoring the fact that there were Indians living on its shores. For a moment I reflected on how unfair it was that Lake Erie showed no signs of aging, while my appearance was changing constantly with more gray hair, more wrinkles, and less muscle. It also depressed me that the shoreline marked the end of my northerly migration. I had come seeking a better life and no farther north could I go. A cold wind off the lake snapped my mind back to immediate concerns and I quickly made a decision to double my efforts to get a job with the SM&N. It came down to the fact that I wasn't happy being a businessman and I had become bored being a station master. Maybe working in the new interurban industry would provide something of both occupations.

I went inside the boarding house and reserved a plain but surprisingly clean and tidy room for two bits. I then walked back to the West House and entered the old, stately hotel. I sat in the lobby on one of the overstuffed chairs, the kind that a salesman would sit in to take a break from his appointments and smoke a cigar while he read the newspaper. There I sat, and while I pretended to read a gazette, I studied the clerk and listened to him interact with a couple of guests. I decided after observing his friendly nature that it was worth a try to enlist his help.

"Good day my good sir," I said to the clerk as I approached the desk.

"How may I be of help to you sir?" he inquired politely.

"I was wondering if the hotel would be willing to accept messages for me."

"Are you a guest here?" he asked.

"To be honest my good man, I am not, but I am staying with a friend, and I needed a place close by to accept messages."

"Your friend's house would not be one of those along the docks that charge fifteen cents a night by any chance?" he smirked. For a moment I reflected on the fact that I could have saved ten cents if I had looked a bit longer for a room, then I searched my mind for an appropriate answer to his query. Before I could say anything, the clerk said kindly, "Relax my good man," obviously mimicking my use of the phrase. "Times are always hard for the working man. I'll be glad to take care of your needs according to your story. I have had to use many a ruse myself. For instance, my name is Randall Speers here in Sandusky, but back in Russia my mother would know me only as Yakup Ostrovich, which is my Jewish-Russian name."

"Well, your background does not disturb me," I answered. "Western civilization owes much to the people of the Torah. Only the ignorant do not recognize the accomplishments of the Jewish people, especially under the difficult circumstances of having no homeland." I realized I was "spreading it on too thick" trying to gain Randall's help by complementing his ancestry.

Randall let out a good laugh. "I believe you are a man of intelligence and you have no further need to impress me. I now know your secret as you now know mine."

I was puzzled by this last statement but figured he was referring to revealing his ancestry to me while I informed him that I falsely told someone else I was staying at the hotel. I gave Randall my name, and in return he said the hotel would accept messages. Randall put the paper in his pocket and said, "I will buy you a drink and maybe even dinner at the place down the alley from Jones Tavern on Perkins Avenue. I will be there five minutes after seven o'clock tonight. Again, that is down the alley next to Jones Tavern. "

I didn't know what to say. Why would a clerk invite me to dinner? It was so unexpected that I accepted his invitation, because I didn't know what else to say. He seemed quite cultured and maybe was starved for an intellectual conversation. After a moment I felt pleased that I could make such an impression, and I shook his hand and walked back to the SM&N office to tell Miss Marchant the lie that I was staying at the West House. Next, I went to the telegraph office to inform the Clyde station I would be late to work the next day. By then, it was almost five o'clock and I was wishing that I was going to dinner with Miss Marchant instead of having a drink with Randall. But I was smart enough to know this was no time to mix work and romance.

I found the Jones Tavern, which was most inviting with quite a few people inside laughing and having a good time. I walked cautiously down the alley next to the tavern towards a single light from a crude lantern hanging on the wall. I felt uncomfortable, as I always had in alleys since I looked down the barrel of Billy's gun in that alley in Nashville. I had the odd feeling that this was another dark passage to trouble. Why on earth did Randall choose this place instead of the tavern on the street? There was no sign on the door, and it was locked. I rapped on the door and it opened a crack. A voice from within asked me my business. I told him I was there to see Randall Speers, and with that the door opened wide and I was welcomed inside. It was almost 5:30, and I saw that Randall was already seated alone at a table. He stood to greet me and welcomed me to sit. After a few minutes of small talk about the weather and Sandusky, I looked around the place. Across the room I saw none other than Miss Marchant sitting at a table with another woman. In fact all three of the tables on that side of the room were occupied by women and all the tables near Randall and I were occupied by men. "Randall," I said, "there is no place in Clyde where women congregate to drink, and if there was, all the men would be trying to get their attention, including myself. Do you think we could invite Miss Marchant and her friend to join us? To be honest, I find her quite attractive."

Randall gave me a very strange look and after what seemed to be a very long time, he said, "There is a terrible mix up here. Why did you not deny staying by the docks for fifteen cents?"

I answered, "Why should I, it is my business where I choose to stay."

"The fifteen cent rooms by the docks are for one purpose only as I figured you damn well knew." He took another long look at me and said, "You really don't know what is going on, do you? You didn't know that the reference to fifteen cent rooms by the docks was a code. This would be laughable, if it weren't for the fact that I betrayed the trust of.... Say, you're not a copper are you?"

I was disturbed and responded defensively by saying, "I don't have any idea what you are talking about or what this place is about. I think I better leave."

"Nite, let me put it this way to you. Miss Marchant does not like men and I don't like women, just as you have eyes for Miss Marchant and not for me."

I understood him clearly at this point and chose my words carefully. "I know there are people who are either psychologically troubled or do not know right from wrong and thus prefer their own kind."

Randall cut me off and snapped back, "And so you think we choose to be this way. Well, I don't. I would like to walk around town not keeping hidden what God made me. No one chooses this life. I have no psychological problem, but you and the other fine citizens of this country have a serious problem. Go ahead and categorize the people here if it makes you feel better, but I'm sure if I looked hard enough I'd find plenty that you are hiding."

I was shaken by these words and for a moment I thought about Professor Pennington's lessons about tolerance. I believed I was tolerant, but I was not prepared for this moment and could not accept homosexuality as normal or morally right. I felt frightened, maybe even more than when I was in the war. I thought I knew about everything and I had heard about homosexuals, but I never imagined I would meet one, let alone be in a place that specifically catered to their kind as if it was normal. Then I began to fear that I had been seen entering this place, and became alarmed by the presence of the person I was sitting across the table from, for I did not know what he would do next. I knew what I had to do. I told Randall I had to leave, and I got up and stumbled for the door. I glanced back to see Randall looking down at the table.

I headed down the alley to where it intersected with the street, and looked in all directions to make sure no one was about. I walked quickly back to the boarding house, feeling dirty, and wondering if I should check out and start back for home. But at this hour, the only way back would be to walk, and it was too cold for that.

All night I tossed and turned. I was afraid of seeing Randall on the street if I should live and work in Sandusky. And how could I possibly work with Miss Marchant? At other times I thought that both Randall and Miss Marchant seemed like intelligent and reasonable people. I also started remembering about burying Owen all those years ago. I started questioning his story of being in the Yankee prison. Something was not right about his story, such as the other prisoners hating him for being assaulted. And why did he leave the security of his mother's home after his release? Would his mother, a respectable Southern woman, openly carry on with a Union officer that soon after the end of the war? If Owen was a homosexual, then what did it mean that I held him in my arms the night he died?

I realized such thoughts and worries were a waste of time. Just because I may have associated with homosexuals did not mean I was one of them. I never thought about men. Yet I had been Owen's friend, maybe his only one. Did it make any difference if he was homosexual or not? It felt very strange thinking that maybe it was normal for some people to be that way. Once again, I was learning the hard way about how little I knew. I once thought I could live the life of a scholar. Instead I again proved myself a fool.

I never did find peace that night. I finally fell asleep only to be haunted by crazy dreams. The one I remember best was showing up in the morning at the SM&N office naked. Apparently, I had forgotten to dress in the morning, and I was totally exposed to the world. At that point, a rap on the door woke me up. A woman said, "Mr. Nite, it is nearly nine in the morning. This is your last chance to come have some breakfast."

"Yes, ma'am," I answered, "I will not be eating this morning, thank you. I will be down in a short time to check out."

"Suit yourself," was all she said. After she departed, I realized I was no longer dreaming and began to have paranoid thoughts that the woman knew where I was last night. It was a ridiculous thought, but it again had me wondering what to do. Should I just leave town, or still see about a job with the interurban railroad?

I shook with fear as I walked to the SM&N office. I decided I better go, or Mr. Coen and Avery would be suspicious and maybe look into my activities of the prior night. On the other hand, I would have to face Miss Marchant, and I had no idea what she might say or do. Shouldn't she be the one to be afraid, I asked myself, for I was the normal one? I had no idea what she now thought of me, for I had no idea how the abnormal mind of a homosexual worked. I arrived at the office and hesitantly turned the door knob. There was Miss Marchant at her desk just as she was the day before. She spoke first. "I trust you had an interesting evening in our fair town, Mr. Nite. I gave a message to Mr. Speers, but he said you rose and left the hotel quite early. So I held on to this telegram, hoping you were still in Sandusky. Mr. Speers wanted me to tell you that our good town could benefit from a man with your abilities, and he wanted to again express the hotel's apology for the mix-up last night concerning giving you the wrong key. He hoped you would be able to judge our town favorably in spite of that incident and it could be forgotten." She then handed me the telegram and said Mr. Avery would meet me at 1 p.m. when he returned to the office. The telegram read:

Avery—STOP—I do remember Mr. Nite—STOP—My gut feeling is that he is the kind of man we could use—STOP—Recommendation is that you find him something that needs fixing—STOP—I think you understand—STOP—Coen.

I stood there dumbfounded before Miss Marchant. Then she spoke up. "Mr. Nite, neither Randall nor I saw you last night, if you know what I mean. The only thing I am asking is that you too never saw me last night. If you cannot agree with this, then so be it. I will pack up my belongings and move on to another place. I have done it plenty of times before, and I will land on my feet because everyone needs a good secretary. Randall has more to lose, but you must follow your conscience. As a girl growing up not far from here, I heard many stories about slaves trying to escape through Sandusky by catching boats to Canada. Some helped hide slaves, some declared it was against the law, and others were too afraid to help. Then there were those who could not make up their mind about what was right. Who of that group do you think I despised the most?" Without waiting for a reply, she answered herself, "None of them, for we are all slaves either because of the color of our skin, the gender we are attracted to, or our own thoughts, which may be the greatest enslavement of all. So whatever you decide is fine, but I think you should take a job here, for Mr. Coen is not impressed easily and if he remembers you after a year's time, I am sure he also checked into your background and was pleased. What needs fixing are the stations in the area. They have no supervision and need to be brought up to proper standards."

I wanted to tell her I could maybe help her and Randall find some way to change, but her words were so powerful that all I could do was agree that I had not seen her or him the night before. With that I left the office and walked the streets until my appointment with Mr. Avery at one o'clock. The weather had warmed considerably, and when I looked out upon the lake all the ice was gone.

The Northern Shore

Some folks, who make their living on the docks, call the Great Lakes the Northern Shore. Everyone knows that the east and west coasts mark the borders of the United States. Only a few brave souls venture out from there on ships that may or may not again see land. So too, the shores of the Great Lakes mark a boundary of water for the country. Although it is a short distance to Canada by boat, a traveler will lose sight of land and can be caught by the surprise of a sudden storm. The bottoms of the lakes are littered with ships that failed to reach their destination.

Just as cities and towns had been established on the ocean coasts, population centers abounded on the Great Lakes because of the advantage of transportation by water. Goods such as iron ore, lumber, and wheat are delivered by huge ships into large ports like Chicago, Detroit, Cleveland, and Buffalo, as well as into smaller ports, like Ohio's Toledo, Ashtabula, Lorain, and where I found myself living and working in 1897, the city of Sandusky. Once an important Indian trading post, Sandusky became a sought-after prize by the French, the English, and the Americans. Sandusky promised protection from violent storms because of its large bay nearly enclosed by the Catawba Peninsula. It remained an important transportation hub at the end of the nineteenth century not only for water travel, but also as a terminus for land travel.

The latter was the reason I was in Sandusky. I had been hired as a station inspector for the Sandusky, Milan, and Norfolk Electric Railroad. It was not a powerful position, but it was important for the stations had to be properly maintained for passenger safety and convenience. My job was to check on large stations as well as those that were nothing more than a sign next to the tracks. The best part of my job was riding the interurban cars between stations. I loved the power and the speed, especially out in the country where speeding past trees, meadows, and plowed land offered a new perspective of rural America. Every experience was compressed in time. A slow meandering creek might be crossed in a few minutes as a fast flowing brook, and then soon after that as a river of commerce emptying into Lake Erie. The night skies, however, remained the same at any earthly speed, and in this case it was the speed that could take one from city to country on a clear night that was special. Out in the country, one could get lost and forget the struggles of life while observing a full sky of bright stars unimpeded by the lights of the city. Speed could equally provide the excitement of challenge. During the day we would occasionally speed past carriages and wagons on dirt roads being led by clip-clopping horses. Once in a while, a rider on horseback would try and race us, not to be left in the dust, but instead by the smell of oil spewing through the electric motors of the trolley car.

Avery (I never did learn his first name) was my boss. He was an okay fellow, but always seemed nervous and very hesitant about making decisions. He told me that he expected Frederick Coen would be returning and be in charge. This prediction became somewhat true in a couple of years when the SM&N was sold to a new owner, and Fred Coen visited every once in a while, indicating that the Everett-Moore group of Cleveland was at work behind the scenes. The word was that eventually there would be one large interurban railway serving the area. This would be accomplished by incorporating several small railways into one large system to be called the "Lake Shore Electric Railway." The goal was to connect Cleveland and Toledo and all the points in between.

Little change occurred, however, and SM&N continued normal operations. We maintained our small local office with the main office and car barns housed in the Milan and Norwalk area. Occasionally Fred Coen would stop in to see Avery, and he always made it a point to also talk to me. He liked my suggestions and it appeared I might have a bright future if Coen's star should continue to rise.

I continued to travel the line making sure all trolley stops were kept in good operating fashion and helped plan the location and services of future stations. The larger stations were much like the Clyde Train Station in that tickets were sold and baggage organized for storage in the cars. Special baggage cars had to be occasionally coupled at stations to move local freight. When I started work for the SM&N, there were three stations on the Sandusky, Milan, and Norwalk line, and numerous outside stops along the tracks marked only by signs on posts. I came up with the idea to put simple wooden shelters at these stops and post the schedules on the walls behind glass. Avery thought it a waste of time, but I kept pushing the idea. Eventually, I told Fred Coen, and in no time construction of the wooden shelters began. Soon, perhaps realizing his time with the company was coming to an end, Avery left his job, and Coen told me that he recommended to the owners that I take Avery's place. I could hardly contain my excitement and said "yes" when the job was formally offered to me.

I proudly walked into the office my first day as manager, only to find no one there. The rooms were empty except for the two desks, a few papers on Avery's vacated desk, and that damn railroad calendar on the wall. On top of the papers was a note:

> Due to an opportunity in Cleveland, I am forced to give my two-week notice of resignation effective today. Respectfully, Miss Anne Marchant. P.S. I will be in late today for I need to begin making arrangements for my relocation.

I felt terrible. It was not so much that I would miss her help handling all the directives coming out of Norwalk and Cleveland, but instead it was the reason she was quitting. She entered the office at about eleven o'clock. Without saying hello, I said to her that it was not necessary that she resign. "I am afraid it is Sir," she responded. "You're just too good and too naïve. Avery was no worry because I knew plenty about him. On you I have nothing, but you have everything on me. Even worse, you go out of your way to be nice. You think I have a problem and you are going to help. I have a problem for sure, and it is not of my doing. It is a problem of this stinking world. Working for you will just become more and more a reminder of that lousy fact. So, no offense, go ahead and try to do some good and help solve the problems of this world, but I'm sorry, it is not going to be at my expense."

I quietly walked back to my office. Was her being nice to me before this day an act? Why was I trying to be a good person and help others out? At that moment I felt tired of caring about others. For that matter, I felt tired of looking for truth in this "stinking world" as Anne Marchant called it. I sat down at my desk and wrote a letter accepting her resignation. In it I stated that if she wanted to leave immediately that was fine by me. She accepted my offer and was gone within the hour. For the rest of the day I sat there feeling miserable. Why should this be? I was the normal one. All I did was try to help her.

I spent two more weeks in that office occasionally scribbling down ideas to improve the business. Then I told Mr. Coen I would prefer to have my old job back. He made a special trip all the way from Cleveland to ask me why. All I could think to tell him was that I could not stay in a room alone all day and be productive. I missed riding the rails, and I was not up to the challenge of management. Fred Coen, who believed strongly that business and enterprise were the pillars of America, could not understand why I felt the way I did. His job was his life, but I had never found a job worth my total dedication. Coen enjoyed a sense of accomplishment whenever the company laid down one more rail, and I suppose that gave meaning to his life. As for me, I was chasing something that no one has ever caught. I wanted to know the purpose of my life, and you just can't catch something of meaning, if that meaning does not exist in human terms. I was an unsatisfied dreamer. Everything had to be just right, and the dose of reality administered to me by Miss Marchant killed my latest dream more quickly than a bullet shot from a gun.

Frederick Coen reluctantly arranged everything with the owners, and I was back at my old job as Station Inspector. I settled into a regular work routine and the weeks, months, and years began to roll by. Soon it was January of 1899 and I was not far from the age of fifty. Not all was bad. I enjoyed the freedom of working on my own away from the office, and I made enough money to cover my few expenses. On the negative side, I did nothing but work and spend my off time reading. But now I no longer read books of science, literature, or history, but instead cheap dime novels, the local newspapers, and occasionally sporting papers about current play in the professional baseball leagues. I figured I would die in my room alone and miserable. Then something happened that jolted me back to life on a cold, clear winter evening as the sun was setting over the lake. Before I walked home, I picked up a newspaper at the station stop on Perkins Avenue. As I glanced at the front page I noticed a small story about a man being badly beaten and near death in the Sandusky Hospital. There was nothing unusual about such a story, because when ships were in the harbor, Sandusky was a rough port town with all types of men on the streets. Life as a seaman was dangerous and hard work, and a night in port usually involved drinking, which could easily result in fighting. This time, however, I knew the name of the beaten man in the hospital. It was Randall Speers. I occasionally saw Randall on the streets and would nod my head uncomfortably or reluctantly breathe a soft hello. When I read the news, I felt terrible for having never greeted him as I would a friend.

I knew I had to go see him, if for no other reason than to say I was sorry for being so distant. The next day I entered the small hospital when I finished work at 6 o'clock. I was not prepared, as I entered the room, for what I saw. Randall's face was unrecognizably swollen from repeated kicks to his head. His legs were broken, his torso wrapped in bandages that were sweating blood. He could barely breathe. Yet he immediately recognized me. In a struggling voice he said, "Samuel Nite, I knew you were a good man. Please try and understand that I am a good man too."

"I never thought you were a bad man Randall. I just can't understand your life and that scares me. I am afraid because I always believed that without understanding there is no hope."

"You try too hard Samuel. There is no book or words that can tell you why things are the way they are." In an odd sort of way his words gave me hope, even though I was watching a human being slowly die. For the second time in my life I felt compelled to hold another human being in my arms for an entire night as their life ebbed away. In the early morning, I walked out of the room and informed the nurse that Randall had passed away. I went out in front of the building and looked up. The sky was clear over the lake, and there were stars above. But as I moved my eyes downward, I also saw lights on the lake where boats were passing. Eventually, the lights would pass into complete darkness. I thought about the phrase I used to tell the nurse that Randall had died: "Passed away." What an odd description of death. One makes passage from a known point to another known point. By morning the boats would be in Cleveland or some other lake port. I could travel to one of those ports and prove this fact. As with the boats, we say

Randall, too, passed to somewhere else. Unlike the boats, however, no one on earth can travel to that place. We cannot prove that the place even exists. Passage is an earthly term.

A nurse from the hospital made me jump when she shouted from the front steps, "Sir, may I see you for a moment?" She asked me how well I knew Randall and mentioned that no one else came to see him, not even others who worked at the hotel. No one seemed to know anything about him. She asked if I could take responsibility for the body.

"I'm afraid I can't. I only knew him because once, when I was a stranger in town, he offered to buy me dinner. I didn't have dinner with him and from that point on he was a casual stranger. I do know this—he was a good normal man." Then I said something that must have struck the nurse as being very odd, but at that moment I didn't care. "You know, Miss, I once thought they never had slavery in Ohio. I'm truly sorry that I do not know anything about Randall that can be of help for I was truly a stranger to him." She did not say anything, so I said, "Good evening," and walked away.

For January it was a warm night; the temperature felt to be about forty. So I kept walking until the sun came up. I then quickly walked to my room and fell asleep. The next thing I remembered was a loud knock on the door. I figured it was someone coming to wake me because I was late for work. Then I heard the words that one dreads to hear. "Police officer, open up!"

"Could you please wait until I get dressed; it will not be long," I answered, hoping it was about a routine matter. I thought I had nothing to fear because I had not done anything against the law. I again hollered, "I'll be ready in a moment."

Then the door was kicked in and apparently not well. "My damn foot!" yelled the officer. I stood there flabbergasted. "Turn around and put your hands behind your back!" I was scared at this point and quickly did as I was told. The policeman shackled my hands with iron cuffs and grabbed the back end of my trousers, jerking the pants up my legs, cursing the whole time about his foot. My shirt was already on and I fumbled to put my boots on as he directed. Then, he roughly led me out into the street in silence. The skies were now cloudy and the temperature was dropping as it began to snow. A handful of bystanders gazed at the spectacle of it all, and I felt totally humiliated as I was led off in chains. As we reached the corner of First Street and Meigs, I asked the officer to tell me what I had done and where we were going. "You knew Randall Speers, did you not?"

"Yes," I answered. "I was with him when he died last night."

"Is that so?"

"Yes, I went to visit him."

"Save your story for the judge," and then he tried to kick me with his good foot. I saw it coming and just moved far enough away for him to miss and slip on the thin layer of snow on the ground. He fell down and landed with a thump followed by a yell of pain. The crowd of spectators snickered. For a second I thought to run, but I knew it was no use, being in irons and all. The policeman was back on his feet grumbling, "You bloody queer," and he smacked me hard in the back, on the neck, and across the face with his night stick. The rest of the walk to the station was spent with me being pummeled with the stick and shoved, all to the continued laughter of the crowd that was now following us down the street. I could barely walk once we arrived at the police station and was forced to stand at a desk while I was booked for murder. After a horrible spell of being asked questions, followed by a smack when they did not like one of my answers, I was taken back to a room containing exactly eight ten-by-ten cells. "Put him in with the nigger," said the constable back in the cell room.

"There ain't a whole lot of difference between a homo and a monkey," one of them said, followed by a chorus of rough laughter.

The Negro helped me to the one cot in the cell. "You are hurt bad, why did they beat you so?" The best I could, I answered that the officer hurt his foot and took it out on me. "Well, you just go ahead and sleep now, I'll be here when you wake up." I did as he said.

"There now, I was afraid you were not going to wake up," said a voice I remotely remembered. "You have been out since about this time yesterday." Sunlight was streaming in through the cell window. I started to remember what happened and where I was. There was dried blood all over my clothes and I had several oozing wounds. "Do you want to just sleep some more? Go ahead; I don't mind lying on the floor." I answered no, for I feared that I might not wake up again if I slept. The man helped me sit up.

"Please talk to me," I said. "I must stay conscious."

"Okay," he answered as he paused a moment apparently thinking about what to say. Then he spoke. "My name is Douglas Frederick Brown, might I ask your name?"

"Samuel Nite," I struggled to answer.

"You will be okay Mr. Nite. They have no evidence that you committed the murder. You and I are the fourth and fifth men they have brought in. In my case I was walking down the street for the first time in this fair city, which has not proven so fair to me."

For some reason I was at ease with this stranger. Slowly and painfully I told him about the events leading up to my being held in the cell. I even told him about Randall's club in the alley, because deep in my heart I did not consider him an equal because of his skin color. I believed I had nothing to fear from what he, a Negro, knew about me. Later, I was ashamed that I still innately felt whites were superior to Negroes. It was soon obvious to me that Douglas was superior to me in education and spoke with a confidence that I lacked. After discussing my reason for being in the jail, I asked him, "Are you not scared you will be blamed for this murder?"

"My friend, if I feared being accused of something that I did not do, then I would be scared all the time. I am here now with you for some mysterious reason, yet it is for a good reason, I am sure. Let us make good use of this time together, for I am confident we will be out of here soon and I will again be on the move. They are just fishing."

"Moving where?" I asked.

"Same direction as always, north."

My laughter made my bruised body ache, but I still responded for I liked this man and so I continued to ask him questions. "If I, a white man, have not found freedom of mind and spirit here in the North, what in God's name are you hoping to find north of here, especially with nothing but water as far as you can see?"

Douglas looked at me in a funny way, like my question was ridiculous, and then blurted out, on a whole new train of thought, "I am a preacher of sorts. Here, take one of my pamphlets."

The front page of the pamphlet read in big letters, "TEN SUGGESTIONS FOR FINDING YOUR OWN RELIGION BY DR. DOUGLAS FREDERICK BROWN." Inside, preceded by numbers, were ten statements, or what Douglas liked to refer to as the

Non-Commandments. They were:

1. Be willing to engage members of established religions in polite conversation. They may share with you some powerful insights. However, do not allow them to convince you that their religion and theirs alone has the correct doctrines and practices.

2. Avoid easy paths that place the responsibility for your salvation on accepting the teachings of an historical personage. You may learn from both past and present teachers, but no one can reveal the truth through the words and languages of man.

3. Be thankful for scholars, historians, and other learned men who clarify the mistranslations and misinterpretations of words and knowledge. But, do not fall into the trap of holding such men as superior and more intelligent than yourself or others.

4. Find your own religion. Accept no converts. Tell others to find and travel their own path.

5. Do not base your religion on finding happiness. Instead, have courage to face the only possible conclusion of human life—death.

6. Say goodbye to all guilt thrust upon you. Guilt depends on fear like the existence of Hell. Hell does exist, for you are already in it. You are also already in Heaven. Heaven and Hell in the afterlife are human inventions. Ignore talk of their existence.

7. Love, compassion, selfishness, and pain are mysterious aspects of truth. They can enrich your spirit and just as easily lead to destruction. Love and compassion must lead to sorrow for those who you bestow it upon must die like you. Thus, one may choose to ignore them and lead a life of self-pleasure, and indeed be happy; that is until one is near death. Then one will experience loneliness equal to a lifetime of sorrow.

8. Redemption does not come by saving others from pain and death. Free a hog from the slaughter house and it will be torn apart in the wild. Give a beggar a penny and it will add a penny's worth of time for more suffering. Save a life and that life may result in the death of others. Yet, we must strive to be kind for kindness is appreciated on every path when given free of cost.

9. Be free of easy answers. Remember that true faith believes in meaning, even though you cannot possibly know the meaning of life. Those who say they know, need faith not, for they know and thus

do not need faith. Do not let them impose their knowledge on you. Instead go bravely into the world and create your own religion and be sure that it is your religion alone and it will die when you die.

10. Disregard the previous ten tenets except for what you may find useful to help you probe for wisdom in the mystery of life.

I had never read anything like this before. The writer was either a genius or an idiot. And a Black man could only get in trouble for possessing such ideas. "What is this all about?" I asked him.

"Why, I wrote it during my six years at Oberlin College studying philosophy. What you just read was accepted as my thesis for graduation."

"You are Dr. Brown and you had this accepted as your thesis when it simply proposes that one find their own religion. Why, that is ridiculous. It appears like you don't believe in anything. And besides, a thesis cannot be merely two or three pages long."

"On the contrary, Mr. Nite. First of all, is not poetry the most powerful form of writing and yet most compact? I spent much time in order to succinctly state my views on religion and true faith." There was a long pause between us before Douglas spoke again, "I also believe everything has a purpose. I believe finding ourselves in this place together to be no accident. But I cannot tell you why and you cannot tell me either. Yet, there is a reason, maybe a different one for each of us, but a reason sure enough that the two of our lives have intersected at this point in time. Nothing in the evolution of life is a wasted moment. Have you never thought of such things?"

"No, things just turn out the way they turn out," I said. "I am going to lie down on this cot and sleep. Please do not bother me with any more of your ridiculous talk."

"You may be right my friend," said Douglas. "You know, however, that two opposites can co-exist and both be true. In other words, I believe there is some luck and there does exist a random happening of events; however, everything that happens does so at an unavoidable intersection where time, matter, intelligence, and spirituality all meet. Evolution is not just physical, but also applies to what one feels, sees, and believes. Think about that. Nothing connects by accident, nothing."

As much as I didn't want to engage in a philosophical discussion, I could not help but respond to this last remark. "First, how can luck co-exist with the fact that nothing happens by accident. And second, Darwin's Theory of Evolution, as I understand it, involves the weak dying off. I see no spiritual factor in that."

"The physical does not die off but evolves into a different form," he answered. "The ashes or dust of all who have lived still exists and so does the spiritual essence of everything that was once what we call alive. Nothing is static and everything down to each minute thought still exists. As for luck, didn't you ever hear the phrase "Luck is what you make it."

I was totally confused and could only respond by saying, "You are a preacher, and you preach quite a bit for one who believes that everyone should have their own personal religion."

"That is how I preach, for I have no words to tell you that make perfect sense, for nothing does. You cannot prove concepts like luck and determination, but you may believe in one or the other and that can be part of your own religion. Everyone does have their own religion. Some of us choose to ignore that fact while others of us practice it with purpose so that their being evolves in a beneficial way. From the things you have spoken in your sleep the last 24 hours, I know that you work on your faith."

Instead of asking him what I said in my sleep, I lay down to sleep some more for I did not want to work on my "religion" any more; I wanted to forget. But I could not fall asleep and I still feared that sleep would bring death as I had experienced with Owen and Randall. Instead, I thought about Douglas talking about Darwin's Theory of Relativity as if it was a religion as opposed to scientific belief. The rest of the country, for the most part, saw it as either anti-religious, akin to atheism, or even the act of the devil. Why even the great William Jennings Bryant had said as much.

I finally fell into a half-sleep where I was somewhere between consciousness and sleep. I was again in the Clyde Cemetery with Red, and I thought about all the variables that had to happen for us to be there at that time, at that moment, or was it this moment. No I thought, this really happened, but I could not remember where in the frame of time it actually occurred. Then I felt a power or force calling to me, telling me that I was meant to be where I was at any given moment, and everyone I met was also at that same point for a reason. I even realized there was a reason I had met the police officer who kicked me with an incredible hate when I did not even know the man. Out of nowhere, despite my lack of religious faith, I saw Christ on the cross accepting the necessity of His ordeal as strangers jeered and mocked Him. The scene changed to Socrates calmly drinking hemlock as ordered by those in authority. "There was a reason for it all," shouted a voice, but I somehow understood that the reason could never be explained in words, and humans did not have the choice to either accept truth or deny it, for it was not meant to be known. Long ago humans chose the desire for insight into the meaning of life or "Knowledge" as it is referred to in the Bible story where Adam and Eve ate fruit from the Tree of Knowledge. "But knowledge is good," I shouted and suddenly I was falling straight down only to be caught.

I was on top of Douglas on the floor. "Relax Sam," he said. "You are okay."

"No," I shouted. "It is not fair for there to be a reason, yet wrong for us to search for it through knowledge." Douglas said nothing, so I pulled away from him and said, "I have had a terrible nightmare."

"From what you were saying in your sleep, I think you were having an experience like those written about in the Bible."

"What do you mean by that?"

"You were wrestling like Jacob did, and you climbed your own ladder to face your own truth. You were twisting back and forth, and you even swore at your angel or devil or some combination of the two. Such a moment is powerful, and that is why the Bible is holy. It speaks the truth, but in the same way as Shakespeare. It is not spoken as people want it. No, they want it like a pledge of allegiance where it is all simple and there are those with the right truth who must fight those with the wrong truth."

Before I could say anything there was commotion in the cell block. A police officer, followed by Mr. Coen and a man dressed in business clothes, had unlocked the heavy outer door and the three men were walking towards our cell. The stranger in the business suit spoke in a harsh but concerned voice, "Look at this man, Frank. He has been beaten. Who was responsible for this uncalled cruelty?"

"It was Officer Musfay who done it Commissioner, yes it was," answered the officer who had led the party to our cell.

The man in the suit looked at me and turned to Mr. Coen. "Fred,

I cannot believe this was done, I can only apologize." Turning back towards me and Douglas he said, "I hope you men do not judge our city by what has transpired here. Our city has a proud heritage of helping strangers. Please don't judge us on these actions." He turned to the policeman named Frank, "And especially don't judge us on the actions of some idiot, who without authority took it upon himself to use violence in the name of the law to unjustifiably beat a man who holds a post with the Sandusky, Milan, and Norwalk Interurban Railroad! Now go deal with this Musfay, Frank, and see to it that he does not wear a badge in Sandusky again!" Frank began to leave, but the commissioner grabbed him by the sleeve and instructed, "Let these innocent men out of this cell first, and arrange an escort to the hospital for this man who was so savagely beaten." With that the commissioner walked out with Mr. Coen.

By the time Douglas and I stepped out in front of the police station, Mr. Coen was waiting there alone. "Are you all right Sam?" he said to me. "I thought they were going to take you to the hospital?"

"No," I answered. "They gave me a note for admittance and treatment. Douglas here is going to accompany me."

"That's good, and I thank you for trying to help Randall. He comes from a fine Jewish family and I tried to help him when I was first here, that is before I went to Cleveland. His father, who himself refused to visit Randall because of his reputation, telegraphed me and told me what happened including your arrest. Early this morning they found an ore boat crewman trying to hawk a ring in a pawn shop. You can figure out whose ring it was. I got here as soon as I could. You go to the hospital now and I will be along later to see you."

Douglas and I walked to the hospital where I was immediately admitted and placed in a private room. Douglas insisted on staying with me. To make conversation, I asked him how he came to Sandusky and how he came to his conclusions about religion and faith.

"I don't know Sam, if I may call you by that name." I nodded in assent. "I just have a feeling for myself that it makes sense. To me true religion is a personal feeling that keeps one going. Now this perception has got me into trouble. People want something solid. They want their religion to be based on indisputable fact. They also believe that one can go to a fine educational institution like Oberlin to learn what is already known and from that place add new discoveries. Yet, when you finish your studies, you find that people, including one's professors, and your father who paid your tuition, do not really want things changed in the fields of religion and philosophy. If you present new ideas that threaten held religious beliefs, there is a price to pay. You know that to be true Sam. It is the same in other subjective studies like sociology and history where new ideas threaten accepted notions about life. By your accent, I detect you are a Southern man, an educated man. You likely attended the university of the Civil War, or at least its aftermath. The whole nation has been to that school. So where are we now? We were both in jail because you made the acquaintance of a homosexual and me because of the color of my skin."

I simply could not take this all in. "Douglas, if I may call you by your given name, how did you come to these views? I have never met a man, especially a Negro, who talks of such things in the way you talk about them."

"I understand Sam. You need a background for the place, the time, and the person you now find yourself with. I'll tell you my story. My grandfather was a slave in Tennessee, a house servant with a rather enlightened master who was alone and childless. The master was married twice. The first wife was unable to give him a child before she died of fever, and a second wife who also failed to give him a child ended up running away. Because he was childless, he decided to share his fatherly instincts with my grandfather who was a house nigger, which was a privilege for a man of my color in those days. Being a house servant instead of a field hand was like working in the accounting office of Andrew Carnegie as opposed to loading coal into one of his furnaces for twelve hours a day. A seeker of knowledge, the master shared what he learned from his readings on science, philosophy, and history with my grandfather. In other words, he treated my grandfather like the white son he never had in terms of education and probably also affection though he kept that part well hidden, especially from any white acquaintances. The relationship came to light only after he died and the provision of his will that freed my grandfather and named him as the plantation manager, but without ownership of the home and the land. He tried to spell this out in the will choosing a nephew to inherit the land if that nephew would agree to the liberal terms he set forth regarding my grandfather. The master's will did not go over well with anyone, and the nephew resented having to treat my grandfather as a near equal. My grandfather's former fellow slaves, who always secretly resented him out of jealousy, now began to openly show hatred, knowing that the nephew had no intention of treating my grandfather as an equal. More important than anything was that the law was not going to recognize the will as a legal document, instead eventually opining that it was a veiled attempt to allow a Black man to have ownership over what was legally a white man's property. Luckily, my grandfather was still allowed his freedom, with the implication that to keep it he should move out of the area, which he wisely did.

"He headed north, first to Southern Indiana, where my grandfather found work in 1842 helping lay track for the Jeffersonville, Madison, and Indianapolis Railroad. He was a proud man and his soft hands and body, as well as his pride, must have suffered hard doing that grueling work. He found a wife, a Black woman who lived as a servant on a farm that the new railroad passed near, and on one of his visits home from railroad work they created together a child. Unfortunately, the mother died giving birth to a son. The boy was left for his first eight years with his maternal grandmother, as my grandfather continued to work on the railroad. Determined to use his education, he started a small school in the newly created railroad town of Seymour, Indiana, in 1852 and brought his son to the town to live. The school was a success. Most people thereabouts were not threatened by the few Negroes living in the area and were just happy to have a learned man to teach their children. Then, in 1856 some slave hunters claimed the rights to a poor Black farmer working about ten miles outside of Seymour. Grandfather went to help the man and was shot dead by the slave catchers. The son, my father, named Socrates Brown, fled Seymour for farther north where he thought he would be safe. He was ten years old.

"He walked dark roads at night prepared to hide in the bushes at the sight of a stranger. He thought he was traveling due north, but in fact was he was moving northeast. Then he was caught stealing food from a farmhouse on the outskirts of Akron. The farmer and his family were Christians and abolitionists and took the boy in, interested in his story. Socrates had landed in the right place. John Brown, the famous abolitionist, had lived in Akron until a year earlier when he left for

Kansas to fight for the anti-slavery forces determined to see Kansas enter the Union as a free state. There were still many abolitionists in Akron who followed the preaching of John Brown, and Socrates was well taken care of by them. He was sent to school with mainly white children, and already equipped with a keen mind and a thirst for learning from his father, quickly advanced so that by the age of thirteen he was an apprentice in a local bank. Then came the war and in 1863 and he left Akron at the age of sixteen for Massachusetts where he heard that Frederick Douglas, the great Negro abolitionist, was actively organizing Negro troops to fight for the Union. He was accepted into the army and fought mainly in Northern Florida. There he became quite ill with influenza and was transported home to die. Somehow he recovered in a soldier's hospital in Akron where he met a Black nurse who became his wife. Socrates went back to his apprenticeship and was soon a bank officer. His wife, Sandra, gave him a girl and a boy in the first two years of their marriage. The girl died at the age of two and the mother lost her will to live and died during an influenza outbreak two years later. Socrates was a strong-minded man and he forged ahead, becoming one of the richest Black men in Akron. He demanded that his son, that would be me, obtain the best education available and sent him to Oberlin for a college degree in the year 1887.

"I advanced quickly with my studies, and to my father's horror, chose to study philosophy instead of a more practical field of study. I developed a rather peculiar religious philosophy as you know from reading my pamphlet. For a few years, I disgraced my father by working on the railroad while I decided what to do with my philosophy degree. Eventually, I formed this fool idea that I could form a church, sort of a church with no doctrines where people could learn to think for themselves. I thought Oberlin would be a good place to start, so I rented a small house outside of town with money my father gave me to establish some type of business, and advertised what some might call a "camp meeting." About 100 people showed up expecting a good old-time revival. About fifteen minutes into my "preaching," as the people chose to call it, I was treated to a cacophony of criticism for delivering godless ideas. I was soon physically pulled from my makeshift stage and chased down the road. I have not stopped running since, as word of my shameful talk has spread from town to town. Here in Sandusky,

I was the perfect suspect for committing an act of murder. Now, that is the whole story, and lucky for you, I am tired of talking, so Samuel get some sleep so that you will feel better.

"What are you going to do, Douglas?" I asked.

"I am going to sit right here and enjoy the shelter of this building."

"No, I mean what is next after today?"

"I'll be doing what my family has always done. I will be heading north. And Sam, you should come with me, for even though your friend Coen apparently has much influence around here, I suspect life will not be easy for you, with one of their own, this police officer named Musfay, losing his job."

"Douglas, there is no north from here other than a huge lake that you can't even see the other side of. This is the end of America. That's Canada on the other side, and you will need papers to get in there."

"Not the way I'm going," answered Douglas.

"You are crazy," I told him. "Where are you going, and why are you going?" Douglas just looked at me and answered my questions in no set order.

"Tomatoes," at first is all he said.

"Well?" I finally asked.

"I would have a hard time as a Black man with my recent trouble obtaining the land here in Ohio to harvest tomatoes, but I have a tip that the land across the lake near the town of Leamington is fantastic for growing tomatoes."

I answered him, "I do not know of anyone who relishes the acidic taste of the tomato."

"Sam, you have to do research and be aware of what is going to be big in the future, and there is going to be a demand for tomatoes to be made into soups and sauces, even beverages."

"You are crazy, but I will admit that you are an amazing man, Douglas."

"Thanks for what I'll take as a vote of confidence," he answered.

I shook my head to a shock of pain, courtesy of one of the strikes of Musfay's stick. After the pain relaxed, I said to Douglas, "You are amazing in mind, but crazy in practicality. I still do not understand how you are going to migrate to Canada with no papers?"

"I will walk."

"You are going to need more than your own religion to walk across Lake Erie."

"That is not true. As you know, the Lake usually freezes over for periods of time during the winter. I have my plan and I have a route. I will make my way from the tip of Catawba Island, which is easily reached from the Catawba Peninsula. From there it is less than three miles to South Bass Island. I will have a three-mile walk to the northeastern tip of that island from which it will be less than a half mile walk across the ice to Middle Bass Island. It is about three miles of land and ice travel from there to North Bass Island, where I will spend the night. I'll need to build a fire and bring blankets and provisions, for it will have to be a very cold day to make sure the lake stays frozen for at least two more days."

"How will you know when there will be three consecutive cold days that meet that requirement?" I asked.

"There is a national weather service as part of the U.S. Signal Service formed for the most part by a man of vision named Cleveland Abbe." In jest, I remarked, "Yes, I did hear something about that," and then I proceeded to tell him how I worked for Mr. Abbe.

"Why Samuel, now I am certain you should come with me."

"We would freeze out there," I answered, "or worse fall through the ice and never be heard from again."

"That's ridiculous," he answered. "Besides, sooner or later all of us are never heard from again. Listen, I have carefully planned this, but your help and weather observation skills would be of great help."

"Douglas, I am not interested in growing anything, let alone tomatoes. I once wanted to work in a vineyard, but now that only brings back sad memories of lost love. I will, however, travel with you as far as the Bass Islands and help make sure the conditions are right and that you set off in the right direction."

"I will accept that help," said Douglas with a huge smile, "for I will need to travel seven miles across the lake and another seven miles to the northern point of Pelee Island to spend the second evening. The third day I must walk nearly ten miles to reach Pelee Point. From there it is all land travel to Leamington, and there I will buy my land."

"How will you buy the land?"

"The land is now inexpensive and I can buy it with the little money

I still have from my father, but I must go soon for I will need every last penny I have and there is no telling when the land costs will go up. I have a deal with someone to buy land without citizenship papers. Once I can prove I purchased the land it will be no problem getting citizenship papers from the Canadian government."

"How do you know all this, and how do you know people up there?"

"You forget, many Negroes found safety in Canada before the Civil War, and my grandfather knew many of them. Contacts were kept." I could believe this, but I wondered why Douglas could not find an easier way to migrate to Canada. Maybe his arrest record would be a problem, maybe there were other incidents in his past, but whatever the case I decided to ask no more questions and again agreed to help him start off in the right direction.

The next couple of weeks I hid Douglas in my room on the first floor. In the evening I would sneak him through the window and made sure he was out early in the morning. During the week of February 5th 1899 it became very cold. It was reported on February 10th that at one spot in Ohio the temperature reached minus 39 degrees, which set a record for the lowest temperature in the state. Douglas declared that we must leave the following day, a Saturday, after I finished work. The timing was right, for I was off on Sunday. It would be good to travel, for it was nearly impossible to keep my first floor room warm, and more than anything, the lake was frozen solid.

That Saturday night it was miserable trekking across the bay and making our way to a place called Catawba Point. There we found an abandoned shack and spent the night huddled around a fire we were able to make after much difficulty. Dawn finally arrived with a view over an expanse of white in all directions, including the ice between us and South Bass Island. To our surprise there were men already on the lake in makeshift huts ice fishing, a means of getting food in the winter by drilling a hole in the ice to catch pike and perch that swam below.

We threw the last log on the fire and cooked some bacon Douglas brought. It was our last chance to talk. Douglas took the opportunity to offer some last thoughts on life. "Try and be restful of mind, Samuel," as he more and more called me instead of Sam. "Remember our talk about knowledge. Knowledge seems to be a good thing, and it may be to a certain extent. Knowledge is power, but the ruthless pursue it for the wrong reasons, and this is what has brought the world to the sad state it is in. People use knowledge to feel superior to others, and once they feel so, they have no problem in destroying other people's lives. The father of the woman you loved had you beaten because he felt he had the right because of his superior knowledge. Now, I am going to tell you something that I very well could be killed for in certain quarters. God the Father of the Bible represents all encompassing knowledge, and he demanded that His people take other people's land and lives. All through history we have had father figures called kings, lords, plantation owners, and Captains of industry exerting their rights because they claim superior knowledge. Christianity was supposed to defeat this hunger for ultimate knowledge. Adam and Eve could not resist it and neither could the Israelites as they killed off the Canaanites and created their brief period of glory. Then came Jesus Christ who conquered the hunger for knowledge and power by not leading the people back to the power of King David, but instead taught acceptance of the one known truth on earth, that we must all experience misery and eventually die. If you accept that ultimate knowledge is unattainable and that death is certain, yet have faith that there is meaning to life, you have a chance at true happiness. Don't struggle for knowledge that leads to conflict with those who believe they have knowledge. I am not telling this to you as one who knows the truth for I sin many times by searching for knowledge to get ahead. And, the phrase "getting ahead" clearly implies that doing so will be at another's expense. I tell you this because you genuinely care about others, I will remember you with kindness forever. I have done all the talking, but you have done the teaching. Now that is enough of my Sunday morning preaching. Shake my hand and see me off."

We got Douglas's gear together. I made him promise to write, and he slowly disappeared out onto the ice, making his way to South Bass Island. Some tears froze on my eyelashes as I turned to walk back to Sandusky. I walked at a slow pace and found myself on the ice of Sandusky Bay when night arrived. There were no stars in the sky, but the lights of the city showed me the way. Normally, I would have been terrified in such a situation, but this time, I felt happy and at peace with my life in the present.

CEYLON JUNCTION

Safely back in my room, I crawled under as many blankets as I could and quickly fell asleep from exhaustion. I woke up early the next morning, and my first thought was whether or not the events of the last couple of days were real. Did I actually watch Douglas head off across a frozen Lake Erie on foot? As I walked to work, I concluded it was true, and I asked myself how I could allow a friend to undertake such a dangerous trip alone. I worried about Douglas the next few days and hoped I would receive some word that he was safe in Canada. Such a message never arrived.

The month of February 1899 was not only very cold in the north but set record cold temperatures as far south as Florida. I remember seeing a photograph of a snowball fight on the steps of the Florida Statehouse in Tallahassee. The dirty snow began to pile up everywhere, and the euphoria of the moment when Douglas and I separated soon turned to lasting doubt and depression. Everywhere I looked in Sandusky, whether it was the dirty factory walls, the muddy streets, or the advertisements in the business district, I was reminded of mankind's pitiful attempt to give order and permanence to the changing and unpredictable world.

Musfay was not fired from the police force but instead served a short suspension and was back walking his beat. To many, he was a hero for trying to clear the town of homosexuals, while I was a villain for having associated with them. Musfay was greeted with smiles; I was greeted with looks of disgust. The odd thing was that Musfay seemed changed. Now, he would nod at me on the streets, a gesture that indicated he was genuinely sorry for what he had done. I wanted none of it because my heart was filled with hate and anger that extended to just about everyone and everything in Sandusky. Soon, my feelings grew to encompass the entire country. Since the Civil War, a new system of slavery had been established in America. Industrialists worth millions of dollars employed workers who toiled twelve hours a day six days a week for twelve cents an hour. I had the luxury to think about this injustice because I had the fortune to work for a rural streetcar line away from the inhumanity of the factories, slaughterhouses, and coal mines.

There was a new war of independence being fought. The battles had names like Homestead and Pullman and they were fought between striking workers demanding decent wages and the business owners who felt they had the right to run their businesses as they saw fit. The latter believed they earned their position of ownership and were under no obligation to workers who could leave if they didn't like their treatment. The truth was that the unskilled workers had nowhere else to go to make money to feed themselves and their families. It depressed me to see so many men walking the streets, unable to survive without work and unable to adjust to the inhumanity of work when they could find employment. In coal mining communities, coal barons owned the stores, gladly extending credit so that the miners became indebted servants. In this manner, the free enterprise system created a new type of royalty with the same old story of the few dictating to the many. On the whole, most people believed this was the only workable system. I had heard the same argument growing up in Virginia concerning slavery, which stated that the slaves needed someone to take care of them, and they should be thankful to the few, who kept them clothed, fed, and sheltered. To the powerful, this was the way God had planned it and so be it. As always, religious doctrines were adjusted to support the status quo.

The powerful won the battles of the labor wars of the 1890s with guns and money. Labor lost in the streets and on company property, but just as important, they lost in the political arena as evidenced by the presidential races of 1896 and 1900. William McKinley defeated reform candidate William Jennings Bryan both times because big business used their money to "educate" people that they would lose their jobs if Bryan won and implemented his reform ideas. I was certain these lies would eventually tear our country apart and thrust us into violent class wars like those seen in Europe. It was inevitable as the gap between the rich and the poor grew wider and wider.

However, America still possessed patriotic fervor, and the people willingly marched off to fight in another war. It was 1899, only 34 years after the bloody Civil War ended, when we fought the Spanish, not because they posed a threat to us, but to expand our power and join the elite colonial nations of Europe. Victory over the once proud Spanish empire came easily, as did McKinley's win in the 1900 presidential election.

I did not understand why poor people would support the war and McKinley. I was disgusted and held little hope for the future. Then, two things happened that renewed my spirit. By accident, Theodore Roosevelt became President of the United States, and I met Thelma. Roosevelt was not supposed to be President. He was a progressive Republican who supported many of labor's demands. The powerful men who represented the interests of the rich were afraid of his popularity, so they placed him in the least powerful political position they could find, the office of Vice President of the United States. What they did not figure on was the assassination of President McKinley. I was happy about the change but not in the fact that it took an act of violence to put a reformer in the White House.

While there was progress and hope in Washington, Sandusky remained a private hell until one evening I was on the Number 12 Car headed home after inspecting the small station at the Soldier's and Sailor's Home. Three stops short of my destination I saw an older woman was struggling, carrying several bags and a cane, trying to exit the streetcar. I just wanted to get home, but I decided someone had to help her. Once we got off the car, she raised her cane at the driver and announced that, "It was about time the trolley system provided help to the elderly." I tried to explain that despite my uniform I was not helping her in an official capacity, but she stopped my words by saying, "Come along. My house is just down the road, and you will be back in time to catch the next car."

Not knowing what to do, I finally waved the driver to move on. I picked up her bags and I followed her down the road. It was dark, and it was cold for October, so I wanted to get this chore over with quickly, but she insisted I enter her house for a cup of tea. I set the bags on a table barely visible in the fading light, and I managed to light her kerosene lamp before it was too dark. She opened the door to a small room that had a small swinging door close to the baseboard. The purpose of the layout was soon apparent as she carried the lamp into the room, for running to her from the door was a small dog and a medium-sized cat.

"Come here Jennings and Bryan," she called. Ignoring me, they both ran to her. "I found these critters when both were about a month old," Thelma explained. "They were left on the streets to fend for themselves. They don't know they are supposed to hate each other. It is a virtue they have, just like you."

"What do you mean by that?" I asked.

"I mean, you damn fool, that I know who you are, and you did the right thing about that boy who died from the beating. And every time I see that Musfay man, I let him know it too. I also see you moping around town. You don't even notice me watching you on the trolley, or on the streets. Stop feeling sorry for yourself! It is only a few idiots acting like you're the fool. There are plenty of us about who know who the real fools are. Sandusky is not all bad."

Finally able to sneak a word in, I said, "I don't see any enlightened souls here."

Thelma raised her cane as if to hit me, and in full voice said, "You are not looking. Where do you spend your spare time? Have you thought of going to any of the church socials, dances held up at the Breakers Hotel, or to the book subscription library readings? Most of all, have you looked around for a way to help others, to do something useful for someone? You still have your health Mr. Nite. Use it!"

I was stunned and felt that I wanted to run from the house and keep running until I could run no more. Before I could act on this thought, Thelma ordered me to sit down and drink the tea she had prepared. I did so and spent two hours answering questions about my life. Thelma listened, occasionally nodding or shaking her head, until about eight o'clock when she told me to leave in order to catch the last streetcar home. As I thanked her and walked towards the door, she said, "I'll be expecting you for dinner at six p.m. sharp on Thursday when we will continue talking. In the meantime, think of something worthwhile to do, something worthy of your talents and experience."

I did as she told me and returned to her house on the correct day at the correct time. She opened the door and started laughing, "Did you see in the paper what Marc Hanna said about Roosevelt?" I knew Marc Hanna was a Cleveland industrialist and campaign manager for the late President McKinley, but I had no idea what he said. She raised her cane at me and in a loud voice said, "You are not even reading the newspaper! You are a young man wasting his life." Then she added, "That damn cowboy is in the White House." Before I could say a thing, she said, "That is what Hanna said."

"Thelma, I turned fifty about a month ago. I am not a young man."

"Nonsense! I am eighty-two and damn lucky to have reached this age. I survived the Sandusky cholera epidemics of '49, '52, and '54. My first husband didn't. Then, my second husband ran off to war just in time to get killed at Cold Harbor. My third husband lasted till 1884 when he went down in a ship trying to make one last run in November of that year. The damn shipping companies should never send a boat out on the lakes as late as November. A huge, unexpected storm claimed more than one boat that night." Returning to the subject of her age, she said, "I have the right to say I am old, but damn if I'll say it. Samuel, it is by the grace of God that you are alive, and I'm sure it is not to waste your time doing nothing."

I liked being called Samuel. It reminded me of Dr. Pennington. "Okay," I simply said. We ate dinner, and between bites of a delicious stew, I answered more of her questions. I could not get her to tell me anymore about her life. Upon leaving, I promised her I would look for something useful to do on my off time.

"Good," she said. "Now my mission is complete." I looked at her trying to contemplate what she meant. "Don't look at me like that. It is just a common phrase. Of course, there is a truth behind every common and ordinary thing in life. Now get out of here before you miss your streetcar."

I looked for Thelma the next few days, but I did not see her on any of the streetcars, or anywhere else. After four days, I decided to go to her house one pleasant Sunday afternoon. No one was there and I didn't even hear Bryan barking. So, I went to the neighboring house. A man around my age answered the door and asked what I wanted.

"My name is Samuel Nite."

"Yes, I know who you are. " After a pause that seemed to last forever, he said, "Good for you. Musvoy and his type have been bothering innocent people for years. People have a right to do what they want if they are not hurting anyone else. They call themselves Christians, yet they make it a crime to visit someone dying in the hospital. What can I do for you?"

"Do you know where Thelma, the woman who lives next door, might be?" As I asked the question, I realized that I didn't know her last name.

"I'm sorry Mr. Nite, but she passed away, we believe three days ago. We went over there yesterday because the dog was making such a fuss. Because no family came forward, or anyone else for that matter, the authorities thought it best to bury her this morning. I'm sorry that we did not know you were an acquaintance." I did not know what to say, so after a short while the man spoke up again.

"All I can tell you is that she was buried in the pauper's cemetery. No one really knew her. She kept to herself and nothing over there had her name on it, She had just moved in about three weeks ago and we came to find out today it was not even her house. The place was still filled with Judge Ryan's furniture and belongings. We thought she was a Ryan, but the judge's daughter down in Kenton told us she was not." The man kept talking on and on, telling me the daughter was going to move out the judge's possessions later, and how the authorities gave the dog and cat to a local orphanage.

Just then, the streetcar stopped up the road and off stepped a woman who walked towards us. She looked very sophisticated and pretty, and her hair was dark and curly under a hat like those seen on Euclid Avenue in Cleveland. The man excused himself, but not before saying, "Here comes trouble. That is the judge's daughter now. Good luck Mr. Nite," and with that he quickly stepped inside and shut the door. Meanwhile the woman walked past where I stood on the porch and turned up the path to Thelma's house. She hailed me as I left the porch of the neighbor.

"Sir, will you please accompany me inside. I do not want to enter a vacant house alone." I nodded and walked over to where she stood. "I see Mr. Carson next door is still afraid of me," she said.

"Why should he be?" I asked.

"Because of my forward thinking," she answered. This confused me some because the man whom I now knew as a Mr. Carson seemed forward thinking, judging from his remarks about my incident with the police.

"My name is Thelma Ryan," she said extending a manicured hand. I awkwardly introduced myself, taken aback that her first name was the same as the old woman who had been occupying the house. "You look like you have seen a ghost," she remarked, and just like the older Thelma, she gave me no time to answer, but instead immediately said, "Well, come on. Let's enter the house, and would you please look around to make sure there are no more vagrants lurking inside."

I took this as a criticism of the now deceased Thelma and I said, "Thelma was not a vagrant."

"So you knew her, and you are mistaken to think I believed her lower than myself. She must have been a strong, determined woman to take action like she did to secure shelter. Tell me about her."

"I did not know her for long, but I liked her. She was feisty and did not view herself as being inferior to men. She encouraged me to do something with my life and she would not accept my age as an excuse for not doing something."

"So what have you decided to do?"

Ignoring her question, I remarked, "I think you are just like her."

"How?" she snapped back.

"You both have the quality of getting right to the point, and you certainly do not defer to men."

"Well, you certainly have deduced much about me in such a short while."

"You can tell a lot by watching the way one walks down a road," I answered. "Also, I could tell a lot about you in the way you practically ordered me into the house."

"Well, is confidence a bad thing?"

"Not in itself. You may be a shallow, egocentric person or as spirited and exuberant as Thelma."

She seemed to relax a bit and even laughed. "Well I guess it might be a good sign that I too am a Thelma. Please stay a bit and I'll prepare you a cup of tea. Please address me as Thelm, like my close friends do." I had never met a woman, especially one giving off an air of sophistication, who would go by a shortened form of her name as if she was an army mate.

At any rate, I could not help but chuckle because Thelm reminded me so much of Thelma, including her enticing me to stay by offering me a cup of tea. She made me feel good about Thelma's life, instead of the sadness one normally feels when a friend dies. I felt at peace and was glad to be with Thelm. We sat and talked for hours. Unlike Thelma, once she relaxed, Thelm made no effort to control the conversation. She knew how to carry on a two-way conversation, knowing when to talk about herself, and when to listen when I spoke. After I had told her the story about heading west to find pink Catawba wine, she had a good laugh, excused herself, and returned with a big smile and a bottle of wine from the cellar. It was Pink Catawba of course. "Father loved it so," she exclaimed.

She told me about growing up a judge's daughter with no other surviving brothers or sisters by the time she reached twenty. Three of her older brothers had died in the cholera epidemics. She was determined to become a judge like her father, but in this man's world that would not be easy. She secured a partnership in a law firm in Kenton, Ohio, partly by romancing one of the senior partners. Unfortunately, he was married and she had to act very discreetly, carefully playing the role of a single woman forced to work due to the lack of a husband. She was forty but looked thirty. The future of her law career would be hard enough, but she confided in me that she was between one and two months pregnant with the child of the senior partner. She seemed unashamed of this fact, openly talking about it, and I liked her for her honesty and determination. She took cases for many women, with the conviction that women should be treated as the equal of men. She confessed to me that the tough exterior was not her real self but had been cultivated by her in order to compete in a man's world. At about one in the morning I told her about the incidents surrounding my love for Kathleen. As the older Thelma had advised, she said, "I should search for her until my dying day, because love is so hard to find." After a long awkward silence, she changed the subject, telling me like an excited school girl how she had once met the famous lawyer Clarence Darrow in Chicago. Then, she stood up and returned to her feisty disposition and demanded I sleep in the guest room because she did not feel safe in the house alone.

"What about the scandal such an act would cause?" I asked.

"Samuel, I couldn't give a damn about that, and from what you have told me you have already been condemned here in Sandusky by the gossip mongers." Then, softening her voice a bit, she added, "Besides, don't worry, I'll let you out early in the morning onto the back alley where no one will see you leaving."

I did as she said, cleaned myself with a basin of water she supplied, and lay down on the guest bed and tried to go to sleep. I knew sleep wouldn't come easily, for my mind was agitated from the evening's events and quite frankly spending all that time in conversation with a beautiful woman.

About an hour after lying down, I was still awake when the door quietly opened and Thelm came in wearing a pink nightgown. She climbed into my bed and began kissing me. We were still in bed together and awake when dawn broke. I told her I wanted to see her again. "Samuel," she responded, "how would that be possible? I am going to return to Kenton and have James's baby. And James, though married to another woman, is going to take responsibility for my son or daughter."

"So James is his name," I said feeling a strange sort of jealousy.

"Yes, and he is a good man who can be a leader in Kenton, just as you can accomplish much here in Sandusky as your dear friend Thelma told you. I will never forget this wonderful night and if the situation were different, who knows?" Then, with a beautiful smile completely sincere for the first time, she said, "Samuel, I never thought I would meet a gallant Southern man, especially one with such high principles. Now get dressed, and I'll show you the way to the back alley. And find Kathleen. She is your true love."

I did as she told me and exited through the back door, but not before one long, last kiss in the kitchen. I was elated, confused, sad, and feeling optimistic all at the same time as I walked down the back alley towards the downtown area. In a week's time I had met two women named Thelma, and I loved them both, but now they were both gone, but leaving me with hope. I knew that I could never have lived with Thelm. She would have twirled me around her finger. For that matter, I could not have been around Thelma for long. They were both hardheaded women who had definite ideas about the way things should be. They were right about Kathleen being my true love, but there was no way I was going to write to her or travel again to Erie. I had once before let my friends convince me to search her out and I was rewarded with a beating. I still loved Kathleen, but she never attempted to write to me after my experience in Erie. I figured she must have been long married to someone else, and the thought of verifying my suspicion was too much to bear. The prospect of another beating was not exciting either.

I decided to do nothing. I would, however, have an open mind for any opportunity that life might offer. Time flew by, and before I knew it, I was 57 years old and it was the year 1907. I continued to work, and I still enjoyed a level of mental contentment, but my physical body began to experience aches and pains. Up to this point I had been lucky. Between serving in the Civil War, being trapped in Billy's outlaw gang, nearly dying of the fever in Mount Vernon, and being exposed to the influenza and cholera epidemics of the time, plus the beatings in Erie and Sandusky, it was amazing I had lived so long. I believed there was a reason I was still alive and that I was destined for something special to still happen in my life.

I thought about trying to find Douglas Frederick Brown in Canada. I still had his pamphlet about finding one's own religion, and I had continually hoped to hear from him, but I never received a letter or any other type of communication. I wondered if he made it across the frozen lake. Did he buy land and start his tomato farm? He was right about the bright future of the tomato. Henry Heinz of Pittsburgh was successfully buying land and creating sauces, the most popular being a tomato and vinegar mixture called ketchup. Many people were also dining out at Italian restaurants that most effectively served dishes using tomato sauce. Italians and other Europeans had migrated to America and introduced Americans to their fine European cuisines.

Despite the encouragement by Thelma and Thelm to do something, I had found nothing I wanted to do. To be honest, it was because I did not look for anything new. The LSE continued to grow, which made my job more interesting. On August 18, 1907, a second route opened between Cleveland and Toledo. One route ran through Sandusky and the other one branched off at a place called Ceylon Junction and traveled through Norwalk, Bellevue, and Clyde before rejoining the other line in Fremont. I began station inspections at several new stops, including the new interurban Clyde Station. It was nostalgic visiting Clyde, but also lonely, for my thoughts returned again to Kathleen. She was the only reason I had moved to Clyde. I never met a woman I wanted more than Kathleen. Even as I approached sixty, I could not get her off my mind. Her father was surely dead by now, but I was still sure she was married by this time, and finding that out would be worse than another beating.

As fate would have it, everything changed on a winter evening in 1910. I was travelling between Huron and Sandusky having just finished an inspection in Huron. The winter sun was setting over the snow-covered fields. In the distance Lake Erie was covered with ice and a few stars began to shine in the northern sky. I was feeling pretty good for a 59-year-old man as I stood up to stretch my legs. I looked towards the rear of the car and there was a woman, who looked about 40 years old, staring at me. When I looked back at her she quickly turned her head to gaze out the window. It took but a second to realize it was Kathleen.

Overjoyed, I hurried to her seat and exclaimed, "Kathleen is that you?"

"Mr. Nite," she answered, "You have a lot of nerve. Please leave me alone." I could not believe the rejection. If nothing else, at least she should have been happy to see me again as she was once in love with me. I just stood there as if frozen to the spot, unable to speak. While I stood there dumbfounded, she continued, "After what you did to me how can you just stand here like nothing happened?"

That lit a spark. "Plenty happened," I replied, "but I never blamed you."

She looked at me for about ten seconds and finally said, "Blame me? When someone asks for money in return for agreeing not to see a person they supposedly have affection for, well I should say that that someone hardly has cause to blame anyone other than himself."

With a raised voice, I answered, "Who told you I asked for money not to see you?" Before she could answer I continued, now on the offensive, "Don't answer, for I now see the picture. Your father lied to you. What really happened was that I went to Erie to ask your father for permission to see you. I waited for his response at a hotel and I got one all right, in the form of your father sending a couple of his thugs, who drove me out to the countryside and gave me the beating of my life."

Kathleen tried to block her ears at first and then screamed, "How dare you accuse my father of lying, especially now that he is in the ground! How dare you!" Then she jumped up and rushed forward to the conductor and demanded to be let off.

"Why ma'am, we are not at a stop," he replied. "I know Mr. Nite to be an honorable man; you must be mistaken in your charge."

"How is it any business of yours?" Kathleen yelled. "Now let me off!" The conductor, Joe Wilson, looked at me.

"Well Joe," I said and then gave him a nod. "You better let her off at the next stop."

The next stop was at the entrance of a road that followed a narrow spit of land out into the lake. At the end of this peninsula was the resort known as Cedar Point. Still fuming, Kathleen did not hesitate and stepped out into the darkness. The streetcar pulled away and went around the bend where I told Joe to have the driver stop the car so I could exit. He did so and I walked back around the bend to where Kathleen sat on a bench sobbing.

I quietly approached and sat down next to her, wondering what would happen next. She looked me in the eyes and asked me to hold her. After a minute she started talking. "I always suspected father was not honest about you. I once heard my mother say to him, 'Love is more important than age and social standing.' But I could not believe he would put those things above my happiness. When I was a girl he treated me like a princess. In fact, that is what he always called me, 'his princess.'"

"Listen Kathleen, your father did what he did because he loved you. I forgive him and you must also." I surprised myself with these words. They surprised Kathleen too.

"Are you saying he had you beaten and you forgive him?" I responded with a yes. "I don't know why, but I believe you," she said.

All I could say was, "I'm here."

We sat in the cold and when it began to snow, we arose and walked up the dark peninsula road that had turned a fresh white from the newly fallen snow. We walked for at least five miles to the entrance of the resort. I told her how I had settled in Clyde, eventually leaving for a job on the LSE. She told me how she had attended a small teacher's college in Erie and taught school there for a few years before arriving one year ago in Sandusky in answer to an ad for a teacher's position. "Why Sandusky?" I asked.

"Because my father was dead and no one else could stop me from coming to this part of Ohio again. In fact, my mother encouraged me to come here."

"Were you looking for something?" I asked.

"Yes," she answered.

"Do you think you will find it?"

"I have found it," she said smiling. Then we looked into each other's eyes and kissed.

It must have been two in the morning. No one was around, so we entered the resort and found a group of unlocked cabins. We entered one and stayed the night, together. We woke to the sound of someone chopping wood. Then, the chopping stopped and after a short while we heard the thump of logs hitting the ground next to the door. A voice called out, "I see you found wood for a fire last night. Here is some more. The cabin is one dollar a day. If you have it you're welcome to stay. I'll expect you to come up to the caretaker's cabin by the road with the money within two hours. If you don't I'll expect you to be gone with no questions asked."

In the meantime Kathleen and I were alone with each other in this cabin along the Lake Erie shore. We had spent one week together twenty years ago. Could we have truly fallen in love in that one week? If yes, would we be able to pick up where we left off twenty years later? I think we were both asking ourselves the same question. Could this be real? In addition, Kathleen must still have had some doubt in her mind concerning her father's allegation that I used her for money.

Before all this could be explored, I got up and put some logs on the fire and walked over to the caretaker's cabin. A sign above the door read, "Capp's Cabins of Cedar Point, Bryan Capp, Proprietor." Mr. Capp was a huge man, more muscled than fat. He told me to come in, where I was greeted by his wife Roberta. Several small children looked up at me with a look of amazement, I figured from rarely seeing another person out here in winter.

The Capps were generous people and exceptionally kind, seeing that we were trespassers. Bryan spoke in an accent I had not heard in years, and they seemed curious about my manner of speech as well. It turned out the Capps were from a place called Midlothian, Virginia, outside Richmond. Bryan had actually worked digging coal in Midlothian up until two years ago. He explained that the coal had been basically dug out twenty-five years ago, but an attempt to dig out some more was recently given a try. Apparently, the effort died out quickly when the chief investor was elected mayor of Richmond in 1908. "Well I guess that's a first," I remarked. "Most politicians would have used the office to make gains on their investment."

"Not Mayor Richardson," Bryan replied. "He is as honest a person as one would care to meet." I couldn't help but ask for Mayor Richardson's first name. "Why, let's see here," Bryan paused, "Oh yes, it is David Crockett. I can't help but remember that name." As I was speculating, it was none other than good old Davey from Parker's Battery who had helped Owen and me build our winter quarters on the Howlett Line. In that moment I felt as if he was still watching over me, helping me become a man. He was always studying the law and I knew he would use it to do good. As Bryan indicated, his honesty and genuine interest in people's welfare must have made him very popular with the voters.

As I stood there lost in thought about Davey, the Capps stood patiently. They asked no questions. They were like Davey himself, representing the best virtues of the South, like being kind to strangers and friends alike. It is a certain type of friendliness unique to the land I came from.

Bryan had to go into Sandusky that day, and I asked him to take a note to any streetcar conductor he found explaining my absence from work. Luckily, it was Saturday so it would cause little problem. Kathleen was not due back to teach school until Monday. Before Bryan headed out he accepted three dollars for the cabin and cut us more wood. I never saw a man carry more wood on his shoulders in my life.

The most gracious Roberta prepared us some food. While she cooked and we sat at her table, she told us how a couple of years before Bryan had seen an ad in an out-of-town newspaper about managing these cabins that were part of the Cedar Point resort. After the coal mine revival had failed, he was frustrated with the lack of work in the South. He was willing to head north but not to a big city. "There is lots of work in the summer, but not much in the winter," Roberta explained. Bryan and Roberta never asked how Kathleen and I ended up in the cabin. They just treated us as if we were customers with a reservation. I also think they knew we needed privacy and left us alone except to supply us with wood and food. Being alone together was awkward for Kathleen and me, but everything that caused us to fall in love twenty years earlier was still there, and we were able to pick up where we left off. We took long walks along the frozen lake shore. To the north we could see the Erie

Islands, separated by time and space but connected by the solid force of ice. Eventually, the connection would melt, leaving water, which is a less solid force, but one that creates a deeper bond as exemplified by all the life that lives on the surface and below. So it is with love. In the beginning we lose ourselves to the other. This exclusive connection is slowly replaced by a different love, less passionate, less centered on each other, but in many ways deeper and richer from a fuller engagement with life as a whole. We knew we had to reach down deep, below the ice, to be part of the life-giving water in which all secrets are stored and life is given in order to trust each other once more. For certain, the gravity of her father's influence on Kathleen would remain for the rest of our relationship on earth, as would my resentment at him ordering my beating. There would be arguments, and when they raged it would be as if Mr. Jenkins was in the room. But our advanced ages would soften the blows of life that are taken so seriously in youth.

I never would accompany Kathleen back to Erie to see her mother, despite her mother being my ally. I always welcomed her to visit us in Ohio, but visiting Erie would bring back memories of that week I spent near death because of my unworthiness in Kathleen's father's eyes. We learned not to talk about the issue and accept our feelings about a time and place that offered good memories for Kathleen and bad memories for me.

After our soul-searching weekend, our relationship was strong again and we decided to enter uncharted territory for both of us. In 1914, with Kathleen 44 years old and me 64, we married in a small service held in Sandusky. Since the Capps had sold off their cabins the previous year, we spent the honeymoon at the cottages of Mr. and Mrs. Jeffers just north of Ceylon Junction on Lake Erie. After the honeymoon we remained in Sandusky. I continued working for the LSE and Kathleen continued teaching. The truth was, however, that Kathleen still harbored a desire to be a librarian.

Out of the electricity of space conducted by wire arrived a telegram presenting the opportunity to do something as urged by both Thelmas fifteen years earlier. The telegram read:

TO MR SAMUEL NITE OF SANDUSKY OHIO—
STOP —THIS TELEGRAM IS DIRECTED TO HIM BY
WAY OF THE OFFICES OF THE LAKE ERIE SHORE

ELECTRIC RAILROAD—STOP—THE RECENTLY DECEASED THELMA RYAN OF KENTON OHIO HAS LEFT IN HER WILL THE BOOKS AND CONTENTS OF THE LIBRARY OF HER LATE FATHER JUDGE PATRICK RYAN'S ESTATE AT 3003 CASTALIA ROAD SANDUSKY OHIO—STOP—PLEASE CONTACT THE LAW OFFICE OF PETERS AND RYAN KENTON OHIO FOR DETAILS IN TAKING POSSESSION OF THE ITEMS AWARDED TO YOU AS DIRECTED IN THE WILL BY THELMA RYAN.

I was shocked to hear that Thelm died and surprised she would have thought enough of me to leave me her father's books. After more thought, I realized that she did it for Kathleen, for I had told Thelm that Kathleen planned to be a librarian, and Thelm must have had the utmost confidence that I would find Kathleen again. I pondered how I would explain a woman leaving me such a gift, but as it turned out Kathleen never asked. She seemed to be so overjoyed to have the books that she always referred to it as a gift of the judge and spoke to others as if Judge Ryan and I had enjoyed a long friendship together. I think Kathleen simply did not want to know any more about my life because of the difficulty she had dealing with the truth about her father.

We immediately began the project of creating a public library. We took some of her inheritance money and invested it in a small building in Ceylon Junction where the Lake Shore Electric separated into a southern and northern route. It was a spot near the Otto family's refreshment stand, an excellent location because many passengers transferred at this spot and often had time to kill in a manner of speaking. The library would serve LSE passengers as well as the local families in the area. Kathleen quit her teaching job and became totally absorbed in the project. She even wanted some expert advice. So one day in October of 1915, I rode the LSE into Cleveland and visited the city's public library. I was informed that two men had actually set up a library consulting business in Cleveland with a grant sponsored by a foundation of William Carnegie. Their goal was to help people establish libraries whether it was a public, church, or university library.

I left the Cleveland Library and walked a short distance to the office of Holloway and Donaldman on Superior Avenue not far from

12th Street. The receptionist with the pretty name of Laurel asked me to take a seat and told me someone would be with me soon. John Holloway appeared in less than two minutes and welcomed me into his office. After I described the project, Mr. Holloway quickly suggested a plan. An associate of the firm and a library director in Akron named John Lessman would recommend a basic design for the building. Jim Donaldman would help us set up policies and procedures for everyday library operations. Finally, Mr. Holloway would advise us on raising money and long-term governance. A public library, we all agreed, needed to be free to all and not a money-making proposition. Kathleen would use her inheritance to get the library started, but after that some dependable flow of funds would be necessary to keep the library open.

Since Ceylon Junction is a part of Erie County, our hope was to establish the library and then have the county take over the operation. Erie County already operated a library in Sandusky. In 1899 Andrew Carnegie gave Sandusky $50,000 for a public library and in 1912 Erie County began granting funds for the library under terms of an annual contract. Mr. Holloway believed that if we properly established the Ceylon Junction Library, Erie County would be willing to supply some funding. Kathleen now became fully absorbed in making the library a success. By July 1916 the renovations to the building were finished. Shelves were put along the walls followed by tables and electric lights. A desk was placed near the main entrance. We were helped the whole time by Jim Donaldman, a good-natured man, who loved to tell and hear jokes while he worked. At the same time, however, he was a very serious and talented librarian. He showed Kathleen how to purchase a starting book collection, how to classify the books using the Dewey Decimal System, and how to inventory each book on a set of cards. The cards were placed in a specially made cabinet where library users could look up books by authors, titles, and subjects.

On April 13, 1916, the Ceylon Junction Public Library opened to the public. Use started slowly until passengers waiting for interurbans discovered they could borrow books for free. If they would not soon pass this way again, they were simply requested to ship the books back to the library for free under an agreement we made with the LSE. Kathleen ran the whole operation and was extremely happy. Talks began with the Erie County Commissioners, and word was that the library would receive some county funding beginning in 1918. It was good news because Kathleen's inheritance from her father was just about gone. Kathleen did not want to ask her mother for money so we put all our hope on the county.

Everything was going well except for the fact that I worried about my advanced age. What would Kathleen do after I died? I was still working for the LSE thanks to the graciousness of Fred Coen. But I was beginning to notice a trembling in my fingers that eventually became more pronounced and then spread to my arms and legs. Kathleen noticed it too, and convinced me to visit a doctor in Cleveland. A Doctor Cross was recommended to me by a doctor at the Sandusky Hospital. I took the interurban into Cleveland and found Cross's office on Prospect Avenue, away from the main Cleveland business district. Dr. Cross was a young man in his thirties and he seemed excited to see me. "Tell me sir," he asked, "the information I have here says you are sixty six years old and originally you are from rural Virginia."

"That is correct," I answered.

"I guess you were too young to fight in the Civil War, but I bet as a boy you saw some of the armies march by. That must have been quite exciting seeing those fancy uniforms and the proud look on the faces of the soldiers from both armies. Those were gallant times, proud days in American history." I wanted to tell him it was nothing like that, but I did not want to bring back the bad memories, especially finding my parents' place burned to the ground and both of them dead. So I just told him that I did see some of the soldiers go by and they looked brave and all those patriotic lies people liked to believe about war. Many people wanted to revel in such nonsense in anticipation of the United States soon joining the conflict in Europe. They had to convince themselves that it would be an adventure because they knew their boys would not be invited to fight; they would be forced to fight.

After we finished the flag-waving small talk, the doctor gave me a thorough examination and told me to put my clothes back on and meet me in his outer office. I dressed and took a seat next to his desk. After about ten minutes he came in and sat at his desk and smiled. "Yes, those must have been some exciting times back then when the Blue and Gray battled. Imagine, brother against brother. That happened a lot you know. Well let's see what we've got here. I have seen a few cases where patients have these shaking or trembling symptoms. Normally it is nothing to worry about. You know Mr. Nite you are no spring chicken, but I'd say you are in pretty fine shape for a sixty-six-year-old man. The worst case scenario is that you have something that according to an article I read by a Doctor Charcot from a ways back, maybe even fifty years ago, is that you might have something he called Parkinson's Disease, named for a doctor who about a hundred years ago first defined the symptoms. There are some drugs we could try, but if I were you I'd just take it easy and see if this shaking gets any worse. Do you have any questions?"

I only said, "It sounds like you know nothing for sure, so I guess I have nothing to ask and you have no guaranteed cure."

"Well I guess you could derive that conclusion from my examination, but I will be here and if you visit on a regular basis I can monitor changes."

"Okay then, how much do I owe you?"

"I'd say five dollars should handle it." I could not believe my ears. I wanted to say something, but could not come up with anything. I dug around my pockets and pulled out exactly four dollars and seventeen cents. Seeing me count out the money, the doctor told me to just pay him what I could after leaving enough carfare to get back home. I was entitled to ride for free, so like a fool I gave him the whole amount I had, and left the office stunned by the cost of my visit. I was hoping to stop at a stand and get a bite to eat, but now I had a long ride home on an empty stomach and no remedy for my malady. I got home and stubbornly told Kathleen that I was through with big city doctors. Doctor Cross charged me nearly ten times what good old Doctor Hannibal charged for such a visit, and all that for him to tell me that he was not sure what was really wrong. Kathleen hushed me up and called me an "old goat." She said we should just keep an eye on my condition and then we would figure out something else.

So I continued working for the LSE. It was, however, becoming very difficult. I turned 67 years old in 1917 and I began to find it hard to climb on board the streetcars even though I still loved riding on them. My appendages began to shake more, and I did my best to keep it hidden from Kathleen. What I could not hide from her was how I began to be more and more unsteady. Also, I began to be much more forgetful, not about things that happened long ago, but things like names and where I put my pocket watch. Kathleen begged me to go to the doctor again and I said I would. This time, however, I stopped in Clyde to see if Doctor Hannibal was still practicing medicine. To my joy he was indeed still in his old office on State Street. One to always tell his patients the truth, he told me about a few cases like mine that he had seen in older people. He confirmed what the doctor in Cleveland said and called it Parkinson's disease after the doctor in England who described the symptoms about 100 years ago. Dr. Hannibal checked my hands and studied them carefully, saying they were more rigid than normal. He wasn't sure if anything could be done, but he knew of people who went on a long time in such a condition. Then again others went downhill quickly. He suggested I seek out a specialist in Cleveland, a type of doctor called a neurologist. "You know Sam, this world sure has changed a lot," Doctor Hannibal said as he got up with me to leave. "I have to get over to the draft board. No one wanted to sit on a board that has to select boys to go fight, so I volunteered because I'm the only one around here who would honestly check these boys out. They don't know what they are getting into, and they will lie about their hearing and vision and everything else if you just go by what they say. The war in Europe is like it was in places like Petersburg in the Civil War, except a hundred times worse. Every day hundreds come out of the trenches just to be mowed down by machine guns. If only we would spend as much money on things like figuring out this Parkinson's disease instead of inventing better weapons we would all be a lot better off."

Changing the subject I asked Doc if anyone heard from Jobby. "As a matter of fact," he answered, "Jobby has a book published called Windy's Son or something like that. I got a copy, but I don't have the time or the eyes to read it. Next time you are in town, I'll give it to you." I thanked Dr. Hannibal for everything, and went home and gave Kathleen the news. I was determined to heal myself. I did not want to see a specialist in Cleveland. Kathleen begged me to go, but instead I cut my work hours in half and started a strenuous exercise program. I walked as much as five miles a day, usually on the road connecting Sandusky and Vermillion. Soon my walks became shorter and shorter and the naps at home longer and longer. The days I didn't take those naps I found my thinking to be confused. I don't know how to explain it, but my mind just felt different. I was in touch with reality, but reality felt a little strange. It was not necessarily bad strange, but in a way that made me understand that the everyday problems of life were no longer that important because they were not going to last.

When I did worry, it was mostly about Kathleen. The love between Kathleen and me continued to grow. She loved the library, and we spent much time together choosing and reading books. She often read to me, for my eyes, even with glasses, were starting to fail and I quickly fell asleep when I read myself. I worried about how she would survive after I was gone. The library paid little, and despite the county aid, the library was near broke by 1922. I had been able to work until I was seventy because I was apparently one of the lucky ones where my Parkinson's deterioration had moved slowly, but our funds were very low. I had retired from the LSE, and we both knew that the library needed an additional source of funding. Donations were down, and Kathleen's inheritance was depleted.

It did not help matters that the country's economic picture was not bright. Despite the progressive reforms of Teddy Roosevelt, the United States experienced problems after entering the terrible war in Europe. England, France, and Germany lost so many young men in brutal warfare that it made the Civil War look like a minor skirmish. Thankfully, our country's involvement did not last too long and by 1919 the war was over. However, by 1922, a postwar slump in the economy was causing hardship all through northern Ohio.

I remember talking to Fred Coen on a visit to Cleveland in early 1922. Fred was still a major figure with the Lake Shore Electric. He was a bit worried and told me that due to production cuts and major layoffs, ridership on the LSE had significantly dropped. In fact, wages were about to be cut from 60 cents an hour to 54 cents. Hard times were upon us and there was little money for projects like libraries. Nonetheless, Kathleen was determined to find funding. So on a cold November day in 1922 she set out on the interurban for Cleveland to seek money from a couple of foundations. I remained behind to keep the library open.

I always feared for Kathleen when she took a trip on the interurban. I loved them, but they were dangerous. Accidents included fifteen passengers injured in 1898 due to a brake failure near Avon, fifteen passengers were injured in 1902 near Fremont when their car was hit from behind by a freight motor car, and six people killed in 1904 in a terrible collision at Wells Corners. An LSE car, loaded with vacationers, was hit by a local streetcar near Vermillion in August of 1906, and four died near Toledo due to a derailment n 1907. The first accident with an automobile was reported in 1912, and a powerhouse at Beach Park exploded in 1918. The good news was that there were fewer accidents in recent years, a testament to increased safety measures.

Despite the improved safety record, I was full of anxiety as Kathleen's car sped away that November morning, I continued to fret all morning and afternoon. I felt relieved at the station when I saw her car coming in right on time near 4 p.m. in the afternoon. The car came to a complete stop and Bill Greene, a conductor I knew, stepped out. This was unusual, especially at Ceylon Junction where traffic could quickly back up because of the many streetcars that met at this spot. Bill came right up to me and in a hushed voice spoke: "Sam, I have some bad news." Blood rushed into my face, and I almost fell over but Bill grabbed me and took me to a bench. He then simply said, "Kathleen is dead." Apparently, she had been hit by an automobile as she exited the streetcar near Public Square in Cleveland. I never had thought of a person being killed by an automobile. There just was not that many of them on the road. One thing for certain was that there would be many more, but there would never be another Kathleen in my life.

Lake Erie, China, and Beyond

It had been eight years since Kathleen died. I had gone from a self-sufficient, seventy-two-year-old man, to a dependent old man of seventy-nine. The country was on a "hot streak," to borrow a phrase from baseball, with plenty of money floating around and lots to spend it on. It was the last year of the Roaring Twenties and most Americans enjoyed plenty of options, both in entertainment and goods. I was not one of them. My Parkinson's condition progressed slowly, but combined with my age, it had made getting around and doing things an ordeal.

Once Kathleen passed away so did the Ceylon Junction Free Library. Luckily, Mr. and Mrs. Jeffers offered me a place to live at their new cottages on Lake Erie, west of the town of Vermillion. In return I picked up trash and performed other chores like wiping the dew off the metal chairs in the morning. Simple tasks become hard work when your body begins to fail. Most of the time I sat in the shade offering a half-hearted hello to the vacationers headed to their cabins or to the small beach on the north end of the property. I missed Kathleen and even that darn library. Everyone I knew had died or was living somewhere else. I didn't even see the Jeffers anymore, for they had put Mr. Jeffers's nephew Andy in charge of the Vermillion cottages. Every day was the same and every day was different. I'm sure it sounds like I was unhappy, and to a young person it would be a boring life, but my mind had drastically changed. I saw the grand mystery of life in things that I'm sure others seldom noticed, like the way the mist would settle or rise from the lake, the deep low sounds of the horns of the big ore boats far out from the shore, the interchange of day and night, and yes the incredible night sky. I marveled when I thought about the fact that the light I saw from some of those stars was emitted from a time before I was born. Life is associated with the waking activities of day, but it is at night that we are privileged to see our past intermingling with our present. Reality is not bound by time as measured by clocks. We belong to a larger spectrum of time, like the light of the stars, born incomprehensible distances away in a homeland now possibly dead, but through their light constantly reborn in the far reaches of infinity.

Although all my old relations and friends were gone, I had plenty of strangers visit me from time to time. I could not remember where I knew them from, but they seemed to know me quite well. In fact, they would make themselves right at home whenever they visited, as if it was their own home. There was Joe and Belle Hamilton, Mrs. Rice, and a war veteran, like myself, simply known as Ridge. Every time I would mention them to Andy, he would laugh at me and tell me they didn't exist. I remember complaining to Andy that Ridge, in particular, was staying overnight more and more and did not offer to pay a penny of the rent. Andy answered, "In the first place, Pops," which he liked to call me, "I'd see these people coming and going. In the second place, you can't even describe them to me or tell me what you talk about with them, and in the third place you don't pay a penny of rent yourself."

After a while I stopped insisting that the strangers were real. Sometimes weeks would go by without any of them visiting. And, after some more time only Ridge would visit. The other people had from the start seemed more shadowy than Ridge and then they disappeared altogether. I cannot tell you anything about them other than their names. Ridge, on the other hand, was quite real. Sometimes, when he spent the night, I would sit up outside all evening because I could not stand the way he snored so loud. I knew he was a veteran, because he snored just like all the boys did back on the Howlett Line, like every breath was their last. It was the cacophony of young men sleeping to the fullest, because sleeping was the best part of living when you were in a war.

Sometimes sitting up all night in front of my cottage I would wonder why I was still alive, almost eighty years old and Kathleen, so many years younger, already dead. And then I would think back to Owen and Billy and Thelm and all the people I knew who died way before their time. With Ridge there was no time. I had no past with him I knew of, yet he would insist that I was the most important person in his life. At these times it felt like there was no time. Time never is the same anyhow. When you sleep for five hours it does not feel like being awake for five hours, and seven years alive in my seventies felt shorter than seven months on the Howlett Line. Despite this, we comfort ourselves by thinking thoughts like, "I might still have ten more years of life ahead of me." It is funny and sad at the same time.

One late summer afternoon I was enjoying some peace and quiet looking out towards the lake watching and listening to the summer come to an end. There was the buzzing sound of the insects, so different from the noises they made in the spring when they were beginning life. Now they seemed just satisfied to go about their work. It was the same with the squirrels, now laboring more intently at gathering food for the winter. The domesticated animals, like the dogs and cats, on the other hand, were lazy this time of year, contently sleeping in the unshaded areas, enjoying the last warm rays of the sun. I turned to look towards the road where the automobiles now passed with windows shut, lacking the noise of springtime when children yell out open windows with vacation excitement. Suddenly, my thoughts were interrupted by the sight of Andy walking towards me. I was sure he was coming to give me some task to do. I didn't mind, for I was having one of those days when my mind felt clear, at least clear in the way most people define clear. In other words, Ridge was not around pestering me. "Hi Pops," Andy greeted me, "Are you alone today, or are some of your imaginary friends inside sleeping?" Before I could answer, he said, "Today is your lucky day, at least I think it is going to be. There is a real, living man inside the office who wants to see you." He handed me a card signed Edward Connelly. "Are you in trouble, Pops? Do you know this guy?" Andy would say "guy" often and it always took me a while to figure out he meant a fella. "Whatever the case Pops, he wants to see you. Do you want to see him?"

"Why not?" I answered. "The worst that could happen is I would be arrested and it wouldn't be the first time." Andy looked at me strangely, and with a shrug, he said he would go get my visitor. So I waited on the bench in front of my cottage. I figured this would be some kind of trouble. I fell into my usual pattern of thinking, which was that nothing works as planned, and that I never accomplished anything important in my life. While I sat there, I even convinced myself that it would be an army fella coming to tell me time was up, and I was being arrested for not taking advantage of the opportunity given to me by

General Thomas. I figured I would be taken off to join the rest of Billy's outlaws in prison. I remembered that name Connelly from somewhere and believed he was probably one of General Thomas's staff officers.

My crazy thinking ended when up walked a man I judged to be about twenty years my junior, not dressed in a uniform, but instead in a buttoned-down shirt with the top two buttons unfastened. He wore no hat and had a good head of gray hair. There were whiskers on his chin that for some reason I felt were there not because he forgot, or was too lazy to shave, but instead by choice. His confident walk led me to surmise that he left nothing to chance, or, maybe it was that he controlled chance. He carried a heavy suitcase. He greeted me about fifteen feet from where I sat. "Hello, are you Samuel Nite who was raised in Nottoway County, Virginia?"

I saw no sense in withholding this information, so I simply said, "That would be me."

"Incredible! I have found you and I have a package for you." He pulled out from his bag a cylinder about the size of a large can of beans wrapped in paper. He also had an envelope, but suggested I open the package first. I did so and discovered it was an old glass jar. Suddenly, I knew what it was. In the jar were the forty or so gold coins that I buried on Ma and Pa's land some sixty-five years ago. In the envelope was a check for $432.00 made out to Samuel Nite. Accompanying the document was a letter dated 1868 from General George Henry Thomas authorizing Joseph Connelly of Blacks and Whites, Virginia, to act as caretaker and sales agent of the Nite land, with the provision that eighty per cent of the income from the transaction, plus any coins that might be eventually found on the property in a glass jar, be forwarded to Sam Nite of the Proctor and Gamble Company, Cincinnati, Ohio.

I quickly fumbled in my pocket for the card Andy handed me. The name on it was Edward Connelly, Lynchburg, Virginia. "Connelly? Are you...."

"I'm Joseph Connelly's son," Edward interrupted. "My father searched for you until his death in 1887. I was born in 1869 and grew up hearing about the legend of Sam Nite. You were a mystery to all those in Blackstone, or what was once known as Blacks and Whites. Father contacted Proctor and Gamble, but a return letter said there was no record of you ever working there. He increased his efforts after 1883 when he finally sold your land. Dad inspected the land prior to the sale, and something on the ground near the creek bed caught his eye. It was a bottle covered with dirt. We figured your bottle somehow surfaced from the soil due to erosion. Four years later, when he was dying of cancer, he asked me not to give up trying to find you."

"So, how did you find me?" I asked.

"It was because of a lecture I was presenting a few months ago in Marion, Virginia. It just so happened that the author of *Winesburg, Ohio*, who now lives in Marion was in attendance. Mr. Anderson runs two newspapers in Marion and he requested an interview after the lecture. We talked about where I was raised and he seemed quite interested in the early details of my life. I told him the story about the gold coins and he immediately recognized your name. He mentioned that on a visit to Clyde he inquired about you and was told you went to work for one of the local interurban railroads. I took this information with me and visited the Lake Shore Electric's offices in Cleveland. There I was told that you indeed had worked for their company and their records listed you as retired and living in the Ceylon Junction area. So, I travelled to that place, and an inquiry at an automobile service center led me here. It wasn't really that hard once I narrowed down your whereabouts."

I asked Edward to come in for some tea or coffee and he gratefully accepted. At his request, I told him my life story. I had a good recall for things that happened before I ended up living in the cottage working for Andy. When I finished, I asked Edward to tell me about his life. He obliged me for he seemed to be a very patient man, not in a hurry like most people.

Edward was twenty when he left Blackstone to travel, encouraged by his father to get out and learn from experience. We laughed when I told him how his father tried to get me to stay so I could attend his school. Edward said, "If there is one thing I have learned, it is that what is right for one person may not be right for another person. I've also learned that timing is everything."

Edward traveled out west and found few prospects for work, so he joined the Army. The Indian battles were over and eventually he found himself on a ship headed to the Philippine Islands to fight in the Spanish-American War. The war ended before he arrived, so he was immediately dispatched to China to join a battalion protecting American interests in that country. He laughed saying, "It was a case of being in the wrong place at the wrong time. I soon learned, though, that because of some unseen forces we are always in the right place." He found himself in China during an event known as the Boxer Rebellion. Boxers, members of a Chinese secret society so named because they practiced fighting techniques in local gymnasiums, were against the rapid growth and establishment of Western ideas and economic privilege. Their goal was simple; drive all foreigners out of China. They especially targeted missionaries, many of whom were killed along with the Chinese they converted to Christianity. The movement exploded into mass violence in 1900 when many houses, churches, and schools associated with foreign missions were burned to the ground. When a large contingent of foreign troops set out for China to quell the rebellion, the Chinese government officially joined the Boxers and declared war against all foreign powers on their land.

Edward was with a handful of Americans assigned the impossible task of defending the American embassy in Peking until the relief troops arrived. While out on a patrol searching for Americans hiding from the Boxers, Edward was separated from his platoon. Lost in the huge city, Edward appeared to be doomed when an elderly Chinese man appeared from what seemed like nowhere and told Edward that he must go with him. Edward had no choice. He needed the help of this man who spoke excellent English despite being dressed in traditional Chinese clothes. The man hid Edward in a wagon parked close by and then travelled back streets, alleys and dirt roads until they were in the country. Eventually, they neared a small village where the man, named Ch'en, told Edward he could come out of hiding.

They were on a huge plain with mountains visible to the west. Ch'en guided the mule-driven wagon into town and stopped in front of a store where a man came out and Ch'en spoke to him in Chinese. The man went inside and soon emerged with two other men, all three of them carrying food and supplies, which they loaded into the wagon. Soon, Ch'en and Edward were traveling again, this time on a road leading out of town. Edward said, "Amazingly, none of the townspeople raised an eyebrow upon seeing me travelling with Ch'en. I later learned this was because he commanded the greatest respect from the people, not because it was forced upon them, but instead because it was earned." They left the town behind them and the road soon turned into a dusty path with no one in sight. They traveled for hours on the flat plain, occasionally crossing small bridges over fast-flowing streams coming from the mountains. Eventually, they reached the mountains and entered a canyon. Around a bend in the road, which was barely wide enough to accommodate the wagon, there appeared a small stone structure alongside the stream that roared down the canyon. They were met by several men who helped them down, unloaded the wagon, and took the mule and wagon away to a small thatched barn.

At this point, Edward began to tell the story in more detail. "Ch'en asked me to please follow him up a path into another small canyon formed by a small creek that was not more than six feet wide. The sun glimmered off the creek, brushing the canyon walls with gold, and small trees with jade green leaves shimmered with the wind. The scene was reminiscent of an impressionist painting. After about a hundred yards, the path turned left and climbed steeply uphill. After what I estimated to be a mile, we came to an incredible sight. Up ahead was what looked to be a huge castle but was really a Taoist monastery. It sat precariously balanced upon a jagged mountain top and was embellished with giant carved dragon heads. Comforting and frightening at the same time, It was like nothing I had ever seen in the West."

At this point Edward told me about Taoist beliefs and culture. Much of it had to do with magical practices that assured one of living a long life. Of greater interest to Edward was what he called Classic Taoism. Based on statements allegedly made around 500 B.C. by a contemporary of Confucius named Lao Tzu, Classical Taoism is a philosophy on how to live one's life.

Edward laughed when I told him it sounded like a religion. "Yes and no," he said, "but it certainly has no doctrines. An essential Taoist message is that he who says he knows the Tao, a Chinese word for truth or the meaning of life, does not know the Tao." Edward explained many other Taoist ideas that I admit made a lot of sense. For instance, everything has an opposite and cannot exist without it. There cannot be good without bad, for good is meaningless without the concept of bad.

Taoist philosophy teaches that individual peace is found when one stops striving for happiness. Instead one should follow his spirit or inner voice like water flowing down a river. The water will reach the ocean not through struggle, but instead by taking the course of least resistance. Water in a stream does not try to force its way right through a boulder. Instead it effortlessly flows around the rock. Edward said we should live our lives the same way.

Somewhat frustrated by this whole concept, I blurted out, "Edward, I do not understand how an analogy about a stream will help me at this stage of my life."

"Sam, neither the Taoists nor I can tell you what is right for you. You have to listen to your inner voice. If you do something contrary to your feelings, you will suffer."

"Okay," I replied, "In order to help correct social injustice should I have become a social reformer instead of standing off to the side watching history go by just because I was not inclined to follow a path contrary to my feelings. After all, no one wants to be a martyr."

"Well," stated Edward, "I think if you would have become a social reformer under such circumstances, you would have made a bad social reformer despite your good intentions. Following your inner voice instead, you would have a better understanding of how you should lead your life. Eventually you would effortlessly find your place in life, and it is in that way you would accomplish your unique mission in life. From what you have told me, and the questions you have asked, I have a feeling that you have followed the voice of your soul. Your mind says you should have done more in your life, but your heart knows your life has been quite meaningful. The river you started on has taken you to this point. The best one can do is to follow the contours of their river, for struggle or not, we all end up in the great ocean of oneness. The Taoists would say don't fight it, just go with it and be at peace."

Edward later continued his story, including how he lived at the monastery for about a year until the time was safe for Ch'en to take him back to the American embassy. After returning to the States and leaving the army, he took it upon himself to study Asian philosophy and become a lecturer on the subject. We drank another cup of tea and talked about the local weather and the beauty of Lake Erie. We then shook hands, and he left. As I watched him go, I thought about the Taoist belief that there was a balance or dependence between good and evil and other opposites. I thought about how all lives were disappointing and satisfying at the same time. Personally, it was fine that things did not work out as I had hoped and desired. I thought of how a life of resistance or obsession blocks any hope for peace and understanding. If I had spent a life obsessing about the coins, I'm certain I would have shared the fate of Billy, who wanted them so desperately that they cost him his life.

Neither do I believe that what happened the next day was a simple twist of random fate. Despite my enlightened moment about "going with the flow," as Edward put it, I began to fret about the jar of coins and the check. I started thinking about how I had no one to trust and I knew Ridge would return one day and see them sitting on my table or shelf. I decided to hide the coins and the papers below a loose floor board. There was just enough room for me to fold the papers and place them in the jar, and just enough space for the jar to fit under the floor. I completed the job by placing a faded blue rug over the loose board. I obsessively checked at least once a day to make sure the jar and the papers were still in their hiding place.

A few months went by. One January day it was unusually mild, yet the crisp air by the lake foretold a storm, and that winter was far from over. Nonetheless, I felt at peace for the first time since the day I received the package from Edward. It was a strange peace though. I felt partly alive on earth and partly beyond life. I cannot explain this feeling except that when you have it you no longer make plans for the future. You don't think about things like what you will be doing tomorrow, or next week, or next year. I spent the day doing a few chores and sitting in front of the cottage feeling odd, but content. For once I did not worry about the jar of coins and the check from Mr. Connelly.

That night the wind howled and it turned bitterly cold as I fell fast asleep. I dreamt a dream that I often had as a child in which I am sitting at the top of a fifty-foot cliff. The cliff collapses, and I begin to fall but wake up suddenly. It had always been a terrible nightmare, but on this night it felt normal, even comforting. I got out of bed in the middle of the night with an energy I had not experienced in a long time and went over to sit at my table where I noticed a letter I must have placed there and forgotten to open.

When I opened the letter I found it was from Douglas Frederick Brown insisting I immediately visit him in Canada. I got up and walked outside where the storm had calmed and there was a clear, dark sky which was suddenly lit by stars, which grew bigger and bigger until the sky was silvered. It was not night, but it was not day either. And then I was certain I heard Douglas's voice, as if he was ten feet away, beckoning me to come to him in Canada.

Without hesitation I walked across the lawn and began to descend the steps leading down the cliff to the beach. I must have been wearing my coat, for I was warm; and without remembering fetching them from their hiding place, I was carrying the jar of gold coins. As had always happened in my dream, the cliff began to give way. Miraculously, I found myself at the bottom of the cliff on the beach facing a great expanse of ice covering Lake Erie. I walked onto the ice and headed towards Canada.

At least I thought I was headed to Canada. Before long I was out on the ice with no land in sight. Then it began to snow, harder than I ever remembered in my life. It must have lasted less than an hour, but it was enough to cover all my footsteps. I was lost, with no idea in which direction to go. The ice was covered by white snow under a sky that still could not be described as day or night. After a while I figured it was the night sky, but the stars were so large and illuminated the landscape so brightly that I felt completely absorbed in white.

When frozen, Lake Erie is not a smooth sheet of ice like one might imagine. Instead, there are many drifts that look like frozen waves. I was not sure if these were indeed frozen waves or drifts of snow on the surface. As I walked, I kept thinking about this question and concluded that on the lake there would always be at least small waves and naturally they would freeze in place. Then I asked myself how something in movement could freeze in place. I could swear I heard a voice loud and clear say, "Sam, it happens all the time, little by little. Have you not seen icicles. It is a property of time that very small moments lead to an illusion of non-changing permanence." With that I thought that even if I kept moving I would freeze in place, yet moving was my one chance to make it to Canada. My mind became awfully confused; especially when I realized I now had no idea in which direction I was headed or where the mysterious voice had come from. I realized another puzzling fact. I felt strong and capable of walking like I did on that night a long time ago when I hiked from Cleveland to Oberlin. What happened to my Parkinson's disease? It was gone.

I kept walking for what seemed like at least ten hours, but the landscape and the sky did not change. So I sat on one of the frozen waves. I gazed in all directions several times until I saw a small figure on the horizon. It was soon apparent that it was a person who was walking towards me. My spirits picked up a bit, but as I thought about it, they were never really down. Was it possible that a lifetime habit of alternating good and bad feelings was gone? I felt a perfect balance between all opposites. I had never felt this way before. Still, I was aware of my situation, and I needed someone to save me. Certainly, I thought, this had to be Douglas approaching. After all, it was his voice that called me to come to Canada; he was the only one expecting me, the only one who could possibly be out looking for me.

As the person got closer I realized it was not Douglas; it was Ridge. "Hi there Sam," he said once he got within speaking distance. "You feeling okay? Of course you are," he answered his own question. "This is the greatest peace you have ever felt." He spoke in a way I had not heard in a long time.

"You wouldn't remember me, but way back in 1865 I looked right at you from about fifty yards away. You were standing next to a Rebel officer and that was who I was aimin' to get. I couldn't help but notice you fidgiten' with your gun like a real Johnny come lately to the war. You see, I had seen it all, in fact I had just returned to the ranks after suffering a flesh wound at Spotsylvania. I was there where you was, except I was with a bunch a fool young Yankees, officers included, who had no idea what they were doin' in makin' a wild charge. I alone knew enough to stop, and aim my gun at that officer next to you."

"I remember now," I said. "That was Colonel Parker."

"So he was the top guy an' I would have got him too, if it ain't for the darndest thing."

"What?" I asked.

"It was you. Like a darn fool you didn't have your mind on what you was doin', which was tryin' to kill charging soldiers, so like a fool you shot right into the ground and your bullet hit I'd say no more than 20 feet ahead of you. Little did you know that damn bullet kicked up out of the dirt and went right into my chest fifty yards away? You killed me Sam. Yes you Sam, the fella who has spent all these years trying to do right. And, on top of it you set off a chain of bad things. My mama in West Virginia, 'Bertha the Unionist' they called her, who loved me so, started a campaign after she heard I died, to make life miserable for every secesh that lived in the area. The first were Belle and Joe Hamilton. They was pretty good folk, but when they was found dead and their place burned down after the war, it was believed it had to be the doing' of my people and it kicked off a feud, which is just another name for a war right there in what was once peaceful Pochohantas County. It lasted on and off for about twenty years and it was all your doin', Sam. You've done some good for sure, but in spite of your best intentions you have done some bad too. In the end, like all of us, you have just done."

"Does this mean I'm done?" I asked.

"Now ain't that clever. It is certainly hard not to like you Sam. Fact is though that no one is ever really done, or let me put that different, you are done seeing yourself as an individual. That is, you won't be a separate thing from anything else in terms of space and time. Damn, there just ain't no words for it. It just ain't like anything one thinks it is as a human. I'm sayin' the words, but I don't rightly know where they is comin' from. I just can't explain it to you in words. I reckon you just can't explain it to another if there was another, for the truth is you ain't separate from anyone else to begin with, not anymore anyway."

With that Ridge was gone. I believed I was sitting, but then again I don't think I was sitting. Was Sam Nite sitting on a snow bank on frozen Lake Erie? Of all things, I thought about how stupid it was that the census taker from all those years ago spelled our name N-I-T-E. It would have been so much easier if it was K-N-I-G-H-T, or even N-I-G-H-T. It now made sense though. I never lived like a knight, that is I was never on a crusade for a cause, and I never lived the life of a mystic or one who believes in the night more than the day. I thought of one of Owen's corny jokes about my name and laughed as hard as I ever laughed in my life and then I just sat there, I think. I had no sense of time, and for that matter the sense of "I" was disappearing too. I knew there was nowhere to go. I was passing or passed over. It got really warm, I think, because the lake was no longer frozen. I was falling down towards the bottom of the lake. The jar I thought I was still holding must have got away from me, for up ahead of me in the water was a bunch of gold coins spreading out, floating and dispersing in the water like a bunch of golden feathers falling from the sky. It was incredibly beautiful, with them all spread out against the dark sea the same as the stars spread across a dark sky.

Back in the cottage of a man who was once known as Sam Nite, Andy stood talking to a well-dressed Black man. "We found him here in bed. He must have died in his sleep. That's lucky I think—no pain, no idea you are about to go. Yep, Pops deserved it; why he wouldn't hurt a fly. I have seen him struggling to get them to fly out the door instead of swatting them like I'd do. Once I saw him carry a live mouse out of the cottage in a box. Don't know where he took it, but he was gone a long time before he returned. A fool thing to do if you ask me. I'm sure the minute he let it go a snake or an owl got it. But that was Pops."

The men stepped outside and Andy continued, "Well here is the box," as he handed the Black man a carefully wrapped package in brown paper, tied neatly with string. "Sounds like something rattling in a jar. I feel bad for you coming all this way to get it. I'm sure it is worthless. Here is the envelope with the note inside that he left leaning against the package, just as I found it, saying to deliver this to Douglas Frederick Brown of Leamington, Canada. Well, he had talked about people who did not exist, so I didn't want to mail it to the post office up there. I spent enough time and money as it was, calling the newspaper office in Leamington and placing the ad. That way I could say I at least tried. I sure didn't think someone would read it and show up here, especially a nig..., I mean a Negro."

Finally, the well-dressed Black man spoke up. "You say he is buried across the road under that big tree."

"Yep, you can't miss it. You can still easily make out where the hole was dug. It is quite fresh."

After a moment Douglas spoke. "Well, if you don't mind, I would like to visit the grave alone, pay my respects, and open this package in private."

"It's your call Pops," Andy responded. Douglas politely nodded and walked towards the road with the package in hand. First, he crossed the Interurban tracks that were showing a little rust because, as of late, few streetcars were riding its rails. Then, he had the much harder chore of crossing the road with a good deal of automobile traffic speeding down its concrete. Finally, he walked into the small graveyard, and just as Andy said, he easily found the newly dug grave with a headstone about the size of a cinder block that simply read on the first line "Sam Nite" and on the second line, "1850-1930." Douglas removed his derby, and after a short pause he opened the envelope. "I, Sam Nite, on this day of November 13th, 1929, do declare in my will and testament that I leave the contents of this package to Douglas Frederick Brown of Leamington, Ontario, Canada. If after a reasonable effort, Mr. Brown is not located, I request the package be buried with my body under the big tree in the cemetery across the road. I assure any interested party that the contents are worthless, except to Mr. Brown, who might have an interest in what is inside."

Douglas knelt next to the grave and spoke softly. "Sam, I never did try to contact you once I got settled in Leamington. It's not that I didn't care, but I found financial success up there quickly, maybe too quickly. I felt ashamed and did not want you to see how quickly I abandoned the spiritual side of life. I soon had one of the largest tomato farms and canning plants in the area and then sold everything to the Heinz Company. I enjoyed the life of a rich man, the life a Black man could not have lived here in the States. Please forgive me."

Next, Douglas carefully unwrapped the box and first found an envelope marked "To Douglas Frederick Brown." Douglas opened it and read the note inside. "Dear Douglas, I hope you are reading this and not, as I fear, on the bottom of Lake Erie. I once told you while we were in jail together about the hidden jar of gold coins back on my parents' land in Virginia. It is unbelievable, but they were delivered to me in the summer of 1929. Most people would put the contents to foolish use, but I know you would not do so."

Douglas wept for a good ten minutes. He looked up at the big tree and the few stars that were visible in the early evening sky. It was for Northeast Ohio a rare warm March day. Douglas knew somehow, someway these coins would change things and that his life was about to change. His life of leisure living off the profits of his investments, stocks, and bonds was about to end. Something more meaningful he felt certain was ahead. Like all living things, he had no idea what that would be.

Epilogue
The Big Tree

Close to a hundred years after the spirit of Sam departed in time and space, a middle aged man living outside of Vermillion, Ohio, recalled a huge tree that lived near his childhood home. As a boy, he had spent many a day climbing it to the top where he had a magnificent view of Lake Erie. He felt so strongly about the tree that he felt compelled to write about it, and thus he did as follows:

I called it The Big Tree. It stood magnificently about fifty yards from our house. I would run to the tree every day after school. The area around the tree was the perfect place for a ten-year-old boy to get away from people and to think about life. It was a good climbing tree, and atop it, more than anywhere else, I was free from the demands of growing up.

The Big Tree appropriately sat in an old overgrown cemetery, for it seemed half alive and half dead. Burn marks from lightning and the sockets of severed limbs marked the way up. But it was sturdy and still very much the king of the nearby forest.

To climb the tree, I first mentally prepared myself by being still and listening. I could hear but not see the cars going by on River Road, which was hidden from view by small trees and vegetation. I next placed a loose grave stone under the tree. On the stone I could make out the word "Sam," with the rest of the inscription no longer readable. After I returned to the ground, I always carefully put the stone back in the place I found it. Even with the stone, the first maneuver to climb the tree was the hardest. I would stand on the stone and jump up and grab the first branch with both arms. Holding the wooden appendage, I would start swinging my body until I had the momentum to pull my legs up around the limb. Then, with one last effort, I pulled the rest of my body up on the branch and slowly moved backwards until I sat with my back to the trunk. Now secure, I carefully stood up. At this height I could see Lake Road and beyond that the remnants of the cottages of the old Lake Erie resort. Turning my attention back to climbing the tree, I began an upward journey following a planned route of forks and limbs. The climb had become so routine that I could have given each section a name, like those used by mountain climbers for places like Mount Everest's Hillary Step or the Rock Face. Soon, I would be above the other tree tops. The limbs up there were smaller, and although strong, they would sway in the wind making me feel like I was flying. From the top I could see boats far out in the lake; you could even see downtown Vermillion some eight miles away. For a boy, the thrill was unmatched.

One summer day, as I sat in my parents' living room, I became aware of some commotion near where the Big Tree stood. It was more than the normal noise of the construction crews who had been in the area for quite some time preparing the land for new houses. A few days before, I had watched them remove the human remains from the cemetery. I remember seeing them pull out a crude casket of rotten pine wood from under the tree. As they moved the box, an arm of a skeleton fell down through a hole in the wood. There was some laughing as they placed the arm back in the box, loaded it on the truck, and covered it with a big blue tarp. Now, the time had come for the living in the cemetery to die. As I now watched from afar, men yelled out commands as buzz saws went to work. With no other warning, the Big Tree fell with a great thud, the high swaying branches hitting the ground last. At the time, I found the act of destruction exciting, like any normal adolescent boy would. The years immediately after the tree was cut down I gave it little thought or concern, for I was about to move on to more important things like going to college, sitting behind a desk in an office, being a fine upstanding member of society, being another bee in the hive. I would be climbing, this time not towards freedom, but instead social responsibility. Only in my later years would I think of and sadly miss the Big Tree.

Looking back to that day when the Big Tree had been cut down I did not sense the tree displaying any signs of fear or sadness. My guess is that the Big Tree was over one hundred and fifty years old at the time it was cut down. That means it was far from civilization when it was a seedling around 1800. It had survived everything nature had in its arsenal until it met the saw. Near the end, I imagine the tree had no regrets. It had survived for many years. Unlike man and animals, the tree did not have parents. Its days of youth were times of great strife. There was stiff competition with the other trees for the energy of the sun. Animals threatened its life by eating its leaves. There were diseases killing nearby trees, and there always was the threat of violent storms and periods of drought. I'd like to think the Big Tree's best times were when I would arrive after school and hug its bottom limb as I pulled myself up, giving the tree all my attention.

I am certain the tree knew it was a good time to die. Its habitat was being replaced by a forest of houses, built with the remains of once proud and tall trees. The houses were merely painted wooden skeletons.

I remember asking my grandmother, when she was close to my current age of 62, what age she would choose to be. She thought of the joys of youth and responded that eighteen would be her choice. I don't think she carefully considered her response for she was eighteen in the year 1913. She had before her much anxiety, for she was a gentle but nervous person. I'm sure she worried about my grandfather being drafted into World War I. He wasn't, but he did become a Cleveland policeman and that could not have been easy on my grandmother's nerves. He walked a beat during the Prohibition when hoodlums ran the streets and an honest cop could easily end up dead in an alley. I'm sure she was worried sick during the Great Depression. One pink slip or a bullet finding my grandfather could have lost the family house and everything else. The worst had to be when her only child shipped out to the South Pacific to fight the Japanese in World War Two. Every day she lived with fear of a telegram or an official visit with bad news. Maybe the Fifties brought some peace for all she had to worry about were things like nuclear bombs and a war that no one could win. After surviving all of those potential disasters, I would like to think that before we moved to Vermillion she found real peace rocking me on her lap singing a nursery rhyme. Then in 1962, about five years after we moved and around the time the Big Tree was cut down, all her worries ended after a short battle with cancer.

I myself do not want to be younger. The past holds some good memories, but more than anything it was filled with anxiety about the future. I can see it in my sons (age 15 and 13) today; filling their hours with questions like: What am I going to be when I grow up? What about girls? How do I know whether or not I am gay? Are my parents not together because of something I did? Why don't other people like me? What about all this terrorism and the climate change? These are just a few of the anxiety-producing thoughts that I'm sure run rampant in their minds.

Because I love them so, their worries are my worries. I will not have to deal with them though. Most of their personal crises will come and go without my knowledge. In fact, probably for most of them, I'll be dead.

I still have my own worries about my future. They are fewer, now centering more than anything on my mortality. Everybody likes to say they don't worry about death, yet everyone my age describes their birthday like another nail in the coffin, which I suppose does accurately describe birthdays. We just don't know how many nails the carpenter plans to use.

I don't want to go backwards, and I am in no hurry to go forwards. I want to live in a peaceful present. As for the future, the best Western religion can offer is faith.

I have no argument with this tenet, but I don't understand the connection between faith and knowledge. Faith is not needed by those who know the truth and exactly what God wants. A mathematician does not need faith to understand that if he has one apple, and if he is given another one, he will have two. A Christian does not need faith if they know the Bible was written by God and it clearly states what will happen at death. They know they are saved and will enjoy eternal bliss in God's kingdom. I'm happy for them and everyone else who knows the truth by way of their religion. It is people like me who need faith, for we do not know. I need faith that there is a purpose to my consciousness while on earth. I need no proof, just courage and trust that there is something beyond my understanding.

At this point the man stopped writing. His thinking was making him tired. He put the paper down on his desk next to the old gold coin he had found washed up on the shore of Lake Erie, many years ago.

BIBLIOGRAPHIC ESSAY

Several historic characters are depicted in this novel. Many were famous in their time but are somewhat forgotten today. George Henry Thomas was a Union hero after the Civil War on par with Grant, Sherman, and Sheridan. Cleveland Abbe's scientific contributions were so noteworthy that he has been referred to as the "Father of Weather Forecasting." Simon Kenton was every bit as daring a frontiersman as Daniel Boone. Author Sherwood Anderson, at one time, was equal to Hemmingway and Faulkner in popularity. The great Shawnee Indian leader Tecumseh is as important as Sitting Bull and Geronimo who are more well-known because of our fixation on pulp westerns, which give the impression that all Indians lived west of the Mississippi. Johnny Appleseed is remembered in mythic terms; however, his real name, John Chapman, and his actual story are known to few.

Many of the named members of Parker's Battery were actual people. David Crockett Richardson studied law in the trenches and indeed became mayor of Richmond in 1908. Lieutenant John Thompson Brown was an inspirational leader. Captain (later Major) Parker, besides commanding the battery, was a gifted doctor and an important figure in Richmond before and after the war. Joe Mayo, Parker's servant during the war, was an actual slave purchased by Parker for $ 700. Parker and Mayo formed a close relationship that lasted after the conflict.

The book *Parker's Virginia Battery, C.S.A.*, second edition revised, by Robert K. Krick (Wilmington, N.C.: Broadfoot Pub. Co.1989) is a thorough study of Parker's Battery from its formation in Richmond to its surrender at Appomattox and beyond. Any study of the unit's history should start with this study. Also, well worthwhile is a visit to the Parker's Battery historical park in Chester, Virginia. The park is a division of the Richmond National Military Park and has a fine interpretive trail.

No author more passionately defends General George Henry Thomas's military career than Benson Bobrick. *Master of War: the life of General George Thomas* by Bobrick (New York: Simon & Schuster, 2009) is an excellent overview of Thomas's life. Bobrick's The *Battle of Nashville: General George H. Thomas & the Most Decisive Battle of the Civil War* (New York: Alfred A. Knopf Books for Young Readers, 2010) is beautifully illustrated and appropriate for young students as well as adults.

There are several other biographies of Thomas, including *Rock of Chickamauga: the Life of General George H. Thomas*, by Freeman Cleaves (Norman: University of Oklahoma Press, 1948) and *General George H. Thomas: the Indomitable Warrior: a Biography* by Wilbur Thomas (New York: Exposition Press, 1964)

Little has been written on the life of Cleveland Abbe. Most of the information on Abbe used in this book was found in general American biographical reference sources such as *Webster's American Biographies* Charles Van Dorn, editor (Springfield, Mass.: Merriam Co., 1975).

More basic, but brief, information on Abbe can be found in a wide variety of books dealing with the historical aspects of meteorology. Only one biography devoted to Abbe's life was available in the Library of Congress online catalog: *Professor Abbe and the Isobars; the story of Cleveland Abbe, America's First Weatherman* by Truman Abbe (New York: Vantage Press, 1955).

Factual information on Cincinnati places, events, and people were found online. Of particular interest is a site on the 1867-1870 Cincinnati Red Stockings baseball club (www.19cbaseball.com/tours-1867-1870-cincinnati-red-stockings-tour.html).

An online article (http://en.wikipedia.org/wiki/Proctor_and_gamble) includes a history of the Proctor and Gamble Company plus a list of 26 source notes. A similar site for the Cincinnati Observatory (http://en.wikipedia.org/wiki/Cincinnati_Observatory) also includes references.

The life of John Chapman, better known as "Johnny Appleseed," is found in the well-written *Johnny Appleseed: Man and Myth* by Robert Price (Bloomington: Indiana University Press, 1954)

Two other interesting giants of the frontier age are Simon Kenton and the Shawnee chief Tecumseh. Intertwining the lives of these two men is *The Frontiersmen: a narrative* by Allan W. Eckert (Boston: Little, Brown and Co., 1967). Eckert thoroughly researched the topic with copious footnotes and cited references. For a one volume overview of the entire story of the battle for the Ohio River country see Eckert's *That Dark and Bloody River* (New York: Bantam Books, 1995)

Historical maps were used extensively in the writing of this book. Maps of cities and towns, routes of railroads, and the Ohio canals, were found in various online sites. These include www.atozmapsdata.com where the author found excellent 1867 and 1882 Ohio railroad maps. A Historic map of 1870 Mount Vernon, Ohio, is at www.worldmap-sonline.com. The site http://upload.wikimedia.org/wikipedia/commons/1/13/Baltimore_and_Ohio_RR is good for information on the famous Baltimore and Ohio Railroad. For well written and researched material on the Ohio canals see www.dnr.state.oh.us/parks/canallands/canalhistory/tabid/22230/Default.aspx.

Much has been written about Sherwood Anderson, who was known as "Jobby" when he lived as a boy and young man in Clyde, Ohio. There are, of course, primary sources from Anderson himself since he made his living as a writer. However, one must keep in mind that Anderson's autobiographical work is not overly concerned with fact.

One may start at the obvious place and read Anderson's most famous work, *Winesburg, Ohio: a Group of Tales of Ohio Small Town Life* (New York: B. W. Huebsch, 1919). This book heavily relies on Anderson's memories of life in Clyde. Another recommendation is Anderson's *Horses and Men: Tales, Long and Short, from Our American Life* (New York: B. W. Huebsch, 1923). The psychological characterization of being a young man in Ohio during Anderson's lifetime is rendered flawlessly in several of the stories.

There are numerous biographies and literary criticisms about Anderson and his work that could fill several library shelves. Two recommendations are *Sherwood Anderson* by Irving Howe (Stanford, California: Stanford University Press, 1951) and *Sherwood Anderson* by Kim Townsend (Boston: Houghton Mifflin, 1987)

The Lake Shore Electric Railway was one of many interurban electric railway systems in America at the end of the nineteenth century and beginning of the twentieth century. The internal combustion engine led to the demise of trolley service not only between towns and cities but also within them. Today when we debate creating high speed rail, it is amazing to recall that we had such a system in place less than 100 years ago. Three highly recommended books on the Lake Shore Electric Railway are *New Lake Shore Electric, Trolley Trails Vol. 4* by Harry Christiansen (Lakewood, Ohio: Western Reserve Historical Society, 1978); *The Lake Shore Electric Railway Story* by Herbert H. Harwood, Jr. and Robert S. Korach (Bloomington: Indiana University Press, 2000); and the book of photographs from the *Images of Rail* series—*Lake Shore Electric Railway* by Thomas J. Patton with Dennis Lamont and Albert Doane (Charleston, S.C.: Arcadia Publishing, 2009).